S0-ADN-966

No Turning Back

The Harrowing Journeys of Hattie Sheldon

LANE DOLLY

Copyright @ 2014 by Lane Dolly

All rights reserved. No part of this publication may be reproduced or transmitted in any form or by any means electronic or mechanical, including photocopy, recording, or any information storage and retrieval system now known or to be invented, without permission in writing from the author, except by a reviewer who wishes to quote brief passages in connection with a review written for inclusion in a magazine, newspaper, broadcast or online forum

International Standard Book Number 978-15031-3084-5
Printed in the United States of America

Editorial development and creative design support by Ascent:
www.itsyourlifebethere.com

To *my* late grandmother,
Wina Rae Latta Calhoon,
for her commitment to faith, her tenacity
to overcome obstacles, her example of lifelong scholarship,
and her loving reverence of Hattie Sheldon
who was her own grandmother.

Introduction

*J*ust as technology transformed 20th Century America, Hattie Sheldon's life in the mid-19th Century was posed to change for the better due to new opportunities in education. The kind of schooling she received at Amherst Academy in Amherst, Massachusetts and Utica Female Academy in Utica, New York wasn't even dreamed about by her mother or other women born earlier in the 1800s. Very few women continued their studies beyond common school and an even smaller number were privileged to attend brief summer terms of education.

So it was that, as Hattie reached young adulthood, the opportunities that lay open before her far surpassed those of every previous generation of women.

Tradition still held on, though. Young people coped with society's lingering expectations of marriage, family, and community involvement. Yet, Hattie found she could not accept the domestic roles still associated with well-bred young women.

In her soul, a greater purpose called her beyond ordinary, safe, or local role models.

Perhaps the volume of stories she read through freedom of the press gave her ideas. Or maybe her choice was born from an altogether spiritual vision of life.

What we know is that Hattie Sheldon left behind the known in favor of a journey into the unknown. Armed with only the first notions of the human need that awaited her in Indian Territory, she set out to a place far from home—a place rife with danger and daunting challenges—to find her way in the world. Less than a quarter of a century earlier, the unprecedented, forced removal of the Cherokee Nation from the southeastern states led to its rebirth in a rugged territory separated from progress and the rest of civilization.

Once there, Hattie had surprising and harrowing encounters with what we think of today as "hidden aspects of American history." Through the tapestry of her life, I have woven facts about some of America's most compelling lessons learned from our westward expansion.

My hope is that Hattie will serve as a source of inspiration, because her values and devotion remind us to appreciate our ancestors and pass the lessons of history along to generations to come.

—*Lane Calhoon Dolly, McLean, Virginia*

CONTENTS

CAST OF CHARACTERS

THE SHELDONS—A family in Utica, New York

Harriet Ann "Hattie" Sheldon—The protagonist. Born in 1833, she was educated at Amherst Academy in Massachusetts and Utica Female Academy in Utica, New York. She left New York to teach in Indian Territory in 1856.

Ebenezer Sheldon—born 1796. Hattie's father owned a saddle, trunk, and harness business, first in Burlington, New York, then Utica, New York. He was an abolitionist and native of Massachusetts, where his father had served in the American Revolutionary War.

Helen Sheldon—born 1804. Hattie's mother was a New York state native.

Amanda Sheldon Moore—born 1827. Hattie's older and only surviving sister. She is married to LeGrand Moore. Their little daughter is named Mary.

George and Albert Sheldon—Hattie's older brothers who do not appear in this book of the series.

Artemas Sheldon—born 1836. Hattie's little brother.

Mary and Cornelia Sheldon—Hattie's late, older sisters who died during a two-month period of sickness when Hattie was just a young girl.

Aunt Mary Brown—Ebenezer Sheldon's sister from Massachusetts.

THE WORCESTERS—a missionary family in Park Hill, Cherokee
Nation, Indian Territory (pre-State of Oklahoma)

Reverend Samuel Austin Worcester—born 1798. A Vermont linguist
and pastor educated at Andover Theological Seminary. His
service to the Cherokees is legendary due to the famous Supreme
Court case, Worcester v. Georgia. After his incarceration and
the removal of the Cherokees from their ancestral homes in
the southeast United States, he established a mission in the new
Cherokee Nation under the sponsorship of the American Board
of Commissioners for Foreign Missions, a Boston-based organization. His first wife, Ann Orr Worcester, died in childbirth when
their sixth child was born. He remarried quickly.

Erminia Nash Worcester—born 1801. Second wife to the missionary preacher and teacher. A New York state native, she was a
former mission school teacher at a neighboring mission in Indian
Territory.

Ann Eliza Worcester Robertson—born 1826. Worcester's oldest
daughter was educated at St. Johnsbury Academy in Vermont.
Like her father, she became a linguist and teacher in the Creek
Nation alongside her husband, Rev. William S. Robertson.

Sarah Worcester Hitchcock—born 1828. Worcester's second daughter
was a graduate of Mt. Holyoke College in Massachusetts. She
taught at the Cherokee National Female Seminary and retired
when she married a physician, Dwight Hitchcock, MD, the son
of other Indian Territory missionaries. He was a graduate of
Amherst College and Bodoin Medical College in Maine. Their
daughter was Laura.

Hannah Worcester Hicks—born 1834. Worcester's third daughter. A lack of funds denied her an eastern education. She married a mixed-blood Cherokee man and had a large family. Her husband was Abijah Hicks, a farmer who worked for her father's mission. Their children were Percy, Emma and Ann.

Leonard Worcester—born 1836. Worcester's oldest son. Educated at St. Johnsbury Academy in Vermont.

John Orr Worcester—born 1838. Worcester's youngest son. Educated at St. Johnsbury Academy in Vermont.

Mary Eleanor Worcester—born 1840. Worcester's youngest child was born just before her mother died. She was educated at Thetford Academy in Vermont.

THE LATTAS—a large, pioneering family that established the community of Vineyard in old Lovely County, Arkansas, which was adjacent to Indian Territory. Vineyard was later renamed Evansville.

John Latta, Sr.—born 1790. The patriarch, a widower, was a native of South Carolina.

James Latta—born 1827. The love interest of Hattie Sheldon.

John Stewart Latta—born 1821. A Deputy U.S. Marshal in the western district of Arkansas with jurisdiction in Indian Territory.

Martha Latta Pilkington—born 1833. A seamstress married to Fred Pilkington, a teacher.

William R. Latta—born 1823. A wagon-master, six-mule team teamster, farrier, and blacksmith.

Seven other siblings join the story in succeeding books.

PEOPLE FROM HATTIE'S PAST

Margaret—Hattie's girlhood friend. A composite fictional character.

Reverend Philemon Fowler—the pastor of First Presbyterian Church in Utica, New York.

Moses Bagg, MD—A descendant of one of Utica's founding families, he was the Sheldon family physician in Utica, New York.

Professor Alexander Colquhoun—a retired ex-professor of French and Indian ancestry who mentored Hattie at Amherst College. A fictional character.

Professor Cornelius Thorne—a troubled professor at Amherst Academy. A fictional character.

PEOPLE IN PARK HILL, CHEROKEE NATION

Jacob and Nancy Hitchcock—retired missionaries from the nearby Dwight Mission who came to live in Park Hill.

Dwight Hitchcock, MD—a physician in Park Hill will serves the mission and the neighboring area.

Jesse—Dr. Hitchcock's servant who is a freed Negro slave.

George Murrell—James Latta's employer. A plantation owner in Indian Territory and Virginia whose young Cherokee wife had died.

Susan—Mr. Murrell's house slave.

Chief John Ross—The towering leader and statesman of the Cherokee Nation.

Grace Barnes (fictional)—a white mission worker who befriends Hattie. She is married to a half-blood Cherokee, Smith Barnes.

Sweet Berry (fictional)—a shy six-year-old Cherokee school girl who comes to the Park Hill Mission.

Deke (fictional)—Sweet Berry's criminal father. He was widowed after losing her mother, Chesney, a mulatto.

Salali (fictional)—Sweet Berry's full-blood Cherokee grandmother with whom Deke's family is living.

Ida (fictional)—the late Chesney's free, Negro daughter who is age 8.

Levi (fictional)—the late Chesney's free, Negro son who is age 9.

Government Agent George Butler—an official appointed by President Franklin Pierce as federal agent for the Cherokee Indians with responsibility to submit annual status reports to the Superintendent of Indian Affairs.

Rev. Evan Jones—a Welshman who became a Northern Baptist missionary. He traveled with the Cherokees upon removal to the new Indian Territory. Along with his son, Jones worked to translate the Bible into the relatively new written form of the old Cherokee language.

Rev. Stephen Foreman—a mixed-blood Cherokee preacher educated at Princeton Theological Seminary who returned to the Cherokee Nation and became a community leader, as well as Rev. Worcester's Bible translator.

Miss Nancy Thompson—a lifelong missionary assistant closely linked to the Worcester family.

Rhoda (fictional)—the free Negro woman who is the mission cook.

Rufus (fictional)—Murrell's slave who is hired occasionally to do mission repairs and odd jobs.

Mary Covel—an enthusiastic mixed-blood Cherokee student at the Park Hill Mission School whose late father had taught in Indian Territory.

Susie and Taylor Foreman—young Cherokee children of Rev. Foreman who attend the Park Hill Mission School.

Buck and Lucas—fictional school boys at the Park Hill Mission School

E. Jane Ross—a Cherokee teacher who was the niece of Chief John Ross. She was educated at Bethlehem Female Seminary in Pennsylvania prior to teaching at the Cherokee Female Seminary in Park Hill.

Charlotte "Lotta" Raymond—A Connecticut native educated in Philadelphia who became principal at the Cherokee Female Seminary in Park Hill.

TIMELINE

1830   Congress passed the Indian Removal Act allowing the government to force tribes off their ancestral lands in the southeastern United States. Reservation land, called Indian Territory, was set aside for them hundreds of miles to the west.

1836   Rev. Samuel A. Worcester resumed his missionary work among the Cherokees at the Park Hill Mission south of Tahlequah.

1838-39 Removal of the Cherokees from their ancestral homes to internment camps before marching them over 800 miles to Indian Territory. Thousands died.

1839   New Cherokee Constitution adopted.

1842   Cherokee National Council passed "An Act in Regard to Free Negroes." All free Negroes, except those emancipated by Cherokee citizens, were required to leave the Cherokee Nation by the first day of January 1843.

1843   The Great Migration across America to Oregon.

1851   The Cherokee National Female Seminary opened near Park Hill, the first institution of its kind offering higher learning to girls west of the Mississippi River. A male seminary opened, as well.

1852   *Uncle Tom's Cabin* published. Over two million copies sold during its first two years of publication, making a large impact on the anti-slavery movement.

1854   The first homesteaders arrived on the Great Plains. The Kansas-Nebraska Act became law, repealed the Missouri Compromise of 1820, and created Kansas Territory and Nebraska Territory. A provision for settlers to vote on slavery in the new territories led to competition for control of Kansas Territory. Violence erupted, referred to as Bleeding Kansas.

1856   Hattie Sheldon hired as missionary teacher to the Park Hill Mission by the American Board of Commissioners for Foreign Missions.

Prologue

In the 19th Century, United States law specified that when a carefully delineated portion of the unorganized federal domain became amply populated by U.S. citizens, they could petition Congress for territorial status. Subsequently, Congress passed organic acts along with a bill of rights for each territory's residents. A three-part government was established with judicial and executive branches to which appointments were made. The legislative branch was elected by the residents along with a territorial representative. That representative was seated in Congress, which retained authority over the territory. Unfortunately, no organic act was passed by Congress for Indian Territory, where the Cherokees were forced to move. Before 1840, the Cherokee Nation reestablished itself there, but its members were not U.S. citizens. No government outside of the Cherokee National Council was organized until well after the Civil War.

1

Steamboats, Gamblers and Bad Women

*H*attie Sheldon intended to lead the most exhilarating life of any woman in her family. From the beginning of time. Splashing her face with cold water that last morning, she pictured the grizzled men in her father's shop who first told the tales that set her imagination on fire. Since they lived to tell of their adventures and narrow escapes, she was sure she would, too. Her heart was filled with windswept visions of anything but marriage and family in Utica. Hattie was certain her future belonged right in the middle of America's westward expansion.

No other woman she knew had been brash enough to make such a daring choice as hers. Finally, this very day, she was leaving central New York State behind for the beauty and promise of the wilderness. Her bold move had shocked the whole town. That included her parents, who couldn't believe she would choose the unknown over the known.

Already pinning her hopes on a small school in the wilds of Indian Territory, Hattie underlined today's date, July 21, 1856, in her diary. She couldn't wait to lay eyes on her eager Cherokee students in that place west of Arkansas. The moment she stepped into that classroom, her work as a teacher would conclude yesterday's youth and usher in tomorrow's immeasurable womanhood.

Hattie felt confident she was ready. Well, at least intellectually. Surely her energy and strength would return, too, as the doctor had promised. She wouldn't allow any setback to change her plans after investing so much of herself in this goal. That effort had incorporated years of burning appeals for more education and late night studying to prove herself worthy, as well as many fervent prayers.

In a few short days, excitingly narrow passages on the Ohio and Erie Canal awaited her. After that, she envisioned innumerable sights and sounds along the mighty Mississippi River. She expected to skirt beautiful mountain ranges in western Arkansas and traverse hilly dunes as she entered the Cherokee Nation. All this while listening intently to the tips and mysteries shared by other travelers.

Brilliant sunbeams melted through the dawn's blue haze just before departing from her home in Utica that morning. To Hattie, those beams were lighting the way to her new life and job. Both promised to challenge her in untold ways. Deliriously happy about the future, she continued to add to the sea of ideas that had distracted her for weeks.

Right now, however, she was present in the moment to every last detail. Including the time. Looking at the clock, she frowned and began to pace nervously on the front porch. Why was everyone so slow this morning? She hoped her parents weren't having words again.

❖ ❖ ❖

At the sharp sound of the train whistle from the depot, the Sheldon's horse balked and almost reared. When the blast came a second time, splitting the dewy air, the mare startled again. Ebenezer Sheldon, Hattie's ever supportive father, slowed and then jumped down from the carriage seat to restore calm.

"Steady, girl," he murmured.

Hattie had been hearing those same words of encouragement from him in recent days. Now they took on new meaning as the Sheldons continued their approach to the front of the train depot. In a short while, Hattie reminded herself, she would be too far away to hear his voice or enjoy his support.

Arriving at the depot, her father disembarked and reached for her hand. Hattie adjusted her jacket and rose confidently to project strength and balance. She must step down carefully, with the kind of poise that completely hid the sharp pain and lingering weakness in her leg. The truth must remain hidden, especially from her mother, Helen Sheldon, who watched with a grim expression.

Slipping out of the carriage, Hattie placed her weight gingerly on the leg that had broken and healed—or mainly healed. She struggled to banish all memory of the heart-stopping fall that had nearly ended her plans for adventure. Stepping onto the street satisfactorily, she forced a bright and determined look—even though she actually felt less than confident. Was she really as able to make this trip as she had assured her mother yesterday?

"Are you *certain*, Hattie?" her mother asked again, wringing her hands for the fortieth time.

"*Yes*, mother. I'm *fine*," Hattie reacted impatiently while thinking, "*Can't you just be happy for me?*"

"I don't know why your father still supports you in this. How can your leg be strong enough? And you're so —"

Hattie knew the word her mother failed, for once, to voice. *Headstrong.* She had been against this over-reaching, risky venture from the start. Thank goodness she didn't know about Hattie's silent suffering or the depth of her will to conceal it.

"Will you please stop worrying? You'll ruin this wonderful send off," Hattie pleaded. "See, I'm strong and sound!"

Over the shoulder of her cool, linen canezous, Hattie heard her traveling chaperone speaking. Mrs. Erminia Worcester, thick set in a burgundy day dress, carried on a polite conversation as she waited for Hattie. Their journey together would take several weeks to reach the heart of the Cherokee Nation in Indian Territory. She was the wife of the revered Rev. Samuel Austin Worcester, Hattie's future superior at the Park Hill Mission.

Originally, Hattie expected to make this long trip with both Rev. and Mrs. Worcester. However, word had come recently that only Mrs. Worcester was traveling. Precious little had been said about why Rev. Worcester remained in Vermont, where he had relatives, or when he would join them in Park Hill.

Hattie couldn't wait for that day. Just when her search for a teaching position in Utica had hit rock bottom last spring, the inspiring Rev. Worcester had come along and offered her the chance of a lifetime. She was proud of herself for accepting it without asking her parents' permission. Rev. Worcester had promised her a letter explaining the background of the Cherokee Nation in preparation for joining the school there. But it had not arrived.

❖ ❖ ❖

Mrs. Worcester was a slightly dowdy individual with coarse black hair sprinkled with grey. While Hattie watched, she cut her way through the crowd like a loaded supply ship on the Mohawk River. Having arrived in Utica three days ago to collect Hattie, she would serve as guide while they traveled to the mission her husband had founded many years earlier. Hattie had looked forward to Rev. Worcester's polite aid to get in and out of carriages or march up and down gangways into ships. Now that she wouldn't have help, she mustered her own strength for the challenges posed by her leg. This was her private trial.

She had no intention of backing out after these months of planning and dreaming, yet she questioned if she was fit to travel more than a thousand miles—by train, boat, and wagon—into the American frontier. This fact unsettled her as she packed.

Her biggest worry centered on sudden, sharp jabs of pain that sometimes made her falter as she walked. There could not have been a more inopportune accident than the one that broke her leg just after she was hired last spring. During a pilgrimage to her church's baptisms at the Mohawk River, the footbridge collapsed and plummeted her down onto the sandbar.

She had convalesced as long as she dared. Moving around remained difficult, but not enough to curtail her long desired adventure. She could walk briefly without a limp, at least when people were looking, though she barely managed to keep the pain to herself when standing too long or walking too far. Since she was setting out for a foreign territory, her limitation *had* to be kept secret. Surely that wasn't headstrong. It was just her determination in the face of barriers that life threw in the way.

❖ ❖ ❖

Well-wishers and other passengers streamed into the depot now. Hattie pretended to check for her ticket in her handbag, though she was really avoiding her mother's gaze, which was fully upon her. Was her pretense, that she suffered no pain, convincing enough? Hiding her discomfort at this eleventh hour was paramount.

In a moment, her father swung Hattie's trunk down from the back of the carriage, and hurried the ladies through the door of the depot. On the far side, also wide open, were doors that led out to the platform.

"Come along," he urged. "They're boarding."

Hattie hurried as best she could, with her mother at her side, instructing. "You must send us postcards and letters along the way. I want to know where you are. And remember to...."

On and on the list went. Hattie nodded—intent only on boarding the train and getting the weight off her leg again.

Suddenly, her mother stopped her, dewy eyed. "Hattie. Stop for a minute. I want to look at you."

Oh no. She turned warily. "What—look at what?" Her heart pounded for fear her mother had detected her slower gait.

"You ... you look so grown up suddenly," her mother whispered. "I wish you were only going away to school in New England again. Your dangerous dream worries me like you're still a little girl."

Hattie exhaled in relief and relaxed a little. Her mother had a right to this private moment, however ill timed. She had been through so many goodbyes and losses. Having to let her youngest daughter leave was terribly painful. So, Hattie slipped her arm through her mother's and led them forward.

"This is my time, Mother. I've got to make my mark. Of course I will write and, of course, I will miss you. Send me letters often— and make sure Amanda and Artemas do, too."

Huge puffs of steam billowed cloudlike from the engine onto the platform just as a final, shrill, whistle gave notice to passengers.

Hattie glanced excitedly up and down the track. The New York Central line, perfectly on time, was ready to transport her much farther than she could anticipate. The second she boarded this train, she stopped being subject to anybody else's expectations for her future.

Bright rays of sun highlighted features of her father's face that she loved so dearly. His salt and pepper whiskers. The way his bright, kindly eyes crinkled at the corners. He was a caring man who respected all humanity as a good abolitionist naturally would. She valued the security of his bear hug across her shoulders and reached for one of his skilled, creative hands, calloused from years of working with leather and wood. Ebenezer Sheldon had not left her side since delivering her beautiful, new trunk to the train.

Hattie hugged her mother and then turned to the others who had come to kiss her cheek, hug her neck, offer farewell wishes, and remind her of good times never to be forgotten. She was seeing them for the last time in years. When would they be together again, she wondered? Although she would not miss Utica, she would miss all that these people and the past had braided together to define her life.

Shortly after her arrival just days ago, Mrs. Worcester had hastily produced a list of last-minute requirements that took Hattie by surprise. The whole Sheldon family had hurried around to accommodate her wishes. Hattie's mother prepared food. Her brother, Artemas, sped downtown on his bicycle to purchase her new handkerchiefs. Amanda mended her ripped hem, and their father conditioned the leather of her old satchel. These errands weighed on Hattie's mind after she woke up yesterday. Mrs. Worcester was as demanding as Rev. Worcester was gentle and humble.

Rushing to dress and tend her own final particulars yesterday, Hattie paused when her father called her name from downstairs unexpectedly. She peeked over the banister to respond.

"Come down to the front porch, dear," he requested sweetly, his eyes twinkling.

Taking a deep breath, Hattie gathered herself and willed her leg to see her through. This was no time to stumble on the stairs and fall. She must divert attention from her leg and assure her family of her fitness by looking strong.

Emerging from the front door seconds later, to her absolute amazement, there stood the whole family. They had gathered excitedly around a magnificent, leather travelling trunk tied with a huge red ribbon. It was the most beautiful trunk Hattie had ever laid eyes on, not to mention the matching leather satchel, also emblazoned with her initials. She gazed at her father in disbelief.

"Do you like it?" he inquired as he reached to open the trunk for inspection. "Isn't it a beauty?"

"Oh, yes," Hattie gushed, reaching to stroke the leather. "I LOVE it—and the fact that YOU made it for me."

Her father couldn't hide his powerful feelings. "Your mother and I decided on it together," he replied haltingly, which nearly brought her to tears. "It's to honor your commitment to your goal, honey."

Ebenezer Sheldon was the kind of man who usually had more to say. The occasion of her imminent departure left him too emotional to continue. Even at supper, he remained almost as quiet and contemplative as her mother.

Later, he had regained composure, speaking brightly and with enthusiasm. Hattie took his words as encouragement. Occasionally, she had glanced at her mother, who struggled to smile and looked like she hadn't slept much. The same was true of her father, she realized. But she wasn't about to mention it.

"I can't get over the trunk," she complimented instead. "It's finer than anything you've ever made, even for your best customers. It should last me a lifetime!"

"The size of the trunk matches the size of your accomplishments," her father responded. "We may be unnerved that you're leaving us, yet your strengths deserve recognition."

"Thank you for saying that," Hattie returned, hugging him.

"Looking back, it's my fault those trailblazers at the shop filled you with dreams of going out west," he apologized, shaking his head. "Since you're determined to be a traveler, it was only right to fit you out with the best."

Hattie had thought of herself more as an explorer than a traveler. It sounded just fine, though. For she intended to follow the ideals of groundbreaking women who left behind tradition and convention. She was determined. After all, this trip was much bigger than attending a women's meeting in Seneca Falls or going to school at Amherst Academy in Massachusetts. She was traveling over a thousand miles to the frontier. Her contract would keep her away for three whole years.

"I will treasure this trunk more than anything you've ever given me," she vowed, "and let it remind me of you both daily." Then she kissed her father on the cheek and squeezed her mother's hand. Suddenly, a lump in her throat almost made her cry. Words escaped all three of them.

❖ ❖ ❖

There had been plenty of casual or even pleasant goodbyes in

Hattie's young life. This parting as she left for Indian Territory, however, was altogether different. Unlike trips in the past, today's moving train carried a young, almost-adult woman toward a profound, but vaguely defined, destiny. An unsettled feeling gathered in the pit of her stomach about knowing so little. The information letter she had been promised was to come from her employer, The American Board of Commissioners for Foreign Missions. Along with a report about the community of Park Hill and the Cherokee Nation, it should have provided a thorough brief about the teaching position she would fill.

The blast of a parting whistle broke the air as the train chugged away from the station. Hattie waved energetically from the clattering passenger car's smallish window. Soon, she would be distantly separated from her loved ones. As their waving figures faded into the horizon, she wasn't sure which of her many emotions to indulge. Moving to the back car for a final look, she remained there after it rounded a bend and Utica was out of sight. Standing silently for a long while, Hattie never took her eyes off the long, thin expanse of track. Even the spindly church steeple left the horizon, a last memory of the comforts of home and family.

Reaching inside her new satchel for a handkerchief, she unexpectedly retrieved a note instead. It was from her father! When had he slipped it in there without her seeing? Tears gathered in her eyes and tumbled down her face. His swooping penmanship pulled at her heart. She might as well read the note now and have a good cry. By the time she sat down beside Mrs. Worcester, she must be calm and focused.

Pangs of homesickness bombarded her as she loosened the flap of the envelope gently. Opening the card, she noted that he had been quite brief. If her father found himself at a loss for words, he often quoted the Bible. Hattie was overcome with emotion as she read:

July 21, 1856
My precious Hattie,

"Continue in prayer, and watch in the same with thanksgiving; withal praying also for us, that God would open unto us a door of utterance, to speak the mystery of Christ, for which I am also in bonds; That I may make it manifest, as I ought to speak. Walk in wisdom toward them that are without, redeeming the time. Let your speech be always with grace, seasoned with salt, that ye may know how ye ought to answer every man." Colossians 4:2-6

We will miss you terribly. Know that our hearts remain with you daily, even hourly. Please write at every opportunity and I will always answer.

Love, Father

❖ ❖ ❖

Unaware of her ache, the train chugged along its regular route toward Buffalo. Her tears dried, Hattie wondered how much longer her leg would take to heal. The pain stole much needed energy, but she had persevered toward her goal and trusted God to heal it.

Finally settling herself, she looked across at her sole, unexpected chaperone. Mrs. Worcester was already asleep and snoring. Hattie concluded she must be tired after her earlier journey from Vermont to Utica. There were still many hundreds of miles to go, though. What would America look and feel like as they approached the West? Hattie relished the idea of all the new sights she was soon to encounter. Since Mrs. Worcester had made the trip several times, she must have insights that would prove enlightening.

Before asking, however, Hattie savored her last private moments and closed her eyes. During preparations for her departure to Indian Territory, amid the hubbub of packing, and through the ache of parting from her family, she had taken precious little time to contemplate much of anything else. Now, reflecting on the end of preparations, she found herself surprisingly tired at such an early hour.

A jolt suddenly brought Hattie to realize she had nodded off. And she had been crying in her sleep! Quickly drying her face, she glanced at the still-snoring Mrs. Worcester. Thank goodness this show of emotion wasn't detected. Hattie reminded herself that it was time to show strength, not softness. Above all, she must not cry. If Mrs. Worcester caught her tearful, it could detract from the way she treated Hattie. Mrs. Worcester must see maturity, strength and readiness to teach.

Just last week, a little send-off tea for Hattie had been hosted by Mrs. Bagg, her doctor's wife, and Mrs. Fowler, her pastor's wife. They invited several of her school friends and other lifelong acquaintances from the church. Little white cakes iced to perfection had been served with a colorful side of fruit on Mrs. Bagg's best china. After the congratulations ended, the lively conversation turned to the recent engagement of several girls. Hattie and her sister, Amanda, made eye contact over the irony of the topic. Hattie's pursuit of an adventure set her apart from more marriage-minded girls.

What a surprise that her mother appeared almost light-hearted about her lack of marriage prospects. Maybe she was just deflecting attention, Hattie told herself. There was no escaping people's expectations and comments, after all. Where had her mother's new attitude come from? It seemed she was accepting Hattie's departure.

After so much derision, had she accommodated what she couldn't change? How and when had this taken place?

"Helen, Hattie will be back from Indian Territory before we know it," a nosy, grandmotherly neighbor had commented. "What kind of young man do you have in mind for her?"

"There is no good answer to that," Helen returned lightheartedly. "I've gone from worrying that Hattie will be attacked by Indians to praying she doesn't marry one."

Mrs. Worcester's voice snapped Hattie back to the present moment on the train.

"The recommendation letter Rev. Fowler wrote about you was impressive," she offered rather unsentimentally without looking up from her needlework. "He said some awfully nice things."

"He has been so encouraging to me—and said such profound things about your husband, as well," Hattie replied, smiling. "But we both waited in vain for the promised letter from the American Board of Commissioners for Foreign Missions."

"Just call it the American Board, dear," Mrs. Worcester corrected.

"Oh, alright. Anyway, I want to hear more about you. You already know so much about me," Hattie chirped.

"Goodness sakes! There's much too much," Erminia blushed. "I wouldn't know where to begin. You know I was born in the county to your north, don't you? Lewis County, New York, just above Oneida, was my original home. My dear father was a pastor in Lowville. My mother, Olive, was called Livvie and doted on me as her only child. They were honored for me to become a missionary teacher. I first went to Creek Path, Georgia among the Cherokees. My, those were challenging, yet rewarding days. I worked among older missionaries who might have perished were it not for the energies of someone my age. When I ponder the responsibilities they needed me to assume...."

"Who did you work for," Hattie managed to ask as Erminia stopped to breathe.

"Oh, the American Board, of course," Erminia replied, taking up where she left off. "They were the first and best, and still are. Thank goodness they sought me out because I would not have acquiesced to work for any other missionary body. The quality of person they hire is exemplary."

Monday, July 21, 1856

So excited still—beyond belief. Lovely scenery along Erie Canal. Conductor just announced upcoming arrival in Buffalo. Almost dark. So many thoughts. Thank goodness mother packed plenty of food. Mrs. W. said all details had been arranged by the American Board. Spending tonight in Buffalo. Sail from Lake Erie to Toledo tomorrow. Then Cincinnati—the Midwest's leading commercial and manufacturing city.

Days later, with a new exposure to logistics and protocol for women travelers, Hattie found herself on the Miami and Erie Canal approaching Cincinnati. Someone said up to four hundred boats had operated on this canal in recent years. The numbers surprised Hattie, as did the amount of trade.

The landscape had changed dramatically from New York

State's rolling hills, dramatic valleys, and deep gorges. As they crossed Ohio's flatter grasslands, Hattie was surprised to encounter sounder after sounder of swine. Cincinnati was particularly well known for pork, but also shipped huge quantities of flour, whiskey, and manufactured goods mostly down south. Evidently, farmers herded their swine right to the city's edge, where up to 1000 per day were slaughtered, processed, salted, and packed in barrels for shipment.

So far, the journey had not been taxing or subject to bad weather. Yet, every whisper of Utica's mountain air was gone. Until she found herself surrounded by the stench of swine, Hattie hadn't realized just how much she took fresh air for granted.

"Was this the only option for our trip," she questioned. "How long will this odor last?"

"Well, I had hoped we would find favor and be given a respite," Mrs. Worcester returned, as if God should have accommodated her. "Rise above it, dear. This route was the most direct one."

❖ ❖ ❖

Hattie liked watching several powerful horses tow the canal boat via the long, parallel dirt path. Sweat dripped from beneath their thick black manes as they plodded up the incline. She wondered how many workers it had taken to cut away the thick underbrush, dig this canal, and then fortify it. The ingenious design had to overcome significant land elevations. Needless to say, progress via this canal was much slower than on Lake Erie or traveling by train.

Prior to her departure, Hattie's father had traced all potential routes so the family could discuss the specifics at supper. How she missed him already! He said the Miami and Erie Canal, which cost an astonishing $8 million, had been financed by the State of Ohio, just as the Erie Canal had been financed by the State of New York.

Watching bubbles on the surface of the greenish-blue water, Hattie was reminded of his many suppertime lessons over the years. He was transfixed by the idea that, through the sweat of their brow and toil of their hands, ordinary men of enterprise had built America by the minute, hour, and day. This canal was proof of a brilliant plan actually linking the Atlantic Ocean to America's great lakes. The route increased trade by moving goods and people faster than overland. This trip was proving that America was much larger than Hattie had ever envisioned.

"It's absolutely thrilling. Amazing," she murmured, not really to anyone.

"Actually it is regretful to be on this canal," Erminia replied sternly, her brow furrowed. "Disease has plagued this project from its inception, I was told. It is rife with criminals and misfits of every ilk who imbibe alcohol, steal, fight, and cause danger for law-abiding citizens. The sooner we pass through to the Ohio River, the better."

Hattie didn't know how to reply to this smothering of her excitement. Perhaps she should change the subject to prompt Erminia's comments toward something pleasant.

"Maybe you could tell me more about the mission and the school," she responded brightly. "I'd like to learn everything I can about Park Hill."

Instantly, Erminia started talking, her gaze unfocused. Between big gulps for air, she rattled on and waved her hands as she spoke. "It is all encompassing. Reverend is sought out almost constantly for his many skills. He is a leader in the Park Hill community, of course. Because of the mission, we are also called upon for charity. Travelers show up from the far reaches of everywhere, so I keep guests almost without ceasing, in addition to my regular work. No one is turned away. As in any other home, our mission calls upon us to cook, launder, sew, farm, ranch, butcher, preserve, knit, weave, make soap and candles, write letters—in addition to running the school and church. I haven't thought of all that while being away. It makes my head swim! We have toiled dawn to dusk six days a week to build the mission to its present status. By God's grace, the children and I have mustered extra energies, sacrificed long hours, and spent years in prayer, alongside Reverend, of course."

Hattie imagined herself at her father's harness shop in Utica where she had swept, cleaned, and organized. In comparison to the description of the Worcester children's labor, she wondered if her father had really needed her. Certainly Hattie had not worked six days a week at the shop. Thankfully, her father always made her believe he couldn't get by without her.

"So, all your family members have regular jobs at the mission?" Hattie inquired.

"I should say," Mrs. Worcester declared, barely stopping in her haste. "After the boys left for school, we were hard pressed—desperate, really—for labor. It has aged Reverend horribly to toil over upkeep, repairs, and maintenance in addition to preaching, Bible translation, and printing. That's why his time away in Vermont is such a blessing. The family, especially Sarah and Hannah, made it possible for us to take this trip. Under my guidance, they became skilled in the requisite knowledge to keep the mission running under all circumstances. And, believe me, there is no predicting the circumstances."

Hattie hadn't forgotten that all six of Rev. Worcester's children were only Erminia Worcester's stepchildren. She noted that nothing was mentioned about Mary Eleanor, whom she had met earlier in the spring upon the trio's visit in Utica. The girl appeared nervous and troubled. She shared the same name as Hattie's beloved Aunt Mary in Amherst, but the two were as different as night and day. Since Mary Eleanor wasn't on this trip back to Park Hill, she must still be in Vermont with her father. That appeared more than curious, but was really none of her business.

"Mrs. Worcester, what does the mission look like?" she inquired instead, leaning forward. "Are there many buildings? How close is it to other residents of Park Hill?"

"Heavenly days," Erminia sighed, looking up at the heavens. "You must think me possessed of unending capacity to satisfy your inquiries. Soon enough, you will see for yourself, my dear. Now let me shut my eyes for a little rest."

Hattie blushed in embarrassment to find herself characterized as a pest. The last thing she wanted was to bother Erminia. It was just that so many questions were swirling in her mind about her new home, new job, new friends, new church, and new life! Perhaps, in another day or so, Erminia would decide to share more. Likewise, another quiet day without exertion should help Hattie's leg heal and stop aching.

As each hour passed, a new interest of some sort made itself known. Hattie's anticipation about the future was fueled by varying discoveries. For one, she was soon to travel on a steam-powered riverboat. Until now, she had only seen drawings of such vessels. Her younger brother, Artemas, had once made a sketch from a daguerreotype of the 1848 Cincinnati waterfront. Enthused, he had reminded her that an astonishing thirty-five side-wheelers were docked there.

This recollection made Hattie miss him and how he constantly shared his childhood passion for steam and engines.

She also recalled hearing of the risks that could sink steamships: explosions or fire in the boiler, as well as damage from snags or rocks. She had thought Artemas exaggerated when he mentioned the Ohio River. But now that she would soon travel it, the memory wore a little shine off her excitement, replacing it with questions about steamboats. Since there was no other choice, she'd best say her prayers and be grateful she wasn't plodding overland in an ox wagon.

To Hattie's delight, the steamboat operated flawlessly as late July arrived. Far from fear, great anticipation welled up at the sound of the steam whistle and the whoosh of water through the wheel. The beautiful ship, constructed entirely of wood, conveyed trustworthiness and sported freshly painted, smart black railings.

But in the heat on the open water and the confinement of small spaces, the shine wore off. Before long, time began to pass rather slowly. Most afternoons, Erminia preferred to take tea with other ladies in a little gallery. During these distractions, Hattie claimed to be napping, but slipped away to banish her impatience by exploring. Despite the intense summer temperature, she was thrilled to scout around the ship as her leg allowed and, all the more, to listen to the portly captain. One day, he noted her interest and stopped for a chat.

"Did you know that famous people like the Marquis de Lafayette traveled down the Ohio," he boasted. "I had the immense privilege to meet the writer, Charles Dickens, and the famous singer, Jenny Lind, when they visited America. You never know who will be aboard!"

Hattie enjoyed his swaggering, so she engaged him further with questions. Soon, she learned that the steamship carried much more than passengers: it hauled thousands of bushels of coal and stores of food for their provision. It also participated in trade by carrying large lower deck cargoes of molasses, cotton, timber, and rice.

Hattie hadn't considered the challenge of feeding scores of passengers for so many days. It must mean live animals were aboard and somebody down below had to butcher, cook, and clean. No wonder she had detected unsavory odors on occasion. The heat must be intense down below. However, it wouldn't be ladylike to comment or ask direct questions.

> *Tuesday July 29, 1856*
> *Today I walked into a swarm of gnats just above the hatch.*
> *I'm so uncomfortable. Never before has perspiration left white*
> *rings on my clothing. It's unsightly and makes me feel dirty.*
> *The temperature is unprecedented and miserable.*

Her initial excitement having worn off, Hattie searched in vain for ways to pass the restricting, hot hours. Short conversations like the one with the captain didn't make long, stifling days pass any faster. To make matters more trying, the slow, scalding passage of time drove most other passengers out of the sun so they were unavailable for conversation.

Monotony over the length of the journey was beginning to set in. Hattie grew impatient from pain, confinement, and lack of activity, but she pressed herself to stay focused and find things to appreciate. For instance, there were geographical and scientific phenomena her family had urged her to observe. A fellow passenger described the confluence of the Ohio and massive Mississippi rivers at Cairo,

Illinois, which would come soon. Hattie could almost hear her father's didactic reminder through an awed whisper: "*The Mississippi's flow surpasses BILLIONS of gallons of water*," he had repeated, adding a whistle of amazement.

Straining for even a brief glimpse of the far shore, Hattie wished she could narrate for him how far apart the Mississippi's banks were. On top of that realization of size, there were ten times more vessels on the Mississippi than she had ever seen anywhere. Each appeared to be navigated by someone unusual or memorable.

A graceful, vine-thin canoe cut through the water by the muscle of an Indian man slicing his oar in regular time. His long, black hair trailed in the breeze. Off to the starboard side, Hattie watched a team of sweat-soaked, burly men work in concert aboard an old flatboat. Behind it, their rope-connected raft followed clumsily as it bobbed along. A bit further down, two well-dressed gentlemen waved to her from a smart red and black modified canal boat.

Amid the endless panoply of many more sights on the water, Hattie decided a stately, two-tiered side-wheeler was her favorite. Noting it in her diary, she also calculated herself to be well over one thousand miles from Utica. It was a blistering Sunday morning, August 3, 1856. She had gone too far to turn back now, even though the cooler breezes of home sounded soothing.

❀ ❀ ❀

At Memphis, Tennessee, three well-dressed women boarded the steamship with some fanfare and a lot of giggling. Hattie studied their flouncy skirts and exaggerated, colorful hats before scrutinizing their satchels and carpet bags, which were similar to the ones her father made. The women were attractive in a way she couldn't define

exactly. Certainly, their fashionable clothes made the most prominent statement of anyone she had yet seen. Here was more evidence
that women were progressing beyond old customs. After all, these
women appeared free to travel wherever they pleased.

Curiously, Erminia said nothing after spotting them. Hattie
watched her smile and check her own grooming in comparison, however. Without question, Erminia was overly conscious about appearances. After the steamboat was underway again, she gave her attire
another once-over after the women seated themselves nearby. Then
she watched them intently.

To Hattie, the women were merely a source of amusement,
a temporary distraction from the journey's increasing tedium.
Animated conversation filled the air and was peppered with clever
observations. Yet, they kidded and pointed a little too much for
Hattie's taste. Before long, other passengers took notice, as well.
Having lost interest, Hattie gave her full attention to a growing list
of ideas and uncertainties about the Cherokee Nation.

"I was thinking about the Cherokee children," she remarked
thoughtfully in hopes of getting Erminia to comment. "Although
their parents are said to still have heathen ways, the children must be
endearing. I want my teaching to show compassion and incorporate
their traditions. Can you tell me a little more about them?"

"Hattie, Hattie," Erminia repeated in an exasperated tone.
"You wear me out, child. Must I constantly be prodded with questions? I cannot do my husband's work, as well as the Board's. I'm sure
they will write you all those details in good time. You must be more
patient."

Hattie took the scolding with a nod. Yet this time, she did
not let Erminia make her feel foolish. Rather, the dismissal was a
reflection on her chaperone, not her. Erminia simply did not want

to be bothered. She was focused firmly on herself and the present hour. This became all the more obvious when she rose suddenly and approached the three, animated women.

Not invited along, Hattie decided to just watch. She didn't feel a direct sense of rejection. Maybe this was just a vestige of Erminia exerting parental authority. Alternatively, she might just want to talk with new people.

For a while, she flattered the women and pursued a variety of conversation topics. The women shared some niceties, while not expressing the same level of interest. Amused, Hattie couldn't help making comparisons. Erminia had slighted and rebuffed her, but didn't stop talking long enough to blink among these new acquaintances. Her prattle encompassed recent travels in the east, afternoons at tea in Vermont, rides around mountain vistas, and shopping at well-respected establishments. No topic was too tiring or out of bounds, so anxious was she to impress the women.

While Hattie was focused on the display, she hadn't noticed two men who took a seat just behind her. Presently, their exchange caught her attention. Because of their bragging, she wished she could turn around to get a reading on them. That would be rude, however, so she just listened. The more they boasted, the more gripping their discussion became in comparison to the piffle exchanged by Erminia and the three women.

"You hear anything more on those murders week before last?" the younger man asked under his breath. "That killer's surely past the law's reach by now. I bet he's on this very river."

"So what," the other man replied in a raspy voice. "Indian Territory murders ain't news no more. Whites kill Indians. Indians kill whites. Both kill slaves. There's no law out there."

Hattie's pulse jumped. There could be a murderer nearby? She had never encountered such a blasé reaction to coldblooded killings. Rev. Worcester had not revealed that conditions were this troubling. If it were true, who were these men and where were they going?

"We'll hear more once the hands are dealt," the raspy-voiced one added. "Poker brings out the facts as fast as whiskey."

"Poker bought my ticket," the younger man laughed. "I'd gamble forever if I could. First, though, I'll try my luck with one of those gals over there."

"Oh, yeah? I bet they've got designs on bigger fish than us. Some fool's money bought those clothes and made 'em look respectable. But ok, let's flash some cash and see what happens."

The young man's reaction was a subdued, snorting guffaw. Hattie, frozen in her seat, found no humor in what she had just learned. These women must be considered "ladies of the evening!" Suddenly, everything around her took on a sordid feel. Appearances had led her astray. She blushed out of disappointment and embarrassment. For Erminia's sake, she wished it wasn't true. Yet wishes would solve nothing. What should she do? Never before had Hattie even imagined such a situation. She must be wise and handle this carefully.

"That old dame better be careful or they'll pick her pocket," the raspy-voiced man chortled as they stood to leave. "She's way out of her depth. Those gals haven't read the Bible and aren't about to start."

If Hattie needed further proof, it had just come. The men were laughing at Erminia, at how naïve she was to befriend the fallen women. She looked like a missionary, yet they could never know she had no intention except to socialize. How confusing that others thought she was proselytizing, which she actually should be doing anyway.

This misunderstanding joined a pang of compassion, causing

Hattie's protective instinct to rise. What could she do, given Erminia's impatience and frustration with her? There was no clever way to pry Erminia away from the shady company. So, Hattie decided to just keep a sharp eye on the women. If anything became suspicious or dangerous, she would try to create a distraction that might aid Erminia indirectly.

Luckily, there was no need of a rescue. Erminia apparently read the cues and decided there was little prospect of friendship. In a moping posture, she returned to her seat with disappointment written all over her face.

"It is so hard to make new acquaintances," she pouted. "I have been practically devoid of society all these years. It's rare having a chance to make a new friend. Those ladies were so guarded! It's simply inexplicable."

Hattie regretted that Erminia was so genuinely perplexed, but felt obligated to explain. Breaking this kind of bad news was a first for her.

"Um, I don't think they're actually ladies, as such. I overheard something you should probably know. And I apologize in advance for what I'm going to tell you, alright? So, well, it was disturbing to learn that those women only want the company of men, especially the kind with money. The truth is that gamblers bought their clothes and paid for their companionship."

Erminia Worcester's face fell from its self-absorbed contortion. Her eyes glowering, she spun toward Hattie. "I won't abide disparaging talk like that! You'd best mind yourself, Miss Hattie from Utica. It's not your place to judge."

"Oh, I'm not passing judgment on them," Hattie replied hastily. "It came from two scheming gamblers behind me who were watching your conversation. They disparaged the women in no uncertain terms. Yet, they voiced, well, they had a type of concern for you, too. One hoped the ladies wouldn't pick your pocket."

Turning red, Erminia grabbed her pocketbook, grasped it to her breast, and squeezed her eyes shut as if in prayer.

Later that night, the incident behind them, Hattie still had trouble falling asleep. She didn't feel very good and the whole scenario ran again and again in her thoughts. Truth be told, just like Erminia, she could have fallen into innocent conversation with the women. However, she knew in her heart of hearts that she would never, ever have approached them. Then another thought struck her. Was she avoiding the truth about her leg, just as Erminia was avoiding the truth about the women?

Unseemly experiences had been almost nonexistent in Utica. Now, it wasn't just her imagination that there were more of them. Hattie began to feel smacked by the unexpected. She was sensing the threat of unlawfulness in her soon-to-be new home, while dealing with unsavory people in her midst on the river.

Was this what worldliness looked like? The good people and the bad people seemed all mashed together on this journey, whereas life had been perfectly delineated in Utica. With each eye-opening incident, and every drawn-out mile traveled down the river, Hattie moved farther and farther away from anything familiar, comforting, or homey. Even when shading her eyes against the blazing sun, she felt blinded by the glare of the cackling harlots and jaded gamblers, the verbose captain and her unexpectedly narcissistic chaperone.

Her expectations for adventure and purpose had soured somewhat. Was this whole journey ill-conceived and naive? What must be coming next? Her reserves waning, she tried to remain optimistic.

After Monday, August 4, dawned hazily, the steamboat captain gave notice about coming into port. As they docked at the little town of Napoleon, Arkansas, a crowd of passengers clustered in anticipation of walking on solid ground. Hattie felt grateful to be leaving the seamy experiences on the Mississippi River behind. All the more, she was anxious to set foot on this farthest southern state of her itinerary. Soon, she and Erminia would make short work of this trip's last leg. Once they started up the Arkansas River toward Indian Territory, drawing closer and closer to Park Hill, she felt certain she'd get her second wind.

Hattie's excitement was short lived, when familiar voices caught her attention and pulled it back to depravity.

"You think there's much money here?" the young gambler whispered from behind her.

"There's always money. You just have to sniff it out," the raspy-voiced man replied sarcastically. "Every place has a few rich planters. While we're doing business, we'll find out whose money we're up against."

Erminia bristled at this exchange. Keeping her distance, she pulled Hattie back and imposed a long wait for the gamblers to disappear. Hattie's leg ached so terribly she kept shifting her position. Finally descending the plank, she tried not to limp as she searched the mountain of unloaded bags for her trunk. Erminia said goodbye to some passengers and then turned to stroll into town.

"Why are you so slow?" Erminia griped. "For a young woman, you seem to dawdle a lot."

Hattie only nodded as she toiled to keep up. What a hurtful thing to say. But she remained quiet. Block after block, she also kept watch for the little village she expected. It wasn't coming into vision.

Having passed several crooked, old wooden buildings, her hopes withered because the faded facades looked a little scary and stark. Were they even inhabited? To make matters worse, not so much as a blade of grass came into sight. Only weed-ravaged soil surrounded the foundations, along with more than a little refuse.

Further along, Hattie's prospect of enjoying clean shops and freshly painted businesses took another dive. There were no general stores, no decent structures, no attractive signage, and no flowers out front like in Utica. The only businesses in view, a hotel and saloon just down the street, sagged under chipped paint and looked unclean. Where were the beautiful trees dripping romantically with moss like those described in books?

Without warning, a gusty wind swirled a grit-filled cloud in front of Hattie and Erminia. It carried a shocking odor that caused Erminia to cry out in disgust. Hattie, on the other hand, knew instinctively where the odor came from. Seeking more evidence, she had only to look up. There, swarms of black flies formed a dark, menacing cloud leading to a stable around the corner.

All of her life, Hattie had been around horses, stables, harnesses, wagons, and hay; she knew the standards of cleanliness. This place had broken them all. Unswept piles of putrid waste and loitering workers made the squalid place and the pathetic animals inside seem all the more filthy and ignored. If she and Erminia kept walking, surely the worst of the infestation would stay behind them.

"I've seen enough," Erminia huffed as she stopped short. "Napoleon is no place for us. We're returning to the dock."

Taking Hattie by the arm, she thrust her nose away from the odors and made an abrupt turn. As they reversed, however, another unexpected yet even more horrifying sight stopped them. Not twenty feet away, the double doors of a neglected building had just opened. They swayed on squeaking hinges as four young Negro women were led out by a ragged, toothless man. A long strand of raw, bristly rope attached the thin, haggard women to one another. All stared soberly at the ground and struggled to keep their balance, what with their hands and feet shackled.

Stunned by the abject horror of the spectacle, Hattie unconsciously grabbed for Erminia. Simultaneously, Erminia reached across the front of Hattie's shoulders to block her from going further. Now motionless, Hattie's feet became unmovable boulders when she recognized the men before her. Erminia tried to lead her away, but she resisted and stared as the men approached the helpless slave women. To her horror, the young gambler from the steamship slipped his hand inside each woman's clothing and examined her midsection without regard to privacy or common civility. The slave women began to weep silently.

"They seem healthy to me," he reported without a hint of guilty conscience. "Should put in twelve hours a day and birth a baby every fifteen months or so."

"We'll take 'em," his raspy-voiced companion growled. "Put 'em over in that stable tonight. We'll collect 'em tomorrow before we leave."

The sale confirmed, a chorus of giggles arose as the same three tawdry women from the steamship stepped alluringly from the building. Hattie couldn't believe the gamblers had connected with the women so quickly. They swirled their skirts and applauded flirtatiously as the men approached them. How disgusting to make a spectacle of the slave sale, Hattie thought. In response, the gamblers bowed with hats in hand.

Taking one woman's arm, the raspy-voiced man caught sight of Hattie and Erminia. He shot them a long, dirty look and spat on the ground in their direction. Hattie could barely hide her disgust over having been near such decadent behavior. These amoral men were far worse than gamblers. They were also slave traders. For the first time in her life, she bore a sense of smoldering hate.

Tuesday, August 5, 1856
Fighting a poor attitude. Allowed to sleep on steamboat last
night. Bad news: the long drought means Arkansas River
is too low for boats! Our travel plans now scrapped with no
alternative in sight. Good news: seeing better side to Erminia,
although she coughed and wheezed all night.

Later, Erminia at rest under her parasol, Hattie introduced herself to a riverboat official and a well-dressed gentleman who were talking on the dock. Asking a few questions, she didn't get satisfactory answers or reassurance. A looming sense of delay added to her discomfort. When the official excused himself, she learned the gentleman was a cartographer by trade.

He listened to her politely and then let a slow whistle express his doubts. "You'd best get ready for the unexpected in that wild territory, young lady. You're going to be farther from home than you ever imagined."

Unable to help herself, Hattie drew in a sharp, shocked breath as her eyes filled with tears. His bluntness had been unexpected, but so was this emotional reaction. Immediately, he realized his error and corrected it by going on and on about drought, sand bars, shoals, and the resulting delays imposed on travelers. Gradually, she accepted the fact that nobody would be allowed to travel west on the low, unnavigable Arkansas River.

"Don't lose hope," he reassured after they sat on some crates. "Plenty of folks are going your way via ox wagon. I'm sure you can get a ride to the Cherokee Nation that way, if not another."

Hattie closed her eyes as the shocking remark reverberated. *Ox wagon? Surely something better…*

Erminia's sharp voice raised a question from behind them. "When's the next steamship," she demanded, looking like her nap must have been interrupted.

"Well, as I just told your companion, there's not one to Indian Territory," the cartographer replied.

"No, I mean a ship going north—back up the Mississippi," she detailed, sweat trickling from her hairline.

"Not for another day or so. But you need to go west."

"Never mind that. We'll be on the northbound one," she confirmed in a tone that meant business, and then walked off.

Hattie almost fell back from shock. Erminia was more rigid than ever this time. What an unmeasured decision! Hattie's next week—or more—was suddenly too miserable to picture. How could they get hundreds of miles *west* by sailing *north*? The endless Mississippi had been unbearable, yet Erminia was forcing Hattie back onto it. So much for her short-lived belief that that part of the journey was ended. Now, the sweltering, the sweating, and her pain would be lived *in reverse*. She dreaded this ill-conceived detour.

❖ ❖ ❖

Adding insult to injury, the filthy Napoleon Hotel that accommodated Hattie and Erminia for the night was nothing short of disturbing. Even before she caught a whiff of the dank lobby, Hattie nursed a foreboding feeling. Sure enough, she was right. It was a cramped, neglected, musty establishment—and those were the nicest words she could say about it.

Stale and oppressive, the room they shared overlooked the main street. Erminia soon pointed out that noise from the saloon might become a problem, then grumbled further and began inspecting the faded bed linens' cleanliness, the state of the stained wallpaper, and the age of the dusty cobwebs in the corners. Hattie wanted to counter that surely they could endure this one night before embarking on the new, but discouraging travel plans. But she held her tongue.

Lying down should help her swollen, aching leg, she told herself. She must focus on feeling less anxious and overheated. A subtle breeze from the open window brought a bit of moving air but it also shuttled putrid odors into the room. Thankfully, Erminia began to snore only seconds after her head hit the pillow. Silently, Hattie lowered the window, climbed back in bed, and struggled to thank God for getting them this far and keeping them safe.

Perhaps she had only rested soundly an hour or two when loud noises and shrill voices outside jolted her awake. Only a thin ribbon of moonlight reached her bed from the darkness outside. Suddenly questioning her sense of security, she sat up to listen. Obnoxious laughter rose from the street and then something smashed against the building as a man shouted. Hattie jumped in alarm before rushing to the window for a look. Wheezing again in her sleep, Erminia did not stir.

"My bottle's empty," a swaying man howled from below. "I just need one more little drink."

The next second, he stumbled and fell hard near the glow of a fatwood torch. Groaning in pain, he curled into a ball and rolled, soaking himself in the whiskey he had just spilled.

Hattie watched with new eyes. Until now, she thought she knew plenty about whiskey and its evil impact. Abruptly, however, she realized that all her so-called knowledge came from temperance society literature. Those clean, little white tracts only discussed the health damage from whiskey. Watching this pathetic drunk, she realized there were other, terrible aspects to a drunkard's life. Here he writhed in the middle of the night, a nuisance to the public. He must be destructive at home, as well. Several other people loitered nearby, yet didn't help him.

"Hey, watch this," he bragged to the onlookers while reaching for another bottle.

Before Hattie realized what was happening, he stood and threw it forcefully in her direction. Only inches from her window, it shattered loudly and ricocheted off the outer façade of the hotel. Thick shards of glass flew in every direction. Instinctively, Hattie let out a yelp of fear and ducked for protection behind the mildewed curtains. This matched her long ago, mortifying experience during the slave roundup in Utica. Her heart was literally pounding out of her throat.

"Lord, help us," Erminia bellowed helplessly into the darkness. "Is the truce broken? Get the children!"

Alongside her confusion, Hattie experienced a sudden, terrifying loss of strength that left her unable to stand on her compromised leg. What if the man threw another bottle through the window? Panting in fear, she stayed low and crawled toward her companion on hands and knees. Her limbs shook so badly, she made poor progress. Pulling herself up onto Erminia's bed, her leg throbbed with pain and she lost all sense of pretending to be mature.

The weeping that followed was spontaneous and intense. Great sobs came from somewhere so deep that Hattie didn't recognize herself. All at once, fear, hurt, and loss crowded down and nearly smothered her. She had always believed the world was basically good. But these people in this disgusting, dangerous place were very bad. How close had the drunken man come to causing her great harm? Deadly, jagged pieces of the shattered bottle had only missed her by inches. Her night dress wilted from sweat and tears, she chided herself guiltily for such worries. What if she were one of the slave women? In comparison to the stench of their awful night in the horrid, infested stable, how could she dare let herself weep?

If only she and Erminia could get out of here immediately, Hattie wished through the emotion she couldn't contain. All she wanted was to reach Park Hill, to finally settle into the little, safe community that Rev. Worcester loved so much. Life would calm down there and a sense of peace could grow as she began to live out her purpose. It was still so very far and beyond reach, however. Would they ever get there? Hattie buried her head in Erminia's pillow and tried to regain her composure.

Having recovered from her initial distress, Erminia rose and lit the lamp, urging Hattie to stop crying. The expression on her face did not show understanding or support. Hattie found this matter-of-fact response cold, confusing, and annoying. Her mother always showed compassion and embraced her when she needed comfort.

Erminia, on the other hand, displayed no empathy whatsoever for Hattie's broken feelings. Why was she just staring?

"For goodness sake, Hattie," she chided, her voice as warm as mountain stone. "You must collect yourself and put this into perspective. All is not lost. You aren't even in Indian Territory yet. This is trifling compared to everyday events there."

2

Dust and Desertion

The SS Arabia practically groaned as it forced its cumbersome tonnage north at a meager five miles per hour. Progress appeared nonexistent. Hattie sighed, realizing she had taken the Mississippi for granted as they had moved with, rather than against, the swift current.

To pass time, passengers swapped stories. This side-wheeler, brand new in 1853, was special. At one hundred seventy one feet long, she regularly traversed the waters of the Mississippi and Missouri rivers. A while back, she had carried soldiers all the way from Fort Leavenworth in Kansas Territory to Fort Pierre in Dakota Territory. How long must that have taken, Hattie wondered?

"Next month, she'll transport federal troops to Fort Gibson in Indian Territory," the captain disclosed, "and move quantities of munitions, as well."

This perked Hattie up, since Fort Gibson was supposed to be just a few miles from Park Hill. Captain William Terrill, the side-wheeler's new owner, was proud of his purchase. He had a knack for building repeat business, someone said. This must include flattering all the ladies aboard, Hattie concluded, after watching the way he complimented Erminia.

"All the way from Vermont," he marveled. "And not a hair out of place."

Erminia blushed like a school girl. "Why, yes, Captain," she replied. "We're trying to reach our post among the Cherokees. My husband is the Reverend Doctor Samuel Austin Worcester, whose valiant service in Georgia led to incarceration on their behalf prior to removal."

Hattie was so mortified by Erminia's boastfulness she wanted to fall through the deck planks. Erminia was speaking as foolishly and immaturely as Mary Eleanor had acted in Utica last spring.

"You don't say," Captain Terrill returned with exaggerated emphasis. "And where is the good reverend now?"

"Still in Vermont. The press of business on behalf of the American Board of Commissioners for Foreign Missions kept him," Erminia blabbered. "He is their longest serving missionary. Did you know that the American Board places Christian servants on every continent and in most territories?"

"Well, I'm honored to have you aboard," he tipped his hat politely. "We'll have you at your destination in no time."

"Oh, I wish that were true," Erminia continued, to Hattie's chagrin. "We were denied passage on the Arkansas because of drought. So, it's back up to the Missouri River, then south by wagon. I sent an overland letter with a rider to my family asking them to meet us in Springfield. We need transportation there from some port. Where are we docking?"

"This must be your lucky day," he replied, tapping his index finger on his lip. "My son and daughter-in-law are coming from Springfield to Jefferson City to meet me. It will be the first time I've seen my only grandchild. I'm sure they can take you back with them to Springfield."

Erminia smiled upwards while clasping both hands prayerfully in front of her nose. Almost ashamed of her pessimism, Hattie allowed that Erminia's chatter had led to the astonishing offer. They would not end up stranded after all. Hopefully, the captain's family was nice. But how long was that wagon ride to Springfield? Could she endure it?

Thursday, August 7, 1856
Almost glad not to be on the Arkansas River. The cartographer said it went through the richest bear habitat east of the Rocky Mountains.

Friday, August 8, 1856
Erminia's afraid whiskey sellers are on board and that the crates are full of bottles. That makes us game for robbers.

Saturday, August 9, 1856
It rained all day long. We are confined to very small quarters. My leg is killing me.

Sunday, August 10, 1856
Erminia wheezed and coughed all night. I could barely sleep because of it. Captain led a brief service of prayer, but she couldn't go. Much, much hotter today.

Monday, August 11, 1856
Muggy dampness. My clothes may mold. Oppressive in our
cabin. Not much better on deck. Thank goodness we arrive at
Saint Louis this afternoon.

Captain Terrill urged all passengers to disembark at St. Louis. While supplies were loaded, Hattie and Erminia strolled slowly along the river. When they returned, a crew of brawny men worked along the dock. There were two white men and two Negro men. All were muscular and powerful looking, Hattie observed, swatting gnats away from underneath her parasol.

One of the white men scowled repeatedly at the Negroes, which led Erminia to comment.

"Those Negro men are free," she whispered. "See how there's no boss telling them what to do?"

"You mean like an overseer in *Uncle Tom's Cabin*?" Hattie observed.

Several minutes passed, during which one of the scowling white men found a way to insult the Negro men at every turn. He criticized, argued, and made trouble.

"Someone should make him stop." Hattie complained. "The fight he's starting is unnecessary and unfair."

"Just about everything in this life is unfair for most Negroes," Erminia retorted seriously. "You recall that the Bible doesn't promise justice here on earth. Slaves, former slaves, and even free Negroes know that sad fact more than anyone."

"If these Negroes are free, why can't they stand up to that awful man," Hattie pressed.

"Because if a fight breaks out, and it may still, it's the Negro men against the white man's word," Erminia clarified. "I shouldn't have to remind you who would win and who could lose their freedom if the law got involved."

❧ ❧ ❧

According to the cartographer, Jefferson City was a town that controlled the river trade for many miles. More importantly, it was a crossroads for people going farther south. This encouraged Hattie, as she knew they would soon travel south, too.

To pass the time, she took to writing letters, some of which she knew would never reach the post. At least she could pass the time easier by recording observations, feelings, and ideas. Walking on the deck also helped. It could be painfully hot at times, although not as sharp as the hurt in her leg. Stretching helped relieve it somewhat.

While holding onto the rail above the cargo area, Hattie counted crates that were stacked nearby. Soon, two men began organizing them in anticipation of unloading at Jefferson City.

"Not those," a man with the manifest pointed. "They're full of fresh supplies for the soldiers. Get the ones with the stale cargo ready. They're good enough for the Indians."

❧ ❧ ❧

"Why the glum expression, young lady," Captain Terrill inquired later.

"I apologize, sir," Hattie replied. "Some days, I wonder if we'll ever reach the Cherokee Nation. I didn't count on any detours."

"This won't be your Waterloo, I promise," he comforted. "Let me tell you a real live Waterloo tale about an infamous Cherokee man!"

Seating himself beside her, Captain Terrill began a riveting story involving a rich Cherokee, a racehorse, and an ill-fated side-wheeler. A little over a decade ago, Rich Joe Vann, the wealthiest Cherokee in America, got bored running his cotton plantation. So, he indulged in two expensive hobbies: boats and horses.

First, he bought a lightning fast filly named Lucy Walker. She won quarter-mile races up and down the river, which made plenty of money for Rich Joe. He also sold her sought-after colts for up to five thousand dollars each.

Second, Rich Joe bought a spanking new, one hundred forty four-foot steamboat that had just been completed in Cincinnati. Because she was swift like his horse, he also named the steamboat Lucy Walker. Joe's goal was to win both steamboat races and horse races.

The afternoon of October 23, 1844, he left the Louisville wharf and aimed for New Albany, Indiana, then New Orleans. Joe wanted the Lucy Walker to beat another steamboat, the Minerva. This would demand a great deal of power from her three boilers.

The Lucy Walker happened to be full and heavy that day, having drawn passengers from Kentucky and Ohio. Some folks were anxious to follow Louisville's horses in the 1844 racing season, while others talked about the upcoming Presidential election. A few were traveling as a delegation from a Presbyterian Church.

"Lord only knows if they realized that Rich Joe had pushed the captain aside and taken control," Captain Terrill added. "Even worse, he was drunk and focused only on winning the steamboat race."

In his state beyond sobriety, Rich Joe ordered the slave crew around and grew impatient. Then, to his distress, the engines stalled late in the afternoon. Some say the water in the boilers got too low. The slaves scrambled to repair the problem because they wanted to please such a dangerous man. If they lost the race, something terrible could happen.

The boilers got running again, but Rich Joe had lost valuable time. Growing desperate, he came up with a wild plan. Beyond all good judgment, he ordered the slave engineer to throw slabs of bacon on the boilers. Fat could add quick heat, raise the water temperature, and produce more pressure for higher speed. The slave protested strenuously, screaming that the boilers would blow up. Rich Joe got so mad he pulled a gun.

So, the bacon went in. Luckily, the slave had another plan. Claiming he had to check something else, he distracted Rich Joe, then ran like nobody's business and jumped overboard. No sooner had he hit the water than the Lucy Walker's boilers exploded in a massive pyre of scalding hot metal and flames shooting into the sky. Blazing shards of the boat hurled hundreds of feet into the air and onto both river banks. People heard the blast from miles away and saw thick, black smoke billowing up from the river.

"I knew an old crew member from the Gopher, a snag boat nearby," Captain Terrill added, his eyes wide. "He saw it happen and was left partly deaf for months after the blast."

A big chunk of the Lucy Walker was thrown on shore alongside thousands of burning pieces of metal, wood, and glass. The rest of the boat sank slowly, its flames finally extinguished by river water. Nobody knew whether the racehorse was aboard or not.

"That's shocking," Hattie cried. "Was anyone killed?"

"Practically everybody," the captain confirmed soberly. "It wouldn't be polite to tell the ugly facts, ma'am. But some bodies were never found, while others, or parts of 'em, washed up later."

"Eeuuw! That's ghastly," Hattie whispered in stunned amazement.

"But it's not the end," the captain continued. "You see, relatives came from all over to collect their loved ones for burial. Rumor has it that somebody found an arm in a bush. There was a big, fancy ring on one of the fingers, and his family claimed it belonged to Rich Joe."

❖ ❖ ❖

Shaken from the story, Hattie pondered the Cherokees and Indian Territory from a new vantage point. Was she prepared to live there? Tales like this challenged her expectations. A creeping vulnerability wedged itself between her brain and her heart like a constant detractor. Her deflated dream had become longer, slower, hotter, and more tedious than any sane person could ever have guessed.

She and Erminia had been traveling for twenty-two long days. So far, her companion had conveyed precious little information about the Park Hill Mission, the Cherokees, or what she could expect. Tomorrow, with any luck, the river portion of the trip would finally, finally end. She dreaded the overland trek.

Feeling particularly alone and far from home, Hattie wondered if she didn't hold partial responsibility for Erminia's distance. Perhaps she should extend the hand of friendship and not appear quite so independent. If Erminia needed to be needed, Hattie's vulnerability might soften her heart. So, Hattie swallowed her pride and confessed her feelings of apprehension after supper.

"Yes, I have observed that," Erminia replied somewhat warmly. "And I must confess something myself. I was in no state to answer your

questions when we first set off. It was so unexpected for Reverend
to send me home while he remained with Mary Eleanor in the east."

"I was confused by that, too," Hattie admitted. "My questions
got lost or scattered after learning he couldn't make the trip."

"Well, it's not that he couldn't," Erminia paused, her eyes looking sideways. "It was, er, because of, uh, Mary Eleanor's ... choice. I
had so looked forward to some more time in the east. Leaving in his
place was a grave disappointment."

Mystified, Hattie measured her words. "I hope she, I mean,
things work out."

"She's in the Lord's hands," Erminia summarized, dabbing her
eyes.

Wednesday, August 13, 1856

Arrived Jefferson City. Captain found us a nice hotel. We
hope his family arrived safely and look forward to meeting
them. I have my nerve up to ask Erminia about Park Hill
again.

Out of the blue, the best way to approach Erminia had come to
Hattie. It was clear, which gave her confidence. She must appeal to
her chaperone's most evident interest: herself.

"I would love to hear about your work, how you met Rev.
Worcester, and what life has been like for you. Reverend had such
kind, complimentary things to say about you," Hattie began.

This time, Erminia smiled and looked up, almost in an instant reverie of good memories.

"Did he write to you? You said he spends many hours each day in correspondence," Hattie added.

Erminia chuckled. "That man uses more ink than a newspaper. He must write hundreds of letters each year. I'm sure you noticed his brilliant vocabulary, too."

The door had swung open. Erminia proceeded to give a flowery, inflated narration about how she followed her true calling. While working at a nearby mission, she met her future husband, although she didn't think of him in those terms before he was widowed.

Everyone who had the privilege of meeting Reverend Worcester knew they were in the presence of a great man—patient, meek, and humble at all times. He carried much responsibility, but never complained that his burden was heavy. Even more impressive, he took time for each person, need, and problem even as he doggedly pursued his life goal of translating the entire Bible into the Cherokee language.

When his wife died upon the birth of Mary Eleanor, people watched approvingly as he managed his six children well and maintained a posture of Christian leadership. He showed himself to be anything but a martyr, yet the demands soon tapped him. No one was more surprised than she, Erminia revealed, for him to begin to call on her.

"Others had their eye on him, you know," she whispered. "I guess he found me most qualified in heart, mind, and spirit to become his life partner and raise his children."

Hattie only nodded. She had hoped Erminia might include a few comments about the Cherokees. But there was still plenty of time.

❀ ❀ ❀

At breakfast, Erminia gushed about how persistence paid off both with her marriage and finding a ride from Jefferson City to Springfield. Hattie forced a smile when Erminia remarked that hope had returned and they both could look forward to the days ahead.

"Ladies, it's time to meet my family," the captain boomed later and led them outside.

Hattie relaxed at first glance. The Terrills looked like any other, normal family and their baby was darling. Maybe Hattie could let down her guard and not worry about the coming, overland journey. Perhaps if she stretched more often and breathed deeply, the healing would respond. At least they had a plan and could see the light at the end of the tunnel.

"How's the road we'll be taking?" Erminia inquired.

"One of the best ones around," young Mr. Terrill replied. "It goes all the way to Santa Fe."

"Is it safe? I mean from criminals," Hattie questioned, then comprehended that she might sound naive. She smiled sheepishly at Mrs. Terrill and the strawberry blonde baby.

"I reckon as safe as any," he returned. "No matter where you go, there's a chance somebody could hold you up. We don't honestly have anything worth stealing, though."

❀ ❀ ❀

August 15, 1856

My trunk fits. Thank goodness the wagon is large. Crossed a river by ferry. Another tomorrow, then open country. My leg is more uncomfortable than usual.

August 16, 1856

Drought here, too. Soil is so moisture-deprived that dust hangs like smoke in the air. Very, very hot. Perspiration rules the day. Erminia has not let a single thought go unspoken. She wants to be friends with Mrs. Terrill, who is with child again. I do not envy her discomfort. They spoke at length about canning, mending, and colic.

August 17, 1856

The last rain must have been a gusher. Ruts are over six inches deep. Slow going. Even the horses falter over the dangerously uneven ground. I feel that way, too. My teeth are nearly jostled loose. At least I do not have carbuncles, which Erminia brought up, along with potash. Does the sound of her own voice never tire her?

By the afternoon of the fourth day, clouds on the horizon hinted of a change. Hattie had begun to wonder how much longer she would have to stare at the parched countryside. Shortly, the wind shifted, blowing a strong blast against the broadside of the wagon. An unsettled feeling loitered in the air. Was this kind of wind commonplace?

"A storm's coming," Mr. Terrill warned, pointing to a low cloud bank.

Yet, as the front drew closer, it didn't look grey-blue like storms over the Mohawk. Rather, the ominous clouds were brown and churning. Hattie didn't quite know what to make of it.

A few moments later Mr. Terrill sized it up. "Get out your handkerchiefs and roll your sleeves back down. It's a big dust cloud.

In windy, dry times like this, the gusts carry sand that stings your skin like ant bites."

His advice became the understatement of the trip, for the savage gale carried a lot more than stinging sand. Along with its determined force came dried weeds, spiky thorns, and other remnants of prairie grasses, including a few cactus needles. Each fragment hit the travelers' bodies like a tiny piece of ammunition. With their heads down and faces covered, Hattie and Erminia huddled against the angry elements. Mrs. Terrill wrapped herself and her baby tightly in a shawl.

Unprotected, the wagon kept moving despite the onslaught, which seemed to last forever. The actual passage of time, however, was impossible to calculate because dust had blocked the very light of day. Complicating things more, Erminia began to cough and wheeze again. As the minutes passed, she drew her shoulders forward protectively and leaned against the wind. Before long, her whole body shuddered with each spasm. The cough itself sounded so tight and dry that Hattie wondered if the dust caused it. Erminia was growing short of breath quickly.

Such a frightening challenge in the midst of a dirt storm raised critical concerns. The wheezing, now more intense, led Hattie to a conundrum. Erminia's belabored breathing stopped her from uttering one word. She looked so pained that she might pass out. *What am I going to do*, Hattie wondered? *She's always in control. What will happen if I need to make decisions for her? Will she become angry again? Will she accept help?*

Hattie struggled for solutions in the face of few resources. Mrs. Terrill's baby had begun to cry. *How can I help*, Hattie wondered? Immediately, she reminded herself that her responsibility was

Erminia, who couldn't go on much longer with the elements beating against her. What if Erminia could no longer act as chaperone for the journey? Would they have to turn around and go back? Such worries only made Hattie tenser. The more she tightened her muscles, the worse her own leg pounded in pain. She had barely managed to walk without a limp these last few days.

Closing her eyes tightly, she groped mentally for something. Anything. Then, from nowhere, a word popped into her consciousness. Simplify. What? Simplify. Hattie looked up. Had God sent her a message? If she took credit for coming up with it, nothing would change. If she gave thanks to God, however, everything would surely get better.

A first step might be to keep as much dust as possible away from Erminia's nose and mouth. How could she accomplish such a thing? There was no fresh air. Hattie would try anyway. Uncovering herself, she couldn't believe how thickly their clothing was caked with dust. She reached inside her satchel and produced clean sheets of paper, then made a cone to protect her chaperone's nose and mouth. Quickly, she brushed Erminia off, shook her shawl and wrapped her again. Then Hattie looked around to take stock of the greater challenge.

Poor Mr. Terrill, bent from exhaustion, remained at the reins. His eyes must be as dry as a bone. The poor man couldn't cover them or he would lose control of the wagon and team.

"Do you know where we are?" she called to him. "I'm getting worried."

"Yes, I actually do," he replied above the howl of the wind. "We're far from any town, though. This is treacherous for all of us. The horses are losing strength, too."

A few seconds later, Hattie detected a little more visibility.

Turning in all directions, she spied a tiny sod structure down in a dry creek bed. Standing next to an old stone well, it appeared to have no windows and the roof looked secure. Perhaps it might offer shelter.

Tapping Mr. Terrill on the shoulder, she pointed out the shack. He nodded in the affirmative and immediately steered the horses off the road. This gave Hattie a boost of hope and confidence. With any luck, the well might provide some water so everyone could have a drink. She could stretch and get out of the wagon to see about the shack.

Hattie also comprehended something deeper. Despite her aching leg, she must rise to the occasion. It was time to help out on everyone's behalf and become a responsible adult. She could and would do anything to simplify this awful situation. Every previous hardship, trial, and threat had prepared her for just such a moment. She was ready.

Shortly, the little party of weary, parched travelers rested inside the shack with new hope. It was surprisingly sound and dirt free. Perhaps it had only been abandoned recently because some remnants of furniture and a few dishes remained. Maybe a settler had moved on after loading his wagon with all it would carry.

As if in cooperation, the wind began to subside. Mr. Terrill helped his wife and baby get settled and then went to water his horses from a small, mossy tank next to the well. By the time Hattie got Erminia calmed, the baby was already asleep. She went back outside to pump water.

To everyone's surprise, Mrs. Terrill produced a basket that had been sufficiently well packed to keep the dirt out. She removed and lit a little lamp, then offered the others some biscuits. Hattie handed out water, which they drank and used to wash the dust from their eyes. Reaching into her pocket for her handkerchief, instead she retrieved the precious little cross from long ago that the slave woman had made. Holding it close to her heart, she lie down beside the others on their makeshift pallets and fell sound asleep.

❀ ❀ ❀

The next morning, nothing outside stirred after yesterday's violent storm. Not so much as a bird call could be heard. Maybe all of nature was in hiding, afraid to come out of a safe place.

Erminia was sitting up when Hattie first opened her eyes. She wasn't wheezing, but her airway sounded ragged and her drooping posture revealed sheer exhaustion. The daylight's glow streamed in through the door Mr. Terrill had pulled open. It illuminated the fact that Erminia was pale and drawn. Dark shadows hovered under her bloodshot eyes. She stared silently at a wall.

Hattie gave her some water and then followed Mr. Terrill outside.

"I'm terribly concerned about Mrs. Worcester," she told him.

"She doesn't look at all well," he agreed. "Can she travel?"

"I don't honestly know," she confided. "How far are we from Springfield?"

"Not more than half a day's journey," he estimated. "She's going to need accommodation where she can rest. Our home is too small."

"Then take us to an inn. Nothing fancy, just clean," Hattie heard herself decide. "She wrote someone to meet us in that town, although I don't know where. I'll convince her that we need to get there."

In Springfield, Hattie did her best at the spotlessly clean inn to nurse the groggy Erminia. Sadly, there was no improvement, nor did Erminia have any appetite. All night, she continued to cough and wheeze constantly, which left Hattie more than restless. Neither of them got much sleep.

Vexed by the problem, Hattie descended the staircase to seek the innkeeper's advice. Within two hours, he delivered a greying medical doctor to assess Erminia's condition. M. M. McCleur, MD, a formal, portly practitioner, examined her thoroughly. After determining that Erminia was even too compromised to answer questions, he took Hattie aside.

"How long has she had symptoms like this?" he queried.

"Mildly for about two weeks," Hattie estimated. "It was prolonged exposure to the dust storm on our journey that made her so much worse."

"Oh, no wonder," he nodded. "Given the toll it's taken, she must remain in bed."

Dr. McCleur handed Hattie a bottle of liquid medicine to relax Erminia and help her lungs. As Hattie walked him down the hall, she told him about their need to reach the Park Hill Mission. On impulse, she almost asked if he had anything to soothe the ache in her leg, but lost her nerve.

"Keep Mrs. Worcester quiet," Dr. McCleur reminded as he left. "I'll come back tomorrow."

Earlier on the trip, the most impossible challenge Hattie could have faced was keeping Erminia quiet. Now, it took no effort whatsoever.

❖ ❖ ❖

Having hobbled down to breakfast, Hattie rubbed her leg while perusing the newspaper headline about a train wreck outside Philadelphia. She chided herself for being insufficiently grateful that she and Erminia had reached Springfield safely. Soon, Lord willing, they would depart for Indian Territory. How long might Erminia's convalescence last?

She wondered who Erminia had written about meeting them here in Springfield. How would they ever find each other? Would a family member or friends come? She hoped they were as nice as the Terrills because the trip would be another long one by wagon. There were no trains. Progress could be slow, once again.

Staring at the inn's floral wallpaper and glass lamps, she realized her perspective was changing. Back in Utica, her family could take a train nearly anywhere. That hadn't appeared special until the dusty wagon trek.

Looking back at the newspaper as she ate her egg, Hattie saw herself at the library, her place of refuge in Utica day after day, year after year. Her long habit of keeping abreast of the headlines seemed like a distant memory. Inexplicably, now that she was on her grand adventure, the world at large grew remote. Maybe she was just tired after four solid weeks of travel. She also hadn't wanted to admit a sensation of isolation, yet there it was.

I've been foolish to deny the confusion, she mused to herself. *The closer I get to Indian Territory, the more I feel I've gone back a whole century. Only I can't tell a soul!*

A feeling of being disconnected had mounted as the distance from Utica grew. By the time they arrived in Napoleon, Hattie felt cut off from the world, from family, and even from history. Of course, the stench and discomfort contributed negatively, as well. Just last night, she had also dreamed about lumbering along in an ox wagon at two miles an hour while lost in the wilderness.

She was closer than ever to Park Hill, so why was she having mixed emotions? Why did she feel as if she were in a foreign land? Springfield and even Park Hill were not separated from America. They were no less committed to the nation than were towns in the state of New York. The people were no less courageous or worthy than anywhere else. She shouldn't picture this place as separate and distant. It was wrong to think like that. In fact, it smacked of arrogance and privilege. If she allowed such an attitude to take root, she would regret it.

Hattie tucked the newspaper under her arm and headed upstairs. Why had her outlook changed from horizon-seeking to homesickness? Was the pain in her leg dragging her emotions down? She was worried about Erminia, which was legitimate. Perhaps her other mixed emotions were misplaced and just motivated by pain. Her bad attitude must change.

"How do you feel?" Hattie inquired, surprised that Erminia was awake.

"I must admit honestly that I've never felt worse in my life,"

Erminia confessed. "If only Reverend was here and we could go home together."

"Dr. McCleur is coming back to advise us," Hattie countered. "I'll make sure you're well taken care of."

"If only Dwight could do it," Erminia added mournfully.

"Who's Dwight?" Hattie returned.

"My son-in-law. Sarah's husband. He's the best doctor in the Cherokee Nation," Erminia explained.

Just then, a knock at the door signaled Dr. McCleur's return. Smartly dressed in a grey suit, he took Erminia's pulse and listened to her chest. Once or twice, he glanced at Hattie with a look of concern. Patting Erminia and urging her to take her medicine, he took his leave.

Hattie followed him out the door. "What do you think?" she questioned.

"She cannot travel," he whispered with a furrowed brow. "The protracted intake of dust hurt her already weakened lungs. It could take weeks to get her strength back."

"Weeks! We can't afford that," Hattie exclaimed.

"Do you know anyone here? Could you stay with friends?" he pursued.

"No, I'm from Utica, New York. Should I ask Mrs. Worcester if she knows anyone?"

"I'm afraid that's the only option," he advised. "Shall I wait?"

"I'll be right back," Hattie promised.

Returning momentarily, Hattie rejoined Dr. McCleur. "I didn't tell her why I was asking questions. She said a Park Hill plantation owner and friend of Rev. Worcester's, Mr. George Murrell, once spoke of someone named D. D. Berry. They were childhood playmates. D. D. Berry grew up in Baltimore and now lives here in Springfield. Have you heard of him?"

"Yes, as a matter of fact," Dr. McCleur smiled. "D. D. Berry is a merchant, benefactor, farmer, and the wealthiest man in these parts. He's also my patient. Shall I inquire on Mrs. Worcester's behalf?"

"Oh, that would be wonderful," Hattie sighed. Perhaps their problems were solved!

❖ ❖ ❖

While Erminia napped, Hattie rocked on the inn's airy porch and admired a neighbor's rose garden. She closed her eyes against the throb in her leg, letting the faint, fragrant perfume waft through her senses as if it were the medicine she needed. Shortly, a youth rode up on horseback and tipped his hat before disappearing inside.

Moments later, the innkeeper handed Hattie a crisp, white envelope. "It's from Mrs. Berry. Everyone around here knows not to keep her waiting."

The outer envelope's beautiful penmanship addressed itself to Mrs. Erminia Worcester. Hattie's heart jumped with hope that Dr. McCleur had worked so fast. Maybe the Berrys were offering to host them. Truth be told, Hattie needed rest and respite, too. Just because she had kept her broken leg a secret didn't mean it was well. It wasn't. That was obviously why it hurt so badly. Hattie thanked the clerk and took the note upstairs to Erminia.

August 22, 1856
Dear Mrs. Worcester,

It is my pleasure, along with my husband, D. D. Berry, to welcome you to Springfield. Your visit has come to my

*attention through Dr. McCleur. We have all read about and
long admired your husband's commitment to the Cherokee
Nation.*

*It is sad to hear of your difficult circumstances and the illness
that plagues you. I hope you do not consider me discourteous
to intrude on your convalescence. Since I doubt you have
found adequate quiet at the inn, I am happy to host you at
our home for as long as you need to recover. An ensuite single
room will be at your disposal, as will the household help,
carriage and any other requirements to make your stay as
comfortable and rejuvenating as possible. I will have my carriage call for you tomorrow at eleven o'clock in the morning.*

Sincerely yours,
Mrs. Letitia Berry

❖ ❖ ❖

Her mouth gaping, Erminia was pleased to the point of awe.
Such transformed prospects energized her to sit up. Her countenance
brightened significantly. Within a few short minutes, she crawled out
of bed and opened the closet to survey her wardrobe. A change came
over her as energy and strength returned. By comparison, in recent
days she had appeared so frail.

"You must help me clean up this mess," she uttered, waving a
hand toward her strewn belongings. "Such an invitation is straight
from heaven. I can convalesce and enjoy a sojourn in society, after all."

Hattie was so surprised she took a chair and just stared. There
was no question but what Erminia's coughing and wheezing had been
real. What about this sudden recovery?

The gravity of the predicament began to dawn. Hattie slowly

made sense of the scene before her. Erminia was again focused upon making friends, recapturing lost hopes after years of service and frontier sacrifices. She spoke the language of leisure, although she was supposed to be sick.

"After my hopes were dashed..." Erminia trailed off. "This will give me respite I was denied back east."

"You mean your time in Vermont was hectic," Hattie managed to ask.

"It was traumatic," Erminia huffed. "Taxing. I didn't fully understand then about Mary Eleanor. It's come into focus over time. I'm at peace now with her decision."

Clearly, something unusual had happened with Mary Eleanor. Hattie remained curious and even concerned about it. Yet that paled next to the cold development just now.

This hard emotional blow threatened to knock her to the ground. Mrs. Berry had only invited Erminia to her home, not Hattie. From all indications, Erminia did not grasp this fact and if she did later, it wouldn't change her mind. She was going to Mrs. Berry's. Period.

"Give me a few moments to gather myself, dear. I'm so excited I can barely think," Erminia added.

Hattie had nowhere to go but the porch. She closed the door quietly behind her and limped downstairs, all the while turning the tiny handmade cross over and over in her pocket. *Dear God, was Mrs. Berry's omission just an oversight?*

Or did Mrs. Berry know nothing about Hattie? How long could Hattie remain at the inn? Who would pay for it? What if no one arrived from Park Hill? What if Erminia wasn't ready to leave when the people arrived from Park Hill? What if her leg got worse?

Hattie grieved as she scolded herself. *Why didn't I argue for going overland from Napoleon? Why didn't I stand up to Erminia like I finally stood up to Mother? If I had been more assertive, I would likely be in Park Hill already. Instead, Erminia is deserting me over one hundred eighty long miles from there.*

Abandonment. That's what was about to happen. Hattie was going to be rejected by the only person she knew within hundreds of miles. This was a strange and perhaps dangerous circumstance. Even worse, this woman was her superior and the wife of a saintly, gentleman missionary who was her boss. How could this possibly have happened?

These worries and others crowded out sleep for most of the night. Hattie felt dreadful emotionally and physically. By dawn, her symptoms had progressed from pain to what felt like fever. There must be a smoldering fire of anger down inside that was causing this. Yet, Hattie decided to wait and hope against hope that the error might be corrected.

"You must agree it would be rude to turn down this invitation," Erminia reasoned aloud later.

"That depends," Hattie returned quietly as Erminia prioritized her own feelings. "I have quite a few questions about what is going to happen. Who did you write from Napoleon? Where did you say we could be found in Springfield? When are they coming? How will I pay this inn?"

"Oh, I hadn't thought of all that," Erminia replied. "At the time I wrote Hannah and Abijah, I suggested the town constable or sheriff for the contact. Make sure the sheriff knows we've arrived, won't you? "

"Well, what's to become of me? Am I to stay here alone? I have little money. If no one comes from Park Hill, what then? When will you be able to travel? What if I should become ill, too?"

"My goodness, dear," Erminia frowned. "Why are you so out of sorts? Answers will present themselves in good time. I'm sure Mrs. Berry just made an error. Once I'm there and we're acquainted, I'll ask her to bring you over."

Hattie was too tired, pained, and conflicted to argue her case further. While Erminia made final appearance adjustments, she descended the stairs with her selfish chaperone's bags. Hattie's leg throbbed so painfully she almost tripped. The pain bore upward sharply into the center of her body. Hour after hour during the night, she had been awakened by extreme discomfort.

After Erminia's departure, Hattie fell into bed. Why did difficult things happen just when something good was within reach? This had been the case time after time in recent years. The age-old answer from the Bible was not comforting, but she knew she must accept it anyway. Meanwhile, her father's words rang in her head: *"perseverance is in your blood."*

Following a nap, Hattie was clear only about accepting responsibility for herself: there was precious little explanation to account for Erminia. What was she to make of Erminia's choices and reactions? But no one could predict what Erminia would think. The most surprising example was the night in Napoleon. Hattie had come within an inch of being maimed by the drunkard's broken bottle. The incident terrified her, yet Erminia acted puzzled by Hattie's state of upset and even reproached her. It made absolutely no sense.

In fact, Erminia gauged many things by a Park Hill comparison.

As Hattie adjusted to the unexpected, even if she did her *best*, Erminia held her to a standard based on *worse* circumstances than she had ever considered. How was Hattie supposed to tailor herself to the ways of a place she hadn't yet reached?

This latest incident of leaving Hattie behind was very hurtful. Erminia did not comprehend Hattie's wounded feelings. Although her intentions must be good, she gave no credence to how Hattie would fare when left all alone. Erminia just didn't read people or situations well. Even worse, she appeared to always give herself the benefit of the doubt first.

Having reasoned through the distress further, Hattie napped again. Her not-so-sound slumber gave way to vivid dreams of insensitive people, troubling situations, the powerful wrath of Mother Nature, and the inexplicability of fate. Previous to yesterday, the prospect of abandonment was so remote; she'd never considered such a thing. She would have judged any feelings of neglect or desertion as self-pity. Now, they overtook her. All she could do was sob. She had never experienced such sadness or pain or illness in her life.

Nothing had changed by evening. But, drawing herself up, Hattie penned a note to the sheriff, explained the situation to the proprietor, and gave him the note to deliver. It told where she and Erminia were in Springfield, as well as the identity of members of Mrs. Worcester's family who were expected to arrive soon.

Returning to her room slowly and painfully, the thought struck Hattie about how "distracted" she had become. Her dream teaching job was becoming a remote, passing illusion. Her adventure smoldered in ruins now. Even so, if she had learned any lesson thus far, it was that God always had his hand on everything, even the unexpected. An oft-repeated Sheldon family phrase came to mind: *You come into this world alone, and you go out the same way.*

❖ ❖ ❖

Hattie lingered in bed the next morning, as all energy had taken leave of her body. Finally mustering enough vigor to rise and get dressed, her attention was drawn to an envelope that had been slipped under the door. Hopefully, it was from Mrs. Berry! Maybe Erminia had kept her promise. Hattie tore the note open optimistically.

August 24, 1856
Dear Miss Sheldon,

I did not want to disturb you early and hope you have rested well. I pray you find this note soon. A Cherokee man from Park Hill in Indian Territory stopped at daybreak. He asked specifically to see Mrs. Worcester, so I sent him to the home of D. D. Berry. He said he would stop back at the inn later.

At your service,
M. Miller, Innkeeper

The people from Park Hill had arrived already? How unexpected. This gave rise to many unknowns. Dr. McCleur had told Erminia not to travel. Could the people wait until her health improved? What would happen if they couldn't? Just how sick was she anyway?

Pushing herself for want of information, Hattie straightened and packed her belongings while glancing regularly out the window. The effort was a struggle, so she sat down to rest her leg frequently. This was the worst possible time to feel lethargic and feverish. Maybe she was just as incapable of traveling as Erminia. Explaining it would be impossible, however, because in overshadowing her, Erminia had the upper hand.

Soon, a wagon pulled up, let a man off, and departed. Hurrying through the pain, Hattie dreaded the trip down the hotel staircase. Normally, she would have pinched her cheeks to bring color into her face. But today, her face was already quite red. She grasped the railing for dear life and began her tortuous descent.

On the porch, she encountered a handsome young Cherokee man. "Are you Miss Sheldon," he inquired in good English.

"Yes, hello. What is your name?" she responded politely.

"I am Atohi Gunter. It's a pleasure to meet you," he returned.

Atohi Gunter, as it turned out, had been at Hannah's home when Erminia's letter arrived from Napoleon. He happened to be coming to Springfield to visit some relatives anyway and offered to collect Hattie and Erminia for the return journey. Atohi was accompanied by someone named Jesse who worked for Dr. Dwight Hitchcock. Hattie recalled that Dr. Hitchcock was Erminia's physician son-in-law.

"The doctor drafted letters of introduction for us," Atohi added. "We have places to stay on our trip back to Park Hill. Forgive me if I'm prying, Miss Sheldon. I was just so surprised that Mrs. Worcester is staying behind."

Hattie tried not to blink or break into tears at this news. But her disappointed heart almost stopped. Utter disbelief led her to turn and look sideways while trying to collect herself. She paused for a silent moment and set a false pleasant expression. *This upset must be taken in hand*, she repeated to herself. *I must endure it and not show myself as fragile or overly emotional.....even though I've been abandoned by Erminia.* Yet questions crowded into her thoughts even as she continued to make small talk with Atohi.

Momentarily, silent, new concerns joined her mounting questions. She was expected to take this long journey with two men? That was unacceptable where she had grown up. It was beyond the standard of conduct for women! She could not imagine such a thing, or what people in Park Hill would say once they found out.

Hearing the innkeeper approach, she turned politely, yet could think of nothing to say.

"Mr. Gunter here has delivered funds from Mrs. Worcester. Your bill's paid in full, ma'am," he explained. "Shall I bring your things downstairs now?"

Too stunned to reply, Hattie only nodded in the affirmative. Nearly all reason departed as she recoiled silently. She would be leaving Springfield with the two men today. Right now, in fact. There was no more money to stay at the inn, even though she knew she was ill.

One other hope died alongside this shocking development. Her tie with Dr. McCleur and the possibility of appealing for his help was now broken. He would not return to the hotel because his patient resided at Mrs. Berry's home. Hattie should have spoken to him about her pain and fever during his last visit. It was too late now. There was no other option than to depart Springfield.

She smiled weakly as Atohi took her arm. He waved with his other for the wagon to pull up. Hattie worried she might falter as she walked, she was so pained and upset. Her leg throbbed and her head swam at the very prospect of the blazing sun bearing down on her. Only brute endurance would get her to Park Hill. She didn't think she had it. Where would she go if they were forced to turn back?

"My aunt and another lady will be traveling with us," Atohi shared as they descended the porch steps to the street. "We will collect them on our way out of town."

"Really? Oh, thank you. That's enormously encouraging," Hattie sighed, relief joining her exhaustion. At least her reputation would remain intact even if her body didn't.

On the verge of asking who the ladies were, instead she was surprised to see a Negro man at the reins of the approaching wagon. Her mind raced back to newspaper stories of the recent repeal of the Missouri Compromise's former limits on slavery. The man pulled the horses to a halt and jumped down. She wondered who he was and how Atohi knew him, yet had no strength to ask.

"Miss Sheldon, this is Jesse, the man I told you about. He's taking us back to Park Hill with Dr. Hitchcock's team and wagon," Atohi explained by way of introduction.

Jesse, skinny and limber for a man who must be in his sixties, tipped his hat and avoided making eye contact with Hattie.

"How do you do," she replied warmly while mustering the energy to reply. "I didn't catch your full name."

"I just go by Jesse," he returned as he reached to hoist her trunk into the wagon. "Just Jesse."

For the first time, a troubling tremor like she had never experienced left her weaker than ever. If it would help, she might find comfort in just laying back and groaning. But she must grit her teeth and act like a proper lady. The last segment of her nearly endless journey was finally underway. Yet, she was entirely stripped from anything familiar out in this immense landscape. If only she could be excited and ready to appreciate every inch of terrain as they closed in on the Cherokee Nation. Sadly, she realized she barely cared because crippling pain consumed every ounce of effort and attention she could muster.

They departed unceremoniously just as Atohi began to talk with Jesse. Opening her parasol with shaky hands, an overwhelming sense of tiredness left Hattie barely able to keep her eyes open. In retrospect, these were her last vivid memories for a long time.

Her actions and words from that point through the next six

days floated through her mind as intermittent, foggy, and dream-like. She did not recall actually meeting the two ladies who became her traveling companions, but hoped she had acted grateful for their politeness and compassion. They must have helped her.

Vaguely, she recalled that her head flopped forward often as she dozed in the heat. Who were the hosts at night that had accommodated Hattie and the other travelers generously? During occasional lucid times, Hattie could still stir no memory of eating, yet surely she had taken nourishment. Powerlessness came into her life because the fever in her body took control.

Atohi was speaking. At first, his soft, soothing words sounded like a rhythmic poem from far away. Blinking groggily, Hattie gradually became aware that he was talking to her. When had her head come to rest on his shoulder? It was too personal, too close for a mere acquaintance. Fighting her maddening sense of weakness did no good however. She couldn't seem to move. Why did her ears ring so loudly?

The hoof beats of a trotting horse came near, bringing her to attention. A couple of men called out to one another. When had the heat of the day passed, Hattie wondered? She gazed up at the treetops and heard bird calls as evening fell.

"Miss Sheldon, we are in Park Hill," Atohi announced gently. "Can you understand me?"

"We made it?" Hattie uttered weakly as the wagon slowed to a halt.

Just then, the astonishing edifice of a huge, impressive building rose into view. It was the school with the huge Doric columns she had seen in the newspaper article so long ago! Seeing it face to face brought her up short. But she knew it wasn't a dream. The school's brick columns were as immense as any in Utica. And the tall, thin chimneys reached for the sky.

"Can you stand?" Atohi encouraged. "We need to get you inside."

Hattie held two fingers to each temple to quell the pounding headache as she let him pull her up. For so long, her thoughts had centered on taking that first adventurous step onto Cherokee Nation soil. Now that the moment had finally come, she found herself staggeringly compromised and lacking the strength to even look around.

There was Jesse reaching out his hand. He looked directly at her this time, worry gathering on his brow. Guided by Atohi, she was being asked to step down. As she took hold, Hattie caught a glimpse of her own hand and was startled to see how sunburned it was. How had that happened? For that matter, how had they reached Park Hill so quickly? It seemed only hours ago that she was standing on the porch in Springfield.

Without confidence, Hattie took a step forward, but just then the ground went watery. A floating sensation distracted her and seemed to carry her away. Her eyes closed to the restful idea of the Mohawk River back home. Quiet water sounded like the most refreshing thing on earth. She could lie back and float along in its softness.

Fainting dead away, Hattie was caught by the strong arms of the stunned Jesse. Several others who had been alerted by Atohi rushed forward to help. None of them knew exactly what to do.

3

The Promised Land

thereal whiteness lighted the unfamiliar room in which Hattie found herself. She gradually heard and then felt her own breathing. Air brushed her cheek, or had it been that angelic, flaxen-haired spirit that hovered near her? The spirit's face looked like her late sisters, Mary and Cornelia, which almost brought Hattie to tears, for she still missed them so terribly.

Suddenly sad, she turned and rolled into a ball while reaching out feebly with one hand. Hattie wasn't able to touch the spirit, but her hand grazed a magnificent, cool wall. Running her hand over it, she remembered brushing snow off new leather saddles on a wintry delivery day in her father's wagon. If only there was a way to trade the intense heat burning in her core for a crisp and chilly Adirondack ride with him.

An unknown man's soft voice questioned if she was still mumbling. In response, a compassionate woman whispered back that she was beginning to stir. Still believing herself part of a dream, Hattie liked how remarkably real and caring the voices sounded.

Yet from her high perch, winged for freedom, she reached for a cloud somewhere safe and unusually clean. What a respite after the foul town of Napoleon. In response to the horrid memory, Hattie pulled the bed sheet over her nose protectively. The sheltered feeling then transported her much farther back to that suspenseful night of the Underground Railroad rescue. There was her mother, reaching for the black cloth that hid Hattie and the slave child, Sena, from the soulless bounty hunter.

Although she didn't recall opening her eyes, Hattie gradually focused and gathered that she was in a strange place. Why, she even had company! A fair-skinned, freckled man with an anxious, concerned expression was holding her hand. Beside him, a kindly woman with greying blonde hair and blue eyes bore a loving expression. Hattie knew she was not dreaming any longer.

"Miss Sheldon, do you hear me?" the man asked quietly.

"Who are you?" she whispered. "Why are you staring at me?"

"Don't be alarmed," the man with the fair complexion apologized. "I'm Dr. Dwight Hitchcock, the physician in Park Hill."

"You mean, Mrs. Worcester's son-in-law?" Hattie inquired hoarsely. "I'm finally here?"

He nodded with a relieved expression. "We're so glad you've arrived."

"Welcome," the woman smiled through a deep sigh. "I'm Grace. "We'll talk after you're better."

Even though her weak body ached, Hattie still yearned to get up and going. However, she just couldn't help herself from falling asleep. When Dr. Hitchcock visited later, his revelations about her seemed too far-fetched to believe. She had suffered from a terrible fever all the way from Springfield. Atohi Gunter and the two Cherokee ladies had cared for her as best they could. They probably didn't know she was so seriously ill. Without being aware, Hattie had talked, eaten, and rested. Once she reached Park Hill and lost consciousness, Dr. Hitchcock placed her under constant observation. Others sat with her while she convalesced. Yet, she remembered nothing.

His narrow-set, probing eyes gazing through little wire spectacles, Dr. Hitchcock made meticulous inquiries. It was good she found his manner comforting because Hattie was forced to reveal facts of last spring's freak accident that almost destroyed her ability to travel. While leading a procession as part of a baptism ceremony on the Mohawk River, a footbridge had collapsed. Hattie had suffered a broken leg and then pretended to be fully recovered so no one would prevent her from making the trip to Indian Territory.

He considered the story important until the end, when he closed his eyes tightly and shook his head. After a pondering moment, he theorized that the strenuous journey had resulted in multiple setbacks for her leg. Hattie appreciated his manner and lack of scolding, which she deserved, nevertheless.

By the time she told about the dust storm, he was wide-eyed. The troubling facts appeared to coalesce and cause him agitation. He rose and paced as she concluded.

"So, you are saying that the storm caused the illness that required Mrs. Worcester to remain in Springfield?" he repeated incredulously.

"Yes, she wheezed and coughed in reaction to all the dust," Hattie confirmed.

Frowning with concern, he digested Hattie's revelation. "That finally makes sense. You're the only person who knows what really happened to her. We've all been terribly worried."

Once Hattie could stay awake, Dr. Hitchcock began to diagnose her properly. He took a thorough history, assessing how much weight she had lost and then measured her broken leg in comparison to the other leg. Briefly, he inquired about her education and family.

It turned out that he had graduated from Amherst College, an institution that was an outgrowth of her own alma mater, Amherst Academy. The mention brought Aunt Mary's dear face and Professor Colquhoun's wise mentoring to Hattie. How she missed them, as well as her school in Amherst.

With a more advanced Amherst education, no wonder Dr. Hitchcock sounded like an eastern man. It explained why she trusted him instinctively. His professionalism gave her hope at a time when she had few reserves.

Because of his manner, Dr. Hitchcock reminded her of Dr. Bagg, her lifelong family physician, whom she missed. If she could tell Dr. Bagg all that had happened since she left Utica, he would scarcely believe it. And she wasn't even settled in Park Hill yet.

How soon could she return to normal, she wondered? The issue of getting established in her new home had been primary before this unwelcome illness. If only she could jump headlong into her new life and home. Meeting people. Finding her way around the mission and Park Hill. Learning about and getting acquainted with the Cherokees. Starting school. Writing home.

When he finished the examination, Dr. Hitchcock pulled up a chair and took a seat at Hattie's bedside. He cleared his throat and then looked at his notes again. He did not make small talk.

"I wish I had good news, but I do not," he imparted in a solemn tone. "It is clear that your broken bone has not fused correctly. There may be several other reasons why you're feverish, as well. Undoubtedly, one is too little rest after you fell and another is too much activity."

Hattie's expression dropped sharply. She had not expected anything remotely this grave. His concern almost frightened her. Dr. Hitchcock continued to be quite serious as he explained that her illness was far from temporary. The next weeks would be very crucial.

"I can't say whether you'll be able to teach or not," he added quietly.

Amazed, Hattie's chin quivered as hollowness invaded her usually unflappable core. A thousand frantic thoughts brought her up short. How long would they wait for her to heal? What would she do if they wouldn't let her teach? Where could she afford to stay without a job?

Suddenly, these new questions were joined with pangs of regret over past decisions. For this verdict went to the very heart of her credibility and wisdom. Hattie had to admit to herself that she had been too driven and short-sighted in leaving Utica. She ignored all signs and essentially willed her leg to heal. How foolish. Then she had convinced herself that she was strong enough to go ahead with her journey to Park Hill. Yet that was even riskier. Finally, by hiding her intense pain, she had misled Dr. Bagg to her own detriment.

Dr. Hitchcock's point, innocently made, really meant that she was to blame for her own difficulties.

She was staring at remorse, as well as the potential loss of her dream. What purpose had her strenuous education and the tortuous journey served? She almost despaired over the procession of astonishing things she had endured to get here: the searing heat, endless days on the river, cackling harlots, foul-smelling Napoleon, gambling slave traders, horrendous dust storm, deteriorating health, and a chaperone who abandoned her!

The answers had something to do with maturity and character building. That kind of learning usually proved to be the most painful. She couldn't get around the age-old truth that no man was ever promised an easy life. And her problems weren't over! Here she sat, over a thousand miles from home without a single soul to hold her hand.

Dr. Hitchcock broke her reverie because he was still speaking. He had begun to describe how her bone, muscle, and other tissues were in terrible shape. So much so, that a question lingered about her ability to walk correctly and count on her leg in the future. The enormity of it agitated her to the point that her face and ears burned.

"And one more thing," he added before leaving. "I know you're anxious to meet everyone. But I'm asking you to take precautions for a few days. Stay in. Do you understand?"

"No company, then weeks of recuperation?" she repeated with disbelief.

"Miss Sheldon, your health is not sound enough for rigorous mission work," he emphasized. "Only time will tell—if you get enough rest. It's almost September. No one will fault you if you decide to leave. But if you remain, your commitment to your responsibilities is expected. There are many demands to meet."

From her second story vantage point, Hattie stared out the tall window through her tears. Just below, a white stone porch wound its way between column after column. The Cherokee Nation, or what she could see of it, stretched out generously in all directions. Her inability to enter it, however, left her devastated. Beyond her building, the patchy lawn sloped down to a prominent, white fence that must be sturdy enough to keep livestock out. But that fence was also keeping her in.

For as far as she could see, pecan, hickory and walnut trees graced the landscape in various shades of green. Flinty outcroppings broke through the prairie grasses, adding highlights of amber. Acre after acre of rolling hills to the south nestled around small farms. From her vantage point, she could make out individual houses, modest barns, and fields of corn not far away. They seemed to invite her closer. But that didn't change her burden of worries. What was she going to do? When would she get better? Who would decide if she could teach or not?

How curious that she had not expected such beauty in her chosen home. Even more poignant, she now felt like Moses: she could see the Promised Land, but could not enter. Yet, what good did it serve to regard this wonderful place as a prison? She should be thankful. In her spacious room, the puffy feather bed, handsome chest and curved wardrobe served as a makeshift welcoming committee. She appreciated the comfortable, practical furniture, even though it wasn't sanded and varnished like hers in Utica. The fact that her trunk fit in the room brought comfort by connecting her with her father.

Someone had taken very good care to unpack her belongings, Hattie noted as she gave them an overview. Then she paused. How had her least favorite dress ended up here? She loathed that unflattering dress. On second thought, it was perfect for this sweltering climate. Amanda must have stuck it in the bottom of the trunk as a little joke. She could almost picture her sister's gleeful expression upon sneaking it past her.

When Hattie inspected the rest of her garments for damage or mildew, all but one appeared intact. How in the world had she ripped it, she wondered? It was virtually ruined. Given the heat, she would have to get another lightweight, summer dress. Her things also needed a good wash. More than a little dust still clung to the collars, cuffs and skirt bottoms. But she didn't have the energy to wash.

A knock came at Hattie's door, which broke her gathering sense of monotony and loneliness. The woman who peeked inside was the same one, Grace, who held her hand when she first awakened.

"I hope I'm not disturbing you, Miss Sheldon," she asked timidly, smoothing her faded sleeves and skirt. She looked like a woman who worked long hours every day of the week.

"I'm thrilled for some company," Hattie smiled as she propped her swollen leg up. "And please just call me Hattie. Are you the kind person who unpacked me?"

Grace blushed and nodded. After talking for just a few minutes, they fell into instant camaraderie. This woman's kind, loving nature drew Hattie to her. Grace nearly oozed with genuine goodness that turned the edges of her eyes up each time she smiled. When she asked questions, Hattie could tell that Grace's interest was the most honest kind.

On second thought, just as Hattie started to inquire about Grace in return, she hesitated. "Dr. Hitchcock said I shouldn't have company until I'm better. Will he be upset with us?"

"I think he really meant for you to avoid exertion. He's a studious man of theories. The doctors he corresponds with in Massachusetts keep sick people away from mothers and children," Grace explained. "So, you're no threat to me. Besides, I've had every illness in creation and beaten them all."

Hattie already admired this woman and wondered about the history behind her last comment. Grace must not have children or else they were grown. Hattie left that question unanswered, as it might be sensitive. How old was Grace? She couldn't be as old as Hattie's mother, yet her posture drooped. Something about her hinted that she was careworn.

"Alright. So, tell me who else I'm going to meet," Hattie asked, a little spark of enthusiasm lifting her sagging spirits.

"Well, some marvelous people feel they know you already. Several helped while you were sick, like Martha Pilkington, who recently taught sewing in the Chickasaw Nation. She and her husband, Fred, will soon move to Texas, but came first to spend time with her two brothers. From there, let's see. You know that Dr. Hitchcock's wife, Sarah, is one of Rev. Worcester's daughters, right? She's had a bout of intermittent fever and isn't very well. They have a little girl named Laura. Then there's another Worcester daughter named Hannah. Like me, she has a Cherokee husband. Abijah Hicks is his name. He does all the farming and maintenance for the mission. They have three little ones, so Hannah does a powerful amount of work."

"Mrs. Worcester mentioned their names, but I didn't know all that," Hattie related. "I gathered that the Worcester's extended family is fairly large. But how do you know them so well?"

"I've worked for the mission on and off for years. Plus, this is a small place. Everybody knows everybody else's business for the most part," Grace added nonchalantly.

She went on to name other teachers like Jane Ross and Lotta Raymond, who were away but returning soon. Rev. Stephen Foreman, who worked with Rev. Worcester on the Bible translation, had a large family nearby. Dr. Hitchcock's parents had retired from Dwight Mission to Park Hill. Chief John Ross and his extended family lived a short distance away, as did Mr. George Murrell. And from there, the residents of Park Hill were too numerous for Grace to name.

"I've just got so many questions. There's a sense of urgency to get started here. I can't wait to get out and walk around," Hattie sighed. "I want to learn this place top to bottom."

"Sure, that's understandable. I should warn you, though. You mustn't strike out on your own," Grace said slowly with a pause.

"Why?" Hattie questioned.

"It's just that people don't know who you are yet. Better to wait until they see you're not a stranger," Grace explained. "Didn't anyone tell you that?"

"No. I can't believe it," Hattie returned, remembering that the expected letter full of additional information about the Park Hill Mission had never come. "You mean formal introductions?"

"Well, but who knows when Reverend, or Mrs. Worcester for that matter, will be back. Since you're not a member of the tribe, it's like trespassing," Grace added. "I'm just thinking of your safety."

"Are you saying it's dangerous here," Hattie queried, a little stunned.

"Not in broad daylight," Grace related. "But after dark, it can be risky."

❖ ❖ ❖

August 20, 1856
Dear Father and Mother,

*Your prayers have been answered. I arrived in Park Hill all
in one piece. Mrs. Worcester and I have tales to tell from
all along the way—Buffalo, Toledo, Cincinnati, Cairo, and
Napoleon. Just as you emphasized, the Mississippi brought an
endless succession of vessels and travelers. You won't believe
it, but drought in eastern Arkansas forced a detour back up
the Mississippi to the Missouri. We added stops at St. Louis
and Jefferson City before traveling overland with a riverboat
captain's kind family all the way to Springfield, Missouri.
On the way, a tremendous dust storm waylaid us temporarily.
After arriving in Springfield, a succession of the nicest people
came across our path: a wonderful innkeeper, a friendly
physician, a socially prominent woman, and a well-educated,
young Cherokee man. The trip from Springfield to Park Hill
sped like a dream. A dear woman met me and helped unpack
my things. She feels like a lifelong friend already. There
are so many more I want to know better, including Rev.
Worcester's family and others from the mission. You can rest
easy that I'm in a wonderful, second- story room and have a
panoramic view of my new home. Oh—my trunk made the
journey beautifully and rests at the foot of my bed. I will write
more later.*

Much love, Hattie

❖ ❖ ❖

Rocking on the porch, Hattie let the afternoon sun soak into
her spirit. At least she had finally written home, even though the
letter was long-overdue. The situation couldn't be helped because she

had felt much too ill to write since arriving in Springfield. Hopefully, her carefully-chosen words would comfort her parents and keep them calm until she could explore this place and share more.

Meadowlarks called from a nearby grove. Even though agitated about missing church her first Sunday in Park Hill, she told herself rest was healthy and would surely strengthen her leg. The time had been spent wisely. She had also penned letters to Amanda back home, Aunt Mary in Amherst, and her dear childhood friend, Margaret, in Hartford.

The brightness and warmth made her surprisingly sleepy, so she tugged at the brim of her hat and closed her eyes. A few moments after she dozed off, a horse trotted up and snorted. Hattie tilted her head and looked up.

"Good morning, Miss Sheldon," a petite young woman greeted. Auburn-haired and agile, she dismounted like a bird lighting on a branch. "I'm Martha Pilkington. Mind if I join you?"

"I'm glad to know you," Hattie smiled. "Grace mentioned your name. But how did you know mine?"

Martha said many had anticipated Hattie's arrival, which was encouraging. From the way she talked, Martha acted like she already knew Hattie.

"Do you know how I ripped my dress?" Hattie heard herself ask.

"There was a nail on the side of the wagon that snagged it. Thank goodness you weren't injured as you fell," Martha added with a hesitant expression as she reached toward Hattie. "Hannah Hicks asked me to deliver this letter of greeting. I'll be able to tell her you're better."

Taking the note, Hattie thanked her and smiled that Rev. Worcester's daughter had written. Seldom had she visited with someone who talked so fast or knew so much as Martha. This woman was a whirlwind of information and personality. Raised just across the border in Arkansas, she came from a large family at Vineyard, a place her father, John Latta, had founded about 25 years ago. Originally from South Carolina, he had known the Cherokees before President Andrew Jackson's unprecedented Indian removal program uprooted them to Indian Territory.

"That's the first glimpse I've had into anyone's life," Hattie remarked. "I can't wait to meet everyone else and hear their stories, too. But first, I need to see the mission. Do you know when school starts?"

"No, I used to live near here, but not lately," Martha responded. "I'll pass your questions along to Hannah, though."

"Thanks. Is she the best person to talk to about the background on Park Hill? I have so many questions. Like, about Indian removals," Hattie returned. "I assume things have gotten back to normal?"

"Normal? There's no such thing. The Cherokee Nation has calmed down, but there are still feuds," Martha expounded. "Things haven't been all that violent in years, though."

What in the world did *all that violent* mean, Hattie wondered, trying to hide her concern? This place was beginning to sound dangerous. Martha didn't notice and continued. Unorganized territories seemed to draw lawbreakers, she related. Criminals trolled the rivers, swindling others for fast money. Indian Territory was a crossroads for every sordid element of society, every down-and-out wanderer. Because the various tribes each had separate constitutions apart from federal law, criminals were handled in widely varying ways.

"Like everywhere else, there are lots of good people and some bad people around. Outlaws roam this land, using every trick in the book to sell whiskey. They target the Cherokees and their money from the government," Martha added. "Some Cherokees are wary of white strangers and newcomers. So that brings us back to you. Tell me about your trip? I've never been back east."

Hattie shared about her family, in particular her father's conscience, political sense, and abolition work. Her great love had always been reading and learning, which led her to attend Amherst Academy and then Utica Female Academy. The unforgettable article she had read about Indian removals as a girl quickened her senses before the chance meeting with Rev. Worcester, who hired her. She regretted that he had not made the trip from Utica, and then mentioned Erminia Worcester in passing. Martha leaned forward curiously at that mention.

"So, did you manage alright?" Martha whispered. "How was she?"

"Who?" Hattie returned.

"ERMINIA," Martha mouthed silently with exaggeration. "On second thought, you don't have to answer that. Just because I've heard some things from the girls, doesn't mean I should put words in your mouth."

Hattie knew better than to comment. But there was obviously some kind of story worth knowing. "My focus now is learning as much about this place—past, present and future—as possible. But Dr. Hitchcock advised me to stay off my feet. It's driving me crazy."

"Hmm. You're a big reader? That gives me an idea," Martha quipped as she rose. "I've got to go ask a few questions, but I'll be back. You can count on it!"

❖ ❖ ❖

Miss Harriet Ann Sheldon
Teacher, Park Hill Mission School
In Care Of: Cherokee National Female Seminary
Park Hill, Indian Territory

Dear Miss Sheldon,

Welcome to Park Hill! My brother- in- law, Dr. Dwight Hitchcock, has passed news of your arrival and recovery, as has our friend, Grace. I pray you're feeling ever so much better. My sister, Sarah, is also under the weather, but gaining a bit each day. We cannot wait to meet you. I have to depart for Fort Gibson to gather food and supplies for my family, however. Please forgive our inability to greet you in person. We are so excited to have you and want to assist you in getting acclimated. Also, bear with us, as the mission is still undergoing repairs during my parents' absence. It is the first time in many years that we could pitch in with renovations above anything moderate. Father is the utmost conservative manager, bless him. We are thankful to have saved him from the laborious construction he would have done himself. I cannot predict exactly when your quarters will be completed, but we are rushing to finish now that you have arrived. Godspeed until we meet in person.

Sincerely,
Hannah Worcester Hicks

❖ ❖ ❖

Slowly, Hattie closed and returned Hannah's note to the envelope. Its contents gave her pause. She shouldn't have needed the note to clarify that her overly wonderful room was too good to be true. A little frustrated, she now knew it was only temporary.

How naïve of me," she chided herself. *I wanted to believe this new, expansive place was the mission. Perhaps I've been foggier than I even realized. No wonder there was room for me; it's early September, so the students haven't arrived yet. But thank goodness for Rev. Worcester's leadership and close tie to education in the Cherokee Nation. It will help to meet the other teachers and share camaraderie with them*

Somewhat relieved, Hattie read Hannah's note again. It provided much food for thought. Would Hannah have a say as to Hattie's readiness for teaching after she healed? Since Erminia had said the whole family helped at the mission, that must be the case. Reading between the lines, Hannah also seemed to reveal that Rev. Worcester was extremely careful with the mission's money. Had he put the church and the children first? As for doing the heavy construction himself, how could he possibly find the time? He preached, managed and traveled to several mission stations, translated the Bible, looked after education standards in Park Hill, and ran a printing press.

Erminia's words returned to remind Hattie that Rev. Worcester wrote multitudes of letters and was a leader in the community. Did he have any help? What was happening at the mission during his long absence?

These questions on her mind, Hattie climbed the stairs to her room slowly and painfully. Exhausted, she collapsed on her bed for a much needed nap. Were she not so debilitated, the stifling heat might have kept her awake. She fanned while wondering if her illness, not the climate, caused her to suffer so. Then she slept.

❀ ❀ ❀

"Hattie, I've got a surprise for you," Martha's voice murmured while rubbing Hattie's hand. "Wake up. Remember I said I had an idea? Well, it worked! Instead of just sitting here alone with your questions, I got permission for you to read in a private library. You're going to Mr. Murrell's beautiful place, Hunter's Home. No stress or strain on your leg either."

Hattie's hand flew to her mouth in excitement. "How did this happen?"

"My brother has worked occasionally for the mission and knows everyone in town," Martha detailed. "He's made arrangements for you to go there for a few afternoons."

"That the big, white house I've heard about," Hattie brightened. "Did I tell you that Mr. Murrell's friend is hosting Mrs. Worcester in Springfield?"

"No, but I bet he's rich. Speaking of Mrs. Worcester, when is this year's social?" Martha asked. "I guess she'll have to host it since Rev. Worcester hasn't returned."

"What social?" Hattie queried.

"They haven't told you anything, have they," Martha retorted sympathetically. "There's a social every September. People come from the other missions and it's always a great time."

"How exciting! But, I wonder what I'll wear? My good summer dress is ruined," Hattie exhaled.

"You're talking to a seamstress! Show me that dress. Next week, we'll make fast work of the problem," Martha promised.

"Why, thank you! I can't go to the mission for the first time looking bedraggled. Can you possibly take me past there—just for a glimpse—on our way to Murrell's tomorrow?" Hattie nearly pleaded.

"It's not my place, to be honest. And I'll be gone with Fred anyway," Martha blinked. "Grace said she would come for you, so ask her about seeing the mission."

"Good idea," Hattie smiled.

"You'll like Fred. I've got to introduce you soon." Martha added.

"Bring him over one evening," Hattie invited as Martha slipped out the door.

❖ ❖ ❖

Grace rode her tame old mare, Lady, up the lawn, stopping just below the high base of the Female Seminary's porch. Holding onto a column, Hattie had only to accommodate her skirt and slide behind Grace onto the horse's back. It hardly hurt at all. In the future, she would need to find a better way to handle her skirt. Women in Park Hill didn't ride side-saddle as she had back in Utica.

Finally, she was off to get a glimpse of Park Hill for the first time. She crossed her fingers in hopes she wouldn't get too tired on this first outing. Grace said they were headed in the general direction of Park Hill Creek, a subsidiary of the nearby Illinois River. It wasn't far from the mission.

"Can you please take me past the mission? I haven't seen it yet," Hattie asked as they headed south.

"Me? I don't think I should," Grace hesitated. "To be honest, Mrs. Worcester, well, she made it clear that, uh, you're her charge."

Aha, Hattie reacted silently. Now things were making better sense. "You mean she wrote that all the way from Vermont? Now that she's waylaid in Springfield, surely she won't mind."

"You might be surprised what she minds," Grace returned warily. "Since she's the boss, I'd better not. What if she found out?"

❀ ❀ ❀

As Grace narrated, Hattie gathered that the variation in Park Hill's residences was due to uneven success: very poor to very rich. Mr. Murrell's place must fit into the rich category, Hattie surmised. Nobody poor had a private library.

Despite some brightness from the evasive sun, the morning haze lingered as they sauntered along. They aimed toward the creek's little offshoot called the Park Hill Branch. In the distance to the east, a lavender-grey peak of the Boston Mountains rose up to mark the Arkansas border.

As they rode, Hattie chatted to get better acquainted. After a few exchanges, she asked some questions. "Tell me about your family, Grace. You probably told me right after I arrived here, but remind me again. Do you have children?"

"It's just my husband and me. His given name is Smith. We married about 15 years ago," Grace replied.

"Does he farm?" Hattie inquired.

"No, but he hires out to farmers and planters sometimes. He also makes deliveries and does other jobs around the area," Grace added.

On either side of the plain dirt road, Hattie saw small, crop-producing farms of various sizes. Each farmstead had been laid out around a basic little house. Some were painted and others weren't. All seemed respectfully cared for and nestled next to vegetable gardens. But Hattie couldn't see any tendrils or blossoms. Those gardens looked anything but lush and overgrown as they should have been in late summer. Instead, burned edges marked the leaves. In the fields, the sun had bleached corn shocks dry. They made crackly sounds in the breeze, which was evidence of drought.

Hattie thought back, realizing that this ground had been but a prairie and the place virtually uninhabited only a short thirty years ago. The Cherokees, forced to this new homeland, had cleared it and started over. How long had it taken for the fields to produce crops? What had they done for food in the interim? Thank goodness nature's abundance had welcomed them. Rev. Worcester had said fresh, clear water bubbled from underground springs in huge supply. In addition, the countryside teemed with wildlife of every sort.

After going another short distance, Hattie noticed a woman with long black hair carrying wood. Shortly, she saw another laboring on her hands and knees over a stone. Was she grinding corn? Hattie shouldn't be shocked, but she was. Didn't they have mills here?

Beyond a grove of trees, a third woman dressed in a beaded skirt waved at Grace. She was stirring the contents of a big, blackened kettle atop a burning fire. This was more primitive than Hattie had anticipated. Rev. Worcester had said the Cherokees were now a more educated people. Naturally, she assumed that meant they took advantage of more recent methods. Did these people not have stoves in their homes? But she kept quiet out of an abundance of caution. This was no time to act privileged.

Shortly, she and Grace rode around a bend, revealing a much larger clearing ahead. Hattie stopped in mid-sentence as she looked up to an expansively beautiful estate. The home was approached by a stately winding lane edged by a long, vine-covered white fence. From its size, she estimated that the nearby orchard must contain hundreds of apple trees. Other buildings stretched even farther over the ridge and out of sight. Grace turned to see Hattie's expression.

"This must be your first view of a plantation home," she observed. "Next year, you'll see the pink rose bushes in bloom. This is called Rose Cottage. It's where Chief John Ross lives. Wait until you see the other plantations down the road."

As they rode on, Grace spoke of the Chief's long, loyal service to his people. Having been elected chief for life, he was about sixty-five years of age, but still quite the hard-traveling diplomat. He spent considerable time in Washington, DC and, in recent years, had remarried a woman from the state of Delaware. Their young children were his second family. To Hattie's surprise, Grace said the Chief had had a Scottish father and was only one-eighth Cherokee, although his heritage was thoroughly Cherokee.

When Hattie finally glimpsed the approach to Mr. Murrell's "Hunter's Home," she grew wide eyed once again. The house was much grander than her home back in Utica. Fresh and white, its frame structure featured prominent green shutters at the windows. Shadows floated across the gracious façade as the clouds gathered. A dark woman in a starched uniform swept the porch.

Grace said the house was fashioned after similar homes in Virginia, the state of Mr. Murrell's birth. Greek Revival in style, he had named it Hunter's Home because of his fondness for fox hunting. That mention accompanied the barking of several dogs who watched them approach. Tall, stately trees swayed over the expanse of lawn that led to at least three other buildings, one of which was a large barn. The sizable place yawned in three directions with the babbling creek flowing behind it.

"You should know that Mr. Murrell is white, but his young, late wife was Cherokee," Grace explained. "She got sick and died last year. Even sadder, he's childless."

"Oh, how tragic—and heartbreaking. I hope I'm not an imposition," Hattie returned sympathetically.

"He's away most of the time, so don't worry," Grace added. "They had been so happy and used to entertain socially. I don't know if he's ever returning or not. So, now you're on your own here. I'll say goodbye and come back in a couple of hours, alright?"

Hattie started up the walk, but couldn't help detouring slightly to look around the side of the house. Her leg ached, but not enough to stifle her curiosity. Just then, the cross-hatched doors of the barn east of the house opened to reveal stalls. A deeply bronzed man led a striking, sorrel horse out. Clanging sounds from somewhere must mean there was a blacksmith shop nearby. Curls of smoke caught Hattie's eye above another structure to the southwest, which had to be the smokehouse. Two women stood outside, their arms filled with baskets.

My goodness, Hattie exclaimed to herself. *All of these Cherokee people have much darker skin than I pictured. I've never known they were as dark as....*

Suddenly, Hattie's heart skipped a beat. She stopped dead still. Although she had never seen the Cherokees before, a natural instinct told her the people in her midst were not Cherokee. Some wore primitive clothing. They were avoiding her eyes. It seemed impossible, but she stared at them to be sure. Because they looked like slaves. Negro slaves.

Hattie momentarily lost her moral footing, geography, and sense of being. She didn't want to believe what she saw. The scene mirrored Harriet Beecher Stowe's famous depictions in the revolutionary anti-slavery novel, *Uncle Tom's Cabin*. Here she stood in Indian

Territory, not the Deep South. So why were Negroes doing this work in the Cherokee Nation?

Grace's earlier narration had included the word *plantations.* Hattie hadn't ever known there were plantations in Indian Territory. She had only heard about farms. But farmers didn't generally have slaves.

Bowing her head in grief, she turned back toward the front of the house. Her long history of familiarity with abolitionism in Utica had taught that plantation owners, the backbone of the southern economy, insisted they must have slave labor. Every abolitionist knew that fiction.

Something white caught her eye beyond another grove of trees. She walked a few steps only to find laundry on a strand of rope flapping in the breeze. A row of small closely placed cabins stood there, as well. If Hattie had doubted herself, this discovery put all questions to rest. These were slave dwellings. And this whole operation was exactly what her father and all abolitionists detested.

Nearly overcome with the blow of disappointment, Hattie realized she was staring. The last thing she wanted to do was show disrespect of the Negro people in this situation. Gathering her wits, she forced herself to return to the front of the house. Her heart now ached along with her leg.

As she knocked on Mr. Murrell's door, Hattie straightened her shoulders and tried to calm her agitation. When the door opened, her spirits brightened considerably. A smiling, heavy-set black woman looked at her and raised her arms in surprise. It was the same woman she'd seen sweeping earlier.

"You must be Miss Sheldon," she invited with a sweeping gesture. "Come in! Ever' hour I've watched for you."

"How do you do. Tell me your name," Hattie responded warmly.

The woman looked puzzled, as if a white woman had never asked about her before. But she responded in kind. "Well, I'm Susan, ma'am. I heard you were a northern lady."

Warmth and light poured in through oversized windows that seemed to reach beyond the silk damask draperies toward the outdoors. The leafy trees reflected handsomely in a large gilt mirror. Tiny little reflective rainbows sprang from the mirror's edge and hovered high on the ceiling. That led Hattie's eye to the attractive wallpaper in the hall. Grace had said this home was full of imported furnishings. Glancing around as she followed Susan past the parlor, Hattie had no reason to doubt her. The red plush furniture there fairly shouted of formality, as did the fireplace's heavy brass and irons.

"Master's away these days," Susan shared. "I was told Miss Martha vouched for you, so make yourself comfortable in the library. I'll be right near mendin'. Just call if you need me."

The library's bookshelves surrounded a desk topped with a lovely, hurricane lamp. If she were to guess, Hattie would say the late Mrs. Murrell probably enjoyed reading here. There must be hundreds of volumes and other periodicals in this room. She needed to take advantage of this generous opportunity, calm herself, and try to concentrate after her shocking discovery outside.

Surveying her options, Hattie walked her fingers along the shelf while reading the book titles. Most were classics one would expect a gentleman like Mr. Murrell to own. In fact, she had already read most of them herself. Nearby, she found two old copies of Arkansas newspapers and read them front to back. The jaded perspective of Indian Territory's neighboring state, which was a slave state, was to be expected.

Turning back to the shelves, she approached several stacks of handwritten originals and other printed documents from the American Board of Commissioners for Foreign Missions, her new employer! The first document was entitled *Minutes of the 1840 Annual Meeting of the American Board.* Hattie gaped at the subheading that read: *On Monies Raised from Slaveholders.* Quickly, she began to read its declaration.

"That God Almighty cannot receive the products of theft on the gift altar, we concur."

How astonishing! The organization would not accept contributions from slaveholders? That must include Mr. Murrell. Interestingly, the date on the declaration was sixteen years old. A committee of clergymen had been named to study the issue and make recommendations. They reviewed unrighteous methods that had secured money. She assumed that meant slave labor. The document went on to say men who employed such practices while claiming to be Christian were suspect in both their integrity and their intention. However, the committee added, any effort against such men would encounter so many problems as to make action imprudent for the Board.

Hattie blinked and slumped back in her chair, awed by the implication of what she thought she understood. Was she correct in interpreting that the committee recognized a wrong, but then refused to enforce actions against it? Impelled to continue, she next read a report from 1845.

"The committee acknowledges that no existing structure of slavery predominates among Indians of North America with whom the American Board missionaries work, with the exception of the Cherokee and Choctaw tribes. Neither has the Board ascertained that its employees working among Indians in territories neighboring any of the states have been asked to decide on the issue of retaining slaveholders as church members."

The issue was allowing slaveholders to remain members of churches. How extraordinary! Was Mr. Murrell a member of Rev. Worcester's church, Hattie wondered? How could she find out? She wondered if any action had taken place in recent years. It wasn't exactly the kind of question one asked because the answer was probably none of her business. Yet she was now formally associated with the American Board at a mission just down the road from slaveholders!

What if she were tasked with teaching the children of slaveholders? The thought occurred to her that the Board seemed able to excommunicate the parents from the mission church. The thought of it ran shivers up her spine. How could the American Board have sent her to Park Hill so uninformed? She doubted that Martha Pilkington had any inkling of this library's contents when she arranged this opportunity as a favor.

Returning to her reading, Hattie couldn't concentrate for the barrage of concerns in her head. There must be slave children in Park Hill. She must ask who taught them. This gave rise to even more uneasiness as she questioned who really was in the greatest need: the Cherokees or the slaves?

In quite a short time, Hattie's life had grown so complicated. First, her health was compromised, and now her beliefs. She felt naïve for assuming her new life would be cut and dried. That came from her immature desire for adventure when she should have paid closer attention her purpose. Her loving, but often sheltered childhood had not prepared her for anything like this.

While Hattie continued reading, strange sounds occasionally broke her concentration. Eventually, she realized they were bird sounds, but they did not come from outdoors. Curious, she was drawn to investigate. Following the sounds, she cracked a door around the edge of one bookcase, went through it and proceeded beyond the parlor. Craning her neck, she peered into the next room.

To her absolute astonishment, it was a bright, airy chamber filled with an unbelievable number of immaculate bird cages and billows of green plants. Each cage was home to one or more sweet canaries in a variety of yellow and green colors. She remained still and watched as they threw their little heads back and sang to their hearts content.

Again, the unexpected had drawn her. Surely, this must be what Heaven was like. Yet, she was a trespasser, just like she would be if she walked around Park Hill. Hattie closed the door and started for the library.

Passing the window again, she watched a tall, thin man stride across the lawn. He was impressive, imposing even, with an air of authority. Noting that his fair complexion looked slightly sunburned, Hattie scrutinized his weathered features before realizing that he wore a gun belt. He reminded her of many travelers from out west who had traded in her father's shop. Only taller.

As he neared a hedge, a second, lanky man emerged and waved. Hattie's stomach jumped to her throat. He was the most handsome man she had ever seen with coal black hair that glistened in the light. Wide, smiling eyes complemented his brilliant grin. She couldn't stop staring at him. As the men shook hands, Hattie decided they favored one another.

Under the shade of a tree, the men stood, hands in their pockets, and exchanged a few late afternoon comments before turning her direction. Hattie drew back from the window, as she didn't want to be caught watching them. And certainly, she didn't want to meet any man since illness had left her pale and gaunt. She would ask Grace or Martha who they were.

That night, after Grace left her at the seminary, Hattie was nearly overcome with exhaustion. Just as her leg brought pain, her senses ached from the unexpected stories she had read. Confused, she felt overwhelmed by the number of things she had discovered. Accommodating all that Rev. Worcester endured left her almost teary eyed.

On top of that, sticky, humid weather had returned with a vengeance. Even with her window open, nothing stirred the air. She fanned until her arm gave out. This oppressive climate in Park Hill had not been discussed in any library volume she consulted in the Utica Public Library. Had she grasped the near panic of suffocation, would she still have come? There in the dark, all alone, she wasn't sure.

Probably, there was no way to prepare for such heat. How long until my body adjusts, she questioned silently, even as her hair and teeth seemed to perspire. She longed for Adirondack breezes instead of this sweat-soaked existence. Yet, the heat got her mind off her aching leg.

September 1, 1856

Overwhelming discoveries today. I feel like a robber whose
theft hasn't yet been discovered. Father would die if he learned
the mission associates with slaveholders. I might be overcome
with sadness were it not for seeing that unforgettably hand-
some man.

Before the second day of reading at Hunter's Home, Hattie
suffered misgivings. A fitful night's sleep only added to the strain of
her debilitation. What if she nodded off and was discovered drooling
on the papers? She would never live it down.

But the drive to find out kept her pushing ahead; the volume of
information was just too enticing. She couldn't resist the chance to
uncover more hidden background on Park Hill. In all likelihood, she
would not be given another opportunity or source this rich.

On the way to Hunter's Home, Grace took her past another
remarkably large home. Originally owned by Chief Ross's brother,
Lewis, this painted clapboard house kept pace with Rose Cottage
in the elegance of its furniture. Grace had been inside once when
music from the remarkable Chickering piano filled the house. A few
chinquapin trees kept the structure company, while an immense grey
limestone chimney adorned it. That must be the warmest place in
winter, Hattie mused. The property was called Prairie Lea because
its location was so near a patch of unbroken prairie.

"Lewis Ross' daughter, Araminta "Min" Vann, lives there
with her husband, James, and daughter, Fanny. A bit of scandal follows them and their lives are unsettled," Grace revealed. "Don't let

on that I told you this. Once, after returning from a week of work in Fort Gibson, James grew suspicious and crept up to find that Min had a gentleman caller. A scary confrontation played out because James wanted to kill him. If Min hadn't rushed to hide the butcher knife, that's what would have happened."

Hattie grimaced as she envisioned the scene. "That name Vann is familiar. Are they related to the man whose steamboat exploded and killed all those people?"

"Yes, one and the same," Grace confirmed. "James Vann is the son of Rich Joe who died. Dramatic events run in the family. "

When Hattie pulled out a slim volume in the Murrell library later, several yellowed newspaper clippings fluttered to the floor. Taking an excited breath, she sat down to peruse the first clipping from 1831.

THE VALLEY PATRIOT

Serving Otsego, Onondaga and Oneida counties
in the State of New York

Wednesday, April 13, 1831

The state of Georgia is starting to carry out her laws for the Cherokee country. The account that follows specifies, in temperate terms, the details of the first outrage of their implementation.

Office of the Cherokee Phoenix, New Echota, March 19, 1831

This week, we can but issue half a sheet. The reader will interpret the reason below in the editorial.

Georgia's law makes it a serious misdemeanor for white men to reside in the Cherokee nation without having taken an oath of allegiance and acquiring a permit from his Excellence the Governor or his agent. Sunday last, following Sabbath services, the Georgia Guard presented itself and arrested three of our citizens, Rev. Samuel Austin Worcester, missionary for the American Board of Commissioners for Foreign Missions; Mr. John Wheeler, a printer with the Cherokee Phoenix, and Mr. Thomas Gann. Wheeler and Gann, who have Cherokee families, are citizens. They were removed to the home of a Mr. Tarvin and kept at gun point all night. The next morning, they were marched by Etowah where another missionary was taken into custody later that day.

The aim of this report is to provide factual information about what we saw and not to give editorial comments. This situation is early and we must be patient until it concludes.

To be fair to the commanding officer, Colonel Nelson, we report that he conducted himself with respectful behavior to the prisoners. It is regretful, but not all his colleagues were given to his level of kindness. Yet, we feel compelled to make note of an independent behavior. Sadly, we also report that it did not meet with the approval of the commander.

This spellbinding account had occurred before Hattie's birth, she noted. The very fact that the Valley Patriot's reading audience included her home county of Oneida made her pause. But since her parents lived in the country near Burlington, New York, back then, they probably hadn't read it. If they had, would she be here now? Several other stories she found about Indian Territory had also been printed back then. The first article from The Valley Patriot meshed perfectly with clippings that her pastor, Rev. Fowler, had shared with her.

Now that she was actually in Park Hill she could picture more graphically the injustice done to Rev. Worcester and, all the more, to the Cherokees. His loyalty to them had meant nothing to the Georgia government. In fact, for the state to arrest him seemed like open coercion. But he hadn't given in. He had remained loyal all the way to prison. Hattie could almost shed a tear just thinking about it. But, first, she had more to read.

THE NEW YORK ADVOCATE
NEWS FOR CHRISTIANS IN THE NORTH
January 1856

An act has been approved by the Cherokee Nation's two councils for the protection of slavery. It provides for the dismissal of teachers at mission schools who mislead a slave to the disadvantage of his owner. The act outlaws schools from hiring any known abolitionist or individual whose reputation goes in opposition to that of slave holders. Furthermore, it imposes a fine upon any native for advising a slave to the disadvantage of his owner.

Hattie nearly choked and had to pause for air. This article was printed less than a year ago and came from a newspaper to which her father subscribed! He must not have read this. Missionaries misleading slaves? She practically staggered to her chair from the book shelf, pondering if she would have the opportunity to interact with slaves. Whose slaves? She would love to teach them, to know them, to help them. But this story meant she would be watched! How ironic, because she was convinced few people even knew she was present.

The reporter had distinguished a relationship between a missionary and a slave as a totally different thing than a relationship between a slave and his master. Did slaves really have to keep solely to themselves and their plantations? Did their master essentially interpret the world to them? She had encountered such limits back when reading *Uncle Tom's Cabin*, but thought they were just the novel's fictional exaggerations. Now, they felt personal, a legitimate possibility close by in her new home.

Her heart beating fast, Hattie sensed danger and alarm. A certain defenselessness invaded. Her beliefs were sound and her mind clear on where she stood. But, faced with slavery that was entrenched, would her fervent plans be impacted or fall short? When the Worcesters visited Utica, there had been no question but what Hattie and her family supported the abolition movement. Nothing about slavery in Indian Territory had entered their conversations.

This finding turned her entire sense of purpose on its ear! If the reporting was accurate, Hattie might actually be in Park Hill in contravention of the law. She hadn't even formally started teaching, yet the facts seemed to shout that she was already at risk of being removed! She couldn't help but read on.

> The well-educated and politically versed Chief of the
> Cherokees, John Ross, vetoed the act. It did not pass the lower
> house and fell to defeat. The unspoken rumor is that detractors
> seek to end missionary efforts in the Cherokee Nation. They
> are impatient to stop the influence of educators who impact
> the established practice of slavery. Those opponents are said to
> have been successful in getting the bill passed. But Chief Ross
> looks ahead at his Nation's interests, which leads him to veto
> the act. He is to be admired for his philanthropy.

Hattie exhaled after reading this last section. Thank goodness Chief Ross had exercised his veto. It didn't mean the matter was over, however. Her father had talked about politics enough for her to grasp that issues didn't just go away after a single defeat.

Agitated, she watched the clipping quiver in her own hands. She was scaring herself now. It was the first time in her life she had shuddered like this. She still felt quite unwell, but had tried to be careful. This kind of symptom was troubling and would draw a big frown from Dr. Hitchcock.

Yet, she could not pull herself away. His opinion and potential scolding paled in comparison to the staggering accounts she was reading. How had educators threatened the practice of slavery in Park Hill, she wanted to scream. *Is that why I'm the new teacher? Did this impact my predecessor's departure?* Hattie had so many questions rushing through her thoughts that she dropped the newspaper clippings on the floor.

What had happened and why didn't she know about it? Someone was not telling the whole truth. Weighty issues like this demanded openness during the hiring of new teachers. Since Rev. Worcester had not told her, then who should have?

Surrounded by doubts and threats, Hattie tried not to succumb to anger. She wanted answers. But the sad fact was that the Worcesters were not there. Speculating about who she might ask without looking ridiculous, she realized these weren't the kinds of things one brought up to new acquaintances. Yet, in the absence of an explanation, how was she to cope with the feeling of urgency, the threat, and the complications?

The more Hattie fretted, the more her hands shook. Then her mouth went dry. Standing, she found herself a little wobbly on her feet, so she went to the window to stretch and clear her mind. It wasn't long before she was supposed to leave. Making the most of all opportunities must be her goal, she told herself, no matter how ill or upset the information left her. So, sighing deeply, she returned to her reading.

In another stack, she uncovered several copies of what turned out to be girls' newspapers. Momentarily, she envisioned herself back at the library in Utica reading every newspaper in sight, day after day, year after year. Hopefully, the Cherokee girls who wrote this newspaper shared her love of learning and hoped to explore the world in the same way she did.

One of the newspapers was called *Cherokee Rose Buds* and a second was entitled *A Wreath of Cherokee Rose Buds*. The girls had written and published the papers themselves, charging ten cents per copy. Picking up an 1855 issue from just last year, Hattie expected reports on classes, mentions of examinations, or notices about meals and laundry.

Instead, she gaped at the contents. To her amazement, one young author couched her new school environment in idealistic terms; she elevated missionaries and whites, presenting overly perfect images of them. This was quite unexpected. Reading on, Hattie discovered that this attitude was pervasive throughout the issues. Clearly, white culture held much more sway with the Cherokee girls than she had ever imagined. They practically deified the type of society she had so taken for granted and wanted to escape in Utica. The juxtaposition was more than a little troubling.

Up to this point, Hattie still had had little contact with the Cherokees. Perhaps that was good, since she must not understand them as well as she thought she did. If the attitude in these student papers was reflective of most Cherokee students, she had much more learning to do.

Her conclusion was born out during the next five minutes of reading. A truly surprising discovery loomed in the sentences before her, which had been written recently. Hattie found herself shocked by the girls' unfavorable descriptions of their own less-educated and less-civilized fellow Cherokees.

At first, she thought she had misunderstood or misinterpreted the content. Picking up another issue, she began to read an 1854 article. Once again, it placed great emphasis on developments made by Cherokees, only using current-day white society as the guide. The orientation emphasized changes of all sorts—educational, societal, religious, and moral. The girls' wording wasn't just about learning and growing. It was about completely transforming to become like whites.

Hattie squeezed her eyes shut to sort out the confusion. It sounded like these young people were turning on their own. What a shocking reversal after all they had come through as a people. But the relevance of it for the future had to mean something vitally important, as well. She must contemplate how to approach them as their teacher.

Reeling, she straightened the library papers. Her view of the Cherokees would need adjustment and a lot more study. Maybe she wasn't as equipped to teach as she had thought. How could she ready herself for things wholly unanticipated before school started? Amid these concerns, her whole body seemed to turn on her and all she could dream about was resting.

Back at her room, Hattie declared herself an anxious disaster. All the information she had encountered and its repercussions plagued her thoughts. The very success of her big plans seemed to hang in the balance. She had come to Park Hill because she wanted to teach the Cherokees victimized by extreme unfairness. Her treasured mentor, Professor Colquhoun, had called her passion about "the other side of the story on Indian removals" admirable. Now, of all the unforeseen impediments, slavery had reared its ugly head and clouded everything.

She sat down to rub her leg but couldn't get rid of the tension inside. How could she help from overreacting? Park Hill was serving up one troubling surprise after another.

Moping over her nausea and tense muscles, Hattie had to admit she was far from well and even farther from feeling like herself. The very thought of taking the stairs led her to skip supper. Discouraged, she climbed weakly into bed and stayed there, hoping tomorrow would bring better health, more information, and a calmer demeanor.

It didn't. She awakened with a start. The eastern horizon was barely light and, lacking the feeling of refreshment, she truly needed more sleep. The idea of going all day after a short, irritable night was not welcoming.

Sitting up, Hattie rubbed her eyes, only to find that they were crusty and swollen. Her skin felt strangely bumpy, as well. Putting her head back down, she dozed only fitfully. The light of dawn seemed to tease her with promise, yet she could only picture grey confusion. Slaves. Cherokees. Secrecy. Rich. Poor. Drought. Each time she closed her eyes, she saw stars. Which day of the week was today? Sweating profusely, she groaned in agony.

The sound of her own voice awakened Hattie with a start. How strange to have spoken out loud. And the name she had called was "Father." This suddenly covered her heart in homesickness. She missed her father so much. Tears flooded out of her eyes before she was truly aware of her feelings.

Oh no, she chided herself. *Don't cry. It will stuff up your nose!* Sitting up, she thought of getting a handkerchief, but felt too weak to walk over to the wardrobe. Thank goodness she had not made arrangements to go to Hunter's Home again.

As the hour wore on, Hattie's symptoms did not improve. She deteriorated to the point of fearfulness when a more severe wave of dizziness forced her to get help. Unsteady on her feet, the bed served as ballast while she held tight. Quickly throwing on her dress, she made wobbly steps forward and opened her door.

"I need a drink of water," she said aloud as she entered the hall.

An unknown woman happened to be there and approached as Hattie clung to her door. "Are you all right?" she asked in alarm, reaching to steady Hattie.

Uncharacteristically, Hattie didn't even introduce herself. Instead, she grabbed the woman for dear life. Before she knew it, all her strength drained out and she sank down to a seating position on the bare floor.

"I can't endure this heat anymore," she whimpered.

Her own words stunned her as she realized that she had run out of all emotional, mental, and intellectual reserves. The woman quickly sprang to help. She felt Hattie's clammy forehead, got her to her feet, and took her back to bed.

"I'm Jane Ross, Miss Sheldon," she promised. "I'm going to send for Dr. Hitchcock's help!"

The next thing Hattie remembered, she was looking at Grace. Those warm, motherly eyes spoke volumes. Shortly, Martha arrived, as well. They asked her all kinds of questions she couldn't answer. Why did they keep talking about her skin?

"I'm so hot, I could die," Hattie groaned.

"Oh, dear. It's an unbelievably cool morning," Grace whispered compassionately. "There must be another reason why you're so overheated."

"A storm chilled us down last night, Hattie," Martha added. "You're the only one who didn't cool off."

Even with cold water compresses, Hattie suffered with sweats. Then her chills returned. She grabbed the bedcovers to banish her shivers one minute and then threw them off the next. The ladies made her drink water.

Shortly, Dr. Hitchcock arrived. After giving Hattie a good once over, he reported disturbing findings. Overnight, she had broken out in a hostile red rash.

"I'm afraid this illness has entered its second phase," he informed a much-disoriented Hattie. "The rash is a complication on top of your bad leg."

A little shiver of dread ran up Hattie's spine. Nevertheless, she mustered the nerve to look at her arms and legs. They were covered with bright red spots, hundreds of them. So was her face.

"What is it? How do I get rid of it," she moaned.

Dr. Hitchcock looked annoyed. "I don't know, to be honest. The only certain thing is that you didn't stay quiet enough to heal. Look what's come from disobeying my orders. A headstrong spirit can get you—and the mission—in trouble. I'm recommending that you return to Utica as soon as possible."

Mysteries were waiting to be solved out there in Park Hill, just beyond the windows. Yet, Hattie wasn't sure if she would be allowed to go in search of answers. For she could not muster any strength to look out. If only she could clear her mind to think through the troubling information she had just discovered. But anything serious or concentrated made her head throb.

Why had she put mind over matter? Another serious error of judgment had knocked her flat and had repercussions way beyond her health. Would she truly have to pay a life-changing price for her lack of discretion? Not an ounce of cleverness, respect, or foresight figured into the way she had disregarded Dr. Hitchcock's wise advice. Now, she wished fervently for a chance to turn back the clock.

Hattie's fix fueled misgivings. There in her bed, she had plenty of time to just think. The climate was ripe for regret; she knew in her heart of hearts it would lead to nothing constructive. This was no time for blame either. The better choice leaned toward the positive. She might feel dreadful, but the one thing she could control was her thoughts.

How had other people overcome devastating blows? Unknown pilgrims and colonialists long before her time had followed wiser practices than she had. Courageous people in her past had faced down big obstacles, too. From somewhere she couldn't name, a gathering undercurrent of memories reminded her of their grueling trials, inspiring stories, and the way they had touched her life.

There had been her ancestor, John Sheldon, who tramped icy forests three times into Canada before redeeming his captured family following the Deerfield Raid of 1704. Her own father aided the Underground Railroad to secure freedom for runaway slaves. What about wonderful Professor Colquhoun from Amherst Academy? Revered for his debate teaching and history acumen, he educated young people while keeping his politically unusual heritage under wraps. How could she forget Harriet Beecher Stowe who vowed to change history by penning a novel that unmasked slavery's evils?

A tear stung the rash on her cheek as it trickled down. She envisioned her sweet, departed sisters whose untimely passing had motivated her to live like there was no tomorrow. Could she let them and her other towering role models down? No! She must now measure their influence and take encouragement from their brave deeds.

Even though Hattie told herself to be philosophical, she returned, nevertheless, to Dr. Hitchcock's scolding. What an unexpectedly severe rejection! How dare he suggest that she leave Park Hill! The very thought of taking his advice left her rebellious all over again. In fact, she was so mad she couldn't see straight.

Some reason existed for what she had been through—the unbearable situations and staggeringly hot days. What about the contortions she endured with Erminia just to get here? God must have reasons for such challenges. Thank goodness she hadn't been beaten before. But what about now?

Her whole existence up to today amounted to one giant sphere of determination ... for a better education, a break from boring traditions, and to win her parents over. Years of hopes, energies, and dreams reached beyond Utica and delivered her to this very place to fulfill the mission's life-changing work.

Boiling everything down, Hattie wanted to pound tacks into leather like she had time after time at her father's shop when she was upset. There was nothing to pound here! But she refused to give in and would not accept defeat. She had come to Park Hill for a specific purpose—to teach and help right old wrongs. She must not let Dr. Hitchcock's threatening order, her discovery of slavery, and the recent hysteria over abolition in the Cherokee Nation overshadow everything.

The time had come to look carefully at the larger scheme of things. That meant looking up. *Who do I think I am*, Hattie challenged, her idealism fading before her very eyes. *I'm in my own way. Nobody can overcome such obstacles with their own strength.*

These extremes could be overcome. But she must view her work as a mission of *faith*. More clearly than ever, she comprehended anew that she was on God's errand. In fact, she always had been. Ambition and stubbornness had just gotten in the way. Had God allowed her broken leg and then the rash to slow her down? Probably. Maybe he had a very hard time getting her attention.

So, falling to her knees at her bedside, Hattie asked God to soften her heart and show the way. She needed help taking stock and accepting Park Hill on its own terms. And from that prayer came the answer to her questions. This territory was not going to bend toward her. Only with God's help, could she accommodate it. But, oh, it was going to be hard.

A renewed sense of resolution began to offset Hattie's suffering and fears. Nothing about her situation appeared good. But she was alive. And she hadn't burned any bridges with Rev. Worcester. And there were children out there who needed a teacher.

For that, she was grateful. There was a bright side still. And for it, God deserved her thanks and praise. Even through all the trials and her illness, he was probably protecting her from something worse.

> *Dear Lord, help me have greater faith to beat this illness, accept the complications, and learn to respect frontier life. Only with your help can I get well and fulfill your plans for my life, your idea of my role. There's not even a remote possibility that I'm giving up and leaving. Oh, and please help me show Dr. Hitchcock and the others what I'm made of. Amen.*

4

The Real Park Hill

y the hour, Hattie's pen flew to fill pages with ideas, plans, and goals. In terms of approaching her new attitude, relationships had to come first. She must pay attention to every single person and listen carefully to all they had to say. Each one was another potential stair step toward gaining understanding, proving herself, and getting started. She must shed her outsider status.

Coming to terms with the background came second. If she wanted to fit in and do well, she needed to know the unspoken rules of the game, the facts behind this place's uniqueness, and the people who held sway. It was time to familiarize herself with the history of the last twenty-odd years.

Each day, something seemed to pique her sensitivity to unfamiliar events and circumstances. Without an understanding of them and how they contributed to the Park Hill of today, she could not be relevant. She must delve into the past.

Finally, participation rounded out the top three. If she wanted this to become her home, she needed to help out, listen, be available, and become identified around Park Hill. But, as time continued to pass, she must prove soon that she was not a renegade. Following orders was primary—while quietly beginning to carry out her plan.

September 4, 1856
I'm going to the social no matter what. The thought of putting
my tail between my legs and running all the way home to
Utica is repugnant. I'm going to find hope if I have to dig it
out of the dirt.

Martha was a great source of information, yet she was leaving soon for Texas. Until then, Hattie intended to make use of the fact that she was a walking dictionary of Park Hill facts and lore. For starters, she would learn as much as possible about people Martha knew. That included Grace.

"She's already helping Hannah prepare for the social. They've set it for next Tuesday," Martha shared. "Grace really likes you, Hattie."

"I like her, too. And she's been a tremendous help already," Hattie returned, thinking back to Grace's loving demeanor and giving spirit. "But do I detect something else? Forgive me for asking, but she seems quiet too often."

"Well, Grace's life is hard," Martha sighed and then launched into an explanation.

Her startling revelations included the fact that, years ago, Grace ran away from her malicious, slaveholding family down south and ended up in Fort Gibson. Some soldiers there treated her very badly. Rev. Worcester soon rescued her from the kind of awful fate that often befell destitute women. He even offered her hope, and then she came to Park Hill where she met and married a Cherokee man.

"But I hear he's mean, too," Martha punctuated sympathetically. "I think she remains here mainly because Worcester watches out for her."

Hattie could scarcely believe it. For a moment, she fell silent. "That's one more thing I could never have guessed. This place is full of startling stories. I can't believe there's slavery here. Or such complicated politics. Or wealth."

"It will take you a while to figure out the complexities," Martha nodded. "Was Murrell's library helpful?"

"Yes, but, also disturbing—even threatening. Abolitionism gets linked to teachers like me from the north," Hattie declared. "And that's just another complication nobody mentioned. I keep wondering what else I need to know about Park Hill?"

Martha shook her head ironically. "It will take more than a few little chats and afternoons of reading to explain everything. This place is full of twists and turns."

"Life here is so different than I expected," Hattie replied wistfully.

"Indian Territory is unlike anywhere else. There are wonderful people here, as well as murderers," Martha sympathized. "You have to deal with this place as it is. But time's wasting. Let's fix you a decent dress for the social."

❖ ❖ ❖

Martha appeared a little tired, but gave full attention to the challenging project. Surely there was a way to emphasize the good parts of Hattie's ugly dress and sew it to the salvaged parts of the ripped dress. They made a plan, then started to cut and pin the pieces together. Before long, a fairly decent and flattering new dress began to emerge.

As they worked, Martha told stories about her extended family about whom she was very proud. Her eyes glistened lovingly as she told Hattie all about them, one after another. Among Martha's seven brothers were James in Park Hill who arranged Hattie's visit to Hunter's Home, and John Stewart, the Deputy U.S. Marshal who covered this territory all the way to Fort Smith. Eli, Bob and Sam had all but disappeared into the west, while Will survived malaria after a wagon train debacle in Texas. Jack wrote occasionally from his travels. There were also two sisters. Peggy was married with a family at Vineyard and Lizzie still lived at home and looked after the patriarch.

"I think I already mentioned that Father knew the Cherokees well when our family still lived in South Carolina," Martha shared while clipping her thread. "Few understand them better. He arrived in Arkansas even before the government removed the tribes to Indian Territory. If you want to understand traditions and factions, he's the one to ask."

"What factions?" Hattie queried.

"They didn't tell you that either?" Martha declared, incredulously. "Good heavens, Hattie. That's a major issue. There's a bitter history of revenge and bloodshed between two disgruntled groups within the Cherokee Nation."

"But, why?" Hattie pursued as she salvaged good lace from the collar of the ripped dress.

"Wiser heads better explain that. It's terribly complicated," Martha demurred. "I'd rather tell a tale about brother John. I'm so proud of him. You need to keep in mind that the U.S. Marshals Service is the only law enforcement agency with the jurisdiction to enter Indian Territory and other frontier lands. John Stewart's job is to patrol this whole area. You will love how he dealt with a famous criminal."

As Martha's fascinating story unfolded, Hattie learned how a notorious ruffian named Mat Guerring had terrorized with the brazenness of his crimes. Back in 1847, he broke into old Shoeboot's house at Fort Gibson because Shoeboot's two granddaughters had Negro as well as Cherokee blood. Right in front of their hysterical mother, Guerring tied and kidnapped them. He managed to evade authorities all the way to Warsaw, Missouri. Since the girls looked like slaves, he wanted to sell them at the slave market and make a handy profit.

Riveted, Hattie could not believe her ears.

Deputy U.S. Marshal John Stewart Latta was sent to arrest Guerring and a gang of terrible desperados he associated with, the Starrs. But they were on the run. Meanwhile, the Illinois District sheriff, Charles Landrum, followed what he considered to be a reliable tip on the whereabouts of the two little girls. With the help of his tracking buddy, an old scout named Pigeon Halfbreed, they headed for Missouri and ended up discovering the girls unharmed. Things could have ended badly, but there was a very happy ending when they were returned to their family in Fort Gibson. Later, the Cherokee Council appropriated twenty-three dollars to reimburse the sheriff and Pigeon Halfbreed.

"But what about the kidnapper, Guerring?" Hattie begged, almost spilling the pins.

"Oh, right. He was just awful. People really wanted Guerring caught after his string of bloody knifings. He had committed gunpoint robberies and atrocious murders, too. So, John and an old partner rounded up a big posse of Cherokee Light Horsemen and trailed after him."

"Did they arrest him? Was he taken to jail?" Hattie interrupted from the edge of her seat.

"Nope. They shot him," Martha replied stoically. "Guerring met his maker on Friday, June 2, 1848. I'll never forget it."

❖ ❖ ❖

When Martha had to leave, Hattie asked for help later to convert a petticoat into two parts for riding astride instead of side-saddle. The Cherokee women she had seen around Park Hill did not ride side-saddle. Her successful venture with Grace told her she could stay astride like they did and it didn't make her leg ache any more than usual.

As they walked out, she thought she detected even more improvement in her leg. It felt a little stronger! She wasn't favoring it as much as before. What a sign of hope! She counted this as a blessing after months of misery.

Emerging into the daylight, there was Fred Pilkington waiting out front for Martha. Hattie was glad to make the acquaintance of this jolly man with round cheeks, big ears, and a sturdy frame. He related that he had taught recently at the Colbert Institute in the Chickasaw Nation. The opportunity to buy land in Texas was drawing them south, however. But he would teach there, as well.

"Martha's been a godsend to help me sew," Hattie told him. "She's got quite a few tricks I didn't know."

"Now, I must say that Hattie herself is surprisingly handy with a needle—more than some city girls," Martha interrupted. "She'll be a qualified seamstress by the time we finish."

Fred confirmed that even if Hattie had wanted to buy a store-bought dress, it required a nearly five-mile trip to Tahlequah. That could take the better part of a day. Most personal goods and products arrived by steamboat at Fort Gibson and then went there overland by wagon. Residents in Park Hill could buy only basic dry goods at Andrew Nave's general store.

Hattie couldn't help but reminisce about the wide variety of merchants, stores, and goods in Utica. All those wonderful choices from the past brought a nostalgic daydream or two. She could name the exact location of her favorite beautiful ribbons on the shelves at W. Williams and Co. But that was receding into the past; she no longer had access to a large number of choices. The limitation gave her a funny feeling. To make it go away, she decided to feel grateful instead. She had enjoyed wonderful privileges during her childhood.

Goodbyes were said and she was sad to see Fred and Martha go. Just before they drove off, she decided to issue an invitation, maybe to test their interest. "I hear they have sing-a-longs here every so often. Come back and join me one evening soon!"

When Hattie entered the dining hall, there sat her angel of rescue from the hallway, the Cherokee teacher Jane Ross. Prim in a calico dress, Jane stood and motioned for Hattie to join her. She was much taller than Hattie recalled.

They got better acquainted over a cup of coffee. Jane's easygoing manner and kind heart must inspire the young women at the seminary, Hattie thought. She held herself back from commenting or asking Jane about the Cherokee girls' infatuation with white culture, however.

Jane had just returned for the fall term after an extended visit to relatives. Openly, she shared about Cherokee removal and coming to this new homeland with her parents. Since no schools existed yet, she had attended the Cane Hill, Arkansas, school for girls. Her uncle, Chief Ross, then arranged for her higher learning at the Bethlehem Female Seminary in Pennsylvania. After the female seminary in Park Hill opened, she was one of several eastern-educated teachers who joined the faculty.

"Would you mind helping me with some yarn?" Jane inquired. "You must be bored from waiting to get out and meet people in the community."

Hattie appreciated the sensitivity. As she and Jane worked, Jane seemed happy to answer question after question. Her knowledge was impressive, not to mention her close connection with the venerable Chief John Ross. The Cherokee Nation, she explained, was a sovereign entity within the United States: essentially a little republic with a constitutional government all its own. The capitol was Tahlequah, a town just to the north of nearly five hundred people.

Hattie digested that number with interest. Her last recollection of Utica's population was eighteen thousand people. She had never thought of herself before as a city girl, like Martha had called her. But given the difference between Utica and Park Hill, she comprehended there might be more adjustments ahead.

Jane went on to say there were nine districts in the Cherokee Nation. The names were Tahlequah, Canadian, Coo-Wee-Scoo-Wee, Delaware, Flint, Going-Snake, Saline, Sequoyah, and Illinois. It was a surprisingly large area. For a homeland chosen by the government, the new territory was also much better than the Cherokees ever expected.

Of course, that didn't make up for the loss of their homeland. But they managed through both the good and the bad. Fresh, clear water bubbled from underground springs in huge supply. The streams were full of fish and the hills with wildlife. But, the land was rocky and not very fertile. Yet some managed to produce crops of cotton, tobacco, and even goobers.

"Beyond the land, there's great respect for education here," Jane specified. "It's a priority in Cherokee society. Did you know you're one of many well-educated New England teachers to come here?"

Jane was one, too. So was Rev. Worcester's daughter, Sarah. Hattie had heard somewhere that Rev. Worcester worked with the teachers and had supervised both the women's and men's seminaries. There must be great confidence between the Cherokees and the American Board, she concluded.

Picturing Rev. Worcester at the helm gave her a needed sense of security. He definitely had the background and passion for education. Surely that must be why Sarah and her older sister, Ann Eliza, had returned to teach and live near him in Indian Territory. The matter was too sensitive to bring up with Hannah, however. When her time had come to go off to school, the family lacked sufficient funds to send her. It made Hattie sad for her.

Hattie told Jane she had heard that Sarah's alma mater, Mt. Holyoke, had written the Female Seminary curriculum. The goal was to imbue it with knowledge, belief, behavior and purpose for Cherokee girls. She also wanted to inquire about abolitionism and its link to teachers, but thought better of it. Would she be branded as one before she ever began to teach?

Every time abolitionism came to mind, Hattie thought of her father. All of his life, he had revered founder Thomas Jefferson's reminder that all men were created equal and endowed by their creator with certain unalienable rights. She must have heard him repeat it a million times. Equality in law meshed with equality in the Christian belief system, her father said.

"I hate to interrupt our conversation", Jane was saying. "But I've got to be going. Would you like to read our fall student handbook? I'm sure you'll find it similar to the mission's."

As she turned the handbook over later and studied its cover, Hattie was reminded that she hadn't yet seen any of the mission's teaching materials or even the school room itself. She needed to ask where to locate the books. Had Rev. Worcester printed the ones from which she would teach? Another question of primary importance was when school would start. There were many important, but unanswered questions. Each day, they weighed more heavily.

She envisioned a steep, invisible wall blocking her from the Park Hill Mission. She couldn't see over it, touch it, or go around it. Ever sadder, she seemed to be the only person who even detected it. The fact that nobody would take her over there was just strange.

First, Grace had warned Hattie not to strike out alone as a stranger. But that was beside the point since Hattie could only walk short distances. Second, Martha had avoided Hattie's request to see the mission. It was an acceptable response since she had no formal link to the mission. But it was also evasive and widened Hattie's sense of separation. Third, Grace's excuse took Hattie by surprise.

Nobody was willing to cross some sort of unseen line at the mission. It seemed likely that Erminia was behind this.

Or was it just a mild mystery heightened by the anxiety from her rash? Per chance, the whole situation might just be a whopping oversight. She scolded herself that her energy would be better spent on the plans to remain in Park Hill no matter what.

Seemingly, only two remaining avenues existed to get her to the mission: Sarah or Hannah. Surely they had the authority under the circumstances. Had anyone even heard from Erminia, who had the ability to prolong an illness or make it vanish? Given her delirious happiness over staying at Mrs. Berry's, she was too far away to impact the equation.

Sarah or Hannah? Given Hattie's battle with her leg, which showed the outcome of too short a convalescence, she decided against Sarah. Whatever the nature of Sarah's illness, it had kept her silent and separated from the outside world. She was focused on healing. That left Hannah.

Hattie dipped her pen in the inkwell and started writing. Her appeal must use the most convincing, yet polite words she could muster. It would point up her sense of urgency since the September clock was ticking away. Until someone confirmed that she would not be allowed to teach at the mission, she intended to proceed as if she would—and soon.

September 5, 1856
Dear Mrs. Hicks,

*Thank you for your note of last week. Your kind welcome
helped me understand the demands on your time, especially
during your parents' absence. I hear you have taken Dr.
Hitchcock's advice—as has Sarah—to allow time for my*

persistent, fiery rash to heal. It is better and I'm excited to spend time with both of you.

Please allow me to transition into teacher's mode. Now that September is upon us, the impending start of school needs attention. Do you know when it is supposed to begin? I am anxious to see the mission and school room and locate the manuals and materials for review. Where are those stored?

The question of my duties is foremost, as well, because the promised letter containing those specifics never arrived. I also hope to familiarize myself with your father's translation work. Would you be able to show me the press? He spoke so fondly of your enduring assistance.

The unusual circumstance in which we find ourselves calls for a bold approach. I respect the sensitive matters that kept your father back east and know why your mother remains in Springfield. Yet, surely the parents and students who are counting on the Park Hill Mission also wait for reassurance and notice. I have now been in Park Hill over a week and feel a great need to press forward in the spirit of cooperation. I pray you will not be burdened or offended by my appeal and thank you for any help you can offer.

Sincerely,

Miss Hattie Sheldon

Jane's copy of the Cherokee Female Seminary's daily student schedule surprised Hattie. It was even more stringent and tightly controlled than hers had been at Utica Female Academy. Students rose at 5:30am and studied for one hour before breakfast. Next came chapel.

Five hours daily were assigned to recitations, both before and after noon break. Late in the afternoon, students could choose from various forms of physical exercise for half an hour before an early dinner at five o'clock. Two hours of study hall rounded out the evening followed by two retiring bells, the last of which rang at nine fifteen.

On Saturdays, students could run and play, often around the river where swimming was allowed. But not on Sunday, when all students were required to attend church. No activities were allowed on the Sabbath. When did the students have time to pursue interests of their own, Hattie wondered? She had always enjoyed extra time to read books of her own choosing, as well as newspapers and periodicals at the library.

Dearest Hattie,

Hello from home! It goes without saying that we wait in nervous anticipation for word from you. Surely your trip was full of enough stories to fill a book at the library. If you are reading this, it means you arrived safely in Park Hill, which was our greatest concern. Both mother and I have worn out our knees praying—and our brains thinking—of news to share with you. The shop is quieter, of course. Artemas mopes around the house pretending he likes having the run of it. Oh yes, the foot bridge has been repaired over the Mohawk—as good as new for next year's baptisms. How is your leg? I hope it is so completely healed that you've forgotten about it.

*Your mother and I were commenting at breakfast how very
quiet the house is since you left us. The only rambunctiousness
comes when Amanda brings little Mary, whose blonde curls
and milky white skin continue to enchant us.*

At this mention of little Mary's lovely, flawless skin, Hattie was
sent into a dither. Frustrated, she folded her father's letter without
finishing it and began to pace the floor. *My face looks anything but
flawless,* she moped.

She so wanted to go to church on Sunday, but had to admit that
vanity held her back. It was true that some of the bumps had cleared
up and the worst of the rash was over. But, what a mess it left behind!
She still looked alarmingly and severely speckled. If only it hadn't
impacted her face with such a vengeance. How could she make a
decent first impression in this condition? People would either think
her ill or juvenile just when her credibility needed to be established.
This rash could prevent her from coming across as capable and forth-
right. Her decision was firm even as her guilt mounted: she would
not be seen at church.

Back in leafy Utica, her parents' imagination of her circumstances must wander toward an abject wilderness. But that really was
not valid. Park Hill was a thriving community full of busy people—if
only Hattie could meet them!

She knew she should write her parents back, but the truth
couldn't be revealed. They needn't know about the myriad of challenges that bombarded her. If she wrote, the best she could do was
reassure them that she was fine and getting excited to teach. It might

not be a bad idea to echo Jane's point that many of Park Hill's residents placed powerful emphasis on education. Conversely, she would avoid any confirming mention of criminal activity or outlaws nearby. News traveled fast, and who could say but what a story about Indian Territory might pop up in eastern newspapers? The clippings at Murrell's library had proved that. Hattie hoped her parents would never read that citizens and missionaries alike avoided crossing paths with kidnappers, robbers, whiskey sellers, and murderers. She didn't want them asking about difficult things that were true.

"Where have you been? I've missed you," Hattie cried as Grace came through the door.

"We took the ox wagon to Fort Gibson for supplies," Grace replied sheepishly. "Like Hannah does, remember?"

Hattie was so embarrassed she wanted to kick herself. She should have recalled this. When first telling about Hannah, Grace had explained how Cherokee citizens got supplies. Hannah herself had mentioned it when she sent that first note. Hattie had not shown Grace the sensitivity she deserved.

That was the price of becoming too focused on one's self. This had become evident when she heard herself pouting over her skin. Why did it bother her so much to be spotted? All she knew was that milky white skin would make a better impression at church and the social.

"Let's have a look at your rash. Have you ventured out yet?" Grace inquired, her eyebrows raised as she reacted to Hattie's spots.

"Dr. Hitchcock's order is driving me crazy," Hattie whined. "But I have no other choice."

"That's what I thought you'd say," Grace replied with a wry smile. "But a little bird told me the good doctor had to leave early this morning. He won't return for a couple of days, which is another way of saying you won't get caught. I've got a carriage today. Want to get out in the sunshine?"

Hattie was so excited she enfolded Grace suddenly in a bear hug. When Grace shied back, Hattie withdrew out of concern. "Are you alright? I didn't mean to…"

Blushing, Grace turned to grab her bonnet. "You just surprised me, that's all. Let's go!"

When she laughed, it signaled that all was well. The lovely stillness that accompanies a cloudy day greeted the women as they set off. A chorus of chirping birds, invisible in the leafy treetops, set the tone for Hattie's first outing in days. Whatever Grace wanted to show her was just down the narrow country road. Hattie loved surprises.

"You said you wanted to know everything about this place," Grace elaborated. "So, I'm introducing you to something."

Momentarily, an impressive brick church on a rise beckoned Hattie and Grace closer. Obviously brand new, the large, stately structure raised Hattie's hopes. Was this the mission church she had longed to see for so long? How utterly inspiring! She would be so honored to worship here, the handsome, auburn bricks offering the feeling of security.

"I know what you're thinking, but this isn't the mission. It's called Sehon Chapel," Grace explained. "Park Hill is atwitter over it because it's so fancy. Those bricks were made in a local kiln, just like the ones at the Female Seminary."

Hattie didn't quite understand. Rev. Worcester had not mentioned Sehon Chapel. He had just spoken of the mission church, which he played a large part in constructing. Hattie had never remotely pictured a church this large in Park Hill.

"It was built to provide girls at the seminary a place nearby to worship," Grace related, "and there's a gallery above especially for slaves."

Hattie didn't know what to say. Surely Rev. Worcester wouldn't have separate worship areas in his church.

"Someday soon, this chapel will open for services, but I don't know when. It belongs to the Methodists," Grace continued.

Now Hattie knew for sure that it had nothing to do with the mission. The American Board was largely Congregationalist, not Methodist. So why had Grace brought her to see it? Maybe she just thought Hattie should know it was here.

"As you can imagine, it complicates things even though there's no question about its usefulness," Grace added seriously. "Since the seminary opened in 1850, the girls have worshipped at Rev. Worcester's church over at the mission. He's never had a large congregation anyway, so he'll feel the blow when they leave to attend this new chapel."

Hattie stared at Grace. Did this mean competition existed for parishioners? Such a thing just seemed wrong. Certainly, there were enough people and churches in Utica for everyone. On further thought, this joined the challenges she had read about in Murrell's library. Not only did Rev. Worcester cope with the issue of slaveholders, but the number of worshippers had just declined, as well.

"When you start meeting people, you'll find out what good relationships Rev. Worcester has with locals and merchants," Grace summarized as she turned the carriage around. "Some think Sehon Chapel's financing may create friction, though. You should know that Mr. Murrell and Chief Ross paid to make it a reality. They say they want our little mission church to succeed, but they're Methodists at heart."

On the way back, Hattie tried to brighten the mood. She shared her anticipation about the social. Perhaps it was the only time she might meet some of the people. Several were coming great distances from the other missions Rev. Worcester supervised. Grace confirmed that some from Park Hill would attend, as well.

As she spoke, Hattie suddenly had the faintest memory of nervousness about the social from the middle of the night. Had she just dreamed about that strange frame of mind? She pictured herself leaning into her mirror, which was not like her. She had even cried as she examined her spotted face more closely. The words she had spoken also sounded foreign. But she still felt the confusion of them.

"*I want to be … attractive. I want to look … feminine and appealing,*" she had whispered into the dark.

"I can't wait to meet them," Hattie replied, shaking herself back into the present moment, "But I hate this splotchy skin and what they'll think. You don't have to tell me that's vain, because I already know it. The thought of covering it up just won't go away."

"That's a totally normal reaction. And I actually think there's potential with that idea," Grace chirped. "Let's go see what's in the kitchen."

Intrigued, Hattie followed Grace there upon their return. They rummaged around until Grace found what she wanted. In her handkerchief, she smeared a glob of lard and sifted a tablespoon of flour into Hattie's pocket. Then they were off.

Taking stock of the raw materials, Grace sat Hattie down

while grinning rather wistfully. "I used to make myself beautiful. Hopefully, I still remember enough to do the trick for you."

How cheerless that Grace acknowledged her own lack of interest in grooming. What had led to such a comment? But Hattie kept quiet and sat still.

Carefully, Grace applied a thin layer of lard to Hattie's face and then blotted it. Very quickly, Hattie could smile, frown, and crinkle her forehead without discomfort; the dry feeling and flakiness seemed to disappear. Next, Grace took a pinch of flour between her thumb and forefinger, sifting it over the entire face. To Hattie's absolute amazement, it stuck! As a final touch, Grace blotted it and then told Hattie to close her eyes. Taking a gulp of air, she blew a few strong breaths to whisk away any excess flour.

"This is a miracle," Hattie gasped. "I could never have figured this out on my own."

"You shouldn't have to figure everything out alone," Grace returned rather poignantly. "One of life's greatest gifts is a friend. I'm so thankful you have come to Park Hill to keep me company!"

❖ ❖ ❖

September 9, 1856

Tonight I will see Rev. Worcester's house and possibly other mission buildings for the first time. I'm so excited to meet others from the American Board. In some ways, I feel like this is my true arrival here. They don't realize all that I know, however. That includes the trying side of Erminia.

❖ ❖ ❖

Approaching Worcester's white clapboard house, sounds of conversation and laughter joined the chirp of crickets. It was a perfect, cooler afternoon made fresh by brief morning showers. The moisture wasn't enough to end the drought, but much appreciated nevertheless.

Hattie was delighted to accompany Fred and Martha to the social. Their company restored her confidence that had fallen into question over wearing a makeshift dress. Martha reminded Hattie of Amanda as she pointed out how its refreshed floral skirt flowed gracefully and was a nice fit. On top of that, Grace's camouflage trick left Hattie's skin quite presentable. She could relax and meet the guests.

Together, the three strolled onto the lawn where some attendees meandered near a large apple tree while others chatted in groups. Big yellow apples dotted the ground and had filled bushel baskets nearby. Hattie's leg pained her only mildly, yet she reminded herself not to limp. Encouraged by the lard and flour mixture on her face, things were on the upswing.

The first person she wanted to find and thank was Grace. Despite scanning the crowd intently, she did not see her friend. Just then, a familiar chortle caught her attention. Hattie's mouth almost dropped open when, just across the way, she spotted Erminia Worcester. Completely taken aback, she stared because Erminia looked rosy and animated while welcoming guests. She seemed the very picture of health, and strong enough to remain standing while acting as both hostess and host in her husband's absence. Hattie could not believe the transformation.

Her mind raced back two weeks when she had been suffering all alone in Springfield after Erminia left for the Berry's home. Did Erminia even recall how Hattie had nursed her so faithfully? When had Erminia returned to Park Hill? She should have contacted Hattie since she felt so lively and robust. That pampered stay at an elegant home with servants must have suited her.

"Come on. Let's get this over with," Martha cajoled, taking Hattie's arm to approach Erminia.

Hattie should have guessed how the encounter would go. Erminia threw her arms open and let out a squeal of exaggerated surprise. Reaching out like they were long lost relatives, she embraced them both with an affectionate hug.

"Hattie and I became well acquainted on our trip from Utica," she bragged to Martha and two other ladies. "I had to come between some awful gamblers and questionable women to protect her."

Hattie gritted her teeth at the blatant mischaracterization of their experience in grimy Napoleon, Arkansas. If this was the way she slanted the story, it would be a long afternoon. Luckily, someone else caught Erminia's attention so that Martha could lead Hattie away.

"Don't give one ounce of energy to her make-believe," Martha warned supportively. "Just keep walking. We aren't the only ones who know she's full of hot air."

Hattie grabbed a swallow of tea, telling herself it must be her choice to think constructively. She hadn't come all this way to be bested by the likes of Erminia Worcester. Already, she had overcome the journey and much more that Erminia wouldn't even care about. It was a sweet victory, which made this social and all the good people more wonderful.

Hattie spotted Jane Ross a few lengths away and waved. Recalling their conversation, she couldn't wait to hear what nice things others had to say about Rev. Worcester. Since he was still away, she expected glowing reports of his long service and artful coordination of education in Park Hill. When Jane and another woman started walking her way, Hattie waited. Martha turned to talk with the tall man Hattie had seen at Murrell's.

"Miss Sheldon, I know you've been waiting to make the acquaintance of Mrs. Sarah Hitchcock," Jane introduced before someone named Miss Swain distracted her.

Exclaiming brightly, Sarah took Hattie's hand in both of hers. "Hello at last! One ordeal after another has kept us from each other until now. But we will be fast friends very soon! Sit with me for a little while."

Instantly, Sarah charmed Hattie, and not only because she was the most stunningly gorgeous woman Hattie had ever seen. A vision in a green silk dress, brunette tendrils framed her big, doe eyes which were the brightest blue. Her warmth conveyed the regard of an old, treasured friend. And even though Sarah's frame appeared thin and frail, her spirit glowed with interest.

The two fell into easy conversation as Sarah pointed out the new faces with whom Hattie should become familiar. This must be Sarah's only way to help, given her lack of strength. The little briefing brought a much appreciated perspective about the scope of American Board mission stations managed by Rev. Worcester.

Turnout was good this year from Rev. Willey of Dwight, Rev. Torrey of Fairfield, Rev. Ranney of Lee's Creek and Rev. Huss from Honey Creek. As Sarah put faces with names, she explained that their spouses, the teachers at their respective mission stations, and others assistants could not make the trip due to distance, expense and responsibilities. Mr. Archer, the printer, and Rev. Foreman, the translator, joined the pastors. Hattie must meet all of them.

"My husband's gone to Dwight Mission to check on Rev. Torrey's wife, Adelaide. She gave birth there on August twentieth.

It was harrowing. But for his good care, she would have perished," Sarah whispered.

Such compassion and interest came across about everyone Sarah mentioned, including Hattie herself. Evidently, Rev. Worcester had written about his strong impression of Hattie after leaving Utica for Vermont last spring. Hattie blushed at the flattery, but it encouraged her in the way families support one another. This woman, the personification of delicate sweetness, had a special way of making people feel valuable. Sarah's eyes never left Hattie's face.

Without a hint of complaint, Sarah also related how Dwight's parents had come to live with them recently. The household needed reorganization anyway, she excused in the kindest, most patient voice. Little Laura adored her grandparents, who had tended her so lovingly during Sarah's debilitation. Hattie felt guilty for a thought that crossed her mind: would Sarah feel the same way if Erminia had moved into her home and cared for Laura?

"You must come over soon," Sarah pleaded genuinely. "I will send you a note. Please say yes?"

After the two parted, Sarah's charming aura remained with Hattie. She had never met so angelic a person. Hattie watched her walk slowly toward the house. When would her strength return, Hattie wondered?

Had all the work on this social been completed before Erminia showed up? The long white tablecloth had been ironed carefully by someone talented and patient. All the more, several large platters were stacked high with delicious-looking, fresh donuts. Hannah and Grace must have labored long hours to make them.

Just beyond the house, Hattie spotted a stone façade and the ropes of the Worcester's well by a stack of hay bales. A blonde woman there seemed to fit Rev. Worcester's description of his fair, younger daughter. Just as Hattie started in her direction, a Negro man darted from behind the hay bales and added a plate of fresh donuts to the table. It happened so fast that Hattie stopped short. Was he Jesse? She hadn't thought of him since they arrived safely in Park Hill.

Resuming her approach, Hattie admired the woman's two darling little children—and a tottering baby, too. Perfect stair steps in height, they laughed while petting a lively black and white cat.

"Are you Mrs. Hicks, per chance?" Hattie inquired, reaching out. "I'm Hattie Sheldon, the new teacher from Utica, New York."

Hannah's open face beamed as she brushed a strand of ash blonde hair off her glistening forehead. She looked nothing like Sarah, yet her wide-set grey eyes expressed the same warm sentiments. It seemed that Sarah resembled her father while Hannah must resemble their late mother.

"Finally we meet! Thank you for seeking me out. I've been so anxious to talk with you!"

Patiently, Hannah drew her children close and introduced Hattie. There was Percy, who looked just old enough to attend school, then little Emma and baby Ann. She pointed out her husband, Abijah Hicks, who did all the mission farming. He was visiting with other guests across the way.

"I'm supposed to keep grandfather's cats away from the milk," young Percy offered. "My favorite one is Hymn."

"It's actually H-Y-M-N," Hannah spelled as she straightened a tablecloth. "Father named the other cat "Her.""

"Ha, that's clever," Hattie giggled. "I would love to talk with you the rest of the night. But I see how busy you are, so I won't distract you further. Just know that I want to see you soon, help out where there's a need, and talk about the school."

"Will you be my teacher, Miss Sheldon?" Percy asked with endearing eagerness.

"Yes, and I can't wait," Hattie answered, tousling his beautiful head of black hair. "I'm not quite ready yet, though."

"Oh—forgive me," Hannah exclaimed while tending Emma's mosquito bite. "I received your note. Yes, I will be happy to take you to the mission and printing building. I'll have to work it in, so I'm not sure when."

Elated, Hattie clapped her hands and gushed with thanks. It was finally going to happen! The invisible wall might fall soon! Maybe she really could get school started before October. Blowing a kiss to the children, Hattie took her leave feeling great anticipation. The burden seemed to be lifting!

Across the lawn, Erminia Worcester clucked for attention and summoned the guests. Ever confident, she motioned them closer. When they quieted, she thanked them for coming, commented on the weather, and launched into a mention about Vermont. Out of the corner of her eye, Hattie watched Hannah look down and wondered if she did this to cope with her stepmother's ways.

Momentarily, Hattie heard her name called and realized Erminia was introducing her. Following instructions, she waved to polite applause. For a brief moment, she could hear her father telling his children to stand tall in public. *Project an image for the way you want others to regard you,* he had instructed so often during her maturing years.

"In Reverend's absence, I've asked our friend, James Latta, to offer the blessing," Erminia continued, turning to make way for a man behind her.

Hattie's heart jumped. This James Latta was the same handsome man she had admired from the window of Murrell's house!

How surprising to see him here, but all the more to observe Martha standing beside him, beaming from ear to ear. *Oh my heavens,* Hattie marveled. *That unforgettable man must be one of Martha's brothers! Did he arrange for me to go to Murrell's library?*

No sooner had the perfectly stated prayer ended, than James pecked Martha on the forehead. Simultaneously, she pulled his arm toward Hattie to introduce them. Just that fast, James came to stand right next to Hattie, close enough to touch her. But that was altogether unacceptable in anyone's books.

Standing beside him brought Hattie a thrilling rush. That powerful smile of his could melt hearts, and perhaps even the lard off her face. They exchanged a few words before James invited Hattie and a couple of others to a smaller table off to the side. He had brought some freshly cooked game from an afternoon hunt and offered his friends a taste. Hattie soon held a warm nugget with a crispy outer coating of browned meal. What was it? She hesitated as some of Grace's casual comments about game came to mind. Was this bear? Or, even worse, opossum? Where was Grace anyway?

Hattie dared not turn up her nose. This was her chance to impress James Latta, whose dancing eyes and Samson-like coal black hair looked completely irresistible. It went without saying that his sister vouched for him, so the tasty morsel was no trick. Hattie popped the fragment of mammal in her mouth and crunched down while smiling back. Her attraction to this man far outweighed the inconvenience of any bad taste or strange texture. But, wonder of wonders, it was delicious!

"I'd like to try it myself," a loud voice over Hattie's shoulder challenged.

Turning, she came face-to-face with a disheveled, stubbly-bearded, Cherokee man. Had he been clean, she might have ignored the notch missing from his lower left ear. His greasy hair and semi-intoxicated state, however, only raised concerns about who he was and why he came. Sobered by the smell, she stepped back slightly.

"Why sure, Smoky," James agreed through a strained look. He began to walk toward Hattie slowly, however, while keeping his eye on Smoky. Hattie sensed caution.

Unexpectedly, Smoky turned to Hattie and stared too long for her comfort. His voice took on a challenging edge as he stepped nearer. "So, you're the new northern missionary that got here sick."

Hattie stared in disbelief at the man as he loomed before her with his scowling expression. To her relief, James reached her right side just as Fred reached her left. Neither of them spoke.

"My sister was sick like that and pretty near lost her mind," Smoky added too confidently, his gaze cold. "Like you, she talked crazy for days."

"I'm better now," Hattie squeaked, wondering who he was and how he knew about her illness.

"Your secrets are out," Smoky laughed disturbingly. "I'm gonna find out what you're up to…"

"She said nothing of interest to you, Smoky," James retorted seriously. "Miss Sheldon prayed during her worst times. She was dignified even while unconscious."

"That's a big lie," Smoky argued, throwing his head to challenge James.

"It's the gospel truth," James reiterated, drawing himself up. "I was there and saw for myself. Now leave her alone."

"Smoky, I've got some special donuts for you," Hannah called warmly. "Come over here with Abijah and me."

Truly stunned, a rush of fear and disgust left Hattie adrift.

She cast one last look as the ominous-faced man limped off. Uncomfortable, she also felt the weight of too many eyes on her. Martha seemed to read the situation and started a distracting conversation.

Hattie could still find no words. Looking at the ground, a mountain of potentially embarrassing worries seized her. Was James Latta kidding? If he really had heard her pray, it meant he'd been at her bedside. And that left her utterly exposed and vulnerable. Had she actually talked crazy while unconscious?

Fred Pilkington's expression of concern and empathy caught Hattie's attention when she looked up. Because he offered his arm, she took it. Slowly, they walked back to the donut table. Hattie wished she could forget about what just happened. If only she could rush back to James Latta and ask a million questions. But this was not the time or place to resolve such private issues.

She paused, and then glanced back at him shyly. He was watching her rather helplessly. Perhaps he didn't know what to do either.

"T-H-A-N-K Y-O-U," she mouthed silently, before Martha joined on her other side.

Putting the incident out of her mind, Hattie shook hands and soon found herself in the thick of likeminded people. Their genuine interest matched hers, which opened the door for getting acquainted. Nobody was in a hurry.

She heard that the origins of the American Board paralleled America's religious awakening in the 1790s. Concern over preservation of the country's Christian roots resulted in incorporation of the American Board under Massachusetts law in 1812. Within seven years, it found common ground and began to benefit from the Indian Civilization Fund that Congress had established. Existing missions received funds in exchange for keeping Congress informed. The

American Board must submit annual reports full of findings about a given mission's efforts in education and religion, the Indian culture and people, and the status of progress and peace.

Even more exciting, teachers would submit a description of their school and students. Wouldn't that please Ebenezer Sheldon! The very idea that Hattie's account would be published by the highest governing body in the nation was thrilling. Such an opportunity encouraged her tremendously and could help her get through the long wait for Rev. Worcester's return. Once he got back, everything would fall into place.

Hearing her name called, Hattie turned to see Percy approaching her with several young friends in tow.

"Miss Sheldon, these are my friends who will come to school," he beamed.

Delighted, Hattie shook hands with Taylor Foreman, a tanned boy around eight years old, and his darling sister, Jennie, who looked about six. These children of Worcester's translator, Rev. Foreman, appeared so eager to learn. Percy pointed in the direction of their house to indicate that they lived close by.

Hattie heard herself gush with enthusiasm, to which the children responded excitedly. She also inquired about their family. "I haven't met your father yet. Everyone says he's a great leader in the Cherokee Nation."

"He's talking with some other preachers," Taylor explained.

"Our older brother, Austin, died last year," Jennie offered suddenly, the corners of her tiny mouth turning down. "And our older sister, Erminia, is sick in Texas where mother took her."

Hattie gaped temporarily and then caught herself. The innocent, trusting confession revealed more than the sadness in Rev. Foreman's family. Had the children's late brother been named for

Rev. Samuel Austin Worcester? What had happened to him? Was their sister named for Erminia Worcester?

A flash of insight followed her questions. The children wanted her to understand them, to know what was important! Why, these children felt exactly like Hattie had felt when her sisters died. They hardly understood yet how an undercurrent of grief would be with them forever. She bent down, patted them both on the shoulder warmly, and whispered how sorry she was for their loss.

"But, our sister, Susie, will go to the seminary this year," Taylor bragged the next moment.

"Do you have a melodeon," Jennie inquired expectantly. "You have to play while our Cold Water Army sings."

As the social drew to a close, Hattie mustered her resolve to approach Erminia once again.

"Thank you for a lovely afternoon—and welcome back," she began.

"I appreciate that, dear," Erminia replied. "But take notice. I'll only be here a short time."

"Why," Hattie asked unconsciously. Her expectations were dashed again. She would not get to hear Erminia's take on Rev. Worcester's work in the Cherokee Nation. Where could Erminia possibly go this time?

"I've learned that my wonderful son, Leonard, is in Kansas now. Things have calmed down there, so I'm going up there for a long overdue visit. He's a brilliant musician, you know," she bragged. "I will take in many concerts and other functions."

Given this unexpected development, Hattie prioritized her

most urgent need as she tried to be polite. "How nice. But, say, do you happen to know the date when school is supposed to start here?"

"Why, I have no idea," Erminia returned without interest or responsibility. "That is up to you, Hattie. It's awfully late to just now be asking such a question."

Previous to meeting James Latta, Hattie might have let Erminia Worcester's nonchalance throw her off balance. But, suddenly, it didn't matter nearly as much. Instead, she lost interest. Why accommodate Erminia's offenses? She would much rather fix her attention on James Latta. For a young, attractive man to come to her rescue so decisively, so confidently, was a totally new experience.

❖ ❖ ❖

Once the wagon carrying Fred, Martha and Hattie was out of earshot, Hattie needed answers about the strange encounter with Smoky. Who was he anyway? What had she said in her delirium and how did Smoky find out? James couldn't have made up stories about Hattie just to get rid of him. They must be true. Did other people know things about her that she didn't know herself?

"He's just a troubled man," Martha sighed. "He drinks too much whiskey."

"Smoky used to help Abijah at the mission farm," Fred continued. "Don't worry about him. People know you're in town and word gets around when someone's sick."

"How many people were at my bedside?" Hattie questioned. "Did I humiliate myself?"

"No, certainly not. Don't be upset," Martha soothed. "It's just that Dr. Hitchcock wanted people he knew to sit with you at all times. Did I tell you he's James's best friend? That's why he trusted me to sit with you during the days. Fred took over in the evenings. Then James spelled Fred. Grace, bless her heart, came from midnight to daylight."

The extent of her illness suddenly hit Hattie. What made people offer such loving service to strangers? She owed them all a debt of gratitude.

"Did you see Grace tonight?" she broke in. "I couldn't find her anywhere."

"No," Martha responded quietly.

"When I was at your bedside, you talked about Aunt Mary," Fred interrupted. "You must love her very much."

"James said you were upset about a slave roundup," Martha added. "And you wept about your sisters."

Burying her head in her hands, Hattie felt like she had invaded her own privacy. The shock of it needed attention. But so did other things. Every time something surprised her these days, she found herself off balance. That didn't look like leadership. She would be wiser to put her personal concerns aside and get serious. Maybe this was her chance to broach the matter of slavery now that it had come up.

"I've got a lovely family, but two of my sisters died in succession. It changed all of us. My parents raised us in a society of abolitionists and once we helped with an Underground Railroad rescue," Hattie explained. "My father's always reading the newspaper out loud and talks about politics. I can't bear it when people are deprived of freedom. That's one of the main reasons I'm here. But finding slavery shocked me. Would you tell me more about why there's slavery here? It seems to be a touchy issue here."

Within a short time, all kinds of eye-opening information came out. Beyond Mr. Murrell's operation, as well as other large slave-holding plantations, some smaller planters in the Cherokee Nation also owned slaves. Hattie was shocked to learn that slavery had been the norm among some Cherokees even before removal! After all, it was the backbone of the southern economy and they had lived in several southern states then. When President Andrew Jackson threw the Cherokees off their land and out of their homes, they and their slaves marched side-by-side all the laboriously long, dangerous way to Indian Territory.

But heritage issues caused so many problems, jealousies, suspicions, and challenges. Whites had married Cherokees. Despite laws to the contrary, some Cherokees had married Negroes. The law got in the middle of those unions and specified who received Cherokee citizenship and who didn't. It also specified who was allowed to be educated and who wasn't.

Mixed blood Cherokees were generally more well-to-do and reform minded. They had very different ideas about how to live, thrive, and survive than the more traditional full-bloods. That included their ownership of slaves. A long-standing feud between the two factions simmered over unresolved problems. Complete peace and forgiveness could never quite overcome arguments about removal and problems with the government over land rights and payments. Violence erupted on many occasions, and often, slaves got caught in the middle.

"Ever since I read that Cherokee slaveholders resent northern teachers, it's gnawed at me," Hattie divulged. What she didn't share was her worry that, from day one in her classroom, some people would brand her an abolitionist. What could she say to the children of slave holders? She couldn't bear to endure one group of humans owning another. But if she said so, she would lose her job.

Nothing can change history, she reminded herself. She must find a way to deal with both sides of the slavery issue. If what she had learned at Murrell's library was a sign of things to come, she'd best figure it out soon. *Remember,* she told herself, *you're on God's errand.*

Too quickly, they arrived back at the Female Seminary, which cut short the conversation.

"Your confidence means a great deal to me," Hattie breathed appreciatively. "I mean about slavery, as well as my illness. You've been loyal to a stranger in a confusing set of circumstances."

"You're no stranger," Martha protested. "We know Rev. Worcester, his values, and the kind of people he associates with. He hired you because you're the cream of the crop, Hattie! We knew you were going to be our friend forever. People don't come here and then just forget one another. This place and what happens here makes people brothers and sisters forever."

This heart-warming thought stayed with Hattie late into the evening. All in all, she believed in this mission and was learning how to thank God for it, problems and all. Now that a larger body of mission-minded folks showed the way, some of the pressure could be abated. Hannah and Sarah seemed to be on her side. She stood a good chance of convincing Dr. Hitchcock that she was going to teach. And soon.

Callers, Quilters, Chores and Children

*T*he first trace of fall in Park Hill seemed to be at hand. Gone were the humidity and mustiness that marked Hattie's early days in the Cherokee Nation. She ventured downstairs to exercise her leg and then lingered on the porch just to smell the fresh air. It was time to banish the last vestiges of illness. Several vacant rocking chairs with flaking paint swayed gently in the light breeze. Hattie chose one of them and seated herself with her thoughts.

Above her head, a pair of doves had nested, evidenced by their soft call and telltale bits of briar and straw that floated down. From somewhere quite secret, a couple of woodpeckers tapped like conductors against old, hollow tree branches. She closed her eyes and let the sun's warm rays soak in.

"If you stay still, the wild turkeys might come and keep you company," James Latta hinted quietly, only a few steps away. "Or will I do?"

Taken off guard, Hattie recognized his voice, but still jumped in surprise. Unable to contain herself, she turned with a grin to greet him.

"I didn't hear you walk up," she replied warmly. "What brings you over here?"

"There's a certain young lady who deserves an explanation," he returned. "Mind if I sit down?"

As his account unfolded, Hattie learned that Dr. Hitchcock had felt an enormous responsibility to care for her. She couldn't share any symptoms in her semi-conscious state or tell what had happened before she arrived in Park Hill unaccompanied.

Hearing those words softened her heart toward the very direct doctor. His concern also had something to do with the fact that his servant, Jesse, brought her from Springfield. A level of responsibility rested on his shoulders and Dr. Hitchcock took it seriously. Finally, James shared how much the doctor regretted the sad fact that Erminia had left Hattie on her own.

But it was James's mention of Jesse that pricked Hattie's ear. He was a slave? And Dwight was his owner? She couldn't believe it!

Instead of pursuing answers to that question, however, she recalled a word of advice. *Take this place as it is*, Martha had said. That prompted Hattie to stick with the subject. She needed to hear the full story about her unconscious days, not pass judgment on Dr. Hitchcock.

"Forgive me for being so direct with this question," Hattie began. "But was I really talking crazy while I was so ill?"

"Crazy is too strong," James replied. "No, you weren't. Focus on the fact that the doctor wanted you protected. It was really an ethical dilemma because you were unconscious. He cared about your privacy."

Hattie blinked out of appreciation. Shortly, James went on to relate her health to the mission's overall emphasis on protecting health. It turned out that Rev. Worcester had gained significant medical knowledge by studying some old doctor's textbooks during his Georgia imprisonment. Gaining new knowledge had helped him survive the grueling work and deplorable conditions.

After he arrived in Park Hill, Rev. Worcester taught laymen to treat deadly fevers. On that point, it was Dr. Hitchcock's fear that Hattie might suffer brain swelling and more severe complications unless someone tended to her constantly and helped her take nourishment.

"You mean you fed me?" she gasped, covering her face in embarrassment. "Oh, my. I don't know what to say. It's just so personal..."

"Like I said," James reassured respectfully, "you weren't awkward. You acted mannerly, not like a deranged person. You just don't remember, that's all."

"It's also frightening," she replied soberly.

"There's nothing to fear. I haven't said a word beyond Martha, Fred, or Dwight," he related considerately. "And I won't. Ever."

With that, James made a colorful statement about how she was in the west now and then launched into an enthusiastic story. From what she grasped, he had lived through considerable ravages while army freighting as a wagon master in Texas. Animating his tale with sweeping gestures, he explained how he was a civilian hired to haul the bulk of military cargo, often with military protection. Hattie was carried away by the colorful story that featured horse thieves along the rugged road to San Antonio and the threat of dengue fever on the lower Brazos River.

James and his charismatic younger brother, Will, sounded as experienced with six-shooters as their opponents were with bowie knives. In a matter of minutes, she comprehended that his talents went well beyond hunting and cooking the kind of game she had tasted at the social. This man was completely at home with six-mule wagons, the repair of them, and controlling them with a type of whip called a blacksnake.

The mention of a whip reminded her of her father's heroic moment during the Underground Railroad rescue. If James was anything like him, she wanted to know James better. For the first time, maybe ever, a man who wasn't a family member or revered teacher captured her entire attention.

They talked well into the evening, neither of them mentioning supper or hunger. He asked how her family's life and work went, the kinds of topics that filled their days, and what Utica looked like. She inquired about any number of topics, as well, before coming full circle to Dr. Dwight Hitchcock. By then, she had grown comfortable enough to ask the question that continued to linger.

"Is it really true that Dr. Hitchcock owns a slave?" Hattie queried in reference to Jesse.

"I said servant," James corrected. "Jesse was freed by his Cherokee owner some time back. He gets to stay because of good conduct. He works for Dwight."

"I wondered why he wouldn't look straight at me," Hattie related.

"You were a stranger to him," James explained. "But he thinks highly of you now. Dwight said Jesse was telling all his people about your Underground Railroad rescue."

"I told stories in the wagon?" she questioned uneasily.

"Yes, and it sounds like they were good ones!"

September 10, 1856

James Latta came to see me! He called on me! I feel safe and protected by his reassurances. Maybe I didn't make a fool of myself while unconscious. Can't even remember what else we talked about. He's a fascinating man. No wonder Martha brags about him so much.

Hattie borrowed soap and carried water to do some much over-due washing. It was past time to get on a schedule, even if she had the order wrong. On her last visit to Hunter's Home, she had questioned Susan about when women in the south did their chores. Just like northern women, Susan confirmed that Monday was wash day, iron-ing took place on Tuesday, catching up—as well as mending—hap-pened on Wednesday, Thursday demanded churning of the cream, on Friday the house and everything in it got a good cleaning. By mid-day on Saturday, the house smelled good from baking. Finally, Sunday was set aside for worship and to soak clothes in preparation for Monday.

Having hung her things to dry, Hattie heard the canter of hooves and turned to see Grace approaching amid a little cloud of dust. Waving, she called a lighthearted greeting and then gathered her bucket and soap to go inside. But as her friend dismounted, she couldn't miss a purplish bruise on the left side of Grace's neck and jaw. The painful-looking place must be the size of a small plum.

"What happened?" she questioned in alarm, reaching out to Grace. "That bruise looks like it hurts!"

"It does, but don't fret," Grace returned soberly. "I was milk-ing and the old cow got mad. She kicked me right off the stool before I knew what happened."

Hattie had only milked a cow once. In Utica, her family purchased milk from a nearby dairy farmer. She couldn't relate to the power of an angry milk cow. Grace said her bruise was already healing and then handed Hattie a note from Hannah. Hattie stuffed it in her pocket and nodded.

Dwight and Martha had vouched for Grace as having good judgment and being trustworthy. Should Hattie encourage Grace to be more cautious? From all appearances, Grace must hurry to her own detriment. She obviously did the usual chores a woman's home life demanded, but also helped at the mission and in the Worcester household.

Who did Grace trust? Did she have a confidante? Hattie considered herself a good choice as the two women had important things in common. It had been hard enough for Hattie to leave her family as a grown woman. What had Grace faced when leaving her family— forever—as a girl? Hattie chose her words carefully.

"You and I ought to get better acquainted," she suggested.

"You're wondering about my story, aren't you?" Grace anticipated.

Hattie swallowed hard over being too obvious. "Well, yes. But I thought that ... waiting for you to take me in your confidence ... might show respect."

"If I went back to the very beginning, it would start with my wealthy, self-centered parents naming me Georgia Grace and then handing me over. For sixteen long years, I lived down south and was loved only by my dear Negro mammy. When she borrowed a fork one too many times, my father beat her to death. So, I ran away and left my old self and old miseries far behind. Praise God that Rev. Worcester pulled me out of nothingness, which saved my life. I even changed my name afterwards. I told him I had left Georgia behind for better things. His reply was unforgettable. He said, *I know exactly what that feels like.* He meant his imprisonment, of course. So often, he says clever things like that."

Hattie all but shed a tear thinking of the abuse Rev. Worcester had suffered while chained in the Georgia penitentiary. But this conversation was about Grace, not him. And she comprehended that Grace had come to terms with many unspeakable things. Maybe she didn't need to talk about them.

"I just worry because your girlhood was hard and your life still appears to be difficult," Hattie heard herself recap.

"Well, we all have hard times," Grace philosophized. "But Christians believe in forgiveness. We all answer to God while treasuring one another."

September 10, 1856
Dear Hattie,

I wasn't able to sleep after the social for thinking of you. Thank Heavens for your safe passage to us, and then for your deliverance from illness. Now that you are in Park Hill, my spirits feel so bolstered. I'm looking forward to ever so many times together, conversations, and stories about your life in the east. Since my regular chores have been thrown off by the social, I've decided to turn my back on washing and ironing in favor of taking you to father's printing office. Can you come to my home tomorrow at mid-morning? I will have the help of a friend to keep the children and can break free for a few hours.

Affectionately, Hannah

❖ ❖ ❖

Hattie was so excited to go to her future home and the printing building she couldn't contain herself. Finally, finally, after over two long weeks, she would see, touch, smell, and maybe even taste the mission. *Bless Hannah for making my wish come true,* she prayed. Without question, today's tour had been a long time coming. Yet Hattie reminded herself that it must pose a sacrifice for a woman as hardworking and needed by her family as Hannah.

The first thing she noticed was what a fine home Hannah had in comparison to some of the smaller ones where women cooked outside over fires. The substantial Hicks residence was of hewn log construction, featuring a large central fireplace and several glass windows. In front of the rail fence, lively, untamed shrubbery added a friendly touch. Behind the house, a good-sized vegetable garden must have provided for the family, but looked rather dry. It was next to the spring house that stored milk, butter and cheese. A colorful, patchwork quilt flipped in the breeze as it aired on the clothesline.

The wide porch featured a few piles of various rocks the children must have gathered. Just as Hattie approached the door, Hannah opened it and invited her in. A virtual eternity seemed to have passed since Hattie left behind the comforts of her own beloved home in Utica. She had visited the sprawling Murrell plantation since then, but it didn't have Hannah's touch like this warm, more personal place. Taking stock, Hattie appreciated hospitality in a new way. It had become a rare privilege since she arrived and found herself at the seminary most of the time.

Once inside, Hattie was relieved to see that Hannah had a cook stove. While Hannah made coffee, she took a seat and glanced at a basket filled with intricate tatting. Beside it, scissors and a comb waited on the table to cut and groom hair. In the corner, a well-used spinning wheel kept company with balls of yarn.

"Want some coffee? I've just roasted new coffee beans," Hannah shared excitedly. "We were out for a while but a shipment finally arrived."

"I haven't had a good cup in days," Hattie returned.

Silently, she realized how she had taken for granted the availability of coffee and tea in Utica. Furthermore, she chided herself for even noticing that Hannah had no carpet, draperies or niceties like china or a tablecloth.

Instead, Hannah owned earthenware pots. She retrieved one momentarily and ladled up some aromatic, stewed apples. It was their season and the sweet, cinnamon essence made Hattie's mouth water. They sat together at the rough table and Hannah lit a limp looking candle. There was warmth here that she hadn't experienced in a long, long time.

"Forgive the dim light," Hannah commented. "I haven't made candles lately and we're quite low. This beef tallow one is the best I can do today."

"The light is fine. I'm thrilled to be here and grateful you invited me," Hattie relayed appreciatively. "The aroma of the coffee reminds me of home."

Just then, the baby began to cry in another room. Hannah rose, but went to the front door instead. Peeking her head out, she looked both ways before excusing herself to see what the baby needed. Glancing around, Hattie could glean how busy Hannah's family kept her, what with scattered children's toys in one corner and spinning in another. How did she keep her house so spotless with the responsibility for candle making and quilting and drying garden vegetables for winter?

When Hannah returned, her expression had changed. She approached Hattie looking upset. What had happened?

"I'm so sorry about this," Hannah began, "but my friend still hasn't shown up. She promised to come for the day and care for my children. I don't know what happened, but we have no choice. We will have to go to the printing house another time."

Hattie contained her disappointment silently. It was forgotten the very next moment when Percy screeched into the room on his stick horse. That chipper little man seemed to want adult attention just when Hattie craved a classroom full of children. He kept looking at her expectantly and then finally came right over. Innocent and bright-eyed, he began to speak in Cherokee.

"I just said '*My name is Percy. When does school start?*'" he explained.

"My goodness! That was impressive," Hattie bragged.

"My daddy only speaks Cherokee to me," he finished, smiling up at her.

Captivated, Hattie found herself charmed by young Percy.

❖ ❖ ❖

"What was it like growing up in Rev. Worcester's family?" Hattie asked Hannah later.

Hannah smiled. "Father taught us that we possessed innate worth. He always reminded us that we are of great value to God," she answered simply.

"That sounds like my father, as well," Hattie shared as if they had known each other a long time.

"Really? Tell me more," Hannah asked.

Wonderful memories tumbled out as Hattie described her

siblings and parents, as well as their talents and interests. All the while, Utica and her home came alive again. She could almost feel herself running out the door on the way to her father's shop, walking toward Rev. Fowler's office at the church with its tall, spindly steeple, or savoring a slice of her mother's freshly baked bread.

Mentioning her mother made Hattie wonder what Hannah had experienced when Erminia came into the family. Judging from her own time with Erminia on their long trip to Park Hill, it must have been rough going. From that vantage point, Hannah's kind, patient demeanor became a powerful testament to her character and constitution. Erminia had not wilted her.

The thought made Hattie thankful for her own mother. She respected her mother's accomplishments, and even more so in hindsight. As she shared with Hannah about the death of her two sisters, she explained how the orphanage, temperance union, and church all helped dispel the intense grief and brought hope and purpose to her mother. Looking back, Hattie recognized new benefits and examples as a result of her mother's choices. She hadn't realized it before, but her mother had helped steer her destiny beyond the ordinary.

Helen Sheldon was so very different than Erminia in personality. She had remained supportive, even though she and Hattie had not seen eye-to-eye about the future. Her mother never became critical of Hattie's words, manners, or ideas like Erminia had. Hattie saw new reasons to be thankful that her mother had raised her patiently, lovingly, and without harsh reprimands or commentary.

Back when she was young, Helen Sheldon's prospects were far different than Hattie's. She hadn't expected further education because it wasn't available. She only hoped to marry and raise a family.

What about Hannah's expectations? She was Hattie's same

age, but a generation behind in terms of educational opportunities. She had waited for her turn, but it never came. Her life had turned out very different than Hattie's.

A letter last year from Hattie's friend, Margaret, at Catherine Beecher's school in Hartford, Connecticut, contained something Hattie had never forgotten. The parents of Catherine and her sister, Harriett Beecher Stowe, instilled in their children a sense of responsibility to influence the world. The whole world! The Beechers' aspirations were far more elevated than those of most people Hattie knew. Harriet had penned her now-famous novel, while Catherine had begun several successful schools. Their expectations and accomplishments raised the stakes for girls like Hattie. She reflected on it now as a guide for her future. She fully intended to do something very meaningful in the Cherokee Nation.

September 11, 1856
Today has silenced my complaining. Hannah tackles endless, exhausting work. She mothers, cooks, sews, weaves, mends, knits, tats, dusts, scoops ashes, hauls water, dries vegetables, airs quilts, makes soap and candles, gardens, trims hair, and more. I think she is nothing short of a saint because, for all that, she still has the most appreciative disposition. I don't feel so isolated after our visit. She treats me like family.

September 11, 1856
Dear Hattie,

I just learned that several friends and neighborhood ladies who are members of the Cherokee Nation plan to quilt tomorrow morning right downstairs from you at the female seminary. Would you like to join my dear mother-in-law, Nancy Hitchcock, and me? It might be a lovely opportunity for you to get acquainted. I cannot say exactly who will come, but the quilters usually include Mrs. Jane Ross Nave; the Chief's wife, Mrs. Mary Ross; our own dear Mary Covel; Mrs. Araminta Vann, and fellow teachers, Miss E. Jane Ross and Miss Lotta Raymond.

Fondly, Sarah

❧ ❧ ❧

Hattie wondered if she would see Dr. Hitchcock the day of the quilting. She needed to thank him again for his care. More importantly, she intended to address his disappointment after she disobeyed his orders. But he was away.

Her attention was captivated immediately upon meeting his and Sarah's little girl, Laura, before the quilting began. The adorable little blonde child surveyed Hattie one second and reached for her the next. Thrilled, Hattie took Laura in her arms. Any observer would have believed she'd known Hattie forever, which seemed to please Sarah.

"That child reacts to Miss Sheldon like the school children will soon," Nancy Hitchcock confirmed, gliding toward Hattie with her hand extended. "It's wonderful to meet you finally. Just call me Grandma Hitchcock, if you like. Everyone else does!"

Hattie immediately liked the elder Mrs. Hitchcock and prized her affirmation. The vibrant, grey-haired woman's inner glow turned out to be accented by twinkling humor, as well. Her conversation proved she saw the bright side to most issues.

"I know you're anxious to get started at the school. But you can't teach all the time. Quilting and knitting will buoy your spirit and give you rest. I'm looking for your missing spark of interest, though," Mrs. Hitchcock grinned.

Hattie laughed. She knew Mrs. Hitchcock gasped that she could care less about knitting and quilting, but wouldn't say so. The thing that caught her eye, however, was how closely Mrs. Hitchcock and her son resembled each other in their close-set features and intelligent expression. Yet, Dr. Hitchcock must not have told his family that Hattie disobeyed his orders. Had he, surely they would not have been so friendly with her or straightforward about her teaching.

The number of students in Hattie's future class was growing! In addition to Percy Hicks, and Taylor and Jennie Foreman, she learned of others while quilting. There was the twelve-year-old Vann girl named Fanny, as well as the Meigs children, whose unusual names were Return Robert and his sister, Submit, or just "Mitty." To Hattie's great enjoyment, she also finally made the acquaintance of sweet Mary Covel, whose gleeful grin and long eyelashes positively hypnotized her.

"Mary's missionary father, Caleb Covel, passed to the eternal world in 1850," Grandma Hitchcock had explained gently. "Her Cherokee mother, whom we educated at Dwight Mission, wanted us to teach Mary, as well. So she lets Mary stay with us in Park Hill. We absolutely adore her and claim her as part of the Worcester, Hitchcock, and Hicks families."

Hattie found Mary and enjoyed a little chat to find out the girl's interests. "I can read anything I want and they let me play with

Laura. Grandma Hitchcock teaches me to cook and card and spin and weave and knit," Mary boasted appreciatively.

As the conversation unfolded, Hattie could see how endearing, smart, and responsive Mary was for a girl of only twelve. She spoke with awe of her late father, who had been born into a shipbuilding family from Portland, Maine. An explorer, he took to the high seas as a young man and sailed around the world twice. Mary still owned a few dishes he had brought back from China.

After his forays abroad, Caleb Covel returned to America and studied to become a teacher. This led him to Indian Territory, where Rev. Worcester hired him to teach at Dwight Mission. It was there that the widowed Covel met the Cherokee woman he would marry, Eliza Turtle. Mary reveled in being their mixed-blood Cherokee daughter and appreciated the chance to be educated in Park Hill after the Hitchcocks retired and moved there to be near Dwight.

"Oh, Miss Sheldon," Mary gushed. "I can't wait until the day school starts!"

September 12, 1856
I am meeting myself coming and going. The reticent Cherokee
ladies welcomed me so warmly and I found their quilting
beautiful and intricate. They hold Sarah in deep regard. Her
mother- in-law, Mrs. Hitchcock, is a delightful lady full of
wisdom and witticisms. A dear future student, Mary Covel,
will be lovely to teach.

That evening after supper, surprise guests joined Hattie on the porch. Honored that Martha, Fred and James were there, she invited them to choose a rocking chair and enjoy the view with her. Several deer sauntered slowly across the dewy grass of the seminary lawn. For a long while, the foursome made light conversation. Somewhat distracting was the sweet aroma of apples that permeated all of Park Hill. Hattie longed for a taste of her mother's pie, applesauce or apple butter. Dried apples carried many in the Cherokee Nation through the winter when snow covered the ground and gardens awaited spring.

The foursome's rocking slowed somewhat upon noticing two men in deep conversation nearby. Walking slowly, the men appeared extremely serious, hands behind their backs in full contemplation. James identified them as Henry Dobson Reese, Superintendent of Education, and Col. George Butler, Agent for the Cherokees through an office in Fort Smith. Hattie was able to gather that Reese was a board member for something and Butler represented Indian Affairs, having succeeded his late, revered father.

"Someone mentioned Agent Butler recently. Can you tell me about him?" Hattie asked.

"He has pretty good judgment—most of the time—for a guy who's biased. Butler's only charged with keeping peace, promoting education, fixing the debt, and keeping the government informed about the Cherokees," James retorted sarcastically.

"There's pressure to impose new taxes, as well," Fred said. "He also protects slavery."

"Hattie, you should know that Butler's intent on stamping out abolitionism because it upsets the mixed-blood slaveholders," James explained. "That keeps him on guard."

"I've been told that most of my fellow missionaries are northerners who generally oppose slavery," Hattie commented. "Does he think that makes us crusaders for abolition?"

"Probably. Although Butler works for the federal government, he's a southern loyalist through and through," Martha confirmed. "He only pretends to be fair."

"Slavery is the law here," Fred added soberly. "Butler's paid to keep slaveholders happy and quiet."

Hattie boiled inside, but kept a straight face. "So he really is watching all the missionaries? It sounds like he's spying to maintain peace."

James nodded. "He'll be in hot water if trouble escalates on his watch."

Hattie learned later that the other man, Reese, possessed a law degree and leadership potential. Highly trusted, he had declined to practice law in favor of serving the Cherokee people. Reese's relationship with Rev. Worcester was steady and cooperative, which Hattie would have expected, given Rev. Worcester's central role in overseeing education.

"The reason education is even possible is because the sale of Cherokee land funded it," James continued.

"I knew about the discovery of gold on Cherokee land in Georgia," Hattie replied. "Is it really true that a minority group within the Cherokees negotiated a secret treaty to sell the land?"

"That's correct," James confirmed. "They would have been forced out anyway. But they sold and received U.S. registered stocks in return, which they invested. The earned interest—and only the interest—was supposed to support public education. But the key point is that the treaty came through the minority."

"Now, there's disagreement about the funds," Fred said. "I don't think the government paid them on time. Either that or the assets weren't invested wisely. The Cherokees also say they want independence from government funding of common schools."

"Which one is it?" Martha queried. "I heard there's a growing debt."

"Reese thinks there are too many schools," James answered.

"There can never be enough schools in this big territory," Fred argued. "You can ride for miles without a school in sight. If you ask me, there's ample money but too much spending."

"I thought the argument was about where the money should go, like common schools versus seminaries," Martha said.

"This is like a maze," Hattie exhaled. "It's unbelievably complicated."

Unexpectedly, Martha got a twinkle in her eye. "Don't let it worry you. We've got other things to think about. Will you go with us to Tahlequah tomorrow?"

Settling herself beside James, Hattie scarcely believed they were spending the day together. She couldn't have been more thrilled if she'd orchestrated the whole thing herself. In a matter of days, her gusto for teaching was nearly matched by her, well, her curiosity about James.

Ever so many questions had gathered since last night, but it wasn't good to take the lead in conversation. She smiled to herself thinking of her mother drumming that lesson into her head. Surely James would make an opening comment soon.

Until now, she had never given a thought to what other folks would think if they saw her out like this. It could look like they were becoming a couple. Did she mind? Dealing with others' questions would have to come later. It was too late to call it off anyway.

Hattie just had so little experience with courting. There had been forgettable flirtations with immature classmates. She couldn't ever forget the hilarious mismatch with Dr. Bagg's young, dull mentee, Finis Cumbers. Her interest in men had always taken up so little room compared to time spent studying. The fact was, she seemed to be getting a late start. *But I'm twenty three years old, have a job to support myself, and live clear across the country from my parents.*

How old was James Latta? Martha called him her big brother and she was Hattie's same age. He was probably a lot more experienced, too. Looking sideways, she drank in his calm, relaxed demeanor. A shiver of excitement ran up her spine. How could James be such a good-looking man and not seem to know it? That was really the best part. So far, she hadn't detected one ounce of ego or swagger in him.

"I saw you at Hannah Hicks's place the other day," James opened.

"We had a great visit. I adore her already. She asked who I'd met so far," Hattie replied. "When I mentioned you, she speculated about what you fed us the night of the social."

James threw his head back and let out a big guffaw. "That was a trick if ever I've played one. But you were a good sport."

"You're kidding! Well, what was it?" she cried. "I thought I'd best eat it or you'd accuse me of being a prissy city girl from back east!"

"I know," James chuckled, leaning sideways to bump her arm in jest. "But you showed yourself kind at heart, Hattie Sheldon."

Hattie tucked the incident away to ponder later. This man had a sense of humor and a forgivable dose of contrariness. It made her absolutely tingly.

❖ ❖ ❖

A few miles further along, James edged the wagon near a bluff and invited Hattie and the others to have a look. Shading her eyes from the bright sun, she stared hard. Suddenly, she gasped because a gallows came into view. It really was a gallows.

"That's the new one," James said quietly.

"What happened to the old one?" Martha questioned.

"I hope they didn't wear it out," Fred joked.

"Lawmen used to just take criminals to the hanging tree," James confirmed. "Drove up, tied their hands, put hoods over their heads and removed the wagon to let 'em swing."

"That's gruesome," Hattie cried. "Did they die instantly?"

"No. They jerked and sputtered. It was ugly and slow," James replied soberly.

"You're just trying to scare me," Hattie protested.

"Maybe so. It's crucial to bring the dangers of this place to your attention, though," he returned seriously. "Those hangings scare everybody—except the family of the person a criminal murdered."

In Tahlequah, all kinds of people bustled up and down. Cherokee ladies in cotton and calico dresses. Children chasing each other. Heavily worn wagons rested two deep. A barking dog argued with a horse.

As the foursome arrived near Fred's destination, Hattie smelled a mixture of leather and oil. There must be a saddle shop nearby. That nostalgic aroma sent her emotions soaring as if she were at home helping out in her father's shop. She coaxed her companions inside while sharing more about her father's business. James raised his eyebrows, which made her think he liked her knowledge of saddle craft.

When the men went to see about the repair of Fred's wagon, Martha and Hattie wandered up and down the row of shops. Proprietors behind smartly painted store fronts had wares for pioneers, mothers, babies, traveling men on horseback, and soldiers. Probably, she could buy anything she truly needed here. But, it wasn't like Utica where shopping was about satisfying mere wants.

❖ ❖ ❖

Just as they prepared to leave, Martha squealed in delight. Riding toward them was her other brother, John Stewart Latta, looking imposing with his Deputy U. S. Marshall's badge and gun. Dismounting, he greeted the others and introduced himself politely to Hattie, who remembered him from Murrells.

For several minutes they carried on a conversation. John Stewart told a couple of funny jokes and then explained his business in Tahlequah. Taller than James, this character with his shock of salt and pepper hair must turn heads for his sheer size, as well as his magnetism. He was friendly and loving to his family, but she wondered what he would be like while confronting a criminal.

When he mounted to leave, John Stewart wagged a finger as he nodded toward his family members. "Get them home before dark, Miss Sheldon," he winked.

Was that a warning or just kidding, she wondered? Having parted with him, Martha was eager to fill the return trip with exciting tales from her brother's fascinating life. As a young boy in South Carolina, he learned to hunt animals and scout with the Indians in the woods. He had Cherokee friends and spent time in their community well before removal. That experience earned him first-hand knowledge, understanding, and the trust of the Cherokees.

After the family left South Carolina and settled in western Arkansas, John grew to manhood while learning several trades, as was required of the Latta boys by their father. First, he mastered blacksmithing, then cabinet making. He also understood the finer points of being a successful farmer. When he became a lawman, he was among the earliest group assigned to the Cherokees, having been commissioned at Van Buren, Arkansas, for local work prior to his federal assignment. His childhood experiences played a key role because they benefitted many Cherokees after they got in trouble. There was never had a more evenhanded lawman than John, James agreed.

"Before this starts to sound too serious," Martha chuckled, "you need to know that John is the biggest prankster and humorist of our whole family. All the nieces and nephews adore him because he never fails to play practical jokes on them. They can always count on Uncle John to scare them out of their wits."

When it came to criminals and crimes, James shared, Indian Territory could fill volumes with every manner of illegal activity. The Cherokee Nation was an extremely dangerous location for lawmen. Hattie had expected it was dangerous for the Cherokees. But that also turned out to be true.

The fact of the matter was that Indian Territory drew criminal types as if with a magnet. Desperados from many other states and territories would take refuge in the Cookson Hills, and John Stewart was often the one who brought them to justice. He had regular, harrowing run-ins with fugitives. The border with Arkansas was particularly fraught with trouble.

John Stewart had gotten cross ways with misguided Cherokee bandits on many occasions, Hattie learned. But, instead of shooting them, he tricked them. He could hear a false owl hoot from a deep sleep and know it was a signal. Trouble was coming. On one occasion, outlaws had crept up and spotted him through a window, thinking they could knife him in the bed where he slept. He let them think that. But by the time they got inside, he had hidden. They thought they had seen a ghost sleeping in that bed.

James shared other enlightening things. Explosive situations occurred regularly in the Cherokee Nation because of factions. These were between people who shared the same blood, which made things all the more confounding. Martha reminded Hattie that this related to her question last night about the secret treaty.

"That treaty led to reprisal murders of the minority leaders after removal to this new territory," James whispered, dead serious. "We lived near the place where Major Ridge was killed. My father can recount astonishing stories from personal experience."

Peace eventually was restored a few years later because of the concerted, diplomatic efforts of many, as well as concessions from leaders like Chief John Ross. But recently, violence had been on the rise. Whereas one side wanted to maintain old traditions, the other side wanted to accommodate change. One side was mixed-blood, the other full-blood. One side was pro-slavery and the other side anti-slavery.

James interrupted by pointing down to a little hollow. "See that place? An old preacher named Asaph Montgomery used to live there. He was said to have ridden hundreds of miles each week to save souls."

"Here in the Cherokee Nation?" Hattie inquired.

"Yes. At first, Methodists didn't have congregations, so he preached wherever the Cherokees would listen. I don't think he was formally affiliated either, but the Methodists took him in."

"How do you know so much about the Methodists?" Hattie flirted. "You said you were a Presbyterian."

"Because our father sold Asaph his horses," James smirked, getting more tickled. "He was a big, rotund fellow, so he wore horses out and needed new ones pretty often."

"Where's he now?" Fred asked.

"John Stewart said he got too fat to ride," James smirked, a tear springing from his eye. "He kinda gave up and they had to take him around in the back of a wagon. That's when a younger fellow replaced him."

"You mean he couldn't climb on a horse anymore?" Hattie reacted.

"Oh, and then some," James chortled. "That man died weighing over 500 pounds. They had to build a special coffin and hire a tailor to dress him for burial. Folks laughed that that one hundred dollar price tag to send him to the hereafter served the cheap Methodists right. It took 30 yards of black cloth to fit him and line the coffin."

As darkness fell, James shared more about Dwight Hitchcock and told Hattie she should address him by his first name, too. He related how he and Dwight enjoyed a deep respect and affection for each other. It weathered their sparring over politics. He described Dwight as an intellectual who read constantly and analyzed public policy. They recognized their differences, but didn't let them interfere with the friendship.

Hattie had gotten answers to several questions, as well. In addition to serving as the mission physician, Dwight saw other patients and was involved with the Cold Water Army. After the Foreman children had first mentioned it, Hattie learned it was the temperance society. Dwight must love children, she reasoned, because many were active in it. He also once led a subscription school near Tahlequah. His parents had served many years at Dwight Mission to the north. Jacob Hitchcock was a native of central Massachusetts. Hattie smiled because she liked his mother so much; Nancy Hitchcock reminded her of precious Aunt Mary from Amherst. As she had learned earlier from Sarah, the elder Hitchcocks had retired to Park Hill not long ago, which coincided with Sarah's long illness. Thank goodness they could take care of her when their son had to be away doctoring other patients.

As the evening wore on, Hattie began to feel relieved that Dwight must not have disparaged her to James. Just like Nancy Hitchcock, James seemed to know nothing of the doctor's surprising directive that Hattie pack up and go home to Utica. Their respect put Hattie's mind at ease. She must see the doctor soon to settle that issue. By now, however, he probably assumed she was well.

That night after the foursome parted company, Hattie floated dreamily around her room at the seminary. The day could not have been finer. Everything about it turned out so wonderfully. Especially James. James Latta pleased her.

6

One More Slaveholder, Two Less Schools

*A*lthough Hattie didn't expect an inspiring steeple like the one at her First Presbyterian Church in Utica, or even a house of worship the size of Sehon Chapel near the seminary, she still hadn't expected a structure so humble as the quaint little mission church. Its lovely, melodic bell, however, touched her heart not only for the depth of its tone, but the undertaking of having it cast and shipped here. Crowning the brick structure, it proudly called worshippers like Hattie. By happenstance, she had accompanied another teacher she's just met, Miss Lotta Raymond, to church.

Gauging the width of the sanctuary before going inside, she expected pews on either side of a center aisle with no side aisles. Perhaps it was crowded, which encouraged cooperation as congregants came and went. *I wonder if people from both factions attend church here*, she questioned silently.

Small as it was, the church seemed the happiest of places. When melodeon music began to fill the air and urge worshippers to find a seat, Hattie realized that Hannah was playing it. A few children in the back chased each other and hid behind their mother's skirts. Ushered up the aisle, Hattie and Grace were given a seat near Abijah and his well-behaved children. Percy waved vigorously at Hattie.

Rev. Timothy Ranney led worship often in Rev. Worcester's absence, Hattie learned. She had greeted him at the social, but wanted to get better acquainted with this man Rev. Worcester respected. He had served at Lee's Creek since 1849.

As the service progressed, the music almost outweighed the preaching. People sang with rich gusto as they harmonized. Someone with the lowest of bass voices practically made the place vibrate with resonance. When Hattie glanced back, to her delight, the singing man was a Negro. In fact, several Negroes sat in the back. Of course, Rev. Worcester would welcome them as equals in the eyes of God. Or was it that they simply weren't refused, which must be the way Agent Butler viewed it. For that matter, were they free or slaves? The particulars mustn't be allowed to steal her attention, though. After a long absence from any church, Hattie valued this time to worship and found herself most grateful to be here.

Afterwards, people nodded greetings and chatted as they departed. Emma and Ann appeared hungry and cried, so Hannah and Abijah left to take them home. Hattie had no chance to ask when their rescheduled visit to the printing building and mission, a good distance away, would take place.

Grace talked with a woman wearing an elegant hoop skirt of forest green and rich brown. The elder Hitchcocks and Erminia, who had sat together, slipped away before Hattie could say hello. Martha and Fred were present, but not James.

Martha launched into reminiscences about her family singing together and showed Hattie her late mother's well-loved first hymn book. The binding was cracked and the cover worn, but Hattie already knew the title by heart. It was *Psalms and Hymns Adapted to the Public Worship of the Presbyterian Church*. Her own mother had an exact replica.

"There's a sing-a-long at the seminary tonight," Hattie mentioned. "You're probably getting tired of my company, but you're invited."

"Oh, that sounds fun. Soon enough, we will be gone to Texas and won't have the opportunity for gatherings like that," Martha moped. "We'll come if we can."

When Hattie turned to look for Grace later, a couple approached her. The man, who identified himself as Stick, wore a dark coat with a rolled scarf tie at the neck. A long, black braid reached down his back. His attractive wife, Narcissus, smiled under lovely high cheekbones.

"Our children are anxious to know when you're starting school," Stick asked after introductions.

"We have a son and a daughter," Narcissus added expectantly.

Hattie didn't know how to respond. This was a crucial moment for anxious parents. The good news was that she would have their children as students. But, without the benefit of any information about school, what could she tell them? She had to think fast and respond. Try as she might, however, Hattie stammered rather badly.

"We are slightly … delayed … awaiting Rev. Worcester's return. An announcement will … come soon. I can't wait to meet your children."

"Thank you. They've run ahead already, or I would introduce them," Narcissus excused. "We look forward to the announcement."

❖ ❖ ❖

Rev. Ranney had said goodbye to nearly everyone by the time Hattie approached him on her way out of the church. A circle of people continued to talk outside. Hattie waved to Miss Raymond that she was coming. Miss Raymond didn't seem to be in a hurry.

"Well, Miss Sheldon," Rev. Ranney remembered. "How is your initiation to the Cherokee Nation coming along?"

When Hattie hesitated, he looked at her sideways.

"Oh, I've seen that look before. Newcomers often get overwhelmed."

He seemed to read her mind! With Rev. Worcester gone, scores of questions remained unanswered. She saw an opening, so why not take her chance? If she posed a few inquiries to him, maybe he would fill some gaps in her understanding.

He agreed! So, they took a seat in the back pew for a brief chat. The church door swung lightly on its hinges in the breeze, giving Hattie a glimpse of Miss Raymond and Grace out front. She could gauge her timing by watching them. Carefully, she formulated her thoughts for Rev. Ranney, stumbling over her words about the start of school, tribal factions, slavery, and the secret treaty that led to removal. Then she felt foolish for focusing too broadly.

"Let me clarify for you," Rev. Ranney began. "The minority was a small, well-placed faction of mixed-bloods comprised of well-educated and powerful men. However, they were outnumbered at a time when tribal relations had grown particularly troubled: the government threatened to throw all the Cherokees off their homelands. So, this minority faction decided the whole Cherokee Nation's actual existence was threatened if they tried to hold on. Believing removal was inevitable, the minority men sought another alternative. They negotiated the Treaty of New Echota with the U.S. Government on behalf of the whole tribe. As a result, the homelands in Georgia, Tennessee, Alabama, and North Carolina were sold to the government. Their aim was gallant enough—to leave white intrusion behind -and start afresh in Indian Territory.

"But the other side, the majority, included the entire Cherokee National Council. That body wanted to stall, to hold out against white intrusion. Unbeknownst to it, the minority's treaty was ratified shamelessly by elected legislators in Washington, DC. The sale included a promise of per capita payments to support the Cherokees. The majority fought valiantly against the treaty, but to no avail. So, the minority members who supported it were accused of treason."

"One of those who negotiated the secret treaty was Worcester's highly educated Cherokee translator, Elias Boudinot," Rev. Ranney continued, taking a deep breath. "Like you and me, he had been schooled back east, where he changed his name to honor his mentor. He was originally called Buck Watie, and was the brother of the oft-mentioned Stand Watie, who remains in the forefront of Cherokee affairs to this day. Two other well-known minority members were Major Ridge and his son, John. "

"Beyond the crime of treason, some angry members of the majority decided to honor an old law that promised death to any Indian who sold land without permission of the elected Cherokees. After removal to this new homeland, some well-coordinated murders killed Boudinot and the Ridges on the same day. It was blood revenge. But Stand Watie escaped."

"This is just primitive!" Hattie exclaimed. "I've never heard of such a thing as blood revenge. I thought a great portion of the Cherokees had become Christianized by the late 1830s. Hadn't old customs like that ended?"

Rev. Ranney paused. "Only partially. Did you know that Dr. Hitchcock tells how Major Ridge was on his way to Vineyard, Arkansas, the day of his death, to tend his sick slave? Many wish somebody else had tended that slave's illness."

Silence fell temporarily, as each considered his own thoughts. Hattie recalled that Vineyard had been established by James and Martha's father. Had he known Major Ridge? Additionally, she wobbled on the edge of her seat at the close connection Rev. Worcester had to the murdered Mr. Boudinot. How had the Worcester, Hitchcock, and Hicks families, not to mention everyone else around Park Hill, accommodated such a level of threat, such unanticipated barbarity?

"This tragedy isn't often discussed, but you need to know about it," Rev. Ranney continued. "At the time it happened, Elias Boudinot and his family were living here in Park Hill with the Worcesters. Nearby, Boudinot's new house was being built. In fact, he was at the construction site when four men approached him asking for help that day. They claimed to be sick. Medicine was only available through Worcester's mission then. Worester had put Boudinot in charge of the medicines, so Boudinot set off with the men to grant their request."

"On the way, two of the men fell back and attacked him from behind, stabbing him repeatedly and cleaving his head with a tomahawk. A boy working nearby saw it happen. Understanding the gravity of the threat, he jumped on Worcester's horse, Comet, and rode over to the store kept by Stand Watie, who escaped on the same horse. The rest will have to wait for another day. So now you know how Rev. Worcester ended up hiring Stephen Foreman to replace Elias Boudinot as his Cherokee translator."

Hattie was just warming up more questions when Miss

Raymond came inside to collect her. It was time to go. When would she get another chance to learn more?

❖ ❖ ❖

Back at the seminary, Hattie encountered a sizable printed announcement that hadn't been posted earlier. She wasn't sure what to make of it. The fact that it was posted on a Sunday and gave only one day's notice pointed to urgency.

MANDATORY EDUCATION MEETING
All teachers, employees and interested parties
are hereby summoned to attend

5:00 O'CLOCK PM
MONDAY, SEPTEMBER 15, 1856
CHEROKEE FEMALE SEMINARY
Signed, Henry D. Reese, Secretary of Education

❖ ❖ ❖

At mid-afternoon, when she stepped onto the porch to shake her little rag rug, Dr. Hitchcock was passing on the road. They had not seen each other since the day she broke out with rash and fainted. It seemed a world of events had happened since then. Because of many new insights, she had stopped dreading the long overdue conversation they must have. Now, it was about to take place.

Perhaps this was a fortuitous opportunity to show how well she felt. For she had every intention of standing her ground against his advice to go back to Utica. Raising her arm, Hattie waved to him and starting walking in his direction. She took great care to show that her leg was strong as she hurried along.

"Hello, Dwight. I missed seeing your family at church today," she greeted as she purposely called him by his given name.

"I was with a sick patient and Laura's stomach ache kept Sarah busy."

"Aha, but as you see, I do not have any aches or pains," Hattie pointed out.

"That's what I hear," he responded.

"This may be poor timing, but I want you to know that I intend to stay and teach," she related with feminine firmness.

"I knew you would," he replied with a confirming nod. "You just needed a push."

"What? But you said I should go home. You didn't mean it?" she questioned incredulously.

"Heavens, no! We want you in Park Hill now more than ever," he winked. "You look as healthy as a horse. Why don't you come over for supper Tuesday night? I'll send the carriage."

❖ ❖ ❖

Over supper at the seminary that night, Jane Ross and Miss Raymond included Hattie as they caught up on each other's stories. It was a jovial, upbeat atmosphere. Hattie would rather have discussed the impending meeting and what it meant, but refrained politely.

When the conversation turned to school, she expected the other teachers to comment about Rev. Worcester, not only because she was the new mission teacher, but because of his long history of educational supervision in Park Hill. But their remarks remained slightly distant. Of course, they were polite. Yet she couldn't read why they didn't ask more about his return. Perhaps it had something to do with the impending meeting. She would likely look naïve by asking what it was about.

"May I sit with you tomorrow night?" she inquired instead.

Miss Raymond looked puzzled. "Oh, you're coming?"

"Well, since Rev. Worcester's not here, I think I should," Hattie explained.

The teachers hesitated. Then Jane shrugged. "Well, then, certainly."

Hattie didn't understand their reaction, but dismissed it. She was new and still learning. They must not realize how Rev. Worcester's long absence left her vulnerable. Without his guidance, she must push forward on her own to become a part of the educational community.

❖ ❖ ❖

A stripe of orange with smoky blue highlights lingered in the western sky after the fiery, red sun went down. Hattie had not seen sunsets often in Utica because the houses and other buildings blocked the horizon. Every night in Park Hill, however, the sky came alive with a riot of color. That glow followed by the coolness outdoors also represented the fact that worries would come and go. She didn't intend to think about tomorrow's big meeting. Why spoil tonight's sing-a-long?

A conglomeration of folks having arrived at the seminary later, the music began. Seating themselves casually on a comfortable woven rug, Hattie, Martha, and Fred joined the lively voices. Before long, the leader recognized Martha and insisted she help out. Martha led *Come Thou Long Expected Jesus* during which a few more attendees filtered in. She had a sweet, soprano voice, which Hattie balanced with her subtle alto.

With each verse, Hattie felt more at home. If she closed her eyes, singing was like praying, especially when she concentrated on the lyrics. Her father liked the hymns of Charles Wesley, even though Wesley was a Methodist instead of a Presbyterian. Opening her eyes briefly, she was glad that Jane and Miss Raymond had joined the chorus. Their intricate harmony was beautiful.

It had been a long while since Hattie had sung these wonderful hymns, which left her losing track of the time. At some uncertain point, a new male voice added wonderful resonance. During *A Mighty Fortress Is Our God*, his mellow baritone came closer. To maintain her prayerfulness, she kept her concentration even when he seemed to sing right into her ear. Suddenly, she realized it must be James Latta, although she'd never heard him sing before.

Hattie didn't want to give away her excitement, even though hiding her smile was torture. But she managed it, aided by the growing darkness. As the verses continued, the baritone seemed to project his resonant tone ever closer. She peeked once and saw a familiar looking boot.

All signs of light had passed by the time the singers sent their last, worshipful sounds out into the night. It was pitch black, but no one wanted to rise and light the oil lamp over in the corner. To Hattie's complete amazement, the baritone reached over and touched her hand. Turning, she whispered to him.

"James, where did you come fr..."

But James stopped her in mid-sentence. With a kiss.

Hour after hour that magical night, sleep eluded her. She tried to rest, but jumped up again in exhilaration. She was too thrilled to be tired. This man about whom she was absolutely mad had *kissed her*! It was marvelously inappropriate. But, suddenly, her future took on different dimensions. The prospects were so towering she could hardly contain her feelings.

In the middle of the night, Hattie shook herself, realizing she simply must come back down to reality. Relationships were serious. They had lasting repercussions. She must not minimize the importance of handling this situation with James correctly. On second thought, it wasn't a situation. Were they courting?

Sarah showed up unannounced on Monday morning. "Come with me on my errands," she invited.

Looking healthier than last week, Sarah told stories about Laura playing with a baby rabbit Dwight had discovered. Shortly, they stopped by the Nave General Store and then went to Sarah's. Her frame house consisted of the equivalent of two log cabins connected by a breezeway. The structure was covered with weatherboards and featured a handsome stone chimney at one end. Its foundation appeared to be masonry, which Hattie knew kept it dry and free from pests.

"This style is called a dogtrot," Sarah shared.

"It's new to me," Hattie replied with fascination.

"I'm glad you could come today, even though I had hoped to entertain you more formally. Laura and I are going to Tullahassee tomorrow, so I didn't want you to feel neglected."

Tullahassee was the site of another mission school in the Creek Nation. In 1850, Sarah's sister, Ann Eliza, had married another teacher, Rev. William S. Robertson, and left the Cherokee Nation.

Together, they tackled responsibilities of the Tullahassee school. Ann Eliza had linguistic talent just like Rev. Worcester and was translating the Bible into the Creek language. Sarah treasured the infrequent visits she was able to make there to her sister's home.

"You'll meet her one day. For now, I need to deliver some medicine to Murrell's for Dwight," Sarah concluded. "Let's be off."

❖ ❖ ❖

Hattie waited in the carriage while Sarah knocked at the door of Hunter's Home. When Susan opened it, she gave a friendly wave to Hattie before seeing Sarah inside. Hattie fanned against the sun and looked around at the slaves working outside. She couldn't help but feel upset all over again about slavery.

Momentarily, James Latta came around the side of the house. Shocked to see him there, he seemed equally surprised to see Hattie. She tried not to get flustered, given the romantic way they parted last night. What he was doing at Hunter's Home. Visiting? Maybe he farmed nearby? To her chagrin, she realized she had never asked a direct question about where James worked.

"I saw you and Sarah arrive. I keep thinking of things to tell you," he quipped as if nothing had happened the night before.

Hattie searched for words. But, in seconds, James began to explain another aspect of the mission's history. He detailed how Rev. Worcester had pulled many strings with the American Board because some of his church's most loyal financiers, who were mixed-blood leaders and businessmen, also happened to be slaveholders. Without Worcester's intermediary efforts, they would have been kicked out of the church.

The politics staggered Hattie. How had Rev. Worcester found

a way to keep all the parties together? He must be a diplomat in addition to the myriad of other jobs he performed regularly.

"How many leaders in Park Hill own slaves?" she asked hesitantly, not sure she wanted to know.

"Well, people with big operations. Successful people like Mr. Murrell," he replied.

"So, are you saying Mr. Murrell was in danger of excommunication?" she questioned.

"No. I didn't mean to confuse you. He's actually a Methodist and affiliated with Sehon Chapel. But he has supported Worcester's efforts," James replied.

"How do men like him rationalize slavery, as Christians?" Hattie probed. "Surely they feel guilty?"

With that, her thoughts turned to the reasons offered in *Uncle Tom's Cabin*, which portrayed how both sides of the slavery issue thought. Each believed God was on their side and used the Bible to rationalize their stances.

"All slaveholders are not doomed to eternal damnation, Hattie," James replied quietly with a note of annoyance. "Some don't even want to own slaves, you know."

"I have a hard time believing that," she retorted rather flippantly. "Especially here. Surely there are other sources of labor to keep their business interests profitable. I see plenty of able-bodied Cherokee men around here. So, why do slaves do the work?"

James gave Hattie a stern stare. His expression had a note of incredulity about it, like she was not thinking straight. He then proceeded to outline many points about how the Cherokees and Indians from other tribes were not considered to be a labor force. They received money from the government for the lands from which they had been removed—lands that had essentially been stolen in shady deals—even though they were reimbursed. That money supported them. Many didn't trust white men and wouldn't work for them, he continued. So, slaves did the work. Slavery had been common practice for a long time in the South before removal. Slaves did the back-breaking manual labor.

"The south is more complicated than I can believe," she whispered. "I only know how men think and reason in New York and Boston where there's very little slavery. The American Board members live there. To them, it's about each man's heart. And they think slaveholders are wicked."

"And where I'm from, we own slaves and slaveholders are upstanding Christians," James responded evenly.

"What," Hattie cried. "Are you saying you own slaves?"

"Yes, that's what I've been talking about in so many words. I'm trying to get you to understand," James responded impatiently. "Nearly every planter I know owns, manages, or does some kind of work with slaves."

A silent explosion in Hattie's chest cut off the air between them. Her tongue was momentarily disabled and she couldn't see straight. Was this yet another example of something she should have known about the Cherokee Nation? No wonder the American Board's letter never reached her. They probably wanted to keep stories like this quiet as long as possible. She almost felt tricked into coming.

"Are you alright?" James inquired, his expression softening.

"I'm speechless and confused and mad," she muttered. "It sounds like Rev. Worcester, whom I know is against slavery, has to fight *for* slaveholders so his Board won't get rid of them even though they are his most necessary backers. Am I to understand that he won't even preach his Bible-based anti-slavery convictions in his own church?"

"It's even worse than that," James confirmed. "The Board doesn't understand his challenges and never will. They make impossible demands and refuse to send him funds. He endures and tries to appease those demands, but soldiers on because he loves the Cherokees. You can't imagine the sacrifices he has made for them."

Again, Hattie was silent. But this time it was out of pure grief. Or love. Or respect. Whatever it was, it made her heart ache with sharp pains.

"I'm sharing this for your sake," James continued. "It's complicated. But I need to put one more important thing to rest. I don't know if it will surprise you or not."

"Well, after what you just said, I can't imagine what could surprise me more," she replied, a pall over her emotions.

"Mr. Murrell's back. Before he left the last time, he approached me to work full time for him. I wanted a change and needed a raise, so I accepted. Eventually, my job will be managing his lands, his crops, and ..." James trailed off, pausing for a long moment, "and his slaves."

Hattie's mouth dropped open. She wanted to bury her face and sob, but Sarah had emerged from the house and waved excitedly at them. Hattie plastered a happy expression on her face.

Cornbread and green beans with smoked pork bacon fed Jane, Miss Raymond, and Hattie before the education meeting. Since Jane's uncle was the chief, Hattie wondered if she knew something she wasn't voicing. Jane referenced the perpetual rumors about education funds running low. But that had been the case for years, she reminded. Especially during dry times like this one, money was tight because of poor crop yields. All the Cherokees needed, in her opinion, were strong rains and good crops to bring in ample profits. Old debts could be paid, although she didn't know the status of the education fund. Disagreements among various Cherokees made concurrence on a single course of action very unlikely, however.

Shortly, they entered the auditorium, which was halfway full already. A sense of anticipation gathered as the noise level rose. On the stage, two chairs flanked the podium and faced the audience. Jane said one would be for Secretary Reese and a second for Agent Butler. Since Rev. Worcester was away, they hadn't made a place for him, Hattie concluded.

Although Hattie had hoped to make subtle inquiries with Miss Raymond because of her role as women's principal, the time just hadn't presented itself. Miss Raymond must be working terribly hard in preparation for the fall term. She said she had kept long hours.

Presently, all conversation stopped when Secretary Reese and Agent Butler began to file onto the stage. Quickly, the crowd grew attentive. The first impression that struck Hattie was everyone's rather somber expression. Did they know something she didn't? Her concerns rose as people in the audience glanced nervously at one another, then back to the stage.

Reese called the meeting to order and thanked those present for attending. He read a statement that lasted several minutes. Butler rose next and reiterated many of the same points that Fred and James had explained to Hattie. She didn't grasp all that was said, but tried to recall as much as possible for reflection later. At least she had a cursory understanding of the general points. The concern focused upon the lack of funds and its impact on the Cherokee Nation education system.

Reese then returned to the podium and began to speak with a much more deliberate voice. He articulated slowly, saying he would prefer to welcome questions after the attendees had a day or so to digest his announcement. Hattie wondered what was going on. Then he offered his key sentence:

"Therefore, we cannot afford to teach the students or keep these buildings open. I am sad to announce that the female and male seminaries will not be able to offer classes this fall. We will close them in the near future due to lack to funds."

The reaction of the crowd was immediate. People froze in their seats, postures rigid. This elevated Hattie's concern significantly. Without delay, Reese stepped away from the podium, nodded to Butler and the meeting ended. Neither Jane nor Miss Raymond spoke or moved, so Hattie kept quiet, too. She hardly knew what to make of the announcement. Had they just lost their jobs? No classes would be held, but surely the suspension was just temporary and they would start again in the spring.

Along with Hattie's abrupt sense of confusion, a pressing thought arose about Rev. Worcester. How could this happen with him gone? He had started this whole operation, after all. It seemed strange or unfair or even crooked to make such a momentous decision in his absence.

The nearly mute attendees stood slowly and made their way to the door of the auditorium. A few mumbled and several coughed nervously. Hattie found the quiet disconcerting. As evidenced by their stunned reticence, the people were unhappy. They seemed stupefied by the news and hadn't yet digested its impact on them.

Hattie couldn't formulate her thoughts. Jane and Miss Raymond weren't much better. They had one big problem in common: where were they going to stay? How long would they be able to live in their rooms? Hattie wondered if the ladies' contracts and salaries would be honored, since they had no advance notice and might not find other jobs quickly.

Each of the ladies immediately went to her own room. Hattie wilted down into her chair and lit the lamp. Usually, she might reach for a pen because writing helped her formulate coherent thoughts. Not this time. She could do nothing as her mind scrambled over the evening's events. Finally, she climbed into bed, clothes and all. She just needed to take comfort from the closeness.

A gentle knock at the door roused her from a near trance.

"Hattie, what happened?" Martha implored as she stepped inside. "Fred insisted we come over to find out."

When Hattie tried to respond, a frog had settled in her throat. In a scratchy, agitated voice, she tried to tell Martha about the astonishing development.

"Agent Butler said they kept thinking a compromise measure could be reached," she related. "But it wasn't."

"What else," Martha pressed. "What did they announce?"

"There will be no classes this fall. Both seminaries are closing down," Hattie fretted.

"You mean it?" Martha whispered, looking stunned. "Starting now?"

"Yes. The whole crowd was dumbfounded," Hattie related. "All I could think was what a disaster! And I can't even talk to Rev. Worcester about it."

"Fred was afraid of something like this," Martha soothed quietly. "I'm not much help, but I know who is. Come on. We're going over to Murrell's to tell James. He'll shed more light on it."

Just as the late day sun hid behind low clouds, they struck out across the dark prairie. It was a fresh, cool evening that promised a full moon. Hattie wanted to *hear* what James thought, but wasn't sure she wanted to *see* him. He had revealed his slavery background, which put their beliefs in direct conflict. How could they carry on courting while coming from opposite sides of the fence?

Yet, that couldn't be resolved tonight. Given Martha's great support and interest, Hattie needed to think things over. It wouldn't hurt to talk about the schools, especially in the company of Fred and Martha. But getting closer to James might spell trouble.

She calmed down as they got closer. September's chirping crickets reminded her of the intricacy of creation. She needed to take a longer view of problems and form a greater respect for timing. When some resonant frogs began serenading in the background, it felt like confirmation that she must heed God's timing. Nature had a way of putting things in perspective.

Soon, the glow of a lamp could be seen as Fred pointed out James's window. Until that moment, Hattie hadn't known where James lived or that he had a cabin to himself. Some large shrubs flanked it and marked the edge of a rose garden. She smelled the smoke house, which made her mouth water. Several slaves were working outside still.

Martha rapped with light, rapid movements on the roughhewn door and whispered his name.

"What in the world are you marauders doing out?" James reprimanded. "Get inside here right now!"

"We had no other choice," Martha explained. "The meeting announcement has left Hattie and the whole town in a terrible state. Reese and Butler are ending the fall term before it starts!"

"Well, what do you know!" James whistled in surprise. "There must be stiff competition for the remaining funds. I heard today that there's new trouble over teachers, as well."

"Butler said one side wants to redirect the money," Hattie remembered, "and the other side wants to split it. Some don't want to pay the debt, but others want to pay the whole debt first."

"Today, word was out that during the last session of Congress, the Cherokees failed to sell some of the neutral land. So no money was raised and their debt had to be addressed," James shared. "Was Chief Ross there?"

"No, because he was in the minority. The vote gave all the remaining money to the common schools," Hattie replied.

"That means Reese went up against Chief Ross and won," James exclaimed. "This is about factionalism, plain and simple. Ross is in hot water for bringing in too many eastern-born teachers. He idealizes them. Reese—and the majority—want all native-born teachers. They're tired of watering down Cherokee culture."

"Where did you learn all this new information?" Hattie confronted. "You didn't mention it the other day."

"No offense, but I can go places you can't," he answered evenly. "I've been asking around a lot."

"So, how could they do this without Rev. Worcester?" Hattie objected. "He started the whole thing. He's overseen it. Do they just run over him like this all the time?"

Martha and Fred looked puzzled, but didn't answer.

"Well, he wouldn't be part of the debt decision, among other things," James replied, looking at her skeptically.

A new wave of confusion clouded Hattie's understanding. Her expression revealed more than a little exasperation. The hour had grown late, however, and this was no time to sort things out.

"I've got to sleep on this now," she commented as she stood. "It's exhausted me. Thank you—bless you—for helping me through this frustrating night."

❄ ❄ ❄

Hattie looked for Jane the next morning, but found only Miss Raymond. Explaining how she still felt so new and out of her depth, she appealed for information. Miss Raymond, herself uncertain, was open and willing, nevertheless, to offer clarification on the seminary closings.

"I guess the Cherokee Nation is doing what it thinks is best," she told Hattie soberly.

"It's mystifying. How could they do it with Rev. Worcester out of town?" Hattie continued. "He's been so loyal for so long."

"Yes, uh, I've heard that," Miss Raymond added hesitantly. "I haven't had the opportunity to meet him, though."

"But, you are the newly hired principal," Hattie searched. "Didn't he recruit you?"

"Oh no, I was hired by the Cherokee Nation," Miss Raymond detailed.

Blinking out of bewilderment, Hattie's countenance dropped. This was not making sense. She thought the Cherokee National Seminary and the Park Hill Mission were under the auspices of the same general education body. Weren't both begun and supervised by Rev. Worcester? Didn't he do the hiring?

"Can you help me understand better?" Hattie finally heard herself ask.

"Yes. But you must agree to call me Lotta. Right after the Cherokees arrived here, the American Board opened Park Hill's first school at the mission and hired teachers," Lotta began succinctly, like a good teacher would. "Later, after common schools were established by the Cherokees, the demand for higher education grew. That led to the establishment of the seminaries. There was much fanfare when they opened in 1851. Although church-based missions receive some government stipends, that is different money than funds which built the seminaries."

"So, do I have it wrong? I thought Rev. Worcester held a position of prominence to guide and manage all schools here."

"I believe he only assisted during the initial launch of the seminaries," Lotta explained. "He does not play a role with them now."

Hattie's mortification mounted and seemed ready to sweep her over. "I have obviously been under the most astonishing misinterpretation."

"This is a confusing place for anyone," Lotta replied with a kind calmness. "I'll tell you everything I know. Will that help?"

Kind, patient Lotta revealed what she had learned during her interviews—and then some. She began from an historical perspective, wanting Hattie to know the whole story from the very beginning. In 1839, a new constitution for the Cherokee Nation established public schools that were altogether separate from the mission schools. There was understanding and cooperation among the various missions and the Cherokee Nation. The mission didn't have to meet the common-school quotas, for instance. They were followed loosely, but required no fewer than twenty five and no more than sixty students.

Next, the Cherokee National Council required each denomination's mission board to submit a request for any newly proposed schools. The Council would consider the location, as well as the amount and strength of funding and backing. It alone held the power to approve or disapprove. Luckily for Rev. Worcester, most of his requests were approved.

In a few years' time, the growing demand for higher education pushed the Council to build the male and female seminaries. Eastern teachers were recruited from eastern schools by tribal leaders. But soon, a contingent wanted eastern-educated Cherokee teachers instead of white teachers. Many conflicts still surrounded this, like with other issues between full-bloods and mixed-bloods.

There was no denying that old disagreements had gained new strength and grown heated in the last several years. Rumors abounded about funding problems and shortfalls. What funds remained were caught in a tug-of-war over whether the common schools or the seminaries would be funded. The announcement last night meant the seminaries had lost, much to the disdain of Chief Ross.

While all this was happening, American Board mission schools under Rev. Worcester's guidance had done their best to remain open. They continued to be taught by eastern teachers at the various stations in the Cherokee Nation. Other schools existed as well, many run by denominations like the Presbyterians, Methodists, and Moravians. Indian Territory at large did not suffer from a dearth of missionaries, Lotta related. The need was so great and the population so large that many groups—almost too many—set up operations and were generally quite friendly toward each other.

"Their interests for the Cherokees are basically the same as ours: salvation and education," she confirmed.

Staffing challenges existed in all the American Board mission stations and were a constant trial for Rev. Worcester, she had heard. Turnover was high among teachers. Many factors contributed to that fact, including marriage, illness, loneliness, and even death. When a vacancy occurred, a struggle ensued to recruit a new teacher immediately while engaging a substitute in the meantime.

"Last year, Rev. Stephen Foreman's oldest daughter, Erminia, helped keep the Park Hill Mission School going after the teacher left. Then the poor girl became ill and was taken to Texas. That's what led to you being recruited, Hattie."

Staggering inside and wondering where her place was in this web of complexity, Hattie barely managed to hold back tears as she thanked Lotta. She appreciated the fact that Lotta did not hide the more telling, unflattering minutiae. As far as she could tell, though, there weren't many encouraging points.

When or how had Hattie gotten the idea that Rev. Worcester was a big fish in the little pond of Park Hill? From what Lotta had explained, he was a little fish, although well respected. Had Hattie somehow juxtaposed his long, loyal service into great influence that didn't exist? Maybe her imagination had filled the void.

But why had a void existed in the first place? Hattie exhaled in frustration because she already knew the answer. It bothered her more and more as time had passed and she encountered all that she didn't know. If Erminia had entertained even a few of her questions on their long journey together, this misunderstanding would never have happened. Nothing would convince Hattie of any version of events but that Rev. Worcester's intent was lost along the road to Park Hill. She now believed the information in the promised letter she had never received was to have been replaced by several weeks of explanations by Erminia as they made their way south.

And even though Hattie still held Rev. Worcester in the highest regard, it seemed obvious she had elevated him wrongly. She had hung big ideas on a myth. Rev. Worcester was wonderful, but he was just one man in charge of a small, remote mission. She was about to join that most humble effort. Lotta's account only confirmed what Hattie had discovered at Murrell's library. The only towering characteristic about Rev. Worcester's shrinking mission was his character.

Nobody was hiding anything from her. Rather, they must be working mightily behind the scenes to shore the operation up. Of course it did good work, but not lately in her estimation. Rev. Worcester had been gone too long.

One day soon, she would finally tour the mission. By then, this big dose of reality would put her adventurous plans and ideas of righting wrongs into perspective. The disappointments would have to be swallowed whole and digested. She would still join and give the mission her all, of course. By the look of her eager, future students, there was nothing hollow about the good work ahead. Besides, she was the lucky one; Jane and Lotta suddenly had no jobs.

7

No More Holdups

September 16, 1856
Dear Father and Mother,

*Park Hill and its residents have continued to be so welcoming.
Now that I'm getting better acquainted in the community,
ever so much activity keeps me rushing. The annual social for
employees of the American Board in the Cherokee Nation
was last Tuesday. Ministers came to renew friendships, share
news, and encourage one another.*

*A dear-hearted woman of long association with the mission
keeps me company and takes me wherever I need to go. Rev.
Worcester's daughter, Hannah Hicks, and her lovely children
hosted me at their home on Thursday. I joined a quilting
gathering of Cherokee ladies last Friday and learned names of
several future students. Saturday brought a day trip to nearby
Tahlequah and then friends joined me for a sing-a-long on
Sunday evening.*

Everything's going so well. I will write more soon.
Love, Hattie

❖ ❖ ❖

Tuesday afternoon came before Hattie took stock of all that had occurred. Spending time at the Hitchcock residence would be wonderful. Since Sarah was gone, surely the elder Hitchcocks had planned the evening to get better acquainted.

Just then she heard her name called. She hadn't expected Nancy Hitchcock to collect her or that they would leave so early. But, more hours meant more time to chat. In a matter of minutes, Nancy was engaging Hattie in her favorite topic, knitting. Hattie liked Nancy more all the time. But she dreaded knitting. She had avoided it until now.

"You'll need good stockings soon," Nancy reminded color-fully, pointing to a basket at her feet filled with knitting needles and fine, white cotton yarn. She brought it to Hattie's side. "We make our own and they wear out quickly. So it's time I got you started. It's wise to have a pair underway at all times."

"I'm laughing at myself really," Hattie allowed with a grin. "I moved heaven and earth in Utica to spend every second at the library and avoid knitting. But now, I don't have much to read."

"It's no reflection on your intellect, if that's what worries you," Nancy chided later while stirring a pot of vegetable soup. "Knitting nobly addresses the unavoidable aspects of life. I think of that when Laura's kitten tangles all my colored yarns together."

Across the room, Jacob Hitchcock, whom Hattie had just met for the first time, cleared his throat. "No young woman can approach marriage without knowledge and skill at knitting," he proffered, glancing speculatively at Hattie.

She comprehended, but shook her head in a good-humored way. "Whatever you're thinking is far removed from my plans. I'm here to teach. You will find me completely focused upon my classroom and the children in it."

"Not from what I've heard," he quipped, looking up jovially.

"I can't imagine who else has spoken about my future plans," Hattie argued. To her great annoyance, she was thinking of James and struggling to hide the smile that stole her face every time she thought of him. This was no time to send mixed messages. She liked him. But he practiced what her father preached against.

Soon, Dwight entered and showed himself quite the host. His father said Dwight liked practicing his chemistry on food in the kitchen. To Hattie's surprise, he was the one who had "gone whole hog" and made the stew. The appealing aroma made Hattie's mouth water for a change, after enduring the somewhat bland food of the seminary.

In addition to Dwight's considerable intellect, Hattie found he also had a great sense of humor. At school, she had grown accustomed to brilliant men playing serious roles. Or stuffier roles. Dwight's wit was irresistible; he kept a straight face after saying something wordy that made them double over with laughter.

Realizing that these few moments before supper might present a rare chance to gain new information, Hattie asked to hear the family's background. Dwight was happy to comply and began in detail. His parents, enduring a laborious ox-wagon journey all the way from Brimfield, Massachusetts, had helped found the first Dwight Mission in Arkansas in the early 1820s. They named it to honor the President of Yale College, Rev. Timothy Dwight, who was also linked with the American Board as its first signatory member.

Upon Dwight's birth in 1822, his parents used the same, revered name for their newborn son.

"Although I was born in Arkansas," Dwight confirmed to Hattie, "I'm a northerner through and through."

"Well, that merely refers to his politics and eastern schooling," James called from a crack in the door.

Stunned, Hattie turned to watch him enter. She would have to play this evening carefully. James tweaked her on the ear, shook hands with everyone, and took a seat as Dwight continued with his explanation.

Graduating from Bowdoin's Medical School of Maine as a physician, Dwight refuted what James had said. He felt absolute loyalty to his roots in this region, so he packed his doctor bag and returned to live among the Cherokees in Indian Territory. Medical care was wanting before he arrived, he pointed out, unless one counted individuals like old Arch Campbell down the road, who claimed to know about herbs and potions.

"He also was motivated to return because of one impressive individual named Sarah," James added, looking at Dwight with jubilant eyes.

After the story unfolded further, Hattie interrupted to ask how Dwight had come to understand the Cherokees so well.

"It required the establishment of trustworthiness. And I respected their customs. That's especially true for the full-bloods," he returned. "Some of my learning came when I found myself in interesting situations, I'll tell you that."

"What about that blizzard, when you went to see Lightningbug's wife and got lost," Nancy reminded.

"Oh, that still makes me shudder. What poor judgment and lack of preparedness," Dwight related. "People here have lost their lives in sudden snowstorms, Hattie. It doesn't take much. I naively thought I could get home. But I ended up in a hollow tree stump covered with my saddle. Believe me, I was grateful to be alive the next morning."

Hattie frowned. "You just said you knew better."

"Well, I did. But here's the story. I had gotten word that the wife of a friend was in labor," Dwight continued. "Her first delivery had been difficult. I knew the second baby would be large, so I went. Luckily, the baby was just an eight pounder and a strong little rascal, which was a saving grace. I struck out for home in the snow and lived through it somehow. But the next one nearly finished me off."

"You went out in another blizzard?" Hattie asked, wincing.

"No, when I started the weather seemed fine. Then heavy snow started to fall. I came upon some other folks caught unprepared. They were poorly clothed and exhausted, especially their little girl. But they knew their way. Overconfident, I loaned them my coat and blanket before the light waned and I lost my way. But my horse didn't miss a beat. Thanks to his sense of direction, we got home and lived to tell the tale. Believe me, I said extra prayers that night to the Good Lord."

"Those people he helped will never forget his sacrifice," Jacob summarized respectfully.

Shortly, Hattie helped Nancy serve supper, being careful to seat herself by Jacob instead of James. The conversation turned to Dwight's younger brother, Isaac, who was a teacher elsewhere in the Cherokee Nation. While the Hitchcocks shared about his latest letter, James directed his attention to Hattie.

"Dwight's like a replacement for my brothers who left and never came home," he whispered. She let the comment go without a response.

"I have something to pass along to you, Dwight," Hattie kidded, changing the subject. "Last night, Fred Pilkington commented on your good job keeping an eye on Rev. Worcester's family while he's back east. Fred called you the 'biggest toad in the puddle' around here. Is that a compliment or an insult?"

"Well, I'd call it an unusually disrespectful designation," Dwight grinned. "I'll have to remember to thank Fred for giving me credit where it is not due."

Once the table was cleared, Jacob excused himself to retire. Nancy washed and Hattie dried the dishes quickly. Hattie couldn't help but laugh when Dwight and James started singing a harmonized version of the popular tune, *Oh Susannah*. It was quite an exaggerated performance. They had such fun together.

When the time came to see Hattie home, the duo continued their antics before dissolving into storytelling. Having commented on his brothers, James appeared lost in wonderful memories. He shared them for the remainder of the threesome's way to the seminary. Hattie actually enjoyed what she heard, but didn't want him to know that. They parted without him noticing she had distanced herself, which was annoying.

The early fall days had grown shorter as summer's extended daylight waned. Hattie couldn't believe how dark it was outdoors. Even after going inside and up the stairs, the need to light a lamp impressed itself on her. It was foolish to worry, but the dark had always been a little unnerving and was more so here in Park Hill than in Utica.

Opening her door, Hattie felt her toe touch something, but when she reached down, nothing was there. By the lamp's glow, she readied herself for bed, trying to think good thoughts and keep her wits about her over James. It had been such a nice evening.

Some of her troubling feelings about Park Hill had subsided. They were replaced by a growing sense of security. Spending time with James, Hannah's family, and Sarah's family had calmed her down considerably. Their acceptance and openness sent a powerful message of love and sanctuary. If she had their support, she could bear up and endure.

Hattie pulled back the covers of her bed and straightened her pillow, smiling to herself about James Latta's silly singing. Dwight must shake his head at times over the situations James created. There was always a lighthearted side to life wherever James Latta was.

Reaching to extinguish her lamp, Hattie caught sight of something white in her peripheral vision. It was across the room by the door. The lamp had somehow reflected against it. She rose and went over to see what it was. To her surprise, she found an envelope that someone must have slid under her door. Excited, she anticipated an invitation to something nice and rushed back to her bed to read it.

Ripping the envelope excitedly, she pulled out a single sheet of paper and read:

We are watching you, Miss Hattie Sheldon. By now you should know we don't want any more northern teachers in the Cherokee Nation. It is time for Cherokee teachers to do the educating here. This is no place for the likes of an agitator like you. Until you go back to your fancy life in New York, we will be everywhere, always watching you at home, at school, at church, and around Park Hill. If you want to visit the Tahlequah gallows again, all you need to do is go out alone or step out of line. Our reach is long, so if you talk about this warning, it is at your own risk. Get out of the Cherokee Nation or the good people you love will get hurt.

Aghast, Hattie started to shake with uncontrollable terror. There was not as much as a simple lock on her door. Who would write such a thing? When had they sneaked inside the seminary?

A thousand theories crowded her mind. Hattie sheltered herself under the bed covers, uncertain if she should stay there. Her lamp was low on oil, so she extinguished it. Staring into the pitch blackness, the wind outside only made her start at every sound. Once, she thought she heard footsteps and broke out in a cold sweat. Since someone had managed to get inside, they could do so again.

Hovering for want of a plan, she fought tiredness. Her leg ache returned, sending even more discomfort through her entire body. Whoever had written the threat letter meant business. The determined tone of the note left her imagining a fearless criminal. He could steal into her room to end her life swiftly with a jagged knife. Or he might hold off, plotting against her to carry out the demise of her work and relationships.

The sheer volume of evil deeds in Indian Territory—murders, shootings, kidnappings, and robberies—had grown commonplace to others, but not to Hattie. Try as she might to reason around the problems on every side, staggering fears and other worries multiplied as the hours passed.

Shortly after twilight, she finally drifted to sleep, exhausted from her watchful ordeal. Awakening later by a terrifying start, she was horrified to have let down her guard. This letter topped the fact that everything had taken on exaggerated proportions the last few weeks. Many pressing problems remained unresolved. Now, those paled in light of the threat on her life.

Suffering so many things alone now became intolerable. Hattie fought back hunger as she dressed at dawn, intent on being with another person in the midst of such fright.

After hitching a ride from Jane the next morning, Hattie found

Hannah behind the house feeding chickens. Looking up, Hannah brushed a strand of hair behind her ear. She always appeared glad to see Hattie, even when interrupted. But today, her smile dropped when she saw Hattie's expression.

"You look like you've seen a ghost," Hannah said.

Her comment confirmed that Hattie must look frightful. But Hattie didn't care. After last night's scare, all she could envision was companionship and wisdom. Keeping the secret, however, was going to be much harder than she guessed. Her very life hinged on not revealing the threat. How would she cover it up? What was she going to talk about that Hannah would believe?

Hattie realized she was standing stiffly and just staring in her silence. She must have shot Hannah a harrowing glance because her friend stopped working. For want of what to do, Hattie began to pace, her arms folded tightly across her midsection, almost like hugging herself.

"I've never seen you like this. What's the matter," Hannah begged.

The start of school was the safest subject Hattie could think of. At least it was legitimate.

"I am overtaken with doubts. Too many uncertainties are in this situation. I feel so alone."

"My father said the same thing while he was in prison," Hannah replied seriously, never taking her eyes off Hattie.

"Erminia confused me. She said the start of school was my responsibility," Hattie exhaled, showing the depth of her burden. "I didn't know that. And what if the materials aren't at the printing building?"

Hannah shook her head. "Oh, Hattie. That is not what was to happen."

"I don't have the slightest idea which way to turn," Hattie continued. "And I don't think I can shoulder the whole thing. There's far, far more confusion here than I thought."

"What do you mean?" Hannah asked, looking confused.

"There has been one letdown after another. Things are so terribly complicated. It's an uphill battle," Hattie raved, realizing her voice sounded shrill. "I think these things are signs that I need to acknowledge. It's beginning to look like I should admit the obvious."

Hannah did not react with words. Slowly, she reached down to lift her bucket. Looking pensive, she led Hattie to her house and seated her at the table. Hannah disappeared for a few seconds and then returned carrying a little book.

"Have you ever seen this before?" she inquired as Hattie turned the volume over in her hands and opened its pages.

"No, but I think I know where it came from," Hattie replied, tears coming to her eyes as she read its title, *Cherokee Primer*.

"Father printed it. The Cherokee people had no intelligible, written language until Sequoyah perfected an alphabet less than forty years ago," Hannah detailed quietly. "Think how long that was after our forefathers had been reading? The Cherokees only recently gained a written record of their language! Because my father was a linguist, he was chosen to be among the first to turn that Cherokee syllabary into words on the page, words that could educate and transform the lives of thousands. On the timeline of civilization, Hattie, the Cherokees are on the ascendance. It is their time! You are a pivotal figure in making sure that continues."

"No, I am not," Hattie argued, annoyed. "The American Board has let me, your father, and the Cherokees down. All these trials and tribulations matter not. I could sacrifice all for the Cherokees and it would be nothing compared to American Board priorities elsewhere.

But I am a human being. I need sustenance. I need someone to care and back me up."

"You told me yourself that your grandfather fought in the revolution," Hannah countered. "Was all that for naught? You said your father wanted a better life and went west to New York State to start his own livelihood. Was all that for naught? Now you have studied more than anyone ever before in your family. You came to this territory to help the Cherokees that need your heart, your mind, and your compassion. You are poised to meet great, pressing needs. All that schooling, the journeys, your illness and recovery, the mind boggling expansion of your experiences.....was all that for naught, Hattie?"

Hattie turned away from Hannah and bent her head down, weeping bitterly. She felt such a mixture of emotions, but primarily shame. Or fraud. She needed comfort, but had been disingenuous about why.

There was no way she could say what was really wrong. If only her father were here, just to remind her that she mattered and to embrace her with encouragement. Now, she realized, she really could choose to walk away from the conundrum that called itself Park Hill.

"I feel I've come all this way, but have reached a dead end," she whispered.

"It's not a dead end if it takes you somewhere you were meant to go," Hannah replied firmly.

Leaving Hattie with her thoughts, she walked to the stove and spooned up a bowl of porridge in a clean bowl. Setting it before Hattie, she urged her to eat. Hattie had no idea how Hannah knew she was famished, but she was grateful for the gesture. It also gave her the chance to sort herself out further. Keeping the secret of the threat letter was becoming more difficult by the second.

"Take that primer. I want you to read it through," Hannah instructed. "I wish I could drop everything, but I must finish my chores and several other important things. I'm puzzled because you were fine on Sunday. Surely the seminary closure didn't push you into this state? Tomorrow, we are going over to the print building. It will do you good, whether you find the teaching materials there or not. At least you have the primer now. That is enough to start school in a pinch. Now come along, we're going to Dwight's. You're not fit to be alone."

"Good grief, Hattie," Dwight exclaimed after Hannah explained that something dreadful was impacting Hattie. "You were happy and animated last night!"

"Besides this teaching debacle that Mother, uh, imposed on her, there's obviously something she can't tell us," Hannah stated solemnly. "I know it's there, but can't get it out of her."

"What else is bothering you?" Dwight urged. "The cat's never gotten your tongue before. Don't you trust us? We will do anything to help if you'll share what has happened."

"I can't," Hattie replied quietly. "I mean, I can't ... find the words to express all that's wrong. Thank you for bringing me, Hannah."

"Maybe her fever is back," Hannah speculated as she walked out the door.

"You'd probably rather talk to Sarah," Dwight pleaded. "But she won't be back for a week, I'm afraid. There's absolute privacy and quiet here, if that's what you desire. My parents are visiting old friends until later."

"I'll start reading the primer," Hattie whispered.

Closing her eyes, she hated how the rapid beating of her heart grew pronounced. She had never experienced such a sense of unending alarm. Was this how people felt when they were in the midst of war? Was this what it felt like to fear for one's life every minute? If so, she would be a poor soldier.

Hattie tried to follow Dwight's instructions to breathe deeply. How could she be alone again at the seminary after feeling the sense of doom promised by the letter? On the other hand, she didn't see how other people could endure her frantic, secretive presence for very long either. It was a losing situation no matter how she looked at it. Continuing to calm herself, she tried to concentrate on the *Cherokee Primer*.

The next thing she knew, she was awakened by Dwight's voice coming through the open window from outside. He was laughing. She also heard horses' snorts. Glancing at the mantle clock, she was staggered to realize she's been sleeping for hours. Her body had slumped over in the big chair. Dwight had placed a pillow to keep her from falling further and had covered her with a blanket.

"How embarrassing," Hattie whispered to herself.

Soon, Dwight came inside. "Are you any better?"

Hattie labored, rubbing her eyes. "I don't have any strength."

"Hattie Sheldon," Dwight suddenly shot back. "If there's one thing I know for certain, it is that you have tremendous resilience. Hear my words. You are much, much stronger than you realize."

"I'm not, it's not true," Hattie argued stormily, folding the blanket that had kept her warm.

"You've forgotten your true nature, I think. Something powerful has thrown you outside your farthest boundaries. When that happens, people usually react negatively. Once your motivation is restored and you focus on the needs of others, you will be alright."

"I feel I'm letting everyone down," Hattie conceded, putting the folded blanket and pillow on a side chair.

"Then think of Rev. Worcester," he pressed. "Don't you think he felt he was letting people down, even while in prison? His devastated wife, Ann, delivered a child *on her own* then, a little girl she named Jerusha. The baby only lived five months. Rev. Worcester couldn't do anything to help, but he held up. It was in God's hands, Hattie. Everything is in God's hands. After his wife died, he was left with an infant and five other children. He didn't give up against those odds either. And he didn't think God had let him down. Whatever is bothering you, Hattie, it is beyond you. It is in God's hands."

Without warning, James came through the front door while Dwight was in mid-sentence. Was he following her? Every time she came to Dwight's house, James showed up. She looked at him not knowing what to say. He flashed a smile in her direction and she couldn't help but return it.

"Where did you come from?" she inquired as nonchalantly as she could.

"Exercising Worcester's horse," James replied. "And you?"

"Hannah brought her over to … read the *Cherokee Primer* in preparation for the school children," Dwight explained, pointing to the book.

James nodded casually before returning to the issue of the horse. "Nobody's been on old Comet for a long while. He's a fast horse and needs to be ridden. I bet Worcester won't mind if you ride him, Hattie. I didn't realize earlier that no one had offered you a horse."

Hattie opened her mouth to accept. For too long, she had had to rely on others to get her from place to place. In light of the threat, having a horse could add to her sense of security. Especially a fast horse.

But, suddenly, an urgent beating on the door caught everyone's attention. The force of it broke all rules of civility and scared Hattie all over again. A man shouted insistently, which signaled trouble. A woman was weeping. Dwight and James rushed for the door. It was then that Hattie jumped out of her chair in alarm.

"It's Fred!" James exclaimed just as Dwight pulled the door open.

The three gasped simultaneously. There stood Fred and Martha Pilkington, bent by fatigue, severely red faced, and drenched in sweat. Blood ran down the side of Martha's head and across her left ear. She clutched a gritty palm against it protectively while holding onto Fred for dear life.

"What on earth happened?" Dwight cried, reaching to draw them in while making a quick visual examination. James raced to catch Martha while Hattie rushed to clear a bed. Martha was on the verge of collapse.

"Quick, James, pump some water," Dwight directed as he examined Martha. "And wet some rags to cool them off."

"We were overtaken by robbers," Fred panted. "They grabbed our horses and dragged us to the ground. I argued, so they came over and hit Martha on the head!"

"Hattie, give her sips of water and loosen that dress," Dwight directed, taking Martha's pulse.

Fred continued, shaken to his core. "After they left, I carried her part way. I couldn't just leave her out there while I went for help. We've been on foot since. It was too far and too hot."

"James, pull off his boots," Dwight directed. "He's dehydrated. Prop his feet up."

"Martha, are you dizzy?" Dwight inquired kindly, wiping away the dried blood from the gash on her head.

"I'm just so thirsty," Martha wheezed through parched lips. "My legs are cramping."

"Take sips of water from Hattie," Dwight instructed. "She's going to stay by you while I bandage your head."

In less than a quarter hour, both Martha and Fred had stabilized and cooled down. Fred was in the best shape since he was uninjured and wore a wide brimmed hat. Dwight pushed significant amounts of water at them to replace vital fluids they had lost through sweat. He got enough information from Martha to determine she hadn't yet suffered serious heat exhaustion; but she was right on the verge, as well as upset and agitated.

Hattie talked to her and prayed with her. Soon, Martha felt a chill, so Dwight removed the cold cloths and covered her with a light quilt. She fell asleep immediately.

"Were you at gunpoint long?" James muttered while pacing the floor. "I've got to get John Stewart on the trail of these ruffians right away. It's a well-known fact that the theft of horses is a forerunner to even worse acts."

"Even worse? What do you mean?" Hattie recoiled in alarm.

"It's old lore and practice. Horse thefts precede worse crimes and murders. They have even set fires in the past to destroy men, property, and animals," James returned gravely, casting a worried glance at his sister again. "A message is being sent, that's for sure."

"I'm certain they were whiskey dealers," Fred related. "We were flagged down and had slowed too much by the time I realized what was happening. The minute I saw the first guy's eyes, I knew he was a bad egg. At first, their wagon was hidden by a grove. It was loaded with whiskey, but pulled by only one poor horse that had gone lame. Once they seized our team, they put their horse out of its misery."

"Where was this exactly?" Dwight asked. "I often take the road down to Sweet Town. Were you south of there?"

"Well, about five miles south of here near Cookson's place," Fred related. "They had some measure of humanity, I guess. Once I begged for Martha's life and said the horses didn't matter, they went easier on us. Thank God they stopped hurting her. Do you think John Stewart can track down my team? We'll never get to Texas without those horses."

"No, they're long gone," James reacted quickly. "Forget them. I'll get word to Father. He'll find you the best team in the whole country to replace yours."

"Boy, am I glad you Lattas are horse people," Fred responded, trying to sound more hopeful.

All evening, Hattie kept a close eye on Martha while also cooking supper for everyone. The thought that she could have been killed was unconscionable. The others shared her relief, as a sense of gratefulness dominated the conversation. But nobody knew of Hattie's secret or her personal fear because she hadn't revealed the threat letter. To bring it up now seemed inappropriate.

Time flew while speculation mounted about the robbers. Such a broad daylight crime put everyone on guard. How far did the implications go? Hattie blinked back an occasional tear; her mind stuck on the idea that danger was creeping ever closer. This dominated and left her shaky. She almost wept with gratitude when Dwight insisted she spend the night.

Between the threat letter, the holdup at gunpoint, and Martha's injury, Hattie's felt squeezed from all sides. Crawling into bed, she fought for levity and wondered if she could overcome these nightmarish assaults. Struggling to relax herself one muscle at a time, she recalled Dwight's comforting words. *Once your motivation is restored and you focus on the needs of others, you will be alright,* he had advised.

It had actually come true, although in relation to a crime. From the moment Martha and Fred stumbled into Dwight's house, all thoughts of the threat letter or the inability to start the school year vanished from Hattie's consciousness. Concern had replaced those worries as well as service and prayers of thankfulness that Martha and Fred had been spared.

Even more enlightening, Fred and Martha had set a powerful example. They weren't giving up their dreams in Texas despite being robbed and attacked by hardened criminals. Hattie pondered this fact for a long time, putting herself in their place, trying to feel what it must have been like. The gruff, filthy robbers came straight for them, terrorizing them with fears of injury and death.

This vision gave birth to another. Hattie could almost put a face on the person who had written the threat letter. She gave him the same kind of sinister features as the robbers. For some reason, this allowed her to take a step back, to separate herself somewhat from the acute fright. After all, instead of pointing a gun at her, the writer of the letter had pointed a pen at her. It wasn't nearly as scary viewing it this way.

❖ ❖ ❖

September 16, 1856
Rev. Fowler preached that fear doesn't come from God. If I am
filled with worry and trepidation, I cannot succeed. Hold me
up, dear Lord. Show me why I'm here and what you want me
to learn.

In her mind's eye, the children behaved so sweetly when she called upon them to recite their lessons. Eager to learn, they rose on cue and offered their own dear interpretations of the information she had presented the day before. When the last one finished, she would read them a story. But someone began to knock on the school room door.

"Hattie, wake up! Wake up!"

At first glance, Hattie found herself still in bed. By the time she sat up, Hannah had rushed in. Winded, she tugged her bonnet off. She drew a chair up beside the bed and took a long, diagnostic gaze at her sleepy friend. It was still dark outside.

"What are you doing here at this hour?" Hattie questioned.

"I couldn't stand it any longer," Hannah gushed, her voice rising. "News is all over town about the robbery of Fred and Martha and how they made it here first. It was just a guess that you were still here when they arrived. Thank goodness you stayed overnight. But since you were in such a state yesterday, I worried about what the robbery would do to you."

Hattie struggled to smile and her voice wavered. "The last few days ... almost defy description. You won't believe it, but this was the first night I've actually slept."

Hannah looked so confused. She pressed for Hattie's feelings about the robbery, as well as her earlier distraught attitude. "Can you talk about it yet? Has whatever it was—been resolved?"

"No. I shouldn't have mentioned it," Hattie apologized. "Martha is the one who needs tending. Threats against other people certainly put things into perspective."

Hannah leaned to peer directly into Hattie's face. "When you say 'threats against other people,' it sounds like you, too, are in some kind of peril."

Blushing, Hattie got up and fumbled with her clothes in hopes of creating a diversion. She had to make it clear she wouldn't talk. But, oh, how she hated keeping her spine-tingling nervousness quiet.

How could she make a fuss over herself when Martha was so injured? What really mattered was that Martha and Fred were alive and well, that children needed to be taught, and that greater priorities must become her focus. She should be big enough to forget failures and flaws, like Erminia's. She should forgive the American Board's oversights and selfish mistakes. Yet, in the cold reality of her frightening quandary, she could not cast a blind eye to the problems or talk herself out of the fear.

Hattie, the new Hattie, the mature Hattie, the independent Hattie, the seemingly fearless Hattie, had been dealt a serious blow. Try as she might to think otherwise, the last two incidents had wounded her deeply. The threat letter could only be viewed as an extreme measure. Was her future boiled down to life vs. death terms now? What did such a catastrophic point call for? A decision? A departure? She didn't know. A part of her didn't even want to seek God's help, for fear he wouldn't choose the solution she wanted.

"You're brooding, dear," Hannah whispered. "Let's go. We've got work to do."

"Work? Where?" Hattie questioned blankly.

"The printing building," Hannah reminded.

❖ ❖ ❖

This outing was Hattie's earliest morning drive since arriving in Park Hill. Silvery dew drops coated every blade of grass, catching the first glimmers of light. She could almost be convinced these were nature's tears after all that had happened.

Today was a new day and something about dawn's freshness should have brought a hint of comfort. But it couldn't, given the circumstances. She pulled Sarah's borrowed cape tighter around her shoulders. A new nip in the air confirmed that fall would soon lead to winter. Soon, frost would glisten as the children arrived to warm up in the classroom.

What did that room look like? It was the one where she would spend her days. Would she be able to show cheerfulness and confidence by the time school finally started? She couldn't imagine it.

Hannah pointed out areas of the mission as they approached. Hattie strained to take in every detail. Finally, the time had come to see her quarters, to claim her new home, to understand the logistics. She would sleep in a place built behind the school room.

Hattie also hoped against hope to find the teaching materials. Just as important, she would finally go inside the printing building where Rev. Worcester committed so much time and toil. Just then, the Worcester home came into focus, making her recall the social there.

"See, beyond the house? That's the printing building," Hanna was saying. "The other small structures are the kitchen, wood house, ash house, harness room, and pump house. The church isn't near these. There's the large garden plot off to our left. Beyond are the fields where Abijah grows corn and other vegetables to feed everybody."

— LANE DOLLY —

"Can you point out where I will live?" Hattie asked, trying to sound nonchalant.

"It's around the next grove of trees. That construction is finally finished, so it's just waiting for you," Hannah confirmed. "I can't wait to take you inside."

Seeing her quarters for the first time, Hattie stifled a sigh and forced a smile. It was the least she could do while Hannah beamed proudly about the many improvements. What had it looked like before? The humble place must have been one hundred times smaller than the inspiring, brick state-of-the-art seminary building. Weighing the differences made Hattie confront her unrealistic expectations. She felt absolutely foolish.

Only one small window high on the wall allowed natural light inside. That wasn't enough illumination for what certainly promised to be a spartan environment. Her inspiring view of Park Hill from high on the hill would soon end.

"The window's small so a man can't enter through it," Hannah explained, unaware that Hattie was constantly on guard after the threat letter.

What a consolation, Hattie sulked, feeling guilty. *It may be safe, but it's gloomy and dark.*

Taking inventory, she walked around the bed topped by a nice goose quilt. Next to it was a sturdy side chair, makeshift table, cast iron stove and wood storage crib. The main room was equipped with water and ash buckets, a small shovel, white porcelain pitcher and basin, warming pan, and chamber pot. On the wall, several protruding pegs would accommodate her clothing instead of a wardrobe.

236

Opposite her bed, the small corner was just large enough to accommodate her trunk.

"The seminary needs me to move here right away," she related. "But it feels rather isolated. Will I be safe?"

"Oh yes, especially after school starts. You'll have ample company," Hannah assured Hattie. "Abijah's near and a mechanic does blacksmithing and helps with livestock. But we always keep a loaded gun in the corner by the stove."

Hannah didn't seem to notice Hattie's sudden pallor. A gun? She didn't even know how to shoot.

The tour and explanation continued. Next, Hannah told how Rev. Worcester insisted that students learn to produce their own food. They would also be required to help as the cook, Rhoda, prepared it. She would soon return from taking care of a sick relative during the summer. A former slave just like Jesse, she had been freed by her Cherokee owner a few years ago. Rev. Worcester had vouched for her and posted a bond for good conduct, so she could remain. Another employee who was unnamed served as the steward. His job was bringing water and wood, removing ashes and waste, and sweeping Hattie's quarters and the school room.

"A handful of students come from too far away, so they live here in Park Hill with local families," Hannah added. "A few will want to stay near you part of the time or in mother's spare rooms. You'll feel safe and certainly not lonely with them around. They'll be looking to you for guidance."

"To me?" Hattie questioned, surprised.

"You're going to be their part-time mother," Hannah chirped.

"I had no idea," Hattie replied, realizing that her privacy might just have been compromised.

Outside again, the layout of the mission became clear. Hattie turned in all directions and put herself in Rev. Worcester's shoes when he first selected this spot. She could imagine how the tall grasses and big shade trees welcomed his arrival. The four to five acre estimate of the mission's size looked to be accurate.

All she lacked now was the long-awaited tour of her school room. Striding forward with Hannah, her stomach fluttered, partly from anticipation and partly from disappointment. With each step forward, she drew closer to what could only be called a commonplace enclosure.

Hannah continued to narrate and, hopefully, didn't see Hattie's silent observations. "In the past, several school rooms were active," she said. "Now, you're the only teacher."

Exhaling, Hattie eyed the older building where she would spend many hours each day. Smooth, tan boards by the door and on the eaves above stood out from the greyed ones to reveal newly patched areas. Hopefully, she could count on the place staying dry when it rained or snowed. Several windows let warm, south sunshine stream in, which would matter the most in winter. But it was a far cry from her alma maters, Amherst Academy and Utica Female Academy.

Inside, Hattie had to allow that a fresh coat of milk white-wash did wonders for even the most weathered and worn of places. Appreciation was called for because someone's effort had brightened things up. Another encouraging point was how spotlessly clean and dust free it was. Little bits of fiber at intervals meant a good mopping had taken place. This school room might not be fancy, but great care overcame many flaws. Rev. Worcester's family had made this mod-est—even lowly—little endeavor as nice as possible.

Several rows of traditional wooden desks—well used—fur-nished the room alongside a few long wooden benches. Hattie walked slowly between the rows, counting individual slates carefully placed on each desk. Oil lamps rested in a grouping on one of the benches. If she concentrated, she could begin to picture the room full of wiggling children with every seat taken, every eye following instructions attentively.

A coarse wood grain defined her heavy desk and ample chair atop the teacher's platform. This desk with its marks and scratches somehow represented her future, the spot from which she would try to make her own mark on the world. Her treasured little bell, the gift from her sister, now belonged there. Its clear ring would call the students to attention. From her desk, each child would be in plain view as they completed their lessons. Some would follow instructions, while others would try to sneak things past her.

A colorful but lopsided world map hung between two of the windows. That was the lightest spot in the room. Perhaps recitations belonged right there—and early in the day. Sunlight encouraged children far more than lamp light.

Moving along, she ran her hand over the big black stove and imagined the room warm and toasty during the cold of winter. And despite the stark reality of this place, she began to feel a little spark of excitement and anticipation. All in all, Hattie decided she was where she belonged and it would do.

Hannah must have described more, but Hattie's thoughts dominated her attention. Mysteries were made to be solved and this one about the mission was now over. A new chapter—one that began with hope and happiness—was starting. The specter of so many troubles couldn't be allowed to darken her little corner of purpose. This school really was an island to itself, a place where the future took root, where the importance of young lives blotted out all other problems for a few hours each day.

"Oh, there's Rev. Stephen Foreman," Hannah exclaimed,

pointing out the window toward the printing building and waving. "I'm glad we didn't miss him."

Hattie tried to recall what she'd heard about him. "He's held many posts here, right? I saw him at the social, but we didn't meet."

"Goodness, yes! Clerk of the Court, Judge of the Supreme Court, Executive Counselor, and Superintendent of Schools," Hannah exclaimed on their way out the door. "And all while doing translations for Father. He's grieving, though."

"Yes, I heard that his son died in a gun accident last year, and then his daughter fell ill."

Tall and imposing with hands in his pockets, Rev. Foreman waved and then waited for them. A piercing intensity dominated his dark, deep-set eyes. Some of that had to be sheer sadness, Hattie suspected. When he looked at her, surely he pictured his stricken daughter who had once taught in the same room at the same desk that Hattie now claimed as her own.

"My children were excited to meet you, Miss Sheldon," he greeted politely.

"Of course! Taylor and Jennie," Hattie remembered, her spirits lifting.

"And I need to mention Susie. She was to attend the seminary because she's fourteen. But I guess you heard it's closing. Would it be alright if she comes to your class?"

"She's more than welcome," Hattie smiled.

Rev. Foreman inquired about Utica, saying he missed New England. Princeton, New Jersey, held a tender place in his heart, as he had studied theology there. He also wanted Hattie to know he had attended a mission school as a boy and was glad his children would, too.

As Foreman mounted his horse and rode off through the tall grasses, Hattie knew she had just met someone important. His leadership positions hadn't drawn him away from the Bible translations. Such a fact spoke deeply of his values and work ethic. She looked forward to becoming better acquainted with the Foremans once their three children started school.

"How much of the Bible has been translated into Cherokee so far?" Hattie inquired as they entered the print building.

"Let's see," Hannah contemplated. "Prior to this year, they had completed John 1-3, Timothy 1-2, James, Peter 1-2, Luke and Exodus. Before Father left, they completed Genesis and Mark is underway. With the assistance of Rev Torrey, they hope to start on Philippians through 2 Thessalonians, Titus through Hebrews and Jude through Revelation in the near future. I have also heard talk about translating portions of Psalms, Proverbs, and Isaiah."

Hattie tried to imagine how a tiny building produced hundreds of thousands of pages of meaningful, life-changing information for the Cherokees. In addition to the Bible translations, the press was also responsible for hymn books, text books, tracts, and other printed materials. No wonder the place looked slightly messy. Someone needed to tidy up, what with errant pages and other litter on the floor.

"This is father's Tufts Standing Press," Hannah gestured proudly, pointing at a sturdy black apparatus that looked rather like a large octopus. "It's cast iron. If you haven't seen one, it exerts force vertically to press images from the inked letters. The operator feeds papers from above while pumping the foot treadle below."

"Is it true your father gave the Cherokees the first newspaper in their language?"

"Yes, but he won't rest until he's finished the whole Bible, no matter what goes wrong," Hannah continued, smiling wistfully. "When replacement rollers were late recently, he took pieces of deerskin and stuffed them with wool to make little balls for inking."

Hattie nodded, but found herself distracted by a long row of shelves. "How long do we have?" she asked.

"Most of the day if we're lucky," Hannah returned. "You're free to wander while I'm proof reading and binding. I have food when you're hungry."

"What do I have permission to read?" Hattie added on her way to the next room.

"Anything you choose. Before he left, I think Father took his confidential files out of here. They're either at home or in Mr. Murrell's library for safe keeping," Hannah said.

The innocent comment made Hattie's hair stand on end. She had already read most everything besides the books in Murrell's library! Those articles, accounts and documents detailing Rev. Worcester's experiences must be his own records! But, come to think of it, Hannah probably didn't know that Hattie had gone to that library. It was Martha who had arranged the visits on a whim. Hattie's time there seemed to be completely independent of the knowledge of Worcester family members. And James, just new to his job there, had approved it. What a twist of fate!

❖ ❖ ❖

The potential for discovery whetted Hattie's appetite more than the promise of food. It also calmed her nerves that were still frayed by the threat letter and last night's hold-up of Fred and Martha. Inside the first hour, she retrieved every book from the shelf one at a time, flipping through the contents page and the index. This approach had served her well for years when she couldn't possibly read word for word.

When she finished looking up certain parts in several books, she turned her attention to a large amount of old correspondence with the American Board. Across the hall, many volumes of the Bible translation lined the shelves. Before becoming immersed, however, she walked the length of the print building's long, windowless wall, glancing longingly at shelf after shelf.

Paper, in her estimation, had its own scent just as ink smelled of a peculiar odor. The sheer volume of paper suggested she might encounter mildew, but no telltale signs presented themselves. She marveled that, small as this building was, the amount of material might rival the Utica Library. Remembering her days, weeks, months, and years spent in libraries always brightened her outlook.

How long would it take to read everything here, she wondered? Hannah's open invitation, which seemed too good to be true, couldn't go beyond a day or two. Would that level of openness continue once Rev. Worcester returned? Hattie wanted to come here again and again. What if Rev. Stephen Foreman was present? She doubted such open access would continue, so making the most of today was important.

Intrigued by so much, Hattie forced herself to look immediately for the teaching materials. A first clue was the telltale residue of chalk at the end of the hall. Next, she approached the map of America and a decent, though worn, globe.

Stacked in another corner were several thick, tattered volumes, including Webster's 1828 American Dictionary of the English Language. A good quality clock rested on a table, along with several pens and an ink well. Underneath the table, she discovered a box for storage of cord wood. Behind it, another stack of books stood ready. Some had Bible stories in picture form, while a dozen copies of the *Cherokee Primer,* replicas of the one she had just read, waited to be carried to the school room.

Hattie began to feel better, although her thoughts remained somewhat scattered and the order of her actions unorganized. Sitting down, she paused. *Now, I have what I need to start school.* The long- awaited moment should be observed or even celebrated. But she didn't have time.

Since Erminia had said her job was to set and announce the start date for the fall term, Hattie needed to stop hesitating and act. She found a pen and inkwell, took a seat, and began to draft the school opening notice.

To her encouragement, the right wording and information was on the tip of her pen. The page before her filled quickly. Truly, the fruit of today's discovery fed her intention to show she could get school started. She must push ahead and prepare the classroom, as well, to show the Cherokees that their children had a good teacher and that the mission school was one to respect. What about the American Board? They might be surprised at all she had learned and accomplished. One step at a time. But, first, she must take advantage of the opportunity at hand.

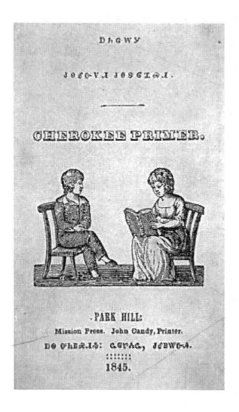

❖ ❖ ❖

Hundreds of volumes filled the shelves from floor to ceiling. All
this was the fruit of Rev. Worcester's labor, his life work. Perusing
book titles that had the Park Hill Mission Press stamp on them, Hattie
next observed Cherokee Almanacs from 1836 to 1855. Above, she
found multiple publications, including the Tract on Marriage, Tract
on Temperance, Cherokee Laws, Methodist Discipline, Address
on Intoxicating Drink, Message of Principal Chief (in Cherokee
and English), Child's Book, Catechism, Selected Passages of
Scripture, Cherokee Hymns, Choctaw Friend, Choctaw Reader,
Creek Child's Guide, Muscogee Teacher, Choctaw Constitution

and Laws, Child's Book on the Soul, Child's Book on the Creation, Bible Stories, and Choctaw Almanacs.

Having read all the titles, Hattie paused. It could take months to review everything in this room. She could only hope to read a smattering in this period of time that Hannah had offered. What should she look for? What did she need to know at this juncture?

She turned over two loose pages before discovering that dividing pages had been prepared by Rev. Worcester to separate the well-organized papers. Each dividing page listed a new topic. She read them as they were alphabetized, marveling at the productivity that had come from selfless commitment. When her eye came to subjects with the letter "S," Hattie's growing curiosity made her stop at a section marked *Slavery*. Looking closer, she saw a document entitled "1855 Mission Slavery Position Legislation." Hattie reached for the whole stack, took a seat, and began to leaf through newspaper clippings, notes, actual letters, and copies of other letters.

The first few minutes were sufficient to answer one of her lingering questions. She could now confirm that Rev. Worcester did, indeed, keep copies of all his correspondence. She should have assumed nothing less, despite Erminia's lack of knowledge about her husband's business and the record of his work. Starting to read the letter on top, Hattie immediately became immersed.

The letter confirmed that, in October of 1855, nearly a year ago, the Cherokee legislature had tried to force all missionaries in the Cherokee Nation to reveal their positions on slavery! This was more on the same topic she had discovered at Murrell's library. As she could clearly see, the threat was explicit: if the missionaries told the truth, they would admit to being abolitionists. And if they were admitted abolitionists, they would be expelled. Hattie's heartbeat quickened as she anticipated how Rev. Worcester might have responded. But as she read further, she saw that the measure had failed. Thank goodness!

But, further down, on a torn slip of paper, a notation read: "add notes about warnings from American Board that we are not as conservative as they require in our policy of hiring occasional slave labor." Hmm, Hattie deliberated. This pointed to how problematic Rev. Worcester's position had been, not to mention the difficulty of enunciating it to the decision makers in Boston. It led her to reflect on how James had practically scolded her when she asked questions about who did labor in the Cherokee Nation.

As Hattie digested this, she came across a picture identified as Rev. Evan Jones of Bread Town. Where was that, she wondered? Jones was a Baptist mission leader and ardent abolitionist, which sounded dangerous. She knew all too well that slavery was absolutely and unquestionably legal in the Cherokee Nation.

Scratchy notes appeared inside another old, dog-eared letter addressed to Rev. Worcester. Some proposed legislation, the letter said, meant that more Cherokees in leadership were aware of politicized missionary efforts like that of Rev. Jones. Conversely, several had commented how Rev. Worcester wanted purely to build respect and repair trustworthiness between Cherokees and whites. The letter commended him: even though his Northern roots were well known, he did not preach abolitionism. *Well, certainly, because the law denied it,* Hattie repeated to herself impatiently.

Replacing this material, she reached for another stack a few inches away. It was marked "1853 Correspondence with Rev. S. B. Treat, American Board: Slavery." On top was a letter from Rev. Worcester to Rev. Treat. The context suggested Rev. Treat might be Rev. Worcester's boss. Beginning with niceties and a few statistics, she discovered heated language on the second page:

"*If I hire a slave and do not have his permission, then I, just as much as his master, engage him in compulsory bondage. If I do so according to his concurrence, then I take no service from him to which he objects. Rather, I engage him as if he were free to come or go as he desired. In giving your permission for missionaries—in times of need when no other labor force can be engaged—to hire enslaved persons, do I understand or not that the committee wants to be recognized as follows? That enslaved persons must not be hired by the mission in the absence of their clear concurrence, nor shall they be forced to continue against their wishes? You communicated a response to me about the option of hiring enslaved persons to do the vital labor for which we have no workers versus my other option of doing it myself while losing my strength or life itself. Please understand that there is yet another option: that of discontinuing service to this mission. Were I to be pressed to choose between hiring enslaved persons or no longer working at the mission, despite this specification about obtaining their concurrence to work, if the absence of their concurrence were one of the main deciding factors, I believe I would not waiver in concluding to resign from the mission and undertake another line of work. I believe I can identify and hire independently as many enslaved persons as are necessary—and anxious to work—until the task is completed. There exist no other laborers available for hire! As a result, I have not been made aware of any missionary who could not identify enslaved persons capable and ready to be employed by him. If your committee and you personally object to clarifying the exact conditions, then your slavery stance, from my perspective, is less conservative than that of,*

Yours very truly,

Samuel A. Worcester

Hattie's stomach jumped into her throat. Rev. Worcester did not have enough help to run the mission! No wonder she hadn't met anybody else. Maybe there was nobody else! And what about the work? It sounded so burdensome that he contemplated resigning! She had to learn more. Why couldn't Rev. Worcester find anybody to hire except slaves? It didn't add up. There must be hundreds, if not thousands, of able-bodied Cherokees nearby. Yet, this correspondence showed they did not perform any of the back-breaking work at the mission. Rev. Worcester's tone signaled clearly that he believed the Board was belligerent, unable to grasp the complexities, and unwilling to offer their loyal, long-suffering servant help. Was the Board wrong? Rigid? Confused? But why? Rev. Worcester's words conveyed so much tension it almost amounted to desperation. If he resigned, was the end of the mission closely at hand? She could scarcely believe it.

Labor problems must pose massive blockades to progress, forcing Rev. Worcester to resort to this level of discourse with a superior. She highly doubted if Hannah had read this or knew about such disagreements. If she knew, surely Hannah would never have given Hattie free access here. These documents revealed a side of mission life which, most certainly, Rev. Worcester would not want to make public.

"Hattie, are you getting hungry yet?" Hannah called from the other room.

"No, I'm still nibbling on the biscuits I grabbed. Go ahead and eat," Hattie mouthed, trying to sound calm.

Now her head was swimming. Threat letter. Hold up. Compromised mission. No labor. Arguments over hiring slaves. Abolitionist preachers. Bewildered, she stood up and stretched while hoping to slow the nervous, rapid beating of her heart.

How could matters grow any more complicated, she worried? James had itemized the conflicts between factions in the Cherokee Nation. Those had bled over into the missionary population. She grieved over the impact, but was powerless to do anything but read on.

Returning to the document, a paragraph noted that the Baptist board, unwaveringly antislavery, had notified Rev. Jones in 1850 that it would withhold funds from the churches he directed. This would continue until he removed all slaveholders from those churches. Accordingly, he notified the short list of full-blood Cherokee slave holders in his churches that their names had been removed from the membership rolls.

Turning to another section, Hattie perused some tediously small notes. A scrawled notation atop one page read: "Information shared with me relating to August 1853." With only daylight from the window as her illumination, Hattie learned that Rev. Evan Jones had attended an American Baptist Missionary Union meeting in Cincinnati, where he testified that every one of the slave-owning members in his Baptist churches in the Cherokee Nation had willingly revoked their membership. A resolution of gratefulness to the Lord was voted upon by the representatives in recognition of Jones's work to rescue them from the impact of slavery.

Then in underlined characters, Rev. Worcester's notes read: "*It was not true.*" Shocked, Hattie squinted as the handwriting grew more difficult to decipher. It indicated that Rev. Jones had taken advantage of the language differences to eject those people from his churches without their full understanding. They were told they would receive letters, but the letters were written in English to people who were more versed in Cherokee.

The next page was in someone else's penmanship. It listed the complaints of persons whom Rev. Jones misled. One man at Lee's Creek received a letter he couldn't read. A woman elsewhere didn't grasp the ramifications of agreeing to withdraw. Nothing came in the form of a letter, so she felt she was still a church member. But because she had agreed to withdraw, she stopped taking communion. Finally, another man wrote that he had no other nearby church at which to worship.

The addition to the content went on to specify: "Members of Rev. Jones's churches did not know what he reported at the Cincinnati convocation. Some read what had happened in the Baptist newsletter." Questioning these complications, Hattie turned to find a copy of another letter from Rev. Worcester to Rev. Treat of the American Board:

"It is my understanding that a church member in good standing cannot be excommunicated legally unless a church vote ratifies it. What you have here is an example of how the Baptists in Cincinnati have been misled into believing they are free from the immorality of slavery in their Cherokee Nation churches. There is no victory and there should be no celebration. Rev. Jones's inability to be truthful with his Board has led to this action that will, no doubt, bring ramifications upon all missionaries in the Cherokee Nation. I pray that no expectation exists within the American Board that similar results can be achieved in Park Hill. Despite Jones's claims, there is no possibility of a complete break between our mission church and slavery, even if the Board demanded that slaveholders be excommunicated."

Hattie leaned back in her chair, almost overcome. What a profound set of circumstances! Rev. Worcester had to deal with a nearby missionary who'd been criticized. It seemed there was a virtual competition between missionary organizations. Rev. Worcester believed that Rev. Jones misled his Board about the extent of slavery in the Cherokee Nation. Even worse, some full-blood Cherokees had been excommunicated.

For Rev. Worcester to keep such content in his papers revealed a crucial point to Hattie: something about it either posed a threat to Worcester or damaged the American Board and its mission in the Cherokee Nation. Suddenly, a worse possibility occurred: what if the mischaracterizations were believed by the Cherokees?

This revelatory worry seemed to be confirmed: the next page emphasized that Rev. Jones and his son, John B. Jones, had turned to Bible translation work. The son had grown up in the Cherokee Nation, earned an eastern education, and then returned to fashion himself a translator. But, as Rev. Worcester pointed out to Rev. Treat, the younger Jones was not a trained linguist. Yet he presented himself as such and guaranteed the full-blood Cherokees that his translations were the best in the world.

This is trouble, Hattie concluded with a frown. Worcester's highly trained efforts must be overlapping with Jones's translations. What if the Cherokees read two different interpretations of Christianity? Which one is correct and trustworthy, she could hear them asking.

So, missionaries from different Christian denominations kept track of one another. Surely, they had enough responsibility elsewhere in a world complicated by wars, barbarity, and evil. Did the Baptists concern themselves with what Worcester and the American Board said or did? She formulated many other questions silently instead of voicing her concerns to Hannah.

This mission was in an astonishing predicament. Perhaps it had been a strong and whole force in the past. But all she saw was erosion. She was simply staggered at all she had learned and all that went on behind the scenes, for it would surely complicate her life, as well. Her expectation of a vibrant organization had withered imperceptibly just today. Not only was the mission itself old and tired, but so were its supervisors in Boston. Nothing gleamed with new purpose or support.

Was Rev. Worcester suffering these difficulties in private? He had not mentioned any of this, nor had Erminia. For that matter, did she even know? What pressure he must endure while trying to protect everybody and the mission. No wonder he needed a lengthy sabbatical in Vermont! To see his ministry compromised after his years of sacrifice and suffering to foster faith among the Cherokees—that would amount to a grave downturn of fate.

Prior to today's revelations, Hattie had struggled mightily to cope with frustration and fear, confusion and commitment. Her idealistic, naive dreams were no more credible than those of the silly girls in Utica she'd disdained. Yet, her rather new troubles were on an altogether lesser scale than Rev. Worcester's. These many years in Park Hill had seasoned him after *multiple* hold ups, *real* threats of all kinds, lengthy arguments via letters, and competition between denominations over Bible translations. To say the least, her upsets paled in comparison to his.

Sobered, her choice now came clear. Or rather, her challenge. The last thing this place needed was a compromised teacher. The only way she could overcome fear while serving the mission and supporting Rev. Worcester was to let her instincts and God guide her. She might not know everything, but she knew enough to pray hard and then allow her trust in God to propel her forward. This mission needed someone to take things in hand, to present strength and leadership, even in the face of threats and troubles.

Just then, Hannah called to Hattie from the other room.

"I've got to finish and get home to prepare supper. Why don't you come and eat with us?"

Hattie swallowed hard as she walked to face Hannah. "That's dear of you. But I have to do some other work. Maybe another time?"

"Alright," Hannah returned. "Do you want to come back tomorrow?"

"Oh yes, and I have a special request," Hattie exhaled, smiling. "I found the teaching materials! Could you possibly print up the notice I drafted about the start of school? We can have 10 good weeks of instruction before Christmas if they're posted immediately."

"Hallelujah," Hannah boomed, clapping her hands in delight. "Yes! I can't wait to tell Percy! I'm so proud of you, Hattie!"

A breeze had kicked up dust since morning. After a long day's work, Hannah and Hattie emerged into the late afternoon blusteriness. High clouds aloft spread themselves thin and wispy like mare's tails. To their surprise, Grace's friendly face greeted them outside the print building.

"Hello ladies. I hope I haven't interrupted anything. Hattie, can you give me a few minutes?"

Hannah locked the door, excused herself, and waved as she departed. "I'll see you tomorrow morning."

8

The Voice of Experience

When Hattie turned from seeing Hannah off, Grace appeared transformed. All warmth and cheeriness had vanished. Unusually somber, her deflated expression tugged at Hattie's heart. For a long moment, she waited while feeling uncertain. Grace shed a tear and gathered herself to speak.

"You asked me to trust you," Grace began, finally.

"I did. And I'll keep your confidence no matter what's wrong. Let's sit and talk under that shade tree," Hattie reassured her while putting aside her own concerns.

"No one must see me crying," Grace countered. "Can't we just talk in your room? "

"Well, I need to check on Martha before returning," Hattie explained. "No one will see us under the eaves of the print building. Those long shadows by the pecan tree offer privacy. You can tell me what's wrong. Then I need you to take me to Murrell's."

Grace followed, politely asking on the way, "Has today helped you? Did you solve the mess about starting school?"

"Yes. That puzzle piece is in place. In fact, Hannah's printing the school notices," Hattie explained. "Abijah will post them around. We'll begin on Monday the 29th!"

Grace nodded, but her eyes betrayed the problem that continued to bother her. "Have you heard this murderous story that's going around," she panted.

"Goodness, no," Hattie returned. "Don't tell me another calamity had happened!"

"Not new, but recent. I'm all but unnerved by it."

According to Grace, a wealthy, mixed-blood Cherokee landowner saw one of his slave women stash food from his garden in her pockets. He told his wife, a white woman, who was vicious and feared. Even he was afraid of her.

When he dozed off after supper, that wretched wife marched down to the slave cabins. She barged right in and confronted the thief. It put that slave woman in a terrible position because she was desperate to feed her children. What the mean boss's wife didn't know was that the children were hungry because the plantation's slave overseer had been stealing the slaves' food! But the slave woman kept that to herself. She also couldn't admit her own stealing because the boss's wife would beat her. So she kept quiet.

"I'll get you one way or another," the wicked wife growled as she left.

That nasty woman had long been abusive toward the slave woman's children, kicking or slapping them, chasing them with a broom, or hitting them with her husband's belt. She was after them no matter what they did. This made the slave woman more and more angry. Now, she knew the boss's wife would beat her sooner or later. As a result, her anger festered. She vowed to get even with the boss's wife before any beating.

The next few times the boss went to town and quiet fell at dark, the slave woman kept watch for his mean wife to come outside. When she did, the slave woman was ready to pounce. Finally getting her chance, she attacked his wife, dragged her away, and drowned her in the nearby horse tank. Then she got help from other slaves who also hated his wife. Quickly, they carted the body away under secrecy of night. Nobody said a word.

When the boss returned from a drunken binge, he didn't seem sorry that his wife was gone! She must have left him again, he was heard to say. But last week, somebody spotted a bit of fabric blowing from a tree way up on the ridge. It looked like a woman's dress, but why up there? That lonely place several miles south of Park Hill was between two rocky crevices and known as a den for huge, old rattlesnakes. Two seasoned snake hunters climbed up to investigate. To their surprise, a skeleton in an old ripped dress lay surrounded by snakes.

Soon, that awful wife's dress and remains were identified by her husband. Immediately, the full-blood Cherokee sheriff put out word of the discovery, but embellished the story. He always caused trouble because he disagreed with mixed-blood Cherokees. One of his tactics was trying to frame people he hated by linking old, unresolved crimes to new crimes. That sheriff speculated that the mean woman had been murdered by a slave while her husband was away. And that wasn't all.

Next, he offered a hefty reward for information on what happened. Meanwhile, the truth had slipped out somewhere, somehow to a troublemaker who drank too much whiskey. That troublemaker found the idea of the sheriff's reward enticing and turned in the murderous slave woman to the sheriff.

"Yesterday, that slave woman herself was found dead," Grace shared, a little pale. "Somebody found her body at the bottom of a hollow. They said she ran away and then fell to her death. But I can assure you that someone beat her to death. I've heard talk that all her hungry little children will be sold, one from another and never see each other again. There is no justice in this world."

"That's the worst thing I've ever heard," Hattie muttered in disgust. "Did you know these people?"

Grace was quiet for a time, just looking across the field. Her arms were folded tightly cross her body, like a shield. "Nobody's going to investigate the slave woman's death. This is more about the fact that that full-blood sheriff hates whites. He plans to use the white woman's death to frame my mixed-blood husband or any other mixed-bloods. You see, a while back, my husband worked at that same plantation."

"So, let me catch up. You're saying the full-blood sheriff hated the mixed-blood plantation owner and his white wife, as well as your mixed-blood husband," Hattie calculated, vexed by the complications.

"Yes. The sheriff also hates me for being the white wife of a mixed-blood Cherokee," Grace whispered. "It's not unusual, Hattie. Many full-bloods insist on the old ways and it's getting worse. To them, all whites have cheated, broken treaties, and caused the deaths of Cherokees. There's even a rumor about a new secret society for full-bloods only. They can't have white friends or even talk to whites."

Not a breath of air stirred. Hattie looked at her friend in disbelief. Grace was the best, kindest, law-abiding woman. She never made trouble. How could a circumstance this confusing occur? It was a blood issue—one about purity—that signaled factionalism once again.

"If anything led to my husband being jailed, I would have to leave this place," Grace continued through shaking lips. "I'm not Cherokee and don't think I could retain citizenship. Leaving would completely break my heart. That full-blood sheriff and many others have no patience for whites here."

"Can't you bring this to the attention of Agent Butler?" Hattie queried, confused.

"That conniving Southerner?" Grace frowned. "He's got no patience for crimes like this. The government wants him to keep peace between Indians. Nondescript whites like me who get citizenship through marriage get brushed aside. If anything, he would likely brand me an agitator because the government's trying to keep whites out of Indian Territory. Rather unsuccessfully, I might add."

"I looked him over at the seminary closure meeting," Hattie recalled. "I didn't know he was that bad."

"That depends on who you're talking to," Grace explained. "I think he's awful. And he would kick me out of here with nothing. Lord only knows what would become of me. It's just too much to face."

"Now Grace, let's not jump to conclusions," Hattie soothed, uncertain about what to do. "You must not give in to fear. I've got to think this over. But it's getting late and I must get over to Murrell's and check on Martha."

Lady, Grace's tame old horse, was by far the calmest of the three as they made their way toward James' cabin. The sun hung low in the western sky and promised a profusion of color at sunset. Hattie's head swam from the complexities she'd just learned, but she kept up a stream of encouraging chatter. Inside, however, she felt battered anew from wave after wave of turmoil. In addition to the hold-up and the threat letter, she'd learned today about steep political mountains the mission must climb. Now, Grace's dumbfounding story added insult to injury. Even if she managed to keep her own wits about her, how could she possibly help Grace?

Arriving at Murrell's, she forced a last remnant of energy into a hopeful, parting smile.

"It's in God's hands, Grace," she reminded weakly. "Meet me again tomorrow afternoon at the print building. We're going to tackle this together."

But as soon as Grace rode off, her eyes became heavy, as if gallons of pent up tears weighed them down. No longer able to figure the Cherokee Nation's catastrophes through, she needed to lay her head on a supportive shoulder and release the flood of anguish. Martha would understand and help her sort out all these problems.

Hattie knocked lightly, shifting her feet from anxiety. No one responded. She knocked again, a little louder. But there was no answer at James's door. She called Martha's name, feeling more and more upset by the second. Silence. James was still at work. Hattie had counted on *not* seeing him, given their unresolved differences.

Walking around the side of the house, Hattie peered through a small window. Inside, the cabin was dark. From all appearances, it was empty! But so was Hattie's ability to cope.

Any other time, this minor inconvenience posed no problem. But today, it added enough extra disappointment to become the last straw. Just when she was on the verge of collapsing emotionally, no one was there to catch her. Endangered, alone, and utterly without support, Hattie's formerly strong façade crumbled. Trying the door handle, she nearly fell inside when it opened. With abandon, she slammed the door behind her and then collapsed onto a bed. Tears began to fall and then multiplied exponentially into a tidal wave. From the depths of her being, sobs convulsed her entire body. She could not stop them.

The great dream of her life, formerly seen as a grand and high calling filled with adventure, had now deteriorated into an unbelievable nightmare. There was no bright light of usefulness warming her life in Park Hill, no one to be found around the mission, no sign that she was on the right track. Her existence had become a grey, cold pile of misery. On all fronts, she felt walled off—from school, safety, mission, seminary, and community.

The only redeeming connection turned out to be the gift of her new, loyal friends. Yet, why did she find herself alone and isolated so often? Even here, at James's cabin, she was taking refuge where she did not belong. Truth be told, Hattie was a trespasser on private property.

The unexpected thought that James might discover her quickened her distress. It would lessen the distance she had tried to construct between them. Previously, she had taken the moral high road about slavery. But, now, that seemed to discount his position too judgmentally. After all, James had never vowed to support slavery to his death. Rather, he was caught by it—unable to change his family history—limited because slavery was the law here—yet planning for the future when he hoped slavery would end.

Given his good heart and that level of intention, did he really deserve to be rejected as a suitor? In her pathetic state, did she want to keep him at arm's length? The answer was a resounding no. She could no longer bear being apart from him. She longed for him to wrap his strong arms around her and hold her close. In the entire world, his embrace was where she most desired to be. Besides, she dare not head for the seminary alone, especially with evening coming so soon.

Her tearful convulsions brought relief, but left her unable to inhale through her nose. Exhaustion loomed as she calmed down, realizing far too much of her attention and energy had been riveted upon losses and disappointments the last few weeks. As tension built, she had become like a maple tree that needed to be tapped. Her tears had helped drain out her hurt. The tremendous tightness in her chest and stomach already eased somewhat. Keeping secrets had rendered her utterly exhausted.

I must stop this, she scolded herself. *I should leave. I should exercise more faith.* But her reserve had fallen to empty. Everything about her life felt depleted and unsettled since she had received the threat letter. Never before had she contemplated the possibility of being killed by the kind of violence which was so common in Indian Territory.

At that thought, she stopped short. On the one hand, the threat letter certainly justified her staying here. But, on the other, what if her presence brought danger nearer to James, too? Or Fred and Martha? She could only stand by helpless if an attack occurred. That was the last thing she wanted!

The very idea of hurting James Latta brought Hattie up short. Suddenly, she came to her senses, alert to new, troubling possibilities. She could not let that happen, even if it meant risking herself. Abruptly, she rose to leave.

But just then, the door opened swiftly and unexpectedly. She drew back toward a corner with a stifled yelp. James grabbed his gun and uttered a defensive growl. In a split second, he aimed and cocked it to fire.

"Don't shoot, James," Hattie cried desperately. "It's just me!"

"Hattie? What in tarnation are you doing here?" he challenged out of sheer astonishment.

"I came to check on Martha, but she's gone," Hattie sniffed.

James lit a lamp and leaned his gun back against the door frame. "I'm not sorry to see you. But you may start the rumor mill on both of us."

When the lamp's glow cast the light of discovery on her tear-stained face, James sobered. Staring at her with compassion, he did not register alarm, fear, or annoyance. Instead, he approached slowly and slid a comforting arm of embrace around her shoulders.

"What tight scratch are you in?" he coaxed in a low, sympathetic voice.

"Is Martha alright," she pleaded, trying to distract him.

Unable to stifle her emotions, however, Hattie began to cry quietly again. James stood close, but seemed uncertain what to do. Leaning against his strong, warm chest, she melted and he responded to comfort her. To feel such tender sympathy cast away all her previous objections to their differences over slavery. She no longer cared that they didn't see eye to eye. The most important things in the world now became companionship and safety.

"Fred has taken Martha to Tahlequah," James whispered. "But that's not the real reason you're here, is it? Tell me the truth."

"I wish I could, but I can't," she sniffed.

"Aw, now. Maybe you need something to eat," he offered, giving her an easy out. "I'll fry up some grub. But you can't eat 'til you spill what's wrong."

"I can't divulge it, James."

"Why the heck not?" he argued. "I've rarely seen any woman with such a red and swollen face. Did a rattlesnake bite you?"

"No. Be serious. If I tell ... people will ... get hurt."

"Hurt?" James repeated. "You mean physically injured?"

Hattie rubbed her swollen eyes and did not respond.

Pulling his hands from his pockets, James went over to the small stove and proceeded to light it. Hattie knew he was turning the situation over in his mind. He placed a big black skillet on top and then returned to stand in front of her.

"I can't help you if you don't tell me," he pleaded in a low, calm tone. "Have you ever heard that I broke people's trust? My brother confides in me about desperate criminals. Murderers. Thieves. Drunks. Desperados who knife people to death. But go ahead and stew over this. Dissolve into *despair*, if you like. But let me define that for you. Despair is total suffering with no hope and not an ounce of meaning."

James's wise words struck a chord. She knew he was right. Trying to hide the threat letter had brought her to the end of herself. Fear had squeezed her so tightly as to force the very life out of her body.

"When I got back the other night," she began tentatively, "someone had slid an envelope under my door. I thought it might be an invitation to something nice. But I was dead wrong."

She stopped and swallowed hard. Every word on the page was seared into her mind. It still made her shudder.

"Well, don't stop now," James urged.

"I don't want to look silly," she pleaded. "I've done my best to be strong. Yet, nothing has gone well."

"Maybe you're not aware of it," James returned seriously, putting strips of bacon in the skillet. "But I realize that. Remember, I am well acquainted with Erminia. What she did to you is shameful. But that's for another discussion."

"The letter said they are… watching me," she whispered, her

chin quivering as the specifics spilled out. "Wherever I go. They hate abolitionists and want to stop me from speaking out or causing trouble. They'll kill me if they find me out alone after dark."

James slid the skillet off the fire and walked back to Hattie. Gently, he pulled her up and put his arms around her again, hugging her tightly. She closed her eyes and hugged him back. Softly, he kissed her forehead.

"Hattie, I'm sorry this hurt you so badly," he reassured. "It's mysterious. My guess is—well, they don't know your determination. And what you don't know is that no teacher has ever been harmed. They wouldn't dare. But I'll alert John Stewart anyway."

"Oh no," she pulled back, alarmed. "They'll find out I've told! Any inquiries will get someone hurt or killed."

"Now, let's not exaggerate. Just leave it with John Stewart. He's savvy. They won't find out," he returned, looking at her intently.

Even though they both would pay a heavy price if anyone found them alone together at night, Hattie let James take her home. He was tired, but did it without so much as blinking an eye. For that, she was grateful. Hopefully, nobody noticed and there wouldn't be a scandal.

Falling into bed later, she more than ached from exhaustion. She couldn't have described her numbness if she'd tried. Today had been more weighed down with one crucial thing after another than any other single day in her life. It all began to tumble back and forth. Her mind raced as she tried to process what mattered the most. Worries about the threat letter left her heart pounding and then gave way to melancholy over her nearly impoverished quarters. Putting anything aside became impossible. All she could do was relive and rethink, all the while more minutes of sleep passing her by.

Fitful, she thrashed to get comfortable, adjusted her bed covers repeatedly, and tried to relax muscle by muscle. But too much had happened and it begged for perspective. How could she possibly continue to keep all her facts straight? Her responsibilities were getting crowded aside by revelations: what should she do with all she'd learned? How would she explain what she shouldn't know? Where could she make use of what she couldn't mention?

At the dawning of what would be her second day at the print building, Hattie drew herself up from bed very slowly. Her body was not rested or refreshed. For a long while, she gathered her thoughts. Then, swallowing hard, she uttered a weak, but genuine prayer for sustenance and delivery.

Today must be viewed differently. Somehow. If she was to overcome so much, she just had to attach the idea of progress to everything she did. Perhaps she could remind herself hourly of hope for tomorrow. Better yet, this must be the day she began to carry the little cross in her pocket. She'd be strengthened just knowing it was there, just remembering the overcoming faith of the slave woman who made it. Should any shock, fear, or downturn arise, she would hold it close and picture herself in the palm of God's hand.

Encouraged, she realized today was no time to pout. Good, caring people were nearby. James's support, in particular, had helped her look ahead instead of back. She was grateful for his kindness and strength. With the confidence that he'd get John Stewart's help, she must trust and get on with her own work.

❖ ❖ ❖

Before printing the school notices, Hannah offered Hattie a brief tour and explanation of her binding work. The print building, though small, was still a complete and prolific production center. True to its goal, all who worked there were propelled forward by a vision. The place offered no comforts. That was certain.

ATTENTION STUDENTS!
THE PARK HILL MISSION SCHOOL
WILL COMMENCE ITS FALL TERM
ON
MONDAY, SEPTEMBER 29, 1856
Please report to the classroom of Miss Harriet A. Sheldon
Promptly at 8:00 o'clock in the morning

❖ ❖ ❖

Now that she held the actual notice in her hand, Hattie's sober brand of hope was joined by a sense of accomplishment. She intended to take James at his word. Her job was teaching and no teacher had ever been harmed. Without any recent influence around Park Hill of Rev. Worcester, some overzealous opponent had just gotten the nerve to try scare tactics. After all, that letter wasn't a gun, like the one the robbers used to bash Martha in the head.

Hattie pushed that awful thought into the past. The notice's big, bold letters shouted good news to Park Hill! In fact, it served as her own kind of weapon to fight back against detractors like the writer of the threat letter. Its strong message would get people talking and preparing. Children like Percy would no longer wait impatiently to come to school.

Taking a little break at noon, Hattie and Hannah pulled rickety chairs up to a side table cleared of paper and books. From a woven basket lined in leftover calico, Hannah produced a couple of chipped crocks, two apples from Rev. Worcester's tree, and thick slices of bread. A peek inside one crock revealed a rather lumpy, brown mass that looked flavorless. But Hattie's first taste brought a murmur of delight. It was a nut butter called canuchi that Hannah had made from crushed hickory huts.

Out front, a horse's snort interrupted them to signal someone's arrival. To their surprise, Sarah pulled up in her carriage, looking gorgeous even in a faded blue dress. She disembarked with her arms open to hug them, having returned early from Tullahassee. Hugs were exchanged and Sarah expressed concern over what had happened in Park Hill. But, beyond that, she fairly bubbled with excitement. She had brought Miss Thompson back for a visit!

"Come over tonight and bring whatever food you have," she invited before departing for the Nave General Store. "We've got to celebrate together while we have the chance!"

After Sarah left, Hattie tried to piece together who Miss Thompson really was. Hannah called her a second mother, saying she had taken charge of the devastated girls, little boys, and newborn Mary Eleanor when their dear mother had died. An American Board mission assistant, Miss Thompson sounded like an angel. Yet she had left Park Hill under difficult circumstances, Hannah shared. The comment raised more questions than it answered, so Hattie decided Grace was the person to ask for details.

"Try to find time tonight to talk with Jacob and Nancy Hitchcock, as well as Miss Thompson," Hannah mentioned as she put away the remnants of food. "I think you'll be rather enlightened by what they have to share."

Hattie respected the elder Hitchcocks, who were wizened from service, sacrifice, and hard work. These days, they found plenty of jobs around Dwight's house that needed attention. What with Sarah's delicate health recently, their help was indispensable. Few missionary couples maintained good health long enough to retire together. Jacob and Nancy Hitchcock were the exception rather than the rule.

Jacob's name had appeared on a page Hattie found right before she and Hannah stopped to eat. It was in a stack of documents entitled "Labor." Already, just after yesterday and today, her insight into the mission's complicated status had grown by leaps and bounds. She went back to the labor pages to learn even more.

A New England reformer by the name of Leonard Bacon had written commentary in 1848. Mr. Bacon asked brave, bold questions about Indian Territory, albeit from afar. "This is of the greatest confusion," Bacon wrote. "Why don't the Cherokees perform some of that labor?"

Once again, here was that touchy issue of who did the hard, physical work in Indian Territory. In Worcester's penmanship at the bottom of the page, his notation seemed to reply to Bacon: "*because the only interested ones are wealthy Cherokees or slaves.*" His words seemed loaded with frustration over the predicament.

Hattie leaned closer to read a curious scribble on the corner of a second sheet. The penmanship appeared hasty, almost like a reminder. It read, "*Jacob Hitchcock's thoughts on this matter helpful.*" She looked forward to getting better acquainted with him, but couldn't mention seeing this.

Further along, a writer at the 1849 Annual Meeting of the

American Board declared that missionaries were dreadfully sinful to hire slaves. He said doing so perpetuated slavery in the most hypocritical ways. Rev. Worcester disagreed, saying the accusation wrongly characterized missionaries as ardent employers of slaves when the opposite was well known and had long been reiterated. Such a wild idea that struggling, remote missions reinforced the massive institution of slavery through *occasional* use of slave labor was ludicrous. The note concluded, saying he and other missionaries had *resorted* to hiring slave labor only intermittently or in desperation.

The last paper in the Labor file showed how Rev. Worcester turned the tables. In a letter, he asked his Boston-based superiors to explain the North's mass consumption of goods produced by slaves in the South. How was that rationalized? Had the board further exonerated its culpability by sending funds to faraway islands instead of Indian Territory? The emotion that such words generated moved Hattie deeply. She had discovered things not meant to be seen. But how the truth lifted her respect for Rev. Worcester.

Although Hattie stayed fairly late at the print building, Grace did not arrive as she had requested. Hattie wondered if perhaps Grace still did chores at the Worcester home while Erminia was away. Grace might be overworked. Would she have time to help out with school? Hopefully, the crisis for Grace's husband was lessening because she had no idea how to help. But tonight offered respite that might give her fresh ideas.

Together with Hannah, she left for the Hicks's home. The idea of gathering food and assembling with the Worcester family gave her energy. What should she anticipate from Miss Thompson? If she kept her ears open, there might be a few quiet comments about Erminia.

Hattie couldn't wait to see Percy, that adorable boy, as well as the other children. They always lifted her spirits. The evening promised plenty of noise, funny games, and singing.

The minute she crossed Dwight and Sarah's doorway, she knew a wonderful night was in store. Laura was darting around after her little kitten. Percy began reciting Bible verses from memory as a sweet-faced woman took baby Ann from Abijah. This had to be Miss Thompson. If Hattie hadn't known better, she could have sworn Miss Thompson was the matriarch of the whole clan.

"This is our new mission school teacher, Miss Hattie Sheldon," Dwight introduced as Hattie took Miss Thompson's hand. Squeezing hers in return, Miss Thompson smiled, her face radiating kindness, patience, and love. She brightened further when Hannah came to stand on Hattie's left and Sarah on her right.

"If I didn't know better, I'd think you were their sister," Miss Thompson raved, reaching up tenderly to pat Hattie on the cheek.

"We think of her that way," Hannah replied. "She's become so important to us already."

"I don't know how we would get along without her," Sarah added.

In a way, Hattie decided the gathering seemed like Christmas, when families so cherished the chance to be together. This felt almost like home. These people were loving, caring, close, and true. They loved this rare chance to relish their common affection. Sarah, Miss Thompson, and Nancy must have cooked themselves into oblivion all afternoon because the table was heaped with lovely, delicious-looking food.

"I want everyone to thank Abijah and Percy," Sarah announced after grace was said. "They supplied the ducks after a successful morning hunt."

Hattie couldn't wait to swap stories with Miss Thompson. Knowing how the girls seemed to treasure the older woman, her goal was to say as many kind and complimentary things as possible.

"I understand you were a vital part of Rev. Worcester's printing effort," Hattie began, then winced that she had brought up the past.

"Oh yes, that was an education," Miss Thompson returned politely. "But my heart was with the children—and still is, even though they are grown with their own families now."

Hattie chose her words. "They are so lucky to have you."

"I miss them desperately, you know," Miss Thompson uttered, almost teary. "Every time a chance comes, I move heaven and earth to get here."

From across the table, Jacob posed a question. "So, tell me, Miss Sheldon, do you have a good supply of candy for your school room yet?"

Several people acknowledged his comment with knowing chuckles.

"Candy? I should say not," Hattie replied emphatically. "That's an invitation to have your knuckles rapped by the teacher's ruler."

"Oh, ho ho! Then you are in for a big surprise," he boomed as the others nodded. "May I share a little story with you?"

Jacob pulled at his wiry sideburns while describing his first days at the old Dwight Mission. He had known little of what to expect from the Cherokee children who came to learn. As steward, his responsibility was to maintain the buildings and grounds, oversee the laundry, handle routine administrative tasks, and provide meals. In particular, he had not anticipated that the procurement of food would entail the purchase of candy.

The fact was, those children entertained more than just a taste for sugar. They exhibited a ravenous need for it! Neither he nor the other new missionaries had seen anything so odd. The mystery wasn't solved for a while and then only by accident.

"After a time, we realized the link was spring water," he explained. "The children got worms from the spring."

"Eeeuuw! That's repulsive! But what does that have to do with candy?" Hattie urged, still confused.

"Oh, I forgot to button up the end," he apologized. "Wormy children always crave the sugar in candy."

Hattie didn't understand. "You mean I could have a student with worms?"

"He's trying to say most of them may have worms," Sarah said quietly, looking sympathetically at Hattie. "Mixing helpful herbs in the candy helps get rid of the worms."

Hattie made a squeamish expression and groaned. "Now I have heard everything!"

"The Cherokee herb doctors make medicines from Jerusalem Oak," Nancy inserted. "They soak the seeds in water overnight, cook them down, and then sweeten the juice to drink. It doesn't taste very good, but the concoction also helps get rid of worms."

"That sounds a bit unappetizing," Hattie reacted. "Tell me more about the herb doctors and medicines."

Jacob was full of information and shared a litany of cures. The Cherokees made medicinal candy from sassafras bark or horehound seeds. Sassafras bark was also turned into tea they drank in the spring to purify the blood. Cherry bark tea was believed to cure chills, while oak bark tea ended stomach trouble. Sage weed broke fevers and helped sweat off impurities. They gave catnip to small babies for stomach ache.

"I'll tell you later about slippery elm, button snake root, and boneset," Jacob concluded, a wry smile on his lips.

"We're always relieved to have survived another summer and its dreaded diseases," Sarah exhaled. "Then we wish fall would last, because winter brings sickness, too, especially if the cold is harsh."

"If it's not whooping cough, it's quinsy," Miss Thompson shared. "Often, like with Ann Eliza, people suffer severe chills. It is a chronic problem and so debilitating."

"Hattie, we sometimes rely on Cherokee medicine because of trouble keeping traditional medicines in stock," Dwight disclosed. "If it's not due to transport problems, we chalk it up to thieves. Medicines are in demand. The profit from a heist can buy many, many bottles of whiskey."

Hannah cleared her throat and glanced at the children to signal that whiskey and thieves weren't good dinner table topics.

"Getting back to the children," she interjected. "Hattie, father taught us to keep them warm and dry. He follows rules and customs from his childhood in Vermont. My favorite one is that fresh air is vital to remaining healthy. But I certainly did not feel warm and dry when he sent us outside for air during the winter!"

Sarah giggled. "How well I remember. He also believes good health comes from eating many varieties of leaves! Did you know that maple leaves start out sour but turn sweet when chewed? You'd be surprised by the tastes of bitter apple tree leaves and sour choke-cherry. Father also chews honeycomb and swears that honey brings the best sleep and treats burns. But his number one cure-all is cider vinegar."

"I concur with that," Jacob gestured. "But, Hattie, beyond food and medicine, we all believe in the ultimate cure. We get down on our knees and pray."

"In particular, we implore God to please send us only healthy babies," Sarah added quietly.

After supper, while the table was cleared, Jacob and Hattie chatted. She liked him, especially his strong Massachusetts accent that sounded like her dear relatives in Amherst. Because he asked, she also shared some ups and downs of her adjustment to mission life. His eyes revealed a deep understanding. Perhaps Dwight or Sarah had mentioned to him about the confusion and lack of information Hattie suffered for so long after her arrival.

"My initial understanding of the Cherokee Nation was shallow," Hattie said. "I came here to serve the suffering people. But it turned out to be quite different than I envisioned."

"How well I understand that, my dear," Jacob replied slowly and thoughtfully. "All of us in this field initially planned idealistic lives of service. We actually believed we could reverse the damage done to the Cherokees by removal and the loss of their homelands. But I have grown well beyond that idea. The Cherokee people, unlike many lost souls served by missionaries in this world, have resources. They receive government money."

Hattie contemplated what she knew. "So, their pressing needs are educational and spiritual more than economic? I thought the government had taken severe advantage of them."

"That's a good start," he replied seriously. "But sympathy isn't entirely appropriate, in my opinion. They've made poor choices in fighting each other and relying on old, deep superstitions. No amount of Christian instruction can penetrate the core to which many cling. Old ways represent security to them."

"I guess I'll encounter some of those ideas through their children at school."

"I don't see their choices as a plight," he continued, deep in thought. "And I remain incredulous at the illiteracy to which a great number remain tethered. Many exist in a condition that we call half-civilized. Yet they're happy."

"But the seminary girls wrote so eloquently about civilized white culture," Hattie queried. "I was shocked to read how they want to emulate it."

"They're a small percentage, though," he clarified. "You'll discover that most of those students are mixed-bloods from affluent families that own slaves. The average Cherokee is poor and just wants to be Cherokee. Many full-bloods resent what whites did to change their culture."

His comment made Hattie reflect on Grace's troubling story. But she couldn't bring it up. "Did you have confusion over slavery at Dwight Mission?" she asked instead.

"I did. That's a primary factor behind many of my opinions today," Jacob said. "I cannot feel much sympathy for an educated and Christianized person who chooses to enslave his fellow man. To me, the practice of slavery removes any claim on suffering."

Unexpectedly, a lively tune began to fill the house. There stood Abijah by the fireplace strumming a brown and orange banjo. Everyone gathered near and began to keep time to the music. Hattie's glee increased when Sarah produced a little melodeon and began to play alongside Abijah. They were going to sing! And dance! Or both!

Producing the sweetest sound, Sarah's small instrument fit in her lap. It featured a right-hand keyboard and a left-hand thumb strap allowing her to both hold it and draw the bellows. Watching her play, Hattie appreciated how naturally the music came to Sarah. For his part, Abijah appeared almost as talented on his banjo, as well.

"As a girl, Sarah accompanied the singing at her father's temperance meetings," Miss Thompson whispered after the music began.

The mention of temperance reminded Hattie to ask Dwight about his and Rev. Foreman's involvement with it. Hannah had just brought it up when Grace suddenly appeared yesterday. From what she gathered, Rev. Worcester, Rev. Foreman, and Dwight helped organize and host Cold Water Army meetings throughout the Cherokee Nation.

Unexpectedly, baby Ann crawled right into the center of the circle looking like she intended to be the primary attraction. Close on her heels were Emma and Percy in bed clothes, obviously unsuccessful in keeping the baby away from the music. Everyone laughed and applauded as Ann clapped her chubby little hands in delight.

Caught off guard, Hattie's emotions soared when James Latta suddenly charged through the door. He looked tired, dusty, and hungry, as if he'd rushed over from Murrell's without any supper. Before she could ask, he grabbed her hand to spin her around. Thankfully, Hattie had danced at her share of boring socials and followed him easily. The others seemed to delight in the boisterous reel and egged James on. Not to be outdone, he motioned Dwight into the dance. Suddenly, Dwight took Hattie's hand and James headed for Miss Thompson!

After the men traded partners again, James made eyes at Hattie as he twirled her around. A shiver of excitement ran up her spine. When the next reel brought them face to face, he came extremely close to planting a big kiss on her cheek. She turned bright red. The favorable applause was thunderous.

Presently, James begged off to go tend some ailing puppies. Sarah pushed a fat slice of bread and butter in his hand as he left. The elder Hitchcocks headed for bed while Hannah and Sarah went to check on the children. Dwight and Abijah retired to tell jokes on the porch, creating the perfect opportunity for Hattie to sit down with Miss Thompson. Without even hesitating, she began to guide Hattie's clumsy fingers around some knitting needles.

"I've waited so long for Rev. Worcester's return from Vermont," Hattie revealed. "Hopefully, Mary Eleanor will be able to return, as well."

"It's tragic that she's so excitable. I grieve over it," Miss Thompson muttered quietly. "I hope Austin found help for her suffering."

Hattie bit her tongue and kept quiet, wondering where the conversation was going. She had never heard anyone refer to Rev. Worcester by his given name. Miss Thompson treated her like a close family friend informed about confidentialities. But Hattie remained clueless as to the actual cause of Mary Eleanor's problem.

"The girls say such loving things about you," she added quietly. "I'm glad you've remained close over the years."

"Our separation has been painful. We grew so devoted after their mother died," Miss Thompson sighed. "Then Austin married Erminia."

"Yes, I heard. She and I traveled together from Utica," Hattie stammered.

"That must have been trying," Miss Thompson blinked. "Did she pretend to suffer from asthma?"

"Why, that's exactly what happened," a totally stunned Hattie heard herself reply. Suddenly, all her gripes about Erminia were validated.

Miss Thompson patted Hattie's hand. "But you've soldiered on ever since, they say. Did she explain anything about Park Hill or just leave you to fend for yourself?"

Wide-eyed, Hattie just stared at Miss Thompson, too undone to speak. It had not been her intention to besmirch Erminia's character, but that wasn't what was happening. This sad conversation merely confirmed the truth. Miss Thompson knew it, too.

"No matter. You'll be alright. God will bless and strengthen you as he has Austin," Miss Thompson concluded. "Poor man. Erminia's influence has aged him. If only he had sought the advice of the elder Hitchcocks before remarrying."

"So, I understand you can tell me more about the Cold Water Army," Hattie plied Dwight later.

"Good grief, I nearly forgot," he apologized. "Yes. Forgive me. It's past time to get busy."

"Do you help Rev. Foreman?" she continued.

"Let's say that we help each other. I'm the Marshal," he explained excitedly. "The annual meeting is October 16 in Tahlequah. Your students must be there!"

Hattie couldn't get over the quirkiness of school children with worms, yet it made her focus anew upon good health and cleanliness. How poignant that Rev. Worcester had studied medical textbooks while imprisoned back in Georgia. He was often called upon to resolve illnesses in the absence of a doctor after that. In fact, just such an absence was the excuse murderers used to lure Elias Boudinot away from safety.

Despite Rev. Worcester's difficulties, she'd also learned of his involvement in ever so many wonderful and historic events. He had developed a powerful sense of balance, she concluded. Maybe she could do the same. It defied her imagination to realize how long she had found her own way in Park Hill without the benefit of his or Erminia's guidance. Surely, he must be on his way home. Once he arrived, her many problems would resolve and things would fall into place.

Thinking of that, wouldn't Rev. Worcester write Erminia about his plans and timing? If only Hattie could talk with her, perhaps she might learn the latest. But Erminia was still away visiting Leonard in Kansas. On a note of pessimism, Hattie allowed that talking with Erminia, no matter the timing, would still require her to do one hundred percent of the communicating. Undoubtedly, Erminia had not changed and would not reach out to share anything even after she returned.

9

Looking Forward,
In Retrospect

reparations of all kinds filled Hattie's calendar for the next few days. Together with Grace, she intended to make use of every waking moment even though she still fretted over the impending move to the mission. Meanwhile, she reexamined Miss Thompson's words in her head.

"What really happened between Erminia and Miss Thompson?" she finally asked Grace.

Grace shrugged. "Where do I begin? Rev. Worcester's orphaned children loved her and the bond only strengthened after their mother died. Then, unexpectedly, he announced he was marrying Erminia. They had barely courted."

"Oh, dear," Hattie groaned.

"Sheer bedlam followed," Grace continued. "Erminia resented

the children's closeness with Miss Thompson. She didn't understand their special little ways like Miss Thompson did. Once Erminia became the lady of the house and the new stepmother, that was it."

"I feel so sorry for Miss Thompson."

"I feel just as sorry for the children, although Ann Eliza, Sarah, and Hannah benefitted early in life from their natural mother's care. The boys fared alright because they spent more time with their father. But Mary Eleanor was raised with Erminia's uneven emotions. People think that's why Mary Eleanor has problems," Grace revealed.

Hattie hung on those last words silently. So Mary Eleanor's trouble was emotional, not physical! She had suspected something similar, but hearing it confirmed was another thing altogether. A very sad thing.

"Does Miss Thompson stay in touch with Erminia?" Hattie inquired as she recovered her wits.

"Heavens, no. Erminia banished her," Grace retorted. "I heard Rev. Worcester just retreated to the printing building in those early times."

"That raises another point. Erminia didn't seem to know much about his documents or papers," Hattie inserted. "But they're all at the printing building."

"Hattie, we both know that Erminia only has attention for her own agenda. I once heard the girls whispering. They were looking over a sad old letter they had written on the sly years ago and sent to Miss Thompson. Well, she saved it. That letter was tear-stained—a cry for help—from a time Erminia brushed the girls aside."

❀ ❀ ❀

Saturday, September 20, 1856
John Stewart stopped by with Martha. Their brother, Will,
the charismatic wagoner thatJames had mentioned, was along.
Nice man, but different than his brothers. Martha's head
is much better. Thankfully, she didn't mention my visit to
James's cabin. I hope she doesn't even know I went there to see
her. John Stewart walked the periphery of the school and my
quarters. I think he's keeping the threat letter secret. Martha
and Fred leave soon for Texas, which is sad to ponder.

After church on Sunday, Rev. Foreman stopped Hattie to discuss the temperance activities of the Cold Water Army. The children's song practices must start immediately after school commenced, he urged. They had to be ready to perform at a rally on October 16. Hattie was relieved Dwight had already told her.

Every fall, tradition held that the children from the mission school, and many others, were invited to attend the Cherokee National Council meeting in Tahlequah. They grew extremely excited to carry colorful banners, march around, and sing. Most already knew numerous temperance songs.

To Hattie's amazement, Rev. Foreman sought her out later with copies of the music. On first glance, some of the songs looked familiar. She smiled to hear that Rev. Worcester himself had written special, crusading lyrics to the well-known tunes and hymns. Long before her arrival, mission school children had used this music to memorize the songs by heart. Each year, they participated in at least two special events.

"In the past, Rev. Worcester personally led the marching," Rev. Foreman continued. "That made the children feel so special."

CHEROKEE COLD WATER ARMY SONG

See us children full of glee,
marching with our banners.
Drunkards we will never be,
nor follow drunkards' manners.
We will not fight with guns or swords,
nor kill one son or daughter;
Our weapons shall be pleasant words
and cool, refreshing water!

—SAMUEL A. WORCESTER

"Do the children really know the consequences of alcohol consumption," Hattie wondered aloud to Foreman.

"Definitely," he confirmed. "Its ghastly side effects are promoted. Everyone knows exactly what happens. Drunkenness is among the most egregious behaviors in the Cherokee Nation."

He said the children were quite well versed in all types of alcohol. With the slightest of prompts, they could rattle off a litany of spirits, including rum, beer, whiskey, and gin. This was due to listening to so many adults at the meetings.

Hattie was dumbfounded to hear of the number of converts from temperance meetings. That number far outweighed the number of salvations at church! After stirring speeches motivated them, imbibers rose from their chairs and went up to the temperance stage. With one hand raised and the other on the Bible, they promised to never, ever drink alcohol again.

After Foreman left, Hattie was grateful for the nice turn of events. This man had come to her. He had shared about an important upcoming rally and helped her get prepared. It was her first experience at the Park Hill Mission of true, collegial cooperation. She respected Rev. Foreman and hoped to turn to him more often when unanswered questions arose.

James visited Hattie after work Monday. But he looked as worn out as she'd ever seen him. When she commented about meeting his other brother, Will, he only nodded. He seemed to shake off his exhaustion shortly and treated her so lovingly, even holding her hand as they rocked on the porch. Hattie could not have asked for greater contentment. This strong, funny, clever man had the power to erase all her burdens.

Since school was set to start on Monday, September 29th, they decided she should move from the seminary to the mission on Saturday, September 27th. The day of the move, he promised to break away from Murrell's for a few hours and help her. It needn't take long to get everything arranged so she would feel settled. He also promised to bring over some crates to move books and materials from the print building to the school room.

James related that Fred and Martha were readying their wagon to leave. He was most excited that his father's gift of the new team of horses had arrived from Vineyard. Breathtaking copper sorrels, they nearly brought Fred to tears; he was very moved, as all his money had gone to the new farmland in Texas, leaving too little to buy a decent team.

"Fred says he's forever indebted to my father," James related. "The new team brought memories of his love for the wonderful team the robbers stole."

"I've been around the love a man can hold for horses," Hattie reminisced.

❖ ❖ ❖

The thought of horses instinctively drew Hattie's thoughts to home and her father's business. Horses were so central to his daily life and work. She could picture him working on a harness or saddle, hammering little tacks into the leather there at his shop. If only she were there. What she wouldn't give for just a few moments together with her family.

Perhaps homesickness had something to do with her inability to write them a simple letter. She missed them all so much. But thinking of her father's shop and the unforgettably wonderful aroma of leather, Hattie felt compelled suddenly to reach out. She was certain her parents felt the lag in communication, but so much bad news had left her unable to put pen to paper.

Now might be a good time, especially after the confirmation of school had lifted her spirits. There were ample stories that could balance the ordinary and the upsetting. If she committed to simple sharing instead of a detailed report, perhaps it could be an easier exercise.

Immediately, Hattie's quill inked the page with abandon. She wrote smaller than usual to pack as much content as possible onto a few sheets. Taking the attitude of a reporter, she covered the who, what, when, where, and sometimes, the why. She was struck by the number of events that had occurred in a relatively short time. From among those, she would choose the ones most likely to favorably impress her family back home.

Encouraged, she scribbled away. Her topics ranged from excitement about the social, to meeting other mission personnel employed by the American Board, to Martha and her impending move to Texas. She described the dress they sewed together and the day trip to Tahlequah before mentioning Fred's new team of horses minus the story of the whiskey robbers' hold-up. Heaping praise on Rev. Worcester's family, as well as his productive little printing press, she described his shelves lined with translated chapters of the Bible. She had been included like a member of the family.

The smiling excitement of Mary Covel and little Percy led her description of the confirmed students and her neatly readied school room. A mention of recent knitting lessons with Nancy Hitchcock sounded much more encouraging than the dispiriting truth about living at the wrong place or receiving a threat letter.

Pleased with her progress, Hattie began to relive her first visit to Hunter's Home all over again. Susan, the slave woman she wouldn't mention, had offered heartwarming hospitality there where Mr. Murrell enjoyed fox hunting and raised a large number of hounds. Beyond this, Hattie's concern was how to mention her relationship with James Latta. It was her primary goal to write just enough so her family would feel good that she finally had a passing interest in a man. She had to get it right to warm them up to the idea of him; only later would she expound upon their growing relationship.

In an attempt to gradually insert James, she approached the subject by writing about Martha's brothers. One was a Deputy U. S. Marshall in Indian Territory, she would begin. Another was a wagon master. The third worked for a revered but widowed landowner who had married into the Chief's family. They were civilized, educated, stalwart supporters of the church. This part had to sound a certain way, so she took extra care in her word choices. Associating James with Mr. Murrell gave him something of a pedigree until she would tell more about him later. First things first. Finally, she added particulars about Park Hill.

Exhaling upon the letter's completion, Hattie felt a sense of relief. She had satisfactorily overcome many misgivings and created the right letter. This should appease her parents well into the holidays and dispel any worries they harbored about her situation. A good feeling of accomplishment finally rested on her shoulders. She had not been overtaken by the adverse elements, which her parents couldn't really understand anyway from such a distance. Now she could focus more attentively on other things without a cloud of guilt hanging over her head.

"Temperance is our long tradition here," Hannah related breezily on Tuesday when she dropped off a note from Miss Thompson. "It instills abstinence as a part of children's morals and beliefs. When I was little, I so looked forward to marching and singing at the big rallies. And the food was incredible. Temperance meetings have drawn big crowds for years because they enlist the best cooks. Every single person is promised a variety of barbecued meats, as well as the most popular desserts. Nobody misses a temperance meeting."

"It sounds like one of our church picnics," Hattie responded, thinking back on her own childhood.

"Ours were almost like part of church," Hannah continued.

"Father also felt temperance activity brought us closer to touching the outside world. Given our social isolation, we encourage our children the same way. Sometimes, Abijah carries them on his shoulders while they wave banners."

Hannah's comment about Abijah brought a recollection. Martha had shared that Abijah Hicks squandered years of his early life drinking whiskey. Because of temperance efforts, he took and kept an abstinence pledge. From that day forward, he never drank again. Thanks to his honorable commitment, Abijah was now a loving and kind husband, father, and businessman. Hattie decided it was unnecessary and perhaps even unkind to let Hannah know she was so informed.

"I wonder how much longer Father can do it," Hannah mused wistfully.

Hattie was surprised by the candor, yet met it with sarcasm. "Well, he *only* does *all* the printing, preaching, mission station management, Bible translation work, temperance leading, song writing, letter writing, and ..."

"Thank you for that respect," Hannah reacted appreciatively. "But he hasn't been as strong since a dog bit him last year. It made him quite sick. His left arm was lame for a long while, so we pitched in during his slow recuperation. "

Hattie recoiled. She had never contemplated that Rev. Worcester was anything but stalwart and in charge. "I'm sorry to hear that. What an ordeal!"

"Sometime later, Dwight also concluded that Father had a type of painful rheumatism," Hannah added. "His energy lessened. It made us realize how much he did, how many things depended upon him. The translation work suffered because that was also when Rev. Foreman's son died."

"So, did you and Abijah take up the slack at the mission?" Hattie questioned.

"Some. But speaking of Abijah, here's something I've been meaning to mention," Hannah continued. "He was told Mr. Murrell won't be in Park Hill during the winters from here on out."

"Where's he going?" Hattie replied, puzzled.

"Evidently, his brother died and left part of a plantation to deal with in Louisiana. It's called Tally Ho. What does James say about it?" Hannah questioned.

"He hasn't mentioned a word," Hattie replied, feeling left out.

"There's yellow fever in Louisiana, you know," Hannah cautioned. "It's dangerous, especially in warm weather, which is most of the time down there."

❀ ❀ ❀

Saturday, September 20, 1856
Dear Hattie,

Wasn't it a special night we spent together with my adopted family? I will relive those healing conversations and moments together many times. How thankful I am for Sarah and Hannah to delight in your good company and loyal friendship. A life in the mission field, a life in the Cherokee Nation, a life apart from culture and society is one that depends necessarily on a few very important and treasured people. It is not without trials though. I doubt Austin Worcester envisioned the way his family is living. But he thinks in an eternal sense, not of earthly comforts or hurts. We all must follow his lead in that.

By the time this note is delivered, your work will be well underway at the school. I will join Ann Eliza's family in prayer that you run the good race, dear Hattie. Before long, Rev. Worcester will return and all will be well. Leave the rest in the hands of God.

A favorite poem of mine came to mind, which is why I'm writing you this before my return trip to Tullahassee. I hope it will remind, encourage, and uplift you until we meet again.

—Affectionately, Nancy Thompson (Miss)

A PSALM OF LIFE

WHAT THE HEART OF THE YOUNG MAN SAID TO THE PSALMIST

TELL me not, in mournful numbers,
Life is but an empty dream! —
For the soul is dead that slumbers,
And things are not what they seem.
Life is real! Life is earnest!
And the grave is not its goal;
Dust thou art, to dust returnest,
Was not spoken of the soul.
Not enjoyment, and not sorrow,
Is our destined end or way;
But to act, that each to-morrow
Find us farther than to-day.
Art is long, and Time is fleeting,
And our hearts, though stout and brave,
Still, like muffled drums, are beating
Funeral marches to the grave.

In the world's broad field of battle,
In the bivouac of Life,
Be not like dumb, driven cattle!
Be a hero in the strife!
Trust no Future, howe'er pleasant!
Let the dead Past bury its dead!
Act— act in the living Present!
Heart within, and God o'erhead!
Lives of great men all remind us
We can make our lives sublime,
And, departing, leave behind us
Footprints on the sands of time;
Footprints, that perhaps another,
Sailing o'er life's solemn main,
A forlorn and shipwrecked brother,
Seeing, shall take heart again.
Let us, then, be up and doing,
With a heart for any fate;
Still achieving, still pursuing,
Learn to labor and to wait.

—HENRY WADSWORTH LONGFELLOW *(born 1807)*

Hattie hated goodbyes as much as when she had left Utica. But the time had come for Fred and Martha to bid farewell. Their presence on so many wonderful evenings would never be forgotten.

In many ways, Martha felt closer than a friend. She had loyally cared for Hattie during her sickness, which would forever bind them together. How Hattie wished Martha could remain nearby to walk with her through the uncertain days ahead, if not for life. But it was not to be.

A tear rolled down Hattie's cheek as Martha reached to hug her one last time. Fred looked a little sad, too, so he turned toward the horses. Hattie tried to thank Martha for as many things as possible in one long, hurried sentence. On the tip of her tongue rested a question held back for some time. Seeing James approach, she realized she'd better talk faster.

She thanked Martha for introducing her to James, trying her best to act nonchalant and not say too much. Luckily, just as she almost ran out of words about him, Martha got the gist of it and spoke.

"You'll never find a more loyal man," Martha assured her, smiling.

"Are you certain he hasn't been courting anyone else?" Hattie inquired insecurely.

"No, I don't think so."

"How can you be sure?" Hattie pursued.

"Because I see the way he looks at you," Martha whispered.

"Rev. Worcester's been through more than many people realize," Hattie wagered to James as they walked together later. The leaves had begun to change color slightly and the cooler air felt wonderful.

He looked at her with a questioning look, but said nothing. Perhaps it was the wrong time to seek his advice on all she had read. Or maybe he was just sad that Fred and Martha were leaving. She wasn't sure what was on his mind.

"Are the seminary teachers still keeping you company," he asked. "What are they going to do?"

"Jane plans to teach at Forest Hill common school. Lotta may be gone because I haven't seen her. I wonder who's helping them move?"

"I'll be there to do your heavy lifting Friday if I can get permission," James added.

"If you can get permission," Hattie repeated, stopping short. "If? Earlier you promised to be here, which reminds me of another issue. I heard Mr. Murrell's responsible for settling a plantation estate in Louisiana. Is he leaving? Does that mean he's put you on a short leash?"

"Aw, don't blame him, Hattie," James defended. "He can't help it. Twice the responsibility fell in his lap. I guess I'll be chief cook and bottle washer when he goes down there. "

Hattie continued to look at James, but with new insight. He truly fit Dwight's description of "dog tired." But she needed to count on his help. It was about far more than just moving from the seminary to the mission. His involvement in her life made a tremendous difference.

"I wish you could stay longer," she whispered wistfully as he headed for his horse.

"Me, too," he answered before brushing her hand softly.

Hattie appreciated the fact that, no matter what happened, he always managed to remain cheerful. James's endearing qualities seemed to grow and grow each time they were together. With him by her side, her hopes had risen, fears evaporated, and confidence soared. When they happened to enjoy the rare privacy of dark and he kissed her tenderly, the tingling from head to toe outweighed every other concern in the world.

❀ ❀ ❀

Shortly, Hattie spied a glimpse of her precious sister's handwriting in her mailbox. Excited, she grabbed the letter and rushed back upstairs. She pictured Amanda's warm, smiling face the whole way. Jumping up on her bed and adjusting the table lamp, she examined the envelope.

The letter had been posted from Utica back in August. Some letters seemed to take forever these days. Surely it hadn't been in her box for long, but she was guilty of forgetting to check lately. She tore into it.

August 25, 1856
Dearest Hattie,

My, how long it seems since you left. August is fleeting, fall is coming. The angle of the sun promises cool days very soon. It is ordinary here, perhaps made more so by your absence. I would love to share enthusiastic stories in this letter, but doing so would be dishonest. The real reason I'm writing is that we are all anxious and agitated over not hearing from you. Father walks out of his way to stop here daily, asking if I have received a letter. He tries to hide his disappointment. Just yesterday, he said he and mother use logic to figure out why you have not written. He assumes you have little or no access to the newspapers or publications you used to devour at the library. Consequently, the nature of your letters might be different, a departure from your past commentary on everything. It is of no matter. They just would praise God to receive even one line in your own, dear penmanship reading "I am fine. Do not worry." Father says things like "she has different matters on her mind now. It is hard coping with a foreign culture. She is so independent, after all." But I can tell he is troubled.

Hattie, there is something else I need to share. You know very well of mother's long support of the church's foreign mission ministry, the Presbyterian Board of Foreign Missions. Father has contributed to it for years, so they receive the PBFM newsletter. Due to your work, they are now reading it more closely. Recently, mother frowned at the front page of the latest edition. She read that many Indians in your region are slave holders! She and father had just discussed their disapproval because the PBFM remained neutral on slavery. Father said he and mother would allow for complicating circumstances— to a point. But the article also provided proof of slavery where father has sent his hard-earned money year after year. It stunned them, so they began to learn more about how Indians could possess the means to own slaves. One night, he dreamed of you teaching Indians whose families used slave labor. We are suffering over you being in the midst of such confusion, so they turned to Rev. Fowler with quiet questions. Equally surprised, he wrote the PBFM and a response is awaited.

Meanwhile, father inquired further with a few friends in confidence. A Congregationalist brought him an American Board article stating that slavery is always wrong and wholly unsupportable. Father learned this position came after the missions were already established. Then his instincts and propensity to analyze politics took over. He saw the American Board's tactic was pure politics. Only after it learned the ugly truth about the tribes practicing slavery, did it announce its disapproval of any mission school or church associated with slaveholders. This, father charged, was its attempt to look innocent and foist responsibility and guilt off itself so its con- tributors would not balk. Father suddenly comprehended what he called "the hidden obvious:" the Indians from down south brought southern practices with them to the new territory.

There existed a range of economic levels within the tribe. The wealthy ones owned slaves, like all other wealthy southerners. They have established plantations in the new territory and live well thanks to slave labor. Father bitterly accused the American Board of irresponsibility for hiring people like you from an anti-slavery family. It did so without as much as a mention of all this. Just yesterday, he speculated that Rev. Worcester, whom he greatly respected, might be caught in an untenable position. Even worse, Father is convinced that you may also be compromised. "What kind of danger might our Hattie face if she innocently states her anti-slavery position in the wrong company or place," he railed. His imagination runs wild with worry.

So, dearest sister, this is our closest explanation for why you have not written in so long. But it is not too late. None of it is your responsibility. If you are indeed compromised, please know that we await your return with open arms. It would please us beyond measure to have you back safely, no matter what you have endured, no matter if you cannot even speak of it. So, I close now with the fervent reminder of our concern. Please let us hear from you as soon as possible.

Ever your loving sister, Amanda

Hattie fell back on her pillow, bringing an arm up protectively to cover her eyes. She didn't want to see the lamp light. She didn't want to see the letter again either, so she tucked it in her Bible. The only thing that felt comforting after such a let-down was lying still in the dark.

Amanda's letter could not have been more unexpected, upsetting, or ill-timed. Hattie had finally returned to a level of happiness after the recent upset. Now this ruined it. She wished the letter had never arrived.

But wishing couldn't make anything better. Nor could she ignore the scolding. Her family had grown uncomfortable and worried awaiting a letter she should have sent from Cincinnati, Memphis, Napoleon, Jefferson City, or Springfield. She must accept responsibility for that.

The second part of the letter upset her more, however. Against sizable odds, her parents had learned the real story about slavery in the Cherokee Nation. Her efforts to protect them by remaining silent about the sad truth now looked suspect.

How truly foolish and shortsighted. She shouldn't have assumed they would wait around for her to educate them about the Cherokees. How could she have been so naïve, misguided, or even arrogant to think they wouldn't look for answers—or that she could keep things quiet from hundreds of miles away? Of course they would harness resources and figure out why their daughter had gone silent.

Reading between the lines, Hattie deduced what her father must be thinking. He might claim that the truth had been hidden. He would ask if the American Board rationalized that well-versed people like the Sheldons already knew slavery was practiced by Indians. Why weren't the facts shared with potential new missionaries up front? What possible good was there in withholding information? If he decided to act, he would not go easy on the American Board.

This was Ebenezer Sheldon's worst nightmare, Hattie fretted. A man of impeccable character and intense loyalty, he grieved that his daughter was enmeshed in an outrage. For a lifetime, he had been clear that slavery was morally depraved and shameful. Now, Hattie was close to slavery every day. Slave owners were members of the mission church. Most of the residents of Park Hill were mixed-blood Cherokees, the sect that owned the most slaves. She hadn't been truthful with her parents about it. And now, they knew that.

Hearing herself go over and over these troubling points, Hattie grew restless and sat up for air. She raised her sleeve again to rub nervous perspiration from her forehead, glancing sideways at her desk. Catching sight of her letter box, she recalled sitting there just this week writing the long overdue letter to her parents. Sadly, it would not reach them for weeks.

Hattie inhaled suddenly, and then yelped. Oh no! What had she written in that letter? Did it conflict with what Amanda had just shared? But of course it did. That was already painfully obvious. Indeed, she had gone into great detail about all the recent circumstances, people, and events that sounded optimistic. She recalled exactly how she had filled her letter with details to make Park Hill look wonderful to her parents. She had skipped slavery. Hopefulness had flowed from her heart, just as it did tonight when she was in James Latta's presence.

The letter conveyed an altogether unrealistic scenario. She even described her view from the seminary that took in horses and pastures, the serene blue sky winking through clouds, and the sun smiling down. That marvelous gift of a shiny, perfect team of horses for Fred and Martha had galloped across her mind's eye and into her letter. And more, so much more.

She loathed this clash of emotions about their widening stances on controversial issues. The timing also played havoc with letters crossing in the post. If only she could return to the enthralling feelings from earlier this evening. If only James were here to comfort her. Picturing him, Hattie knew beyond the shadow of a doubt that all her thoughts and emotions, including those in her letter, had taken on prominence because of James. With him beside her, she truly believed anything was possible: the bad things could improve and the good things could become ever so much better. She had tried not to give away the depth of these emotions in her letter. But now, in hindsight, she doubted if she had been successful.

Something about the scale of this mistake now made Hattie's head feel huge, like it was expanding unnaturally from competing facts and emotions. She could no longer prioritize her parents' point of view: there were simply too many sides to accommodate in the ugly matter of slavery, in her feelings, and in the situation that now surrounded her.

Amanda's carefully crafted letter had brought this to the fore. Family memories tore her attention away from Park Hill, pulling her back to childhood feelings in the midst of the remarkably dangerous Underground Railroad rescue. She had not known both sides of the story then as a gullible child full of abolitionist zeal. The family never undertook another rescue, but she had held on to what she learned. To this day, she still cherished the tiny cross from the escaping slave woman that frightening night. Over the years, it had come to represent her commitment to help the oppressed.

She couldn't mediate between her father's side of slavery versus James's side of slavery. Her situation had grown complicated beyond belief now that the Cherokee Nation's problems were tangled into the fray. Whether Negro or Cherokee, her best effort must always remain with the victims.

Yet that reminder pointed to a source of significant frustration. She'd gotten delayed from acting on her hopes after reaching the Cherokee Nation. Complications of untold proportion had crowded in.

The most recent notwithstanding, she sighed and took stock. She must return to basics and orient herself to her original purpose. The letter's confusion must be set aside so she could begin anew when school started. And her first tool of instruction would be to offer what she wanted most in every circumstances so far: simple respect. That's what everyone needed. Certainly, the Cherokees deserved more than they had gotten. From white people.

Despite this vow, Hattie slumped back on her pillow and let her mind wander. For some reason, she pictured her father sitting opposite James Latta. And, suddenly, she was overtaken. There was no denying now that she had fallen in love with charming James Latta. He embodied the very image of a southern Christian man even though he was a slave overseer. James would never fit her father's definition of a brutal, repressive slave holder in the model of Uncle Tom's Cabin. Yet she intended to hold true to both men. But it wasn't going to be easy.

The tangle of agendas made her picture Nancy Hitchcock's unusual yarns, the ones Hattie was not seasoned enough to work with. The thick yarn might represent her reason and resolve. How strong was it? The thin, cotton strand looked weaker. It represented the past, her parents' insistence on their ways of thinking, and her own naivete that returned unwelcomed through Amanda's letter. Given the differences in the two strands, was the thick yarn of Hattie's vision strong enough to come together with the thinner yarn to create something lasting and whole? Could the two different strands ever be knitted together successfully?

She wished she had written in her letter that the Cherokee Nation and James Latta were just altogether different than anything up north. There was no way to understand them from a Utica perspective. Neither the north nor the rest of the repressive south provided a standard for such judgment. The situation in the Cherokee Nation was a lesson in opposites, an anomaly of indefinable and competing schemes. Maybe Amanda's letter, despite jerking her back several months and hundreds of miles, had actually brought her closer to confronting reality and facing her true feelings.

❧ ❧ ❧

According to Grace, Erminia was back from visiting Leonard in Kansas. Hattie had gotten so used to making her own way around the mission in recent weeks that she wondered if anything would change. Then she took that thought back. Of course it would! Erminia always made herself and her feelings known. She didn't take a back seat to anybody. But what would give?

Reflecting on their last conversation at the social, Hattie had asked Erminia about the start of school. Erminia offered no help. Rather, she had pushed back and thrown all responsibility in Hattie's face. Even though she was the rightful authority, Erminia just shrugged and commented, *it's up to you, Hattie.* This uncomfortable memory rumbled around inside Hattie for a while.

In the early afternoon, Grace left for a few minutes to get sugar at the general store. Before long, a dog barked excitedly outside. Hattie looked across the grassy field to see Erminia striding purposely toward the school room. Her steps created great, noisy flaps as her dark cotton skirt sought to keep up. Whatever was on her mind, Erminia looked ready to address it directly and with great purpose.

Gritting her teeth, Hattie opened the door and managed a constant smile as she waited. When Erminia was within earshot, Hattie spoke to start their conversation on a happy note.

"Good afternoon and welcome back," she called cheerfully. "It's a gorgeous day, isn't it?"

"It is that," Erminia nodded, looking absent-mindedly at the endless blue sky before dispensing with small talk. "I need to have a word with you, Hattie."

Erminia entered the neat classroom, sniffing as she looked it up and down briefly.

"From what I've seen, nothing has been done in preparation for the maintenance of this mission," Erminia began, hands on her hips. "Have you written your plan for student involvement? Where is it? I am here to find out why it is overdue. Progress must be made before Reverend returns."

"When will he be home?" Hattie questioned, her heart lifted unexpectedly. Any news of his travels was too good to be true.

"That is not your concern," Erminia replied curtly. "Your full attention must go toward taking responsibility instead of shirking your duties."

"What duties?" Hattie replied, puzzled.

"You have taken charge to get school started, that much is clear," Erminia shot back, waving a hand in the direction of the globe. "But what about student maintenance? Vital work cannot lag."

"I don't understand," Hattie returned, more confused. "I'm ready to teach the children their academic subjects in this classroom."

"That is just one portion of your job, as I'm certain you know," Erminia huffed as if she had been wronged. "You must show yourself ready to train the students in familial work, as well. The girls will perform chores inside, and the boys outside. The mission requires their help. They cannot thrive in this harsh world on mere academics. Girls must learn to cook, sew, wash, iron, and care for babies and children. The boys will help Abijah with farming, tending the cattle, carrying wood, scooping ashes, and getting water from the well. Both must learn gardening, as well."

Hattie went blank. For a moment she nearly panicked. Surely this was a mistake. Her face and ears had gone hot and red.

"I have never heard one word about maintenance," she managed to say, struggling to keep her composure. Surely they would not expect so much additional work on her same salary of $50 per year from the American Board.

"Hattie," Erminia began anew in a lowered, condescending voice. "Did you honestly expect private quarters only to use the space for yourself? It goes without saying that you use it for the mission, as well."

Hattie had no reply. This subject hadn't ever come up—not during the journey, her illness, the repairs at the mission, or in conversation with Hannah and Sarah. Was she to have no privacy, no time to herself? Was she to cut back on academics in order to accommodate this demand? Why was Erminia so indignant?

Then, something strangely familiar slowed down her worries. Perhaps Erminia's anger, not Hattie's supposed error, was the real clue to this riddle. Was Erminia creating a distraction? That's what Hattie's mother had done so often. She appeared controlling when she was actually scared.

Questions beginning with "what if" began to multiply in Hattie's mind. She decided to remain inquisitive and not irritate Erminia further. That might help uncover the real story.

Probably, Erminia had realized she never told Hattie about the maintenance duties. Or someone else could have commented that Hattie didn't have enough information. Sarah knew the truth. So did Hannah. Maybe, just maybe, Erminia felt a little guilty.

Once again, Hattie grieved over Rev. Worcester not briefing

her. Even though he thought his wife would do right by Hattie, he could have written, too. But he didn't. Should Hattie give him the benefit of the doubt? That was a new idea; maybe he didn't know that Erminia had failed to explain things to Hattie!

Since Miss Thompson's visit, Hattie had proof that the Worcester family went to Vermont last spring because of Mary Eleanor. The trip only appeared to be about seeing family and meeting with the American Board. As parents, *not unlike her own*, they were distracted by Mary Eleanor's problem.

But did that really explain the length of the silence from Rev. Worcester? Nobody in the family ever mentioned receiving a letter from him. Nobody commented on his return either. Given what Hattie had just read at the print building—and considering his earlier letter about leaving the mission if the labor shortage threatened to work him to death—perhaps something tumultuous was underway. Maybe he wasn't returning! He'd been gone long enough to set up a whole new life for his family back east. He could easily show up, gather his family and belongings, and leave.

He definitely had cause, Hattie allowed. And such an option would explain the resounding silence about him. Yet she couldn't make such a scheme fit with his high character. She'd have to think much longer and harder about it. This was no time to allude to him, however.

No, today was about Erminia herself. The aggressive posture and words, especially after her long, silent absence, more than suggested she had a compelling reason to foist blame on Hattie. It had to be a tactic.

Hattie could speculate how it worked. She'd never heard of the maintenance duties, so she couldn't have performed them. But, for the sake of argument, if she accepted blame for not doing them, it gave Erminia what she coveted—a chance to sidestep responsibility. Under that option, Erminia never had to admit she failed Hattie. It was plain old bullying.

Of course! Since Erminia needed to blame somebody, Hattie was the only choice. That's why she was pressing so hard: she couldn't blame her oversight on the distraction of Mary Eleanor's problems. Nobody must ever know about Mary Eleanor's problems because Erminia had played a blameworthy role there!

Hattie felt calmer already. "I don't know what you want to hear," she offered.

Silently, she also said a little prayer for help. In her heart, she realized she must take the high road and set things right. This was no time to be disrespectful or angry to a bad-tempered woman. As unbearable as it seemed, she had to go farther than that. She had to forgive Erminia. But she vowed to be honest.

"You believe I wronged the mission and, therefore, you," she began quietly, picturing herself as Erminia's adult equal. "The truth is, I have never, ever heard about these duties. Something is amiss here ... and always has been. After weeks of silence, your accusation is unfair. But, why don't we correct this problem together? It happened because Mary Eleanor's illness was such a distraction. And despite our differences, you can count on me to keep your secret away from public exposure."

Where did THOSE words come from? Hattie puzzled to herself.

As for Erminia, her face turned as pale as a ghost. Total shock erased her pugnacious attitude, leaving those grey, scowling eyes wide and watery. She stepped backwards clumsily. Sheer incredulity stopped her and she began to cough.

"How do you know that?" she croaked.

"I'm not blind and I'm not ignorant," Hattie retorted quietly.

Erminia must know she has abdicated her adulthood in this situation, Hattie thought. She looked humiliated, sad, fearful, and regretful.

"Who broke our confidence?" Erminia coughed.

"Nobody betrayed you," Hattie explained.

"Reverend will be horrified," Erminia gasped. "He will never forgive me for poor mothering, for bickering. I always knew I was beneath him. Now, I've proven it."

Hattie all but gaped at such a confession from this confidant woman. What stunning words! Erminia was secretly intimidated by her own husband! Hattie really had hit the nail on the head. Erminia was nothing like she appeared, but used many distractions to ward off those who would expose her.

"I've failed as Mary Eleanor's mother," Erminia whined, crestfallen.

"Then vow to be better in the future. I'm quite sure Rev. Worcester will forgive you," Hattie said. "And so will I. But don't treat me this way again."

·❧ 10 ❧·

Moving On

To get her mind off Erminia, Hattie tried to do some eleventh hour organizing for her move. She picked up her Bible from the bedside table only for Amanda's letter to fall out and flutter to the floor. So much controversy surrounded everything. But she couldn't undo what was done. Even if she tried to explain more to her parents about Park Hill and slavery or James and his job, she'd likely not be successful. It was time for their relationship to be about family, not issues.

Hattie reached for her pretty green letter box to file Amanda's letter away. Delicately, she straightened the treasured letters from her family, Margaret, and even Rev. Fowler. Her mother's gently curved hand had an intelligent and unusual character. Her father's penmanship was devoid of straight lines. He managed to write legibly with exaggerated, masculine curls. She proceeded from one envelope to the next, pausing to recall each letter's messages.

But at one of her father's letters, she stopped. It was loose from its envelope. Removing it, Hattie checked the postmark. It had arrived as she was recovering from fever and rash.

She unfolded his familiar, monogrammed stationery and began to read. Oh, yes. It was about little Mary, Amanda's daughter with the head of soft brown curls. How sweet her father had been to share so much detail. Through his words, he nearly brought Mary herself to Aunt Hattie. Mary, with the milky white skin.

The next page began with a change of subject. Hattie read several lines, not recognizing or recalling her father's words for some reason. He related the story of a massacre in Kansas that occurred in the spring. This information was utterly unfamiliar. She felt as if she had never read this portion of the letter before.

Ebenezer Sheldon was extremely agitated. A pro-slavery governor had been appointed in Kansas, he related. Had she heard that an abolition activist named John Brown came there with his sons and raided a Kansas pro-slavery settlement? The Governor's three hundred men were repelled by Brown's forty men. Five died. Slavery's opposing forces were churning, he warned. Open warfare had broken out.

"I need to know if you're safe," he urged. "This is not at all far from where you live."

But Hattie had had no access to such news. Nor had she replied to this letter. What must he think?

Did she remember, he inquired, that the organized abolitionism movement in New York had begun right in their home county of Oneida? The history books would remember a speaker named Beriah Green who had proven that Negroes could learn and become productive citizens. On many occasions, Green lashed his opponents' rationale to bits, brilliantly refuting arguments that tried to corrupt the Bible to defend slavery.

"This is why your mother and I gifted you with the signed volume of *Uncle Tom's Cabin*," her father clarified. "Mrs. Stowe proved that the Bible is opposed in spirit and action to slavery of any kind. And so are we."

At this juncture, Hattie's hands began to tremble. Her father had made his position clear many times before, but hadn't reiterated the entire history of Oneida County to do so. She was halfway afraid to read on, lest he profess new activism with intent to march in the streets. This was a distinct possibility, given his fervency and the fact that Utica was home to a number of anti-slave societies.

"My beloved child," he continued, "your heritage as a daughter of Oneida County places you inside the nation's history. You must stay abreast of this position. One day, you may be called to act upon your beliefs or teach others the unquestioned merits of abolitionism. I remember the important decision your mother and I made early in our marriage. In 1826, we attended a service led by the great preacher, Charles Finney, a fellow Presbyterian. That night brought enlightenment. It forever decided our family belief system, which included the equality of all men under God. And all these years later, here we are."

Hattie suddenly pictured a different man. He so believed in the cause, as she had overheard that night when he and her mother argued without knowing she was at home. To her knowledge, however, they never knew she learned the real reason they stopped all Underground Railroad activity. Their anti-slavery beliefs may have endured, but their action had turned to mere lip service.

The man who wrote this pleading, agonizing letter was compromised. Was it because Hattie now lived far away and wasn't available to shore up his dying dream? Was he pushing her into the activism her mother had forbidden years back? There was no answer.

But many more questions arose—and they didn't relate to her father. Rather, they revealed what was happening inside Hattie, what had already changed. The young woman now reading his letter comprehended that she wasn't the same. Given the chance, would she want to go back home, to be a part of his brand of abolitionism? After her experiences in Park Hill, she thought not. Hattie would make a difference here in her own way.

September 26, 1856

Even though I strive to stay constructive, something disheartening always happens. It's hard not to be dragged into the past. I'm conflicted over what to tell my parents or how. I'm also sad that Martha's gone. It helps to get my mind off the past. I would rather think of the future. Martha calmed me about James and then whispered, "Don't let on that you know, but there will be three of us soon!" Then she just left me standing there with my mouth open! A little stranger is coming to join their family!

Saturday, moving day, dawned bright and sunny. Despite Erminia's confrontation and the letter debacle, Hattie had managed to rest and keep herself focused. This was important in light of last night's discovery and her father's obvious disappointment. That still lingered, but she vowed that her attention must not be captivated by problems today.

Hattie had everything ready for the move except personal grooming items and her bedding. She would tend to these after breakfast.

Thinking of the days ahead, a sense of anticipation encouraged her future life at the mission. It was time. School was starting next Monday. Pouring herself some coffee, she sat at a table, letting the cup warm her hands as she sipped the smoky, bitter flavor of its contents.

This move signified more than her physical location. To have gotten this far, she'd overcome some major hurdles. Every difficult experience had pushed her one step forward. Always, she had to balance the problems with the good things. Lately, she felt more capable of pushing the tough challenges aside faster.

"Hattie, are you ready?" a quiet voice over her shoulder asked.

Swiveling out of surprise, Hattie stared at dear Grace, scratched and bruised from head to toe.

"Heavens above, Grace," she exclaimed, trying not to overreact. "What happened this time?"

"Lady got spooked and raked me under a tree," Grace explained sheepishly. "I can't lift much, but I'm really good at making tea and offering moral support."

"You poor dear," Hattie soothed sympathetically.

"Sarah just pulled up outside," Grace continued. "She's in her buggy and Jesse's in their wagon."

Confused, Hattie rushed to find out why they had come.

"Late last night, James rode over to ask our help because Mr. Murrell sent him to Van Buren," Sarah explained, tilting her head sympathetically.

Hattie had counted so earnestly on being with James today. He had promised to do the heavy lifting. But mainly, she had just counted on him being around. That one fact made this painful transition bearable. Why couldn't he have kept his commitment? It needn't have slowed his departure by more than a few hours. She wanted to cry, but thanked Sarah instead.

"What's the matter, Hattie?" Sarah whispered later while Grace was inside and Jesse loaded the wagon. "You're distracted."

Hattie stammered and then found herself mentioning her sister's worrisome plea and her father's misplaced letter. Hers was a most complicated position, not just within her family, but also over northern abolitionist beliefs. She couldn't believe what she'd discovered in the Cherokee Nation and now her family couldn't either. It was as if the past bore down on the present.

"All my life, I was told slaveholders were bad, evil people," she related. "But I've met some who aren't."

Sarah was silent for a moment. "You're confronting your ideology, aren't you? That may push against the boundaries of your parents' teaching."

"Only one side of the situation was visible in Utica," Hattie added.

"We all must resolve our untested beliefs at some point," Sarah sympathized. "It sounds to me like you've grown and have to choose which torch you'll carry. The decision involves more than carrying the one handed you as a child."

Soon, the loaded wagon lumbered toward the mission. All of Hattie's belongings fit, including her beautiful leather trunk. The presence of her loyal friend, Sarah, was a comfort in James's absence. Nobody could stay somber with Sarah around. Hattie also appreciated that Sarah brought Jesse.

"Thank you, Jesse," Hattie offered appreciatively when he treated her trunk so carefully.

To her surprise, Jesse replied. "It's my pleasure, Miss Hattie.

I'm payin' you back for your kindness to my kin, Susan. And Dr. Dwight's having me check on you now and again."

After everything was unloaded, Hattie insisted that Sarah and Jesse get back to their other commitments. With Grace's help, she would find a place for everything and start to nest. The effort couldn't take more than a couple more hours. Hopefully, the place would soon appear cozy.

"It's amazing what four heads and three sets of hands can do," Grace half-joked.

Hattie laughed. "I never cease to be amazed at your humor. It's always better when things go wrong."

"The only way to look is up," Grace replied with a wry smile.

Yet, as they continued to work, Hattie couldn't look up or get her mind off James. His sudden absence did not feel right. Maybe it wasn't his fault, but she couldn't help it. She needed him. This was no time to rethink her feelings, hopes, and dreams! When would he return?

Later, Grace took Hattie to meet Rhoda, who was stirring up something savory in the mission kitchen. "I told her your move was today. She can't wait to meet you."

Hattie was grateful to Grace, once again, for taking her places. But she looked forward to riding Comet much more often now. His stable was close at hand and James had said he needed to be ridden. Besides, it was time to be freer and go where she wanted when she wanted.

At dusk, Grace took her leave just as a coyote howled in the distance. Finally used to such things, Hattie looked around and wished she had something to read. These long weeks without access to current newspapers had left her so uninformed.

As an alternative, she busied herself by dusting furniture and brushing her clothing carefully. All the while, the effort to keep James off her mind required significant attention.

She had never lived completely alone before and wasn't certain she wanted to learn what it felt like. Perhaps tonight should be viewed as a rare quiet instant, given that children arrived on Monday and nonstop activity promised to follow. Nevertheless, she wasn't quite sure what to do with herself.

After darkness brought the coolest air yet, Hattie made her first fire in the little stove. Soon, it crackled and began to cast a nice golden glow across the dimly lit room. She nudged the logs with the poker, leaving it between them to funnel a whiff of air that fueled the flame. A dancing fire was relaxing to watch, but not as satisfying as gazing on the peaceful meadow from the tall, seminary windows she already missed.

Outside, the sound of stronger winds began to rouse the trees from their silence. Was a storm coming? How frustrating to have no view. Hattie climbed on a chair to peek out her one, high window. But raindrops had splattered onto dust previously caked there. She couldn't see anything through the blurry mess.

For a while longer, she listened as raindrops drummed on the roof and leaves rustled more noisily. Soon, they would turn every hue of gold, russet, and bronze. But what use was the beauty of fall if she couldn't relish it with her own eyes? Cut off from the weather, as well, she grumbled and headed for the door to have a look. Where was her parasol? Hopefully, wind and rain wouldn't blow her off her feet.

Just as she pulled the door open to the swaying trees and sideways rain, an ominous figure lurched from the shadows. Yelping in fright, Hattie recoiled as a tall, hunched man confronted her and grabbed to pull her away. She screamed out of sudden fright, but could barely believe it was happening. The foreboding attacker wore a black hood slit with evil shaped eye holes to hide his identity. Screaming louder, Hattie managed to lean sideways, but was no match for his clawing, gloved hand. The man clinched her left arm in his vicious grip and pulled.

She fought back, even before she smelled his rank odor and the alcohol on his breath. Hattie hated this depraved assailant. A surge of instinct welled up and compelled her to battle with all her might. This despite the driving rain that had already soaked her and threatened her footing. Undeterred, she shrieked the guttural cry of an animal and thrashed even more wildly to get loose. Twisting her torso and steeling herself with clenched fists, she punched, gouged him with her free elbow, thrust a knee to unbalance him, and then kicked his shins as hard as she could.

Surprised at her own speed and strength, Hattie must have hurt him, for his grip loosened with something of a groan. Bending in pain, he staggered for balance, which gave her time to slam the door shut. Her heart beat wildly as she grabbed a corner of her trunk and pulled it to barricade the entryway. Frantic with fear, she rushed to the stove and seized the hot poker from the fire. If the man tried to come through the door again, she would batter him in every way possible.

Hattie leaned hard against the trunk. Had anyone heard her frightened cries against the sound of the downpour? Struck with another idea, she rushed to the corner and grunted angrily for the power to drag her bed across the room. It was big enough to block the door, but she couldn't marshal enough strength. Instead, she grabbed all the clothes she'd carefully brushed and dumped them in the trunk. On top of the clothes, she piled shoes, linens, books, her satchel and other belongings for ballast.

Shaking uncontrollably, Hattie waited. The seconds crept so slowly she nearly despaired. Was he out there recovering? What if he'd gone for backup help and was returning? She would be easy prey if two or more attackers decided to finish the job.

The storm raged unabated and actually grew worse from the sound of the deafening thunder and beating rain. Hattie took this as slight encouragement, if only because the attacker's getaway horses might balk. Without a secure escape, he would be a fool to try again. Yet, she dared not move for what felt like hours.

Finally, she leaned slightly and struggled to fill a dipper of water from her basin. A severely parched throat had left her unable to call for help. The acute, dry ache in her lungs reminded her of the time she'd bolted away from the slave catchers years ago. Then, she knew exactly who she was dealing with. Now, she had no clues to the identity of the awful, hooded attacker.

But several other particulars seemed obvious. This wasn't just another scare tactic. It was a deadly serious assault. The attacker had watched and waited for her to be alone and then made his move. Suddenly, all of Hattie's idealistic and naïve ideas of adventure and excitement in the far flung Cherokee Nation dissolved into nothingness. She could easily have been killed.

❖ ❖ ❖

The night grew as black as Hattie's panic over the near miss. Pacing to fight off the shaking that continued to jolt her, she grieved because no rescuers arrived. Probably there was nobody to hear, even if she had screamed at the top of her lungs all night.

Her sense of security shaken beyond reason, she eventually climbed into bed and stayed there even after the fire went out. Her hands and feet went cold as bricks. Shuddering all alone under her covers became the closest available safe haven. Terrified to her core, Hattie prayed through her tears for God to spare her.

But she couldn't keep her attention on the prayer. Her body had gone limp and the sobbing left her nose stuffy. Meanwhile, her mind raced. That horrible man must be related to the person who wrote the threat letter! The incidents just had to be linked.

From such a vulnerable position, Hattie now regretted keeping the threat letter secret. Even worse, she contemplated a new realization; when she had finally told James, he minimized it. James' should have been much more concerned. And she should have insisted on an investigation, especially in light of his promise of secrecy. Why had she let him characterize her concern as exaggeration? She could hear his exact words now. Nothing explained letting him off the hook except her adoring feelings for him. But backing down because of love could have gotten her killed!

There was even more guilt to accept. She hadn't really taken the letter seriously at its word when it warned her to curtail her activities and movements. Because of her strong-willed attitude, had she brought tonight's encounter upon herself? This assault was proof that her attacker had grown substantially braver since he left the threat letter.

Despite her fear and agitation, she finally dozed off. When she awoke fitfully, it was still dead dark outside. The man had not returned, yet she knew she remained in great danger.

Unable to remove the trepidation from her mind, Hattie stared wide-eyed at her lamp. What if it burned out and plunged her into total blackness until daylight? Against so many frightful realities, more sleep seemed impossible. She dreaded the rest of the night, feeling every wind gust against her quarters' outside façade.

September 28, 1856, 5 o'clock a.m.
I am alive, by God's grace. But forever changed. Life can
end in an instant. Why was mine spared? I have been asking
myself that question since childhood—and now, again.

Hattie found it no coincidence that the next day was a Sunday, the appointed time for worship and rest. She didn't think she could muster an ounce of energy for either. Worst of all, she dreaded moving her trunk and other barriers from the door. Never opening her door again, however, was ridiculous.

Last night haunted her, as if the attacker was the devil himself. But unlike the day after the threat letter, she couldn't run to Hannah or Sarah this time. They would think her weak and overly emotional. If only she could talk with Marshal John Stewart Latta.

Then she was mad all over again. If James had kept his word, he would have been there to protect her. In fact, it seemed perfectly reasonable that the attacker knew James was away from Park Hill. That's what had emboldened him, along with plenty of whiskey. The whole thing looked carefully calculated.

Despite what Martha had told her, Hattie chided herself harshly. The man she had fallen for abandoned her at a crucial time.

James knew the move from the seminary to the mission bothered her. He understood she'd grown attached to the seminary's comfort and company, as well as the splendid surroundings. But did he care?

Before things went any farther, she needed to sit him down for a candid discussion. But, on second thought, that was ridiculous, too. On what basis could she reprimand him? He'd never even acknowledged courting her! They had no understanding of exclusivity or commitment, so she couldn't call him disloyal. Burying her head in her hands, Hattie wanted to sob all over again.

If she were to entertain seriously the idea of going back to Utica, it must be now or never. A needling impulse jabbed her to just climb on Rev. Worcester's horse and head for the Arkansas River at Fort Gibson. After she caught a steamship and was long gone, she'd write and reveal the attack. Who could possibly fault her for leaving?

Perhaps from force of habit, Hattie found herself getting ready for church instead. She couldn't just stay there by herself today even if she was leaving. Her stomach growled hungrily and the sunshine outdoors beckoned her to emerge from her dim quarters.

Slowly she walked toward the little church, being careful to avoid mud puddles. The rainfall had been significant. Acre upon acre of prairie grasses lay nearly horizontal with moisture. Like those grasses, she felt flattened but pressed on and arrived during the opening hymn.

Seeking to be inconspicuous, she slid into a back pew beside Susan and Rhoda. They greeted her warmly, which helped calm her agitated nerves. Rev. Foreman stood to lead the service. Interestingly, today had been set aside for parishioner testimonies instead of preaching.

As if in answer to Hattie's silent suffering, Rev. Foreman's opening scripture was the same one Rev. Fowler shared after the footbridge collapsed in Utica last spring. She hadn't thought of it since, but now it made her homesick. Biting her tongue, she fought back the tears that sought to flow.

"There is no fear in love; but perfect love casteth out fear; because fear hath torment. He that feareth is not made perfect in love." I John 4:18

❖ ❖ ❖

First to the lectern was Jacob Hitchcock. He launched into comments about evil and how to recognize it. "Men and women the world over must take a stand. The best way for evil to triumph is for good men to do nothing," he advised during his time of sharing.

Dwight followed. For a short time, his remarks wandered toward medicine and health. But he brought his point around confidently by concluding, "Only the foolhardy predict what tomorrow holds. We have no power over it. We must live by faith alone."

Sarah went next. With the voice of feminine empathy and love, she explained how God led her to an awareness of people's needs. To live in harmony, she believed, all men must be willing to give their energy and time for the sake of others. "I've been shown that the way to get along is to listen. Sometimes, people's greatest needs remain unspoken," she concluded wistfully.

Hannah, generous of spirit, shared multiple sources of blessing that brought Hattie up short. Even in the midst of her hard life, Hannah's heart overflowed with gratitude. She emphasized how thankful she felt to be surrounded by wise, learned people. There wasn't a hint of regret in her words, Hattie noted. Hannah did not let the past seep into her life. She had been denied the good education that her sisters enjoyed, but was not jealous.

Abijah stood and walked to the front after his wife finished. He began with memories about temperance and how it changed his life. Several men in the congregation nodded. He went on to recognize how many of his fellow Cherokees inspired him. They had not fallen prey to useless living even though many harbored frustration and injustice from their unfortunate circumstances. Before concluding, Abijah expressed appreciation for the dignity shown him and urged that all should abide by the Golden Rule.

By the time he finished, Hattie had a funny feeling somewhere between her heart and her throat. It was altogether new and unrelated to last night. She had heard five powerful messages that somehow seemed personal: for evil to triumph, do nothing; live by faith alone; give time and energy for the sake of others; be grateful for all the good things; and treat others as you want to be treated. These truths soothed her worried mind, but she was too befuddled to apply them.

Once the service concluded, the clamor began. Conversation buzzed. Hattie bragged to Susan that Rhoda was a great cook. As she talked, she watched Erminia leave with Sarah and Dwight. She had wanted to thank them for their testimonies. Maybe she could catch them outside. But she didn't make it that far.

Rushing to her right side, Mary Covel and Susie Foreman launched into an effusive story about their excitement to start school. Before Hattie could even respond, Taylor Foreman and Return Robert Meigs joined them on her left. All the children seemed to talk at once in their exuberance. Percy Hicks and Jennie Foreman approached her next, pushing past the older children to take her hands.

One by one, Hattie recognized them by name and answered their simple, yet endearing questions. Each in his or her own way shared a hunger to read and learn, to listen and practice, to march and sing at temperance meetings. Every dear face told a story of optimism and innocence.

"Well, Miss Sheldon," Rev. Foreman complimented as he passed. "You have quite a number of admirers even before stepping in the classroom."

His words struck a chord. Hattie felt like an imaginary curtain had parted as she turned to look, once again, from one eager child's face to another. Bright eyes. Wide smiles. Open minds. Each special little life gripped her interest and stole her heart. And then, without flourish, she simply comprehended that these children were the embodiment of a direct answer to her dilemma. They inspired the only thing that could drive away her fear: courage. Children needed teachers who used the stories of history to define courage. Her ancestor, John Sheldon, had redeemed his captive children in Canada because of pure courage. If it ran in families, then she must claim it and make use of it. There was no way she could leave these precious children! They were counting on her.

But Rev. Foreman's comment also gave rise to another unexpected revelation. Hattie needed the children just as much as they needed her. They were her reason for coming here—and that mattered fundamentally now. For, nearby, trouble still churned. Significant things really were falling apart in Park Hill. The seminary closures resulted from serious debt. Factions grew. Whiskey sellers and robbers roamed the byways. Abolitionists couldn't stand up against slavery. Illness had struck Sarah and others. Medicines were difficult to procure. Erminia. The mission's status was precarious. Rev. Worcester's whereabouts remained cloudy. And James Latta couldn't be counted on. But the children and their needs represented a constant.

Having come full circle, Hattie's thoughts lingered on the children and returned to how eagerly they approached her after today's testimonies. Blessedly, clarity emerged. If she walked away from this place and the children without solving the riddle of her attacker, evil would triumph and troublemakers would win. She must take up the torch of courage and stick to her commitment while pursuing the truth.

If Rev. Worcester were here, he would likely advise that to survive and thrive, she needed to rely more on faith and less on her own reasoning. She hated acknowledging it, but she really had not lived by faith alone lately. Clumsily, she had stumbled through trials on her own, flawed power. Maybe that's why so many things felt so bad. She'd let blessings go unrecognized and unappreciated. What of her lament just last night about being abandoned, while contemplating a sudden, cowardly departure from Park Hill this morning?

Hattie knew what she must do. Up to this moment, she had viewed her decision to teach and help the Cherokees as the whole story. But it was barely half of a far richer story. Park Hill had life-changing lessons to teach *her*. God had brought her here for reasons she hadn't comprehended before. It was time to pray harder and share her knowledge with these children while she soaked up the richness the Cherokee Nation had to share.

❖ ❖ ❖

Sunday, September 28, 1856

*Today brought an epiphany after the darkest of nights. Where
to begin? I was reminded most soberly that the mission's work
is to advance the kingdom of God. I remember comprehending
it the moment I first met Rev. Worcester. My radical choice
to accept his offer further reaffirmed that admirable purpose.
But somewhere along the rough road to today, I lost sight of it.*

*Horrible, frightening things have happened. Then I discovered
the hidden truth about Rev. Worcester's precarious relations
with the American Board and the poor condition of the
mission. I have reacted like those problems left me no choice.
In short, I became a slave to fate.*

*I'm not sure when, but I also began to see myself as a meek and
timid bystander. Before leaving Utica, my faith had always
been unmovable. Then I let fear creep in when I wasn't looking. And I gave it a foothold. But dying itself isn't what scared
me. Rather, I attached dread and terror to what preceded
death: injury, suffering, and other unfathomable crimes.*

*Waiting for Rev. Worcester—while losing hope with
Erminia—damaged my view of my own worth. I took my
temporary detachment from the mission too seriously. That
uneasy, preliminary status impacted me in embarrassing
ways. I misunderstood many things and sought comfort from
James instead of God. It really is true that I became somebody
besides my headstrong self.... all hunkered down, filled with
worry, and stained with tears.*

*But there's the nugget of truth I missed until now. This was
my time of testing! I just didn't recognize it. But 1 Peter 4:12
clearly says "Beloved, think it not strange concerning the*

fiery trial which is to try you, as though some strange thing happened unto you."

And my trial was at its worst following the attack when I almost gave up and left. My soul all but languished last night, but here I am today. God led the children to me as a sign! I guess I've made it through. Since he wants me to stay, I pray he'll protect me. He has certainly given me to understand the gift of conviction. School starts tomorrow!

·11·

Secrets

*A*fter she polished the fingerprints off her little bell at the end of her first day of teaching, Hattie inspected the room. It had been a marvelous day packed full of goodness without an inch to spare. Well over thirty children had filled that room with every manner of qualities. She must learn their names quickly.

For starters, Lucas and Buck appeared about nine or ten years old. They had kept their distance from the others at first. Yet they minded well and didn't tease the girls too much. She had ended most of the poking, pushing, and pestering, after separating the girls and boys on different sides of the room, as was customary. That diminished some of the ornery ones' big schemes.

With the introduction of each subject—Reading, Penmanship, Composition, Biblical Culture, Geography, Grammar, and Arithmetic—the feeling of community had taken seed. Hattie's sense of belonging grew by the hour. The children wanted to learn. Some seemed to benefit from better discipline at home than others, but she'd address that over time. Another important matter was practicing for the Cold Water Army rally. It would happen tomorrow or the next day.

School was started and her safety was in God's hands. Now, what to do about James and communicating with her parents? She had made a few honest notes, although meager, to begin her letter. Even those looked shallow. If only she could attempt a brief, newsy approach. But, given the attack, she knew her own words would give her away and worry them. So, she procrastinated.

Early one morning that first week as she placed logs in the little stove, Hattie glanced out the window as Lucas and Buck approached. Watching them shove each other playfully, she almost disregarded a little sound behind her at the door. Out of habit, Hattie turned anyway to check.

There, just inside the weathered door stood a tiny, black-haired girl in a carefully made, but worn dress. She stared directly at Hattie, expressionless through the most intent brown eyes. Her seriousness appeared natural; not a hint of a smile broke through. Delicate and thin, she nevertheless held her position as if deciding whether or not to stay.

"Good morning," Hattie greeted with quiet warmth. "My name is Miss Sheldon. I'm glad you've come to school. What's your name?"

But the child did not respond. As Hattie drew closer, the little girl moved sideways and then made her way around the room in the opposite direction from Hattie. So that she would not appear intimidating, Hattie stopped. All she could think to do was smile.

The next moment, Lucas and Buck shoved each other through the door. They always exhibited mischievous behavior so generously. One flicked sluggish, late summer grasshoppers on the girls. The other licked his index finger and ran it down as many necks as possible.

To make matters more complicated, Buck was actually a gregarious, fun-loving boy. He had great sway over Lucas, who was ornery but more innocent. If they weren't pulling Susie's hair, they were pouring water down someone's back. One didn't grasp the moral need for discipline, while the other was simply a follower. Was there a way to link faith and behavior in their minds? *How do I deal with a child who has too little conscience*, Hattie wondered? The idea of right versus wrong seemed foreign.

She called the class to order and had everyone bow their heads. Peeking during the prayer, Hattie saw Buck stick out his tongue and elbow two other students. Before long, he could have a disagreeable impact on her entire classroom. What could be done with him while she waited for the return of Rev. Worcester, whose influence the boy sorely needed?

Meanwhile, Hattie also kept her eye on the mysterious child. Thankfully, she soon chose a seat and settled herself. The boys paid her no attention. Even as the day unfolded, they did not seem to notice the little girl who kept to herself. If anyone approached, she withdrew. Hattie concluded she must be new to Park Hill.

When it came to knowledge about the Cherokee way of life, Hattie felt over her head. How they conducted family business, made decisions, disciplined their children, or spent their time, she knew not. It would be impossible to teach herself these things. She had counted on learning this and so much more from Rev. Worcester.

After two days, the distant little Cherokee child still didn't relate to others. Her big eyes took in the activities around her, but she remained an isolated island in a sea of normal, chattering classmates. Why was she unwilling to distinguish herself with an identity? Hattie had a suspicion that shyness didn't seem to be her problem. Was she suffering something unknown?

While the children were playing outside—and even though this little girl worried her—Hattie took time for some unfinished business. She knew beyond the shadow of a doubt that God had protected her since the vicious attack. During quiet times, however, her thoughts went even further back to an earlier time of trial. She winced remembering the injustice done her by Professor Thorne at Amherst Academy. How poorly she'd handled that suffering. To save her from the same mistake again, Hattie could almost hear the voice of Aunt Mary's reminder from the past: *"I'll give you credit for endurance—unsupported and alone. But it only works for a short time. It's much harder in the long run all by yourself."*

With that memory to guide her, Hattie penned a note to Marshal Latta about the attack. She provided as much detail as she recalled. Could he offer her help? Protection? Security?

❁ ❁ ❁

Growing more concerned about the little girl, Hattie determined to try something new. What if she sought to reach the child through sheer kindness and quiet attention? All she could draw upon was a similar experience at church back in Utica. After trial and error, she accepted that a child would respond only when the time was right.

So Hattie began to pass by the little girl's desk several times each day. Then, in an almost imperceptible way, she touched the child's shoulder or arm with the smallest of pats. Saying nothing, she continued this subtle encouragement. Of course, her attention must of necessity show no partiality toward any child so she kept her efforts understated.

The little lonely girl sometimes occupied herself by twisting a long strand of thick black hair next to her cheek. Soon, to Hattie's dismay, she began to chew on her hair. Something about this raised an alarm. In her understanding of the animal world, notwithstanding animals who groomed themselves, Hattie knew of no species that ate hair. Normal people did not chew hair. (Ebenezer had told her that, sometimes, starving horses did.) So, having concluded the child was not hungry, Hattie chose to gently bring about a change in the little girl's behavior.

Before she had the chance to devise a plan, however, the afternoon's concentration ended with shrieks. There, slowly winding his way inside the school room door, a long snake seemed to seek his winter hibernation spot. Hattie could have screamed; she certainly wanted to. But it would show fear and poor leadership. Catching herself, she moved the children behind her while checking to see if the snake had a rattler. He didn't, but might still be poisonous. Hopefully, he would not strike.

Taking this as a sign of encouragement, she grabbed the water bucket, tossed aside the dipper, and sloshed him with the water. Surprised, he writhed and drew up protectively. Bravely, Hattie slammed the heavy bucket down on his shiny back, and planted a foot to hold it in place.

The snake wriggled its head in pain. That head would soon feel the blade of a shovel that young Percy produced. Mary Covel grabbed it and dug the blade into the snake's flesh. To help her, Percy jumped with both feet onto the shovel's notched shoulders. With his whole weight on the blade, the snake's head was severed. Not a soul moved for a long, tense moment.

Then Hattie broke the silence, "What heroes! You children know a thing or two!"

The threat was over, so a great commotion began. All the children cheered with gusto. For her part, Hattie shook in the aftermath, but took up their goodwill and gave herself a pat on the back. She had never before encountered a snake so closely and didn't want to again. Giving Percy and Mary profuse praise, Hattie encouraged her students back to their seats.

They couldn't stop gushing with questions and comments. All seemed to tell at once that snake encounters were common in Indian Territory. Hattie was genuinely interested in learning more while hoping she wouldn't come face to face with one. As she returned to her desk, she felt a pull on the back of her skirt. Dismissing it amid the mayhem, she assumed one of the excited children had stepped on her hem. Then it happened again, only stronger.

Glancing down, Hattie discovered the silent little girl clutching a handful of dress fabric and straining to remain close. Ashen-faced, the child was shaking and clearly terrified. Almost by instinct, Hattie scooped the child up in her arms. To her amazement, there was no resistance. The little girl buried her face against Hattie's neck and whimpered.

Uncertain about how to proceed, Hattie reassured the others

then turned them out to get fresh air. Maybe running would get rid of their accumulated energy after the snake encounter. The tiny girl stopped crying, but still clung to Hattie, who walked toward a low bench and chose a spot for them to get acquainted.

"Everything is going to be alright," she murmured patiently. "Maybe we can talk now, just the two of us."

Those big, brown eyes looked directly at her for the first time. Hattie waited, smoothing the child's hair while holding her hand. The slightest little chin quiver spoke volumes.

"I think you have something to tell me, don't you?" Hattie coaxed, reaching to raise the child's lowered chin again.

"A snake bit Mama in the strawberry patch," the child whispered sadly. "She died."

If Hattie could have cried a thousand tears, it would have been no relief for the stabbing sympathy over this little girl's grief. Here was an innocent child suffering so much pain—a child wracked with the confusion of loss. Crushing emotions filled Hattie and memories flooded back; she recalled all the anguish and feelings of turmoil that she'd felt as a child when her sisters died. And here, as close as another person could be, was another little girl whose heart was just as broken, whose little mind could not handle the devastation of losing her most important relationship, her mother.

Hattie knew that only God in Heaven could empower her to do the right thing by this child, show compassion, and reveal loving kindness. She prayed with all her might as quickly as she had ever prayed in her life. Bargaining with God was no use, so she threw herself on his mercy and grace.

God answered. Hattie experienced a remarkably different feeling. It wasn't a feeling really. It was the experience of fullness warm enough to radiate right out of her heart toward the child.

"I'm more sorry than you can ever know, sweetheart," she heard herself say as the child stood. And with that, Hattie recognized how her own childhood would inform her role as teacher. She was able to focus totally upon this little girl and pour out understanding, compassion, and even love.

"We can talk about it more. We can cry for your Mama any time," Hattie told the child. "But won't you tell me your name?"

Climbing back into Hattie's arms, the child again rested against her shoulder and sighed. She was relaxing; Hattie could feel it.

"Papa named me Susannah. But I like Sweet Berry, because that's what Mama called me," the child murmured, a little smile coming over her face.

Hattie contemplated the full import of her challenge with Sweet Berry. Who was her father? This little child had already taught the teacher a lesson. What else would the school or the children bring up that might change her life? For that matter, what else did she need to uncover, chip away at, or discover on her rocky road toward mature womanhood?

Most of the things Hattie had previously taken for granted were now in question. It seemed hard to place them all in order, especially with the attack pressing on her mind. Perhaps the most personal transition was comparing who she was versus who she would become.

I'm truly my own parent now, she decided. But that sounded so strange. I *don't need a parent anymore,* she added. Her friend, Margaret, seemed to feel the same way. Margaret's last letter from Connecticut had not mentioned her parents at all.

Hattie mused about the idea of freeing herself from the strong personalities of her parents. As she left Utica, they had assured her she must make her own decisions. Yet, she had continued to yield to them ideologically from far, far away. Was it strange or fortuitous that Sweet Berry had raised the whole idea of parenting?

Before Hattie knew it, the first week of school came to a close. Saturday and Sunday might drag, especially with no word from James. She just had to keep busy or worry might tempt her. Then she recalled Nancy Hitchcock's insistence that she work on new socks. The Hitchcocks had invited her time and again. So Hattie saddled Comet at mid-morning on Saturday and rode to their residence.

Nancy greeted her so warmly. Hattie felt a bond because Nancy shared recently about visiting Utica in her youth. What a small world. While they knitted on the porch, little Laura played outside and Sarah finished her baking. After several games, Laura became thirsty and tearful. It was nap time. When Nancy offered to put the child down, Hattie talked with Sarah in the kitchen.

"I've been meaning to follow up privately on something Dwight mentioned," Sarah began. "You had posed a question about Cherokee support."

"Yes, I did. That's exactly the kind of thing I need to learn," Hattie confirmed.

"According to treaty, federal authorities at Fort Gibson, just southwest of here, keep a watchful eye and supply military defenses for the Cherokees," Sarah related. "They protect against various threats like antagonistic tribes, white interlopers, and every manner of outlaws and liquor. You probably heard that militant anti-slavery factions from Kansas posed a potential hazard earlier this year."

"I think my father mentioned that in a letter," Hattie recalled.

"Despite a barrage of negative influences, including Cherokee hopes that it will be abandoned, the fort continues to honor its mission. It's the Cherokee's primary source for food and other necessities. Rumors circulate, as more Cherokees decide they're independent and don't need that federal help. But we believe the fort plays many vital roles. Dwight says we would be in desperate straits if the federals weren't here."

"I see," Hattie reflected, seeing the seriousness on Sarah's face.

"It's complicated," Sarah said. "At the fork of convergence where traffic and commerce meet, unsavory people congregate. Father and the other missionaries appreciate how Fort Gibson fights their dangerous influence. I am referring to strong drink, hardened women, and gambling. We think the federals maintain civilization and safety."

"I hope Hannah's safe when she goes there for supplies," Hattie commented quietly.

"That's really my point," Sarah emphasized. "Even though it's a grueling, dangerous two-day journey where criminals prowl, Cherokees from here must go there for any food they cannot raise or grow."

"You mean Hannah must get all her supplies from there?" Hattie questioned, suddenly realizing what Sarah was struggling to reveal.

"Yes. Her life is laborious. It's dangerous just to put food on the table," Sarah shared haltingly. "Abijah's tribal practices are awkward for her, too. So, the rest of us—and you, too—must be sensitive to that."

The next week flew and then a rapid knock on the door sig-naled that James had suddenly returned. Nobody else knocked like that. Hattie jumped from her chair, smoothing her dress and hair nervously. Then she slowed down to contemplate her attitude. He had been gone for over two weeks. Was he distancing himself from her? It would be disingenuous if she acted too overjoyed to see him.

When she opened the door, James whistled into the room with a catchy tune and, seemingly, no cares in the world. He barely said hello. What was he chattering on and on about? It sounded dis-jointed. Hattie stood still and faced him without smiling. Couldn't he read the obvious, out-of-character sign of her silence and realize that something was wrong? Was he taking her for granted?

James droned on about going to Mr. Murrell's property in Van Buren, just shy of Fort Smith, and the needs there. His own family operated a farm property at Van Buren, as well. After Mr. Murrell had made decisions about the work he wanted done, he returned to Park Hill, but left James for a second week.

Relating details of his travels, James turned to his journey home. He had encountered ruffians and wondered what trouble they might cause. Unexpectedly, he also ran across his brother, John Stewart. For a time, they rode together on the Whiskey Road. An arrest had been made near there, John Stewart related, for the theft of Fred's team of horses!! One criminal was taken to jail and would soon stand trial. The others were still at large.

James laughed at how much fun they had smashing hundreds of whiskey bottles in a poorly hidden, illegal stash. Scores of whis-key sellers seemed to have no worry whatsoever of being discovered. Travelers had to remain on the lookout, as the dealers were brazen criminals and things were getting worse. They pursued potential buyers mercilessly.

Tomorrow, James said he intended to stop and see Dwight. He was puzzled over why so many people in Van Buren complained of having chills. Some kind of fever must be going around. Why, his mother had suffered chills and perhaps that's what killed her. John Stewart wanted him to pass along a rumor from Arkansas that diphtheria was on the rise again.

Hattie felt like James could just as easily be telling this to some blacksmith or the owner of a general store. Why didn't he tell it to someone who had no need for him *to clear the air*? But he just went on and on without seeing her hurt.

She tried to listen, but mostly she stared at a place on the wall behind James's head. Her emotions were getting the best of her, she feared. He should notice that she was upset. He should ask how she had been while he was gone. Perhaps she'd even reveal the horrific attack. But he was not primed for listening.

This was too much talk, too little perceptiveness of her state, and no asking about her. She sat there realizing that James only thought she heard him. Meanwhile, she was growing so upset she couldn't have repeated a word he was sharing. Her emotions were somewhere else, in a hurt and lost place.

Finally, James appeared to realize that Hattie was not responding.

"Are you sick?" he inquired, pausing from his long report and leaning forward.

"No. But one might say I'm sick at heart," Hattie returned solemnly, unable to force even a pleasant expression onto her face.

"Over what?" James observed, completely oblivious.

"Too many things ..." she trailed off and looked away, tearing up.

"Now, now. Let me ..." he started to get up, reaching for her.

"Don't, James," Hattie burst forth, putting up a hand in protest. "It's becoming clear to me that trying to count on men is not working."

"Whoa! All men? What are you talking about?" he began warily, taking a step backwards.

"First, my father thinks he can dictate how I feel. Then Rev. Worcester and the American Board leave me utterly unguided out here in the wilderness. And now you have been out of touch for over two weeks. I am struggling and have nothing but God's mercy. Time drags on and on. So, is Louisiana next? When are you moving there?" she confronted, almost startling herself with her abrupt approach.

James slouched, his body falling against the chair back. The expression on his face conveyed complete confusion, but also a slight frown of annoyance.

"Why don't you start over?" he requested in a serious tone of voice. "First, just tell me why you're mad at ME. Where did you come up with this bit about Louisiana? "

"I heard Mr. Murrell won't be here anymore during the winters," Hattie explained. "People say you are moving with him to Louisiana. So, are you leaving, just like that?"

Somewhat aware that she was jumping to conclusions, she was caught up in the release of her simmering emotions. James stood and shook his head out of confusion. He put his hands in his pockets and looked at the floor, deep in thought. Frowning, he walked over to Hattie, leaned down close, and said in an exaggerated tone, "I am not informed about the future, Hattie. All I know is that I will die someday! I'll leave then and only then."

He enunciated each word with sharp, clear diction while looking down his nose at her. "I was sent away on business at the last minute. It couldn't be helped."

"How can you just up and leave? I've had no clue about you for weeks?" Hattie pursued. "You could have written so I wouldn't think you were sick. Or dead!"

"Come on, Hattie," James argued. "When Mr. Murrell has a plan, he wastes no time. He doesn't owe me an explanation. I simply have to go. Just now, I got back to Park Hill and came straight here. Any talk linking me to Louisiana is just idle gossip. But what else is in your craw? Let's have it right now."

"Nothing," she responded impatiently, brushing him off. "It's clear that you don't understand."

"How can I solve a problem if I don't know what it is?" he questioned, totally exasperated. "It sounds like you're mad at all men. Stop this childish pouting."

"I don't want to talk about it now," Hattie whined, turning her back to hide the embarrassing tears that wanted out. If only James would just take her in his arms and comfort her. But did he care that much?

"Alright, Miss Sheldon. You may have your way," James said in a low, calm voice. "I can't fix the problem for which you hold me responsible. At *your* bidding, I'm going to leave your poor company and go get some supper."

With that, James walked out the door. Hattie swiveled around in shock and stared at the closed door. James' departure was so sudden and unexpected that she stood frozen in place. Why had he done that? She didn't actually mean she didn't want to talk.

The school children were itching like crazy. Patches on their skin had taken on a mottled, dark appearance. Some had scratched until the patches grew bright red. Hattie simply could not get them to stop. It was more than a distraction, as their attention span was impossibly short anyway.

She found her patience short, too, and nursed a blue mood. A murky pall of guilt had turned into part frustration and part anger over more than the argument with James. She wasn't even close to forgiving herself since writing the fatefully glib letter home. It would surely arrive in Utica any day. In both situations, she had handled herself in a manner unbecoming of who she wanted to be.

With no resolution for the itching after three days, Hattie worried about the Cold Water Army rally. She couldn't possibly take the children there in such a state. There was only one option to end the waiting game. She sought out the doctor.

"Dwight, the children are scratching the skin off themselves," she proclaimed with alarm. "I encourage them to stop, but it doesn't make one bit of difference."

"How long has this been going on?" Dwight questioned, his brow furrowed. "It's funny how you look me eye to eye these days and call me by my given name. If I had a sister, she would be like you, Hattie."

Hattie shook her head, smiling to herself about the compliment. "Three days in a row. And it is not any better. Could the itching be related to bathing in the river—or not bathing at all?"

"How many children are scratching?" he asked next.

"On Monday, perhaps five. On Tuesday, fifteen. But today,

nearly everyone," she griped. "They were miserable and aggressive today, poor little things."

"I can think of a number of perfectly ugly possibilities," he began. "If they have blisters, especially large watery blisters, it is probably poison ivy or oak. They will give it to each other quickly, mind you. But if they are just scratching all over, it is likely the plain old mange."

"Eeeuuw! I thought mange was limited to animals!" Hattie drew back.

"No. And if it continues, there may be other unpleasant symptoms, like hair loss. You have to get rid of the mites," he explained.

"You mean they have little vermin on their skin?" she wailed, throwing up her arms. "This is all I need!" She stared out the window while one index finger tapped her upper lip in a rapid rhythm.

"I'm glad I've got something for you to try on them. It's simple and goes a long way. You can treat them right in the classroom," he said calmly. "But what else, Hattie? I have seen you on edge like this before and you wouldn't tell."

"Oh, I'm just frustrated," she fibbed, avoiding his eyes. "If I could read and stay up with the news, I would feel like my old self. But I have no resources in Park Hill."

"I encountered that same problem," Dwight said sympathetically. "And it led me to subscribe to several newspapers and periodicals. You may borrow them any time."

Hattie looked at Dwight with expressionless surprise. Of course he had resources. This man was intelligent and curious. Why hadn't she thought of that before, when she might have inquired to borrow something to read? He was educated back east and understood!

"Do you mean that?" she breathed in awe.

"With the Good Lord as my witness," Dwight laughed, and

handed her copies of the *New York Daily Tribune* and *The Cherokee Advocate* from a side table. "I also read the *New York Observer*. But I don't buy your story about reading. Something else is the matter. Let's have it."

Turning her head sharply, Hattie caught his well-trained, diagnostic gaze. He was a bright one. She couldn't hide much from his knowing eye. Dwight obviously cared. But since she hadn't heard a word after her letter to Marshal Latta, she didn't have the nerve to mention the attack. If he brushed it off like James had minimized the threat letter, she would be humiliated.

"I seem to have so many concerns. And I feel like crying. Yet, I don't want to be like so many other young women I've known who run from person to person wailing," Hattie explained carefully.

"That's the last way I would have analyzed you," Dwight returned. "Remember, Hattie, I know how greatly the east and the Cherokee Nation differ from one another. This place is a radical departure from your life in Utica. It's a territory, not even a state. The vast majority of people here have a tribal background and a cursory acceptance of Christianity. And, as for this mission, almost everyone you know is married. We have ready partners and never lack for someone to talk to, to support us. That makes for a big difference between your situation and ours. I comprehend the gravity of your circumstances more than you know. And nobody's at the helm of the mission just now. It's a pretty isolated situation for you."

"Why, thank you," Hattie blinked quietly. "You just put my unresolved feelings into words. Yes, I do churn inside over a number of things. "

Those things suddenly gushed out. There was her father and his abolitionism. His beliefs had followed her all the way to the point when she discovered slavery in Indian Territory. Even Chief Ross had slaves, she had heard. But he remained out of sight, like Rev. Worcester. Sooner or later, she needed to meet the chief. Until she could ask an authority and learn for herself, some things would never add up.

"Well, since slaves are on your mind, you need to know about the Cherokee laws governing them," Dwight advised. "You live here now where the rules are different. But being mad won't help. I'll tell you that much."

Some people might have taken Dwight's words defensively. But Hattie appreciated the respect he'd shown her feelings and she admired his professionalism. Could she muster the courage to follow his advice, to let go of her anger and frustration, and accept the reality in her midst?

She nodded yes. "Go on. What else don't I know?"

"Years ago, I guess in 1839, the Cherokee National Council prohibited the marriage of any Cherokee with any slave or person of color not entitled to Cherokee citizenship rights. But I've heard some married freed slaves somehow. The issue is race. Outside of marriage, if there are children and the mother is Cherokee, the children can become citizens. But not if their mother is Negro and their father is Cherokee," he enumerated. "It's very specific. You already know that the agent keeps careful watch over all this. Agents do a thousand jobs, like pursuing runaways. When they're caught, prosecutors pocket half of the fine. It's corrupt and complicated. But it's still better than the situation with slavery further in the South."

There was no need to respond. She nodded her understanding, but still had a vacant expression. He stared at her.

"Why do I sense we haven't gotten to the bottom of things?" he coaxed.

Hattie began to dab at the tears that unexpectedly fell from her eyes. She looked away as she began to speak.

"My early life was under the protection of a strong man," she began slowly. "And now, the men in whom I've placed my trust for life, work, feelings, and future—all of them have left me up in the air." Suddenly, she remembered that Dwight was James's best friend. Would he keep her confidence? She hoped so.

"As a physician, I took an oath to heal," he reminded her rather like a sensitive grandfather. "In this territory doing the Lord's work, I am not here to find fault, but to solve problems."

"Oh Dwight," she apologized, "I am embarrassed and ashamed to involve you. Of course, matters must be faced. But I'm in no position to do so. I overreacted to James's absence, feeling vulnerable about Mr. Murrell's Louisiana place and the needs there. So James and I are not on speaking terms. I would look utterly foolish to write him. Dcorum makes it improper to seek him out. But I miss him and I'm sorry."

"Ah. Well. That IS a big problem. Confusing," Dwight nodded, looking a little sad himself. "I have been married so long I've forgotten the rules of courtship. But let me back up. From my perspective, maybe you did overreact. But who wouldn't, given your situation? You need to know that Murrell doesn't know what he's going to do yet about that plantation. Certainly, he understands this is James's home where he wants to remain. I've not heard that James knows a soul in Louisiana besides some old school chums."

Hattie appreciated Dwight's understanding. But her emotions still left her mute. Nothing was solved.

"My first instruction is, don't let any man in your life decide FOR you about anything. Trust your own instincts, experiences, and education. Live your own life, not your father's, not James's, and not Worcester's," he instructed. "Second, you are seen as quite competent and self-sufficient. That works for the mission's benefit, but some people, like James, may not know how much you need them. So, may I suggest another option?"

"At this stage, I would welcome just about anything," Hattie returned, no longer caring if she looked rumpled and tear-stained.

"I think I will approach James this evening," Dwight began thoughtfully. "On Saturday, I will send Jesse, for you in my buggy. Come to our home. If James agrees to come, as well, then you two can discuss whatever is making you miserable. If he doesn't come, then we will enjoy your good company anyway."

❀ ❀ ❀

Grace stopped by on Thursday. "I've got Mrs. Worcester settled down after that stay in Kansas. Finally, I can help you."

"Oh, thank goodness," Hattie exhaled. "You've got to get me ready to teach domestic lessons. I gather that with winter coming, we'll burn more wood and save more ashes for soap making in the spring?"

"Yes, in the late fall we collect fat when they butcher cattle and hogs," Grace related.

"I'm lost about the details, so I'm counting on you. In Utica, our soap was purchased ready-made," Hattie apologized.

"I'm old hat at this," Grace smiled. "Before long, the cool days will signal butchering time. We can probably help Abijah when he's ready. You'll see the whole thing—start to finish. We'll cut the fat out so we can melt it, strain it, and harden it for making soap later. All the buckets and tubs are stored above in the barn. We should start collecting rain water, too. The basic process involves pouring water over those ashes and packing them down. The dripping produces lye. Did you know we test the strength of lye with a feather? If it dissolves, the lye's strong enough."

"That's all new to me," Hattie replied.

"After butchering, we'll render the fat. When we make soap, lye water gets added to the fat. It's a dangerous process for a newcomer. But I'll show you how to get it thick like pudding so it hardens. Then, we'll cut it into bars. But that's a big oversimplification," Grace explained.

"I'm at your mercy," Hattie begged. "Will you teach me to make candles, too? The days are getting shorter and we need more light."

In the hours it took Hattie to comb through Dwight's newspapers, she already felt more informed than she had in months. Her head swirled with the variety of posts. Both reported stories and notices of events kept her attention. The preponderance of stories ranged from reports about the proliferation of gambling, skyrocketing whiskey sales, illness among federal troops at Fort Gibson, temperance meetings, and the cost of staples. Of particular interest was a news item reporting that Chief John Ross had ordered all Mormons out of the Cherokee Nation. Final comments within the story indicated his displeasure with their efforts to encourage or provoke the Cherokees to migrate to the Territory of Utah.

Hattie read with incredulity an historical reference about the Cherokee slave revolt of 1842. The situation occurred just to the south in Webbers Falls, but participants from the valleys of the Three Forks were involved. Before daylight, a number of slaves locked their overseers up inside their cabins. They proceeded to take everything of the overseer and turn toward the Rio Grande, where free Negroes could settle in a town and not be found or returned. Every Negro in Webbers Falls left the area.

Making a mental note, Hattie intended to ask for more details. Dwight was politically astute and well read, so she could ask him. If James ever spoke to her again, she could also ask him, which might make him feel more comfortable and needed. With each day, she grew more ashamed for not holding true to her intention the day of their argument. When he showed up, she failed to have the serious talk she'd envisioned and got uncharacteristically cranky. Now that she had resolved to stay in Park Hill, she simply must get things between them patched up.

The wait to see James dragged so slowly that Hattie was beside herself. Each day had become slightly shorter as October progressed. Of course, that meant the nights were longer. Being alone in the dark was the most trying thing of all. In the evenings, she tried to relax, read whatever she'd borrowed, or study the Bible for a while by the stove. But she was so anxious that even the attack receded and took on less prominence.

When Abijah happened past and invited her for supper on Friday with his family, Hattie offered a silent prayer of gratefulness. While she had the chance, she also shared with him about Sweet Berry. Without knowing more about the child's confusing situation, how could she help her in a meaningful way? To Hattie's delight, Abijah promised to ask around and find out more on her family and where she lived.

Once all were gathered around the supper table, Hattie bragged on Percy. She recounted the spellbinding steps of how he helped kill the snake. Of course, Percy had forgotten to tell his parents. Hannah let out a moan, while Abijah explained how Percy needed experience killing snakes. Hattie laughed that Percy had been exposed to many things his mother didn't know about.

"What else have you seen that you didn't tell anyone?" Hannah kidded, looking askance at him.

"Last Saturday, I saw Sweet Berry in a tree swing," Percy replied innocently.

Hattie's ears perked up. "This is one of Percy's new classmates," she explained. "She barely speaks in class. Percy, did you talk to her? Or more importantly, did she talk to you?"

"Yes, we had a good time. I pushed her in the swing for a while. We talked in Cherokee," he shared.

"That's good, son," Hannah crooned. "And what else?"

"Her grandma heard us and came outside. She asked me who my Daddy was and I told her Abijah Hicks. Then Sweet Berry asked if her Daddy was awake, but her grandma got mad and stomped off," Percy said.

"What do you think was wrong?" Abijah questioned. "Why was she mad?"

"I followed Sweet Berry. We sneaked around the house and looked inside. A man was asleep all spread out on the floor," Percy expounded. "But I don't think he was really asleep."

"Son, you remember what we talked about at the temperance meetings?" Abijah mentioned quietly.

"Yes, sir. I know that he was drunk," Percy added plainly.

Hattie and Hannah looked at each other silently. The story behind Sweet Berry's unexplained silence was coming into focus.

"How do you know, son?" Hannah persisted.

"I saw whiskey bottles next to him," Percy clarified, taking a big bite of potatoes.

❖ ❖ ❖

To pass the hours on Saturday, Hattie took pride that her students were now settled into the routine of school. Their restlessness during the first few weeks—and acute phase of the mange—had given way. Now, she saw a growing degree of attentiveness and adjustment. McGuffey's readers kept them enthralled. And, sometimes, Hattie told them stories about New York, disguising her family and friends as new characters.

But there wasn't much to keep her busy today. Hattie daydreamed, being careful not to relive the attack. Coping with big problems one at a time proved trying. For this crucial occasion with James, she gave great care to her appearance. Last night, she had washed and ironed her best dress in anticipation of a serious talk between two adults. Using some transparent soap and cologne water, she'd also bathed and washed her hair until it was squeaky clean. After it was dry, she added powder to make it look a little fuller.

At least the outside of her was ready. The inside of her was disorganized, nervous, and uncertain about what to expect. She usually talked herself down from such a level of angst, but not this time. The uncertainty of the evening's outcome left her so restless that nothing short of a bottle of illegal whiskey was going to calm her. Not that she had any clue what whiskey would make her feel like. But she had heard it quickly slowed a person's emotions, movements, and thoughts.

The way Hattie saw it, James was a forgiving man. She had behaved badly; but was it offensive enough for him to withhold charity towards her? Surely compassion would guide him to let her back in his good graces. For after being assaulted, she needed him more than ever. But the problems had to be dealt with one at a time.

Without question, she would never again refuse to discuss something or turn away in a pout. Even though she was sorry, at least she had learned a good lesson about his temperament and limits. Once they got back together, she vowed to be straightforward with him.

If only her mother had armed her with a little more knowledge about getting along with men. In the Sheldon home, her parents seldom argued and never apologized in front of their children. She had only learned certain things by overhearing when they thought nobody was listening.

Sarah greeted Hattie warmly with a knowing look. After a brief chat focused upon little Laura, Hattie spoke to the elder Hitchcocks when they emerged. Nobody acted out of the ordinary. Sarah assured Hattie to take her time, as they were going to a friend's home for supper and wouldn't be back until at least nine. Then they took their leave.

Hattie felt so jittery. Waiting alone in someone else's house seemed odd. Should she face the door or would that look too anxious? If she sat with her back to the door, it might send too nonchalant a message. The last thing she wanted to convey was that she didn't care. How ridiculously untrue that would be.

She did care. Deeply. Why had she made such a mess of their last encounter? After vowing to have a serious talk with James, she just exploded instead. Her demeanor suggested the opposite from what she really wanted to convey.

Then, with no warning whatsoever, the door opened and James Latta simply strolled inside. Hattie's stomach jumped. He looked around, spotted her, and took off his hat.

"Is there anything to eat in here?" he asked casually as if nothing was wrong.

"Uh, I don't really know," Hattie responded, clearly caught unprepared for sarcasm.

"You mean you're not cooking tonight?" he said in an attempt at humor.

"Well, no, since this isn't my home," she replied hesitantly.

"I'm kidding anyway," he began, walking toward her. "So, Dwight has orchestrated this little chat... in hopes it will make him feel better. Isn't that about the size of it?" James challenged a bit confrontationally as he took a seat.

"Make HIM feel better," Hattie repeated, puzzled. "You could be right. But I gathered that his main concern was his two friends."

"That tells me you've come up in his eyes. I wonder if I've gone down?" James laughed nervously. "I'm the old-timer and you're the newcomer."

"Does that matter right now?" Hattie asked softly.

"No, I guess it doesn't really. This is a matter between you and me alone, Hattie," James said, taking on a serious tone.

"Why don't you tell me your grievances?" Hattie inquired, sticking her neck out.

"That's a pretty big word," James replied curtly. "I don't recall saying I had grievances."

Silence fell like a heavy rock on hard dirt. They both looked at the floor as if there might be a hole through which they could escape.

"Alright. Well then, let me apologize to you," she offered, looking up. Her mouth felt horribly dry.

"That's good of you. What are you apologizing for?" he returned, putting the responsibility on her.

"The last time we talked, I behaved poorly and with a lot of immaturity," she leveled. "And I'm sorry for that."

"Accepted. It was an unexpected attitude from you that I hadn't seen before," James added crisply, not letting his guard down.

"I jumped to conclusions about some things, like you moving to Louisiana. It was out of place," Hattie continued. "I hadn't heard from you in weeks and made some erroneous assumptions."

"As I told you then, sometimes Mr. Murrell sends me off on unexpected projects," James explained flatly. "I don't question him. I have to live up to his expectation because I need the job and I like working for him."

"That's something I didn't understand well," she returned, listening intently.

"I know," he said quietly, shifting his position and looking down. "There are many things I don't think you understand, Hattie. It's not all your fault, but that's my main worry."

"What do you mean," she questioned, "main worry?"

"Indian Territory and the Cherokee Nation are confounding. You came here in good faith. But you don't know enough about what's really going on. It puts both of us in compromising positions. For Murrell, I supervise the slaves. I try to treat them humanely while keeping the place operating. There are many trying situations, decisions, and pressures. You appear to just barely grasp what I'm totally immersed in."

Hattie wanted to blurt out how she'd endured a terrifying, heart-stopping, threatening attack. But, instead, she said, "I can't be any more uninformed that other eastern teachers who came here before me."

"Yeah, but I didn't keep company with them," he admitted, to her amazement. "I saw how stunned you were to learn that Cherokees owned slaves. There's no doubt but what Erminia let you down, Hattie. She should have prepared you a lot better. But perhaps her illness is to be blamed. The bottom line is that you need a lot more knowledge in order to get by in this place."

"I know, I grasp that," she countered, pressing on one brow. "But it's not my fault that she left me high and dry. She had plenty of opportunities before she got sick. And—please hear me—I understand your position and how slavery is entrenched. But surely you agree that it's got to stop sometime, somehow."

"There. You've just proved the point I'm making—again," James reacted, sounding agitated. "You are applying your family's utopian understanding to a system you've only read about from afar. That's hard for me to take. I live here and have to carry on. Believe me, to just stop this entrenched way of doing business will either take an act of God or a war. How can we have a future together and go places with southerners if we have such different views? It seems to me that we just disagree fundamentally."

"Well, I don't really think that's true. Remember that I agree with the belief you said your own father holds," she replied slowly. "He says slavery will not stand. But you don't call him utopian."

James frowned and then looked away for a second. He seemed puzzled, as if some sleight of hand had just taken place in a card game. Then he looked at Hattie with a serious expression, but did not speak.

"What places were you thinking we might go together ... where I might not agree with exactly everything you believe?" she questioned softly, taking a step toward him.

"Doggone you, Hattie," James griped. "You don't make it

easy, do ya? I know you're trying debate tricks on me. I see that mischievous look."

"I'm merely communicating clearly like an adult," she reassured, looking up at him with the hint of a coy expression. He seemed not to notice that she had taken ahold of his hand lightly.

With that, Hattie looked James full in the face. For a long while, he just stood there while she kept ahold of his hand. Then he leaned in and kissed her.

By the time Hattie and James arrived at church, she had gotten up the nerve to tell him about the attack. This time, he was appropriately worried. But nothing could be done yet.

Once inside, they heard Dwight telling Erminia and some other ladies about Mrs. Addie Torrey's progress with baby Mary. They greeted Abijah, who asked if Hattie knew that Rev. Charles Cutler Torrey, who was preaching today, was a graduate of Andover Theological Seminary, just like Rev. Worcester. Occasionally, when the two men got the chance, they liked to study the ancient Greek texts together.

"So, we three have Massachusetts in common," Hattie continued.

"Yes. Rev. Torrey was saying earlier that after he finished his schooling, he went to Utica for the American Board's annual meeting last year. Did you attend, as well?"

"No. I didn't know about it," Hattie returned. "I'll talk to him after the sermon."

Just then, Rev. Torrey approached the pulpit and the music started. Everyone quickly found a seat. Hattie had meant to greet

Erminia, but didn't get the chance in the rush. She whispered this to James just as Grace slid silently into the pew beside her.

Shortly, she learned that Rev. Torrey had a great gift with words. So far, he was the best preacher she had heard since arriving in the Cherokee Nation. She particularly enjoyed his original stories of working with the Choctaws before the Cherokees. Some people in the congregation nodded and murmured appreciatively when he said how much the Cherokees meant to him and his family.

"He's a good politician, but has struggled at Fairfield," James whispered to Hattie with a wink. "There's poor Cherokee interest and participation there."

❖ ❖ ❖

After church, Hattie and James worked their way forward.

"Erminia sees herself like a sovereign receiving members of the court," Hattie observed acerbically while picturing the British royal family.

James cast a sideways glance her way and then began to chat with a friend. Hattie joined a circle of conversation alongside Grace. Momentarily, she was surprised to hear James's name called behind her.

"James Latta," Erminia had gushed. "How do you like Murrell's? Any word from your little sweetheart down in Louisiana?"

Hattie felt her body go rigid suddenly. There was no doubt about what she had just heard. Little sweetheart down in Louisiana? The only thing she knew was that James's old school chums lived there now.

"Hattie Sheldon, is that you?" Erminia warbled next. She was showing off.

Hattie strove to look as genuinely happy as possible. Given the new hollow spot in her heart over the sweetheart comment, she strained doubly hard to show warmth. Her burden also included lingering disgust over Erminia's earlier confrontation at the school.

"Yes, it's me. Hello. Have you heard from Leonard since your visit," Hattie inquired, although she was not interested.

"Not yet, but it was a marvelous time. He took me everywhere as his escort," Erminia lilted, as she looked to see who was paying attention.

"How nice for you," Hattie replied.

"But I understand you have been busy, Hattie," Erminia added, her expression losing some geniality. "James just said you have some unruly boys in class? That's just part of the challenge, after all. And before I forget, Dwight told me you want to meet Chief Ross. My advice is, be patient. I will arrange that when the time is right, dear. His wife is a particular friend of mine."

Already somewhat provoked, Hattie bristled. The hair on the back of her neck stood up to Erminia's superior attitude. She needed to reply after Erminia sought to embarrass her. Without so much as one visit during class time, without any first hand understanding of what was really happening, Erminia had closed the door on Hattie's idea. Clearly, nothing mattered as much to Erminia as making good with the chief and his wife.

Rather than take exception in front of all these nice people, Hattie thought it better to attempt a nonchalant or humorous comment instead.

"It's wonderful that you're friends with someone so much younger," she blathered, realizing her comment sounded worse than she meant it. "From what I heard, the Chief really robbed the cradle when he won her hand."

Erminia stared back at Hattie, her smile melting into the look of an affront. James, now standing opposite Hattie, drew his brow into a pinched expression. Beside her, Grace nudged Hattie sharply but invisibly.

"The Chief is young at heart," Grace inserted with a big smile as if nothing was wrong. "Everyone knows how proud he is of Mary."

"Yes," Erminia frowned as her voice trailed off. Nodding stiffly, she turned and pretended to motion to someone across the room.

"Would you like to greet Rev. Torrey?" Grace offered, looking at Hattie with searching eyes.

"I'm afraid we are late and must be off," James chimed in. "Do give him our best. It was a marvelous sermon, wasn't it, Hattie?"

Silenced by the depth of her misstatement, Hattie said goodbye. James took her by the arm, but she was too upset to look him in the face. Together they made their way out of the church in silence.

Once they were out of earshot, James turned to Hattie, his expression strained with disbelief.

"Have you lost your mind?" he rebuked her. "What got into you back there, Hattie? You just insulted your boss's wife in front of people at church!"

"I didn't mean to," she apologized. But then she added, "I don't feel as bad about that as I do about insulting the Chief himself."

"You need more than protection from attackers. You need protection from yourself," he complained.

"Children," Hattie called to the class, "this is Mrs. Grace Barnes. She will be with us in the classroom as well as the dining hall. Please welcome her."

Having Grace at school brought such relief. In particular, Hattie wanted her to keep a close eye on Buck and Lucas. Glancing back at Buck later, she noted that he had the same look on his face as always—somewhere between devilish and contemptuous. It was probably foolish to expect him to pay attention, but perhaps Grace might cajole him into doing more of his school work.

"He looks rather familiar," Grace commented later.

❖ ❖ ❖

"Boys and girls, it's time to practice for the temperance rally," Hattie instructed. "Please repeat the temperance pledge with me."

We hereby solemnly pledge ourselves that we will never
use, nor buy, nor give, nor receive, AS A DRINK,
any whiskey, brandy, rum, gin, wine, fermented cider,
strong beer, or any kind of intoxicating liquor.

"Very good," Hattie encouraged. "We are almost ready! I can't wait to see you marching proudly!"

As she spoke, the children wiggled with excitement. And, for the first time, Hattie noticed that Buck paid attention to her. He was no longer looking down, reaching to pester Taylor, or kicking Lucas's seat. Apprehensively, he glanced back at Grace, seeming to check on her whereabouts.

"He hasn't acted naughty since you arrived," Hattie bragged to Grace. "What have you done to so quickly tame that boy's orneriness?"

"Nothing I can think of," Grace replied, looking baffled. "I said hello and then was able to place him. I'm his neighbor. He looked at me with great big eyes and just nodded."

❖ ❖ ❖

Hattie counted her blessings that the children's itching had subsided thanks to Dwight's help. It would be gone by the rally. Meanwhile, plans were falling into place. Not only was Hannah bringing cakes and pies from mothers around Park Hill, but she had also confirmed that the U.S. Army Band from Fort Gibson would accompany a choir of soldiers singing Rev. Worcester's temperance songs! Parents from Fairfield, Dwight, and other mission stations always contributed barbecued meats, doughnuts, and other delicious foods. Hattie couldn't wait to taste the food.

Rev. Foreman had supplied her with a bright, twenty-foot streamer to lead the children's march around Capitol Square. To complement it, Hattie put the children to work making colorful banners printed with slogans. Girls carried white banners and boys carried pink banners.

Granted, Lucas and Buck's little pranks continued and they showed up late for school, but their worst troublemaking had slowed considerably. How wonderful that Grace dealt with them so effectively. Hattie did not have to tread lightly or exercise caution with any of the other children this week, although they remained in an excited state. And once Sweet Berry decided to trust her and participate, their relationship blossomed further, too.

Hattie could tell that she filled a gap in the little girl's life. Before long, Sweet Berry exposed a few more sad facts about her home situation. Her mother had been a seamstress when they lived far away. Hattie had no way to know how far. After her mother's death, her father came to Park Hill to help on her grandmother's small farm.

Sweet Berry was a smart but sensitive little thing. She needed attention from someone who valued her. When Hattie began to fill that role, Sweet Berry responded to her kindness. On several occasions, Hattie let Sweet Berry visit her quarters before walking her part way home. Sweet Berry had never seen anything like Hattie's clothing, bedding, or magnificent trunk. She stroked the smooth leather and traced the gold monogram of Hattie's initials with her fingertip. Hattie found it dear when Sweet Berry put her little nose next to the leather and sniffed its pleasant aroma. Memories of her own treasured times in her father's Utica shop sprang to Hattie's mind.

Before long, the little girl wanted to help wipe slates clean. In the process, she told some unforgettable things about Cherokee life. One morning prior to school, Hattie casually asked what Sweet Berry had for supper the night before. The answer caught her totally by surprise.

"Grandma made squirrel. We ate until we got full," Sweet Berry replied.

"Oh, how nice," Hattie replied, inwardly feeling queasy. "How does she cook the squirrel?"

"She throws them straight in the fire 'til the fur's burnt off," Sweet Berry replied innocently.

Hattie struggled to keep from thinking the word "vermin" over and over in her head.

"You mean's that's it?" she queried.

"No, then she skin him and put him on a stick. I hold the stick over the fire 'til he's done," the child explained.

"Is squirrel your favorite food?" Hattie asked without really thinking.

"Oh, no," Sweet Berry returned with assurance. "I like Knee Deeps better. But Levi and Ida like squirrel best."

"Why, I've never had Knee Deeps," Hattie commented, wondering who Levi and Ida were. "Tell me about them."

"They are BIG frogs," Sweet Berry answered, her eyes lighting up. "Grandma catch big ones and quick in the pot. I help skin them!"

For Hattie, this story struck a foreign place that sparked indigestion. She found it unbelievable that, in her own adopted town, people would eat—and like—such things. Then she quickly scolded herself. Lest she truly look like a city girl, she changed the subject.

"Is Percy your friend now?" Hattie inquired tentatively.

"Grandma say he's good because he talks Cherokee," Sweet Berry replied, lost in her little project with the slates.

"Does your grandmother speak Cherokee, too?" Hattie continued, acting nonchalant.

"Yes. She can read and write it, but understands a little English. She won't let me talk English at home. But I whisper to Levi and Ida anyway," Sweet Berry added, revealing more clues for Hattie to ponder.

"Can you bring them to school, too?" Hattie ventured, wondering if she went too far. Were Levi and Ida her siblings?

Sweet Berry glanced at Hattie in alarm, and then looked away. She was quiet for too long a time. "Miss Hattie, can I tell you a secret?" she whispered, to Hattie's amazement.

"Why, of course you can," Hattie responded and remained still in anticipation.

"Grandma gets mad. She makes me read to them. It's because my papa isn't their papa," she said with a troubled expression on her little brow.

At this admission, Hattie realized that Sweet Berry's life was far more complicated than she grasped. The child had a non-English

speaking grandmother and two half-siblings who didn't share her
same father. They also didn't come to school. What in the world had
happened in that family? There was no way to figure it out unless she
got more information. That might take some time.

"What are your Grandma and Daddy's names?" Hattie asked
innocently.

"Grandma is called Salali. Papa is called Deke," she answered
without reservation.

"Maybe I can help Levi and Ida read," Hattie suggested gently. "Or are they sick?"

"Oh, no, Miss Hattie," Sweet Berry confirmed. "Papa won't
let them out. He says be quiet or bad men might steal and sell them."

Sell? At this word, Hattie's brain began to churn. Sell? Every
part of her mind searched for possibilities to explain why Deke
would say this about the other children.

Then, suddenly, she had the answer. She had heard of just
such a thing from one of Martha's stories! There could only be
one possibility: Levi and Ida must be Negroes. Sweet Berry had
just explained that they had a different father than Deke. Perhaps
Deke had the other children with a Negro woman. Or maybe Sweet
Berry's late mother had the two children with a Negro man. For her
part, however, Sweet Berry looked Cherokee. But looks were often
deceiving. The whole thing was a puzzle.

All Hattie knew for sure was that Sweet Berry considered
Levi and Ida to be her brother and sister. But something was still
missing. Dwight's words about the 1839 law reverberated in her
head. Did the facts suggest Levi and Ida's parents were not married?
Were they illegitimate? Many other possibilities existed. For one,
Deke could have been married before. If a Cherokee managed to

marry a Negro woman, she must have been free. But this was all just speculation.

If it were true, however, that might explain something else. The law said Negroes couldn't be educated. If Levi and Ida were Negroes, that would explain why they weren't in school. How confusing this must be for them and for Sweet Berry. Hattie ached for the little girl, contemplating how her life was so complicated. For now, Hattie reassured Sweet Berry that she was a good girl and promised to keep her secret.

That evening, James brought up Hattie's brash words at church to Erminia. He insisted she apologize. Hattie eyed him uncomfortably. And she had thought he understood the stresses that led her to say the seemingly tactless things. Now that he was upset again, she wasn't going to broach the pressing issue of her attack, no matter what. He was not appropriately supportive.

"Why are you more upset with me than anybody else, James?"

"What do you mean?" James returned defensively. "Don't tell me others saw you in the right."

"This is about the law of averages, I think," she replied pensively. "There are mistakes I've made, which number fewer than the ones Erminia has made. She's clearly the loser."

"Says who?" he shot back.

"Sarah and Hannah, her stepdaughters," Hattie replied evenly. "And Miss Thompson."

"They actually said that?" James questioned, clearly disbelieving.

"In so many words, yes. Over the years, Erminia was an

unaccommodating stepmother. She didn't act in the Worcester children's best interest," Hattie explained solemnly. "You know she's difficult, James. But you've been wooed by the charming performances she delivers around men. Few know how she's been inside the family."

James was quiet for a moment.

"Erminia returned from Kansas, didn't visit my school room, but confronted me anyway. And she left poor Hannah and her children in tears through her insensitivity."

"Erminia made those sweet little Hicks children cry?" James repeated, unbelieving.

"She most certainly did," Hattie confirmed. "I was busy after school when Percy came back and just stood at my desk. He asked me rather sheepishly if I wanted to come over to his house, saying, 'Mama cried. Will you help me cheer her up?' I couldn't imagine what had happened, so he and I jumped on old Comet. On the way, I learned that Hannah had invited Erminia to a welcome home supper. They ate happily around the table before Abijah left to do chores and Hannah cleared the table. Percy said Erminia suddenly scolded the children and made them cry."

"He's just a child, Hattie," James excused. "You can't make serious judgments based on a child's exaggerations."

"I'm not," Hattie continued. "When we got to the house, I sat Hannah down. She wept all over again. That meal had demanded an additional trip to the mill with the oxen to grind extra corn. They went round and round working the tread wheel in the cold wind. Hannah carried the two younger children and engineered while Percy drove the oxen. All that extra work to welcome Erminia, who wasn't appreciative. She only spoke about how fancy things had been in Lawrence. Hannah had wanted to hear how Leonard was. But Erminia just talked on and on about herself."

"I hate hearing things like this," James exhaled, sinking down onto his chair.

"Hannah couldn't scold her stepmother in front of the children," Hattie added. "But it crushed her. Only Percy, the little soldier, comprehended. Hannah said he just stood beside her in the kitchen and patted her arm."

"Maybe the children did something bad that Hannah didn't see," James offered half-heartedly.

"For goodness sake! They didn't, James," Hattie retorted, shaking her head. "Here are Hannah's exact words: 'Since we are so deprived of society out here, I hoped Mother would share just a few stories to lift us up. But she was picky and petty.' Hannah also told me she felt just like Mary Eleanor did after being reunited with Erminia."

"When were they apart?" James queried.

"During another incident Hannah shared. I guess the Worcesters had a Negro cook named Sukey," Hattie explained. "Anyway, things got so tense at home that Mary Eleanor went to Ann Eliza's. She was great help, as Ann Eliza was ill again with those constant chills. In just a week, she started school there and things began to look up. But then, Sukey got sick and couldn't cook. Huffy Erminia created a tug of war with Mary Eleanor in the middle. She guilted Mary Eleanor into returning and then made her do all the cooking. It was punishment for nothing and it was mean."

"Alright, alright, I agree," James said with irritation.

"Anyway, the reason Erminia stayed so long with Leonard was to get sympathy. She knows she's linked to Mary Eleanor's troubles, but always acts like the one who has been wronged. Rev. Worcester wants it kept secret, but I let Erminia know I'm aware of Mary Eleanor's illness," Hattie continued.

"She's sick? What's wrong?" James questioned.

"Oh James! And you think I don't know what's really going on here," Hattie exclaimed in amazement. "For years, Mary Eleanor's been constantly upset and bursts out with nervous laughter or crying spells. Erminia has been too much for her: the poor girl could do no right in her eyes. That's the real reason the Worcesters went back east."

"I've heard enough," James grimaced, his hands in the air. "Let's not press this anymore. You seem to know these folks better than they know themselves."

"Perhaps. But as for knowing *you*, I have a request," she added. "How about you stop getting short-tempered with me before you know the whole story?"

"Yeah, alright. But listen. Other people's affairs can be quicksand. I don't like much public talk. Be more like Rev. Worcester and keep personal matters private."

"Agreed. That's wise," Hattie soothed, taking a seat herself. "Many more things should be settled privately."

"I'm just trying to protect you," he added in a fatherly voice.

"Alright, then maybe you can do me and the mission a big favor. Grace said Mr. Murrell loaned his horses and wagon to haul children to the temperance rally in the past. The next one is Thursday in Tahlequah. Can we borrow it again?"

"Have you seen Erminia since Sunday," Grace asked Hattie as they rode along. "It's really none of my business, though."

"No, I haven't. But what I said became *everybody's* business," Hattie frowned. "My judgment was poor."

"Most didn't take it as badly as Erminia," Grace allowed. "She thinks she has such authority, but the truth is that she acted rude to *you*, Hattie. You innocently wanted to meet the Chief. But she manipulated it into a chance to control you. Don't forget that people around here know her ways."

"Thanks for saying that," Hattie replied solemnly. "James was upset, which made matters worse. But I think you're right. It's been an uphill battle against her to accomplish what her own husband hired me to do. For her to tell me virtually nothing about this place, then send me here alone, then avoid me; it was too much. I overreacted when she treated me like I'm a child ... in front of everyone. After these last weeks of ordeal after ordeal, I couldn't take it."

"I feel the same way," Grace agreed. "When you come through so very many difficulties, it rearranges your ... innocence."

As the mission teacher, an important part of Hattie's charge was to regularly affirm that God in Heaven ruled over all creation. Daily before school, she led her pupils in a prayer repeated together:

We *thank* thee, Lord, for this new day.
Please help us learn and guide our play.
We *ask* thee, Lord, to bless us all
and teach our hearts to hear your call.
Forgive us, Lord, our pranks, our tears,
and bless our families, so dear.
We *pray* thee, Lord, our souls to keep,
while angels guard us as we sleep.

Amen.

The last line nearly caught in Hattie's throat, for she had prayed to God so often that the attack would not dominate or plague her. But she still wondered what Marshal Latta was doing about it. Pushing that aside, Hattie gathered the children around the globe for a discussion about God's greatest creation, the world.

"God made the land, the seas, the countries, and the people," she reminded, pointing out each place. As each day passed and the children heard about more places, she was pleased they also had new questions and curiosities.

Hattie understood repetition when educating children. One had to retell the importance of revering God and loving Him more than anything or anyone else in the world. That was a principal, as was regular attendance at church. But what she hadn't expected was that some children felt God had local competition.

"Who cares about church? Chief Ross protects and guides us," Buck griped impatiently one day. "He is our leader."

The little boy, as she had learned from Hannah, came from a family that did not particularly trust whites. They held true to many old ways. Hattie had never before encountered this tradition face-to-face. How ironic that this boy ended up at her mission school. Surely she could gradually open Buck's heart.

Two days before the rally, when Buck was bragging about Chief Ross and all he had done for the Cherokees, Hattie stopped to listen after class. Clearly, Buck's words were a repetition of things he had heard at home or in community gatherings. As a child, he might not even understand some of the things he was echoing. But his words revealed respect for authority and Cherokee honor.

Hattie tucked this fact behind her ear for later use. Because James had so many brothers, perhaps he might shed some light on dealing with difficult boys. Hattie also needed him to enlighten her more about Chief John Ross. That very night, even though he seemed a bit distracted with the fox- hunting dogs, she had the chance to ask him.

"Chief Ross is a towering figure," James confirmed, brushing one feisty dog's burr-laden coat. "The man really is godlike to some. He is equally adept in white culture as well as Indian culture. All his combined skills make him a unique leader, spokesman, strategist, and statesman. He's respected in the corridors of power in Washington, DC where he frequently negotiates for the Cherokees. But he's just as capable of standing beside the common man. Probably the biggest anomaly is that he is revered by the full-bloods even though he's only one-eighth Cherokee. "

"I had heard that. And, given the factions, it's amazing. Where did he learn how to be such a man for all people? " Hattie pressed.

"I think it's his background. He had an educated Scottish father and a mixed-blood Cherokee mother," James continued, now inspecting the paws of a limping dog for thorns. "Ross commands respect because he's well-educated, but not too aristocratic. He's experienced life from nearly every vantage point. By the era of his childhood, the Cherokee people were already the most civilized and powerful tribe in North America. As a young man, he started fighting for welfare and autonomy. Yet even though the Cherokees progressed as a people, their land ownership rights were violated by the government. When there's injustice, loss, or destruction, he never flinches. Many credit him with the rebuilding of the Cherokee Nation here."

Hattie petted a little runt from a recent litter. "Well, I don't care what Erminia plans. If I get the chance, I'm going to meet him," she vowed. "Hopefully, his influence can inspire these little Cherokee boys. Grace said he's a Methodist, though. If I invited him to the classroom, would that raise eyebrows?"

"Oh no, he and Worcester are on good terms," James clarified. "He's attended the mission church occasionally and even helped pay for the bell. Those two men endured much hardship for their common loyalty to the Cherokees before removal. When whites ran amuck with greed for land, Ross's home was seized by a lottery winner. Then his wife died on the freezing, heartless trip to this new homeland. You already know how Georgia got heavy-handed over Worcester's Cherokee loyalty and sent him to prison. Those two men have worked together on many other problems for decades and respect each other's commitment."

Hattie revered the character of long-suffering leaders. To hear of their cooperation made her feel secure. How many lessons could she draw, how much harder could she commit to the task ahead knowing that such towering men led the way?

"But what got you so interested in Chief Ross?" James questioned, as he secured the dogs in their pen for the night.

"Those naughty boys disrupt my class. One can't distinguish between Chief Ross and God. I'm not sure what to do when wayward boys cause trouble," she added, going on to explain about Buck and Lucas.

"Oh, bad boys, huh? Well, when they get too mischievous, give them a taste of their own medicine," James responded wryly.

"Like what?" Hattie countered.

"I'd tell them to close their eyes and put their heads down. Then, I would walk the room and read aloud. If anyone looked up or made a sound, they'd have to stay after school and their parents would be informed. I can't speak for you, Hattie, but for the worst offenders, I would drop a couple of fishing worms down their necks. Suddenly, they would learn what their pranks feel like."

"Only a man can do that. I'll have to come up with something else," she said as he brushed her forehead with a tender kiss.

Given James's humor, kindness, and patience with her, Hattie entertained second thoughts about the possibility that he had a Louisiana love interest. When she brought it up to Grace, the response was something she didn't anticipate, but should have.

"That sweetheart comment was just Erminia's needling, in my opinion," Grace frowned.

In exasperation, Hattie placed both hands on top of her head and twisted side-to- side. She had let Erminia frustrate her unnecessarily. The topic wasn't worthy of more comment, so she changed the subject to Chief Ross. Several questions needed to be asked and Grace would have answers.

"Yes, he is a serious man," Grace replied. "You won't really understand until you meet him, Hattie. I bet he'll be in Tahlequah for the National Council Meeting. Maybe you'll get the chance to see him if he comes to the rally."

"Oh, good. I told James I intended to find a way to make his acquaintance," Hattie boasted.

"He's not in the Cherokee Nation that often, from what I've heard," Grace continued. "His work is never done."

"But is his family here?" Hattie queried. "Maybe I can ask some of them to introduce me."

"He's got family all over the place," Grace shrugged. "My husband even whispers that he has a few children that aren't exactly accounted for."

"Why, Grace," Hattie drew back. "Is it true?"

"Your guess is as good as mine," Grace shrugged. "He travels extensively, so he hasn't been without opportunity."

◦ 12 ◦

Deception

OFFICE OF THE U.S. MARSHAL
FEDERAL DISTRICT COURT
WESTERN DISTRICT OF ARKANSAS
FORT SMITH, ARKANSAS

October 13, 1856
Miss Harriet A. Sheldon
Park Hill Mission
Park Hill, Cherokee Nation

Dear Miss Sheldon,

Upon receipt of your confidential letter of 29 September, I dispatched an order for your protection. Since approximately 1 October, your dwelling and person have been under constant guard. An investigation is underway. Proceed with that assurance until further notice.

Respectfully,

John Stewart Latta
Deputy U.S. Marshal

❖ ❖ ❖

The afternoon before the rally, Hattie dismissed the students and tidied the classroom. Unexpectedly, Abijah Hicks appeared at the door. He removed his hat politely when Hattie invited him in. He'd kept his word to learn more about Sweet Berry's family situation. Gathering the facts proved to be quite a challenge, he indicated. There were matters of confidentiality, law, safety, crime, love, and bereavement.

The man Percy had seen passed out drunk at her home was Deke, her father. Years ago, at the crisis of removal when he was a little child, his mother entrusted him to relatives who decided to hide in the mountains rather than die on the endless march to this unknown land. They had raised Deke, although he occasionally saw his mother when she visited. Now in his thirties, Deke suddenly showed up one night in Park Hill with Sweet Berry and two other children. A charming, but angry, full-blood Cherokee, he claimed to be farming for his mother, but mainly he caroused with whiskey sellers.

Abijah had learned these things from Deke's full-blood mother, Salali, when he and Percy walked Sweet Berry home one day. When Abijah told her his link with Rev. Worcester's family and the mission, she nearly wept. Salali revered Rev. Worcester, but didn't come to church since he only preached in English. The woman was wondering whom to trust since Deke brought unexpected upheavals into her life. She said she hadn't even told her neighbors what was happening because Deke warned her to stay silent. Sending Sweet Berry to the mission school was her way of figuring out the challenges. But Rev. Worcester was gone, so he couldn't help.

Sweet Berry's late mother, Chesney, had died less than a year ago. She was not Cherokee, but rather a Mulatto woman from down

South. After she was freed early in life, she fled her original home where she had learned many valuable sewing skills. Later, she married a free Negro man, by whom she had two children, Levi, age 9 and Ida, age 8. Like most free Negro men, her husband had struggled desperately to find work. She sewed for women and kept food on the table. He often had to beg for even the lowest wage, which usually accompanied the most dangerous jobs. Sadly, the place where he worked was so perilous he was killed.

Poor Chesney, also now dead, had struggled alone as a widow with two children. She encountered all sorts of problems. Barely able to support the children, even though she was a skilled seamstress, she was pursued by Deke because of her beauty. Before long, they married and then had Sweet Berry. Salali knew little except through letters from Deke saying he finally had a family. When Deke and the children showed up unannounced in Park Hill, she was stunned to learn that the children had Negro blood. And language challenges.

"The family struggles because Levi and Ida only speak English," Abijah explained with regret. "And Deke is gone most of the time."

Hattie suddenly wondered if learning all this might cause Abijah trouble. He was a law-abiding Cherokee man well respected in Park Hill. Or would his loyalties to Rev. Worcester and the mission take precedence?

As was now obvious, Abijah said Sweet Berry looked nothing like her two half-siblings. She appeared fully Cherokee, which benefitted her greatly. Levi and Ida, on the other hand, were free, but could easily be mistaken for slave children. So, for their safety, Deke and his mother rarely allowed them outside the house.

When Deke began to disappear for longer periods of time, his mother didn't know what to do. This put Levi and Ida in further jeopardy and isolation. They couldn't go to school because an 1841

Cherokee Nation law made educating Negroes illegal. The only redeeming piece of information was that Deke's mother had come to love Levi and Ida.

Hattie blinked so fast she was almost dizzy. Sweet Berry's family story stunned her. Since it felt this complicated to her, how confusing must it feel to the children? Their heritage was impossible to untangle. And how it must hurt Levi and Ida to be alone and uncertain in a strange place.

But Abijah wasn't finished. Rubbing his chin, he began again. "Sadly, Deke is falling more deeply into company with whiskey sellers. He barely farms anymore. His mother tends to say he works long hours somewhere else, but people will soon grow suspicious."

Hopefully, Sweet Berry could remain at the mission school because she spoke English, looked Cherokee, and could "slip by" the 1841 law. Levi and Ida learned almost nothing while sequestered at home where Salali only spoke Cherokee. Consequently, Sweet Berry was forced into the role of translator, which demanded too much responsibility for a little, grieving child who had lost so much.

A trusted, mixed-blood neighbor had told Abijah that Levi and Ida went outdoors at night. They wandered about, sometimes stopping at the slave cabins of nearby plantations. They longed for freedom, but were lonely and scared, not knowing where to turn. If anything should happen to Deke, or if Salali could not care for them, they would be out in the cold. No full-blood would take them in and no mixed-blood would want to feed non-working Negro orphans.

"I'm not sure what will happen if Agent Butler learns of this," Abijah added. "I hope he won't remove Sweet Berry from school."

Hattie just sat there, incapable of formulating her own

thoughts, much less a response. Her mind ran along several trains of thought. Clouded by all the information, she scribbled a few notes as she decided how she felt.

"If ever there were people who need help and God's love, it is Deke's family," she began, trying to gather her wits. "I'm so grateful for all you struggled to learn, Abijah. It would be easy to be overcome and turn away. Much is at stake here."

"I feel the same way, Hattie. It encourages me to hear you say that," Abijah brightened. "I had already decided to deal with Deke man-to-man. He's coming to the temperance rally tomorrow."

"That's wonderful," Hattie brightened. "One way or another, we must fight to offer hope to these people. The mission may have missed a beat or two while Rev. Worcester has been gone, but we can't miss this chance."

October 14, 1856
Dear Father and Mother,

Nearly three months have passed since I said goodbye to you in Utica. In the interim, I feel I've lived an entire new lifetime. The days of travel and then of adjustment came faster and faster as they filled with activity, occurrences, complications, and events far beyond anything I could have expected or imagined.

No longer do I read everything at the library. There is no library here. Yet, excitement surrounds the school, which requires me to teach both academic subjects and domestic skills to both girls and boys. You will chuckle, but I finally learned to knit! Soon, butchering will familiarize me with everything from smoking and drying to curing and the collection of suet. Later, I will learn the processes of soap and candle making so I can teach them.

The children—over thirty of them—are precocious and alert learners. One particularly shy and silent girl stole my heart through her needs and unpredictable home situation. She's joined the singing now as we prepare to march at a temperance rally this Thursday. By then, I hope the children will no longer itch with mange, which we've battled. I'm also learning about herbal candies to treat the worms they get from drinking spring water. I wish I had room and time to write more about my unbelievable discoveries. They would fill volumes.

During this busy season, I have benefitted from the many prayers you undoubtedly lifted on my behalf. The serious objections you voiced about my decision to leave Utica for the Cherokee Nation ring in my memory. While I don't want to add to those concerns, I will merely confirm your wisdom.

My days here have demanded indescribable attention to every level of skill and the resurrection of lessons learned in many arenas. From dawn to dusk, I reason, plan, write, speak, convince, cajole, implement, manage, discipline, learn, teach, rationalize, argue, observe, fix, hide, soothe, explain, explode, laugh, cry, comfort, and pray.

Your letters remind me that families are precious. I do not mean to dishonor ours by the direction my life has taken. Yet, fate has placed me in situations as improbable as they are exhilarating. It is true that slavery is the law here. Most Cherokees are subsistence farmers, but a good many mixed-blood Cherokees, some wealthy, own plantations and slaves. The complications of slavery in the Cherokee Nation, however, are no more concerning to northerners who fund missions like this than to the likes of Rev. Worcester and other Christians who find themselves surrounded by the institution. Literally, slavery is a cross to bear—a rugged, heavy one.

One of those Christians is a man I mentioned in my last letter. A son of Arkansas, James Latta is kind, intelligent, judicious, politically savvy, and responsible. His livelihood requires him to oversee slaves on a plantation here in Park Hill. Like you, as well as his father—an enterprising and inventive land-owner manipulated through marriage into becoming a slave-owner—James believes in the humanity of all Negroes and educates them as best he can for the freedom he believes will come. I respect his integrity, just as I accept Rev. Worcester's occasional, complicating employment of others' slaves amid crying labor shortages.

Simply stated, James Latta inhabits my thoughts, feelings, and every moment I can give him. When we are together, my life becomes something lovely and complete.

I love you with all my heart and hope you can find a way to accept this news, even though you may not understand it.

Your loving daughter,
Hattie

Before daylight, every child arrived on time dressed warmly for the long ride to Tahlequah. Rhoda had prepared some picnic baskets for the trip. As Hattie supervised the loading of two wagons, an endless array of comments and excited questions flew back and forth between the children. Grace would supervise one wagon and Hattie the other. She wished Dwight could attend and lead the procession as Marshal, but he bowed out due to some seriously feverish patients.

It seemed a welcome stroke of luck that the crisp weather cooperated. Ample sunshine began to warm the air as the children settled onto the wagon's fresh bed of hay. The atmosphere was charged with anticipation.

"As we pass places you like, tell me. Maybe there are others you want to visit. Let's have as many comments, dreams, and stories as possible," Hattie instructed the children in her wagon. "Remember, I have something to learn from each one of you."

"I know we're not going past Hunter's Home," Mary Covel offered soon. "But I've talked to a couple of older Cherokee girls who attended a beautiful party there."

"I heard Mr. Murrell introduced some girls to young Fort Gibson officers." Hattie related. "What else did they tell you?"

Mary shared about a certain winter social. The young guests had sipped punch ladled from an immense bowl after dancing in the west parlor. The party had been all the more exciting because the house was decorated for Christmas.

Hattie had walked by that parlor and remembered its tall, elegant mirrors burnished with gold leaf. There had been sparkling chandeliers with crystal prisms that cast rainbows on the walls. Below the limestone mantle, brass fireplace fixtures accommodated multiple logs. Mary's report joined her past excitement and let her picture the amazing birdcage room filled with scores and scores of singing, yellow canaries. Now she wished she had snooped around the house a bit more.

"I hope I'll get the chance to go inside one day," Mary mused.

Hattie weighed such opulence against the slave quarters just outside that house. Riches could cause problems. It wasn't by design, however, that Park Hill was where the wealthiest Cherokees had chosen to settle. Even so, she wished she had known this before accepting her job. Nothing could change it now. No matter where wealth was found, there was usually a lack of it nearby. The haves and the have-nots didn't see eye-to-eye. How could factional resentment be curbed when such differences existed?

"Miss Hattie, way over there is Rose Cottage, Chief Ross's house," Percy commented.

"Has anybody ever been inside the Chief's house?" Hattie inquired.

"My grandma has," Percy added. "She talks on and on and on about it."

I should have expected as much, Hattie thought to herself. No doubt, Erminia had bragged endlessly about visiting such a grandiose, talked-about place.

"Because he's chief, I'm sure he must entertain guests of all kinds," Hattie speculated.

"Grandma talks like he's richer than the President of the United States," Percy continued, clearly awed. "All that silver, she says, closing her eyes. And... *important* china."

"Maybe its *imported* china," Hattie corrected with a warm smile. "He buys it from places like France and has it shipped, I understand."

"And he has a lot," Percy agreed, "because he feeds big crowds of people. That's why he has so many slaves for his smokehouse and dairy."

Hattie hadn't realized before that Chief Ross entertained so lavishly and to that extent. But it made sense. As the Cherokees' main diplomat, he must accommodate many official visitors. And maybe a few unofficial guests. Perhaps that was one reason he maintained such a large plantation.

"It costs a lot of money," Jennie Foreman added quietly. "My father thinks there are better ways to spend it."

Hattie hid her reaction, but took note that Rev. Foreman obviously disagreed with Chief Ross's practices. How much was the chief spending? Where did the money come from? There was much more to learn about the neighbors in Park Hill and their habits.

Mr. Murrell's wagon continued up the road with the children chattering happily. Someone pointed out a grassy meadow where they had played with friends last summer. Even more wonderful, they had picked mulberries from a certain tree.

"Our family went to Rev. Worcester's for supper once," Susie inserted while her little brother and sister nodded. "Mrs. Worcester wore a big, full hoop dress."

"Oh, I see," Hattie responded blandly, wondering why Erminia would dress up so fancy. Did Erminia get along with the Foremans? It was a legitimate question and perhaps an important one. After all, Rev. Foreman and Rev. Worcester had long been close, she knew. If Erminia caused trouble between the men or the families, the Bible translation work would be much harder. Hattie respected Rev. Foreman for continuing the work even though Rev. Worcester was still away.

"When we ate at their house, our oldest brother, Austin, was still alive. That's why I remember it," Susie added. "On the way home, I made fun of Mrs. Worcester's big dress. Papa called me down, but I didn't understand why he was cross. Then I thought he brought up my brother's name. It sounded like he said 'Austin tasteless' several times. He wasn't happy, so I kept quiet."

Hattie wanted to burst out laughing. The comment made perfect sense to her, if not to naïve Susie. It was the funniest moment she had experienced in a long while. The innocence of children never ceased to amaze her. Susie had no idea her father was calling Erminia Worcester *ostentatious*.

Hattie changed the subject so she wouldn't give herself away. Prairie Lea came to mind. It had been built by Chief Ross's brother, Lewis. She had met his daughter, Mrs. Vann, who lived there with her family, at the quilting party.

"Has anyone been to Prairie Lea?" she asked.

"My papa went there once," Sweet Berry replied unexpectedly.

Hattie tried not to frown as she considered such an incongruous piece of information. What had taken a known drunkard like Deke to such an elegant residence? She didn't have a good feeling about it.

"He said Mr. Ross had carpet on the floor and a shiny Chickadee piano," Sweet Berry continued.

"That might be a *Chickering* piano," Hattie commented. "A chickadee is that bird we talked about in class."

But her thoughts were elsewhere. Lewis Ross was a wealthy mixed-blood Cherokee. Was he the sort of person that Deke might dream of associating with? But, from what she had learned from Abijah, the only kind of dealings Deke undertook were swindles. Yet Sweet Berry didn't know that. She just wanted to say something and found her chance.

"Speaking of a piano," Hattie followed up, "I was told there will be one at the temperance rally. Grace has offered to play so you'll have exciting accompaniment while you march and sing your songs."

"I went to Grace's house once," Buck offered quietly.

Grace had never mentioned her house or where she lived. Surely she didn't live in a grand house like the ones they had been discussing. When it came right down to it, Hattie knew little about Grace outside of their times together.

Now, Hattie waited for Buck to add to his comment. Yet, he grew quiet and had a strange, apprehensive expression on his face.

"Go ahead, Buck," she encouraged. "What else were you going to tell us?"

Buck looked around and acted embarrassed, which was quite out of character. Hattie wasn't sure what to make of it. In the last while, he seemed to have curtailed much of his trouble making at school.

"Grace said you are her neighbor," Hattie commented. "Have you visited in her home?"

"Well, uh, no," Buck stuttered, and then turned his back to the others. "Just forget I said anything."

How odd, Hattie thought. There had to be a reason for such behavior. Why had he mentioned being at Grace's house only to change his mind and clam up? Without an explanation, Hattie had to let it go, but wondered what it all meant. Maybe she could figure it out later with Grace's help.

The long trip filled with stories flew by. Soon, they pulled into Tahlequah. Hattie had relished the anticipation of today as much as the children. Encouraging them to talk openly had started things off very well. In fact, she had enjoyed it so much she forgot to think about the attack for a couple of hours. Not once had she recalled the dark intruder.

Other wagons full of children seemed to be everywhere. The much-anticipated temperance rally promised to be larger than Hattie had expected. Aside from the children's participation, she was counting on meeting Sweet Berry's father. Something had to end his drunkenness. Her fervent desire was not just for Deke to attend the rally, but to pledge to quit drinking alcohol. That was the only thing that could make life better for Sweet Berry and her siblings. She also wanted to become better acquainted with the whole family and get Rev. Worcester involved.

Quickly, Hattie made her way to the front in preparation for the march. Directing the children into line, she strained for a glimpse of Abijah. Deke must be the man right beside him. Hattie looked Deke over before they were introduced. She found it interesting that he looked around strategically, as if sizing up the gathering. Did he recognize anybody? Did anybody recognize him?

Deke looked a little scruffy to Hattie, despite being quite handsome. She reminded herself that he was probably still in the habit of drinking. But, hopefully, this meeting would make an impression.

As invigorating music filled the air, the rally got off to a strong start. Grace sat at the piano awaiting her turn. In the wings, Hattie and the children paused while the adult portion of the singing concluded. Their cue came when Grace began to play the opening bars of their marching song.

Proudly lifting their colorful banners, the children entered the hall singing at the top of their lungs. Sweet Berry, in particular, lifted her knees high in time to the music. Hattie knew she wanted to please her father by making a big impression.

Temperance Tune

Loud we shout "Away the bowl!"
Far away—forever.
We resolve with heart and soul,
we will touch it never!
Sweet cold water, now we sing!
Water is the dandy!
Give us water from the spring,
and fling away the brandy!

Chorus: Come and join us, one and all.
Hear our invitation.
Come and fight King Alcohol,
Drive him from the Nation!

—Samuel A. Worcester

Whether Sweet Berry grasped that her father was present for another reason, Hattie didn't know. During the songs that followed, she saw Sweet Berry waving at him. What little girl didn't want her father to notice and be proud of her?

After the children's singing ended, Sweet Berry rushed up and took Hattie by the hand, leading her to meet Deke. Hattie nodded graciously and offered kind compliments about Sweet Berry. Deke, smiling, said his daughter talked about her teacher all the time. The conversation was pleasant, though not lengthy.

Hattie found Deke to be a challenging character. He did not give much away. How he really felt or what he was really thinking was anybody's guess. Beyond smiling at his daughter, his expression did not change much. As for Deke's words, they sounded sincere. But, somehow, he lacked connection and emotion. His eyes were active, however, so Hattie knew he didn't miss what was happening.

Deke's good looks probably opened all kinds of doors, she told herself. How would she describe him? He wasn't really sullen, but something about his nature was oddly detached. For some reason, she felt that Deke was withdrawing from her, but couldn't exactly put it into perspective. Given the circumstances of his life during the last year, she could forgive him acting uncomfortable in a potentially intimidating situation.

Before the speaker urged everyone to take a seat, Hattie settled most of the children on a reserved row of benches. Deke joined Abijah on his right. Sweet Berry perched on her father's lap and gestured Percy over. Hattie knew Percy was interested in improving his Cherokee language skills and would enjoy sitting next to Deke.

Scooping up baby Ann, Hattie took a seat next to Hannah and enjoyed all the commotion. The whole crowd seemed to be drawn by the fervency of the speaker, who made time go quickly. While listening, Hattie played with the smaller children.

When the rally ended, the adults stood around for a time and exchanged pleasantries. Hattie noted with interest that when pledge time came, Abijah did not invite Deke to sign, nor did Deke do it. He had listened to the talks but was not moved. Of course, nothing was said. It just marked the fact that Abijah would need to mentor him more. In turn, Hattie would have to be patient longer. However, she decided she must find a way to visit Sweet Berry's grandmother soon.

❖ ❖ ❖

When they finally got back to Park Hill that night, the hour was late. Hattie yawned from exhaustion. She knew she would sleep soundly. Once inside her quarters, she reached to light her lamp, but kicked something in the dark and nearly tripped. As soon as the flame grew, she leaned down for a look.

It was a shoe she had not left there. Next to it, clothing was strewn on the floor. Hattie gasped, as someone or something uninvited had been there since she left in the early morning hours. On closer inspection, all her belongings were out of place! Clothing and linens were thrown across the bed, as if someone had examined each article separately. Rushing to the wardrobe, Hattie discovered, to her great dismay, that all her winter woolens were gone. Right down to the wool stockings, her entire winter wardrobe had been stolen!

A feeling so personal, so violated charged her emotions. Not again! Marshal Latta had promised he'd posted a guard, but she had never spotted him. Was some sleepy guard shirking his duties? Had he been knocked out by the robber? Maybe the guard was off tracking the criminals!

This crime must be related somehow to the threat letter and the attack. Turning with her lamp, Hattie gasped aloud as she made another terrible discovery. The place where her treasured and beautiful trunk had rested was now empty beneath her window. She let out a mournful cry.

"On no," she cried, "not that. Not that!" But it was true. The finest, most perfectly hand-crafted gift her father ever made for her no longer graced her room.

❦ ❦ ❦

The idea of being fearful never occurred to Hattie. She was too mad. These violations of her person, privacy, belongings, and quarters had gone too far. The deception must be exposed. She was tired of being a pawn in some criminal scheme by staying quiet.

But whom could she turn to? Hannah's house was too far in the dark. Besides, waking up the whole household would scare the children. The same held true for Sarah. And going to James' was utterly improper. Hattie cringed as her only option became clear. As much as she hated the prospect, she would have to take her complaint to Erminia, whose house was close by.

Bundled in her cape and carrying her lamp, Hattie shut the door behind her, ignored the dark, and rode Comet straight to the Worcester home. The hour did not deter her. When she arrived, she didn't even tie Comet at the post. This was his true home, anyway, so he would just stand there.

Rapping at the door with loud and persistent knocks, Hattie waited impatiently until a glowing light showed through the crack. Once it was open, there stood Erminia, squinty in her white night clothes and bed cap. She peered out, annoyed. Immediately, however, her expression acknowledged that something was wrong.

"Whatever has happened, Hattie?" she urged. "Why did you wake me at this hour? Are you alright?"

"I am not alright," Hattie fumed. "Thieves broke into my quarters while I attended the temperance rally."

Erminia looked alarmed as she led Hattie to a chair. "Oh, dear," she sympathized in wide-eyed concern. "I'm so sorry, Hattie. I'll put the kettle on."

"They took all my winter woolen clothing," Hattie raved, shivering from cold. "But worst of all, they stole my treasure—the leather trunk father made especially for me."

"Oh, that's awful! Was it just a random crime, do you think? You didn't draw attention to the trunk, did you?" she questioned.

"No, not really. I had Sarah, Grace and Jesse's help when I moved to the mission. No one else was around," Hattie answered.

"Has anyone else seen your things or visited your quarters?" Erminia inquired.

Hattie suspected the question held a hidden, second purpose of setting her up. Undoubtedly, Erminia wanted to know what domestic skills she was teaching in her quarters. Hattie had ready answers. Sewing and knitting lessons for girls would soon begin. After Grace taught her soap and candle-making, more lessons would follow. She had nothing to hide and could care less if Erminia liked her answer or not.

"Nobody but friends, yet. Except, wait. I brought a new, little student to my room on a couple of occasions," Hattie paused as a painful realization began to dawn. Then she brought one hand up to her mouth in disbelief.

"Who was it? Did you show them your trunk?" Erminia pursued.

Hattie bent forward and folded herself down protectively to rest her elbows on her knees. Cradling her head between her hands, she realized the saddest coincidence.

"It was Sweet Berry," she whispered. "You don't know her."

Erminia insisted that Hattie spend the night in the safety of her home. Having never been inside, Hattie found the house was not just comfortable, but very clean. Attractive homemade curtains framed the windows, comfortable but worn furniture was arranged invitingly, and the house smelled of the apples, just like Hannah's.

Erminia had made good use of the big yellow apples from the tree outside.

Hattie faintly recalled that Erminia hosted endless, unexpected guests over the last many years. What an out-of-character scenario. Yet, it grew in realization as she walked past several attractive bedrooms upstairs. Although virtually impossible to imagine, Erminia must be good at hosting, cooking, and cleaning.

That troubled night, Hattie's fidgety sleep wasn't restful. She suffered scary dreams about thieves creeping up on her while she attended the temperance rally. Sweet Berry had definitely seen and admired her trunk. The memory of her sniffing the leather's aroma helped Hattie draw conclusions. Deke must have learned about the trunk from his innocent daughter and then arranged for the robbery during the temperance rally.

The next morning, Hattie still trusted her conclusion. But question after question mounted. Was Deke also her attacker? The robbery could have been a follow up since the attack hadn't driven her away.

Was Deke working with the writer of the threat letter? Hattie reconsidered her previous theories about that. The letter dripped with distaste for her as a teacher from the north. More Cherokee teachers should be hired, the writer seemed to insist. She'd also heard repeatedly that a growing number of Cherokees thought northern teachers were abolitionists.

On the other hand, perhaps the theft of her trunk simply related to its sale value, which would raise money so criminals could buy whiskey. But how many thieves were involved? Where would they strike next?

When Hattie went downstairs at daylight, she discovered Erminia had been up for some time. Upon entering the warm, inviting kitchen, a full breakfast awaited her at the table. Erminia's linens were nicely starched and pressed. A little plume of field grass graced a tiny vase.

Momentarily, Erminia heaped a plate with steaming food and served it to Hattie. Perfectly round eggs. Smoky, savory bacon. Hot, golden biscuits. Creamy meat gravy made with fresh milk. And the most delicious, cinnamon- infused apple butter she had ever tasted. It practically brought tears to her eyes.

Before discussing the theft, Erminia showed Hattie a letter she had written to Chief Ross about the break-in and theft. Hattie fell speechless when Erminia promised to deliver it in person after she left for school.

Marshall John Stewart Latta happened to be in the area. He stopped by the school that afternoon to bolster Hattie and learn more about the theft. After dismissing her students early, she took him to see her disheveled quarters, recalling that he linked most crimes to the motives of whiskey sellers.

Hattie calmed and started feeling better to have his attention. John Stewart treated her with great respect. Hopefully James had not told him—or the rest of the Latta family—that she was moody and naïve.

"I need a list of all that was stolen," John Stewart requested, perusing the situation.

"It's nearly everything for winter: a waterproof and wool cloak, a dark dress of flannel, a walking dress, several pairs of cotton and wool stockings, and one pair of hard-wearing shoes. But the most valuable and memorable item was my custom leather trunk. My dear father made it for me," she added, biting her lip.

"I'm real sorry, Hattie. It would be nice to give you hope. But honesty is the best policy here. I know of several gangs Deke may run with. Their networks sell stolen items. He might have passed a tip to another network, though. We don't know for sure that he's behind this robbery," he speculated, patting her shoulder. "But your belongings are long gone. Whiskey drinking thieves know how to move stolen merchandise so it can't be traced. They're also experts with alibis in case they're arrested."

"I understand," Hattie moped. "Your honesty helps."

"While we're on that, you need to know something else," he added. "I discussed your intruder with James. He has helped coordinate the guards of your quarters."

Hattie nursed a deep need for support and intended to make the facts public. After school, she headed straight for Sarah's house for a heart-to-heart. It was confession time. What she had to say would come as a shock. But Sarah was very good at sorting out problems. As usual, Sarah welcomed her with open arms.

"Tell me about the children," she began enthusiastically. "I miss being in the classroom."

"It's a menagerie," Hattie said, uncertain where to begin. "Already, I'm faced with what happens behind closed doors."

"That sounds serious," Sarah winced. "Inside our doors, my

Laura and Mary Covel absolutely love you. Mary comes home so happy every day."

"I wish with all my heart to be a positive role model to them and all the others. But someone is trying to prevent me from that. I am in a vulnerable, frightening position, Sarah. And I need you to give me some perspective."

"Why?" Sarah frowned. "What makes you use such words?"

"Because I'm scared. The reason I'm here is to tell you about three terrible things. While you were at Tullahassee, someone sneaked the most awful threat letter under my door," Hattie admitted. "I was warned not to tell, so I kept it secret, well, except from James. Just thinking about it gives me a chill. The letter said I was not wanted here. That's putting it nicely. Some troublemaker is watching and waiting for the chance to grab me. He threatened to take me to the gallows in Tahlequah! By the time James returned, I was desperate for a ray of hope. He promised to have John Stewart look into it. A sentry was posted, but that didn't work."

"Merciful heavens, Hattie! Why?" Sarah gasped, looking up as Nancy joined them.

"Because late Saturday night after the move, a horrible hooded man attacked me and I barely escaped. He almost scared me to death."

"Oh, Hattie," Nancy exclaimed, taking her hands. "That is evil and brazen."

"I can't seem to quiet the memory. He was a tall, thin man in dark clothes and gloves. I'm certain he—or they—knew I was in there alone. It was the most heart-stopping fright of my life."

"This has gone too far," Sarah declared, aghast. "You have no comfort, do you? It's constant terror!"

Hattie nodded soberly. "To make matters worse, I discovered

a robbery after the temperance meeting last night. My trunk and all my winter things have been stolen! The criminals are coming closer and closer. Now I'm on edge every second and shake like a leaf when I'm alone. But I know I should show that fear won't stop me. So, I'm trying my best to go about my business and not give in. It's really hard, though."

"Well, I say it's time to do something," Sarah proclaimed angrily. "Once Dwight's back and the children are in bed, we all need to talk this over by the fire—as a family. You cannot bear this burden alone."

Feeling bolstered, Hattie drew strength from Sarah's action plan. The three of them continued to visit and they reassured Hattie. She relaxed a little, believing that they could and would help.

Then, suddenly, the door flew wide open and banged against the wall. Dwight rushed in, harried and caked with dust. Coughing, he looked left and right, before catching sight of Hattie. Just as his shoulders relaxed, he turned back toward the door. Right behind him, James followed frantically.

"Hattie! Thank God you're here," James exhaled, rushing toward her. "I went to find you and you were gone."

"I couldn't go back to my quarters just yet," she replied, worried anew because more than their good humor seemed to be gone. "What's the matter with you two?"

Sarah and Nancy bolted upright simultaneously. Jacob appeared from his room and walked toward his son looking concerned. Something had happened to James and Dwight. Both were upset, distracted, and exhausted.

To gather their wits, one walked frantically around the room with hands on his hips, looking up at the ceiling; the other bent forward to catch his breath, hands on his knees. Watching them closely, Hattie's fear rose and caught in her throat.

"Say something!" Sarah appealed. "You look awful and it's scaring me!"

Neither man could reply yet. By now, Dwight stood at the basin pouring water on his head while James wiped his face with his shirt tail. For the first time in Hattie's experience, they were speechless. She waited impatiently while her stomach churned.

Sarah became so agitated she filled the silence. "Well, Hattie just revealed her own horror. It's hanging over her head like a swinging noose. Does that have anything to do with what's happened to you?"

"Yes," James choked, still winded. "Abijah ... rode up to Murrell's a couple of hours ago ... yelling for help ... screaming my name ... panic-stricken. He needed John Stewart and his posse, but they were already gone."

Dwight gently pushed James into a chair and handed him a cup of water. He explained how James had flagged him down while looking for Hattie. They had ridden at breakneck speed from one place to the other.

Dwight warned the women that they had bad news. As he spoke, James took a long drink, which revealed a bloodied rip in his shirt sleeve. Startled, Hattie heard the plaintive howling of James's favorite hound outside. Even the dog knew something was wrong.

"I got Abijah down from his horse. He wasn't making sense and kept pointing in the distance. That's when I saw turkey vultures circling above his woods. That always means trouble. I found out that the family was alright, which was relieving. Then, Mr. Murrell rushed up. We got more out of Abijah and then rushed back to the woods together. The closer we got, the more we dreaded what was ahead."

"Go on," Dwight insisted before turning to his mother. "Why don't you put on some coffee?"

"I'm think I'd better sit down," fragile Sarah commented, but in a strong voice. "Whatever it is, we have to face it."

"Abijah led us to his awful discovery in an old, half-dead tree surrounded by those dirty vultures," James revealed, shoulders hunched. "Somebody had hollowed out the trunk and stuffed the corpse of man into the crevice, standing up. He had been dead about a day. The buzzards had pecked out his eyes. He was the new Moravian missionary. Some hellion had actually tied his Bible right to his body. They used the other end of the rope they hung him with."

Nancy Hitchcock covered her mouth with a hand and then hid her face in the hollow of Jacob's arm. Hattie wilted, realizing that missionaries had just become targets.

"My God," Jacob exclaimed. A lifelong missionary, he looked as stunned as Hattie felt.

Only Sarah shot up out of her chair, her face now stony with anger and resolve.

"That's not just any old murder," she condemned, gaining strength. "That's a message. I hear it loud and clear. In light of what Hattie just shared, she has more reason than ever to be fearful."

Within hours, Dwight's house nearly burst at the seams. Among those who crowded in to discuss the developments were his family and parents, Abijah and Hannah, James and Hattie, John Stewart Latta, and Grace. Cherokee Agent George Butler cleared his throat to bring the meeting to order, but nobody paid attention. Multiple comments had interrupted him previously and then the crowd burst into conversation all over again. To a person, they were up in arms over the murder. Hattie witnessed crying, cringing, and cursing.

"Chief Ross contacted me about Miss Sheldon's robbery," Agent Butler practically shouted in a disgruntled tone. "Calm down, folks. The Tahlequah District sheriff and I have a potential lead. All these crimes are happening at once. And then, Marshal Latta's posse caused a stir in another case. They weren't pursuing suspects here with my blessing, though. Yet, under the circumstances of the murder, we have agreed to work closely toward a joint resolution of this deadly crisis."

"Do you know if the deceased had been threatened like Miss Sheldon?," Dwight inquired aggressively.

"Not that I know of," Agent Butler responded. "His wife ... his widow, who is terribly distraught, told me she knew of nothing."

"Miss Sheldon undoubtedly remains a target for revenge, scare tactics, or punishment," James pursued, standing up for emphasis.

"That's correct," Agent Butler confirmed. "We do not know if the missionary's murder is related to her threat letter, attack, or robbery. The best policy now is for her to avoid being alone. I know you all want to help, so I recommend she stay with Mrs. Worcester, where she'll be safe and..."

"No," the voices of Sarah and Hannah replied in perfect unison. Looking at one another sheepishly, Hannah nodded to Sarah, who continued.

"That is not realistic, sir," Sarah argued softly. "Hattie is needed nearer the school anyway. I request that you post more guards by her quarters at night so she can remain there without disruption."

"That seems a bit extreme," Agent Butler argued.

"No, it's not! You need to protect her," James demanded. "She must never be at risk."

Even though she was clammy with fear, Hattie's heart warmed slightly that James would argue for her safety so strongly. She wanted to linger on his comments, but shuddered afresh at the idea of becoming a murder victim.

That poor missionary down in the woods! What kind of vindictive maniac killed one so innocent? He was new to the area! But perhaps that was the point. The poor victim hadn't had a chance to make anybody mad. They killed him because of his role or his background. He must have suffered unthinkable agony knowing they were going to hang him. Hattie couldn't bear it.

"I'll have to run that idea up the ladder," Agent Butler replied evenly to James and Sarah. "I can't promise anybody full time. You people in the community may have to pitch in, as well. Now, I apologize, but we must adjourn. I have a previous commitment over at Murrell's on another matter."

"Before we go," Dwight interrupted, "I'd like everyone's agreement in case there are inquiries about why we gathered here. Until we know more and release the information publicly, just say we met to discuss procedures in case the cholera reaches us. I actually heard of some cases within a few hundred miles of here."

·13·

Waiting and Listening

While trying to keep her mind off the grisly murder, Hattie fumbled nervously with her knitting needles. The senseless killing had joined her earlier fears to set off a reaction in her body that weakened her knees, turned her stomach over, and left her heart racing. For want of anything else to think about, she reflected on the astonishing turn in Erminia's behavior last night. Erminia seemed sympathetic and did nice things to comfort her. But she wasn't sure she could trust a change that sudden. Had Erminia turned over a new leaf or did she feel guilty about something? There were just so many inconsistencies.

Next, Hattie speculated about complications for Sweet Berry and her unfortunate siblings at home. Impatiently, she had agreed to postpone any visits there in light of Deke's almost certain involvement in the threats against her. Had Deke killed the missionary, too? How terrifying to imagine Sweet Berry living with a murderer! Hattie wanted to do something, but took John Stewart's and Agent Butler's warnings seriously now.

Before long, she was to have started making teacher's visits to the homes of students. Sweet Berry had been on the top of her list. If only the lawmen could make a quick arrest so things could get back to normal. But what was normal, anyway?

During the delay while these various investigations took place, maybe she could show Sweet Berry how the mission could assist her grandmother. Since Rev. Foreman had given Hattie some translated Bible chapters, she would send them home with Sweet Berry. Surely, the Bible's teachings would make things better in the household.

The challenge of goals raised Hattie's spirits a little. As she climbed into bed, she asked God to show her the way, open doors, and use her to bless the Cherokees. Beyond them, she needed to be thankful for the others who had protected, befriended, helped, advised, and even warned her. She took comfort from a memory of Jacob Hitchcock's prayer for his family to remain "healthy and together." Hattie had never heard things like that in a prayer before. Perhaps she had taken good health and family togetherness for granted. To people in Park Hill, those things were valuable.

Sarah had prayed with unusual appeals, too. She asked God for safety from dreaded winter illnesses. That, too, reminded Hattie to take stock, be grateful every day, and pray for safety. The warnings around her pointed to how quickly things could change.

On Sunday, the Hitchcocks collected Hattie before church. An unusually good crowd had gathered. After the service, she made her rounds to speak to people. James acknowledged her, but had been drawn into conversation. The animated neighbors talking to him seemed engrossed in a way they hadn't been before.

"Yes, arrests were made," he was saying. "More of the thieves have been caught."

Hattie could barely contain herself. Hope swept through her heart as she waited to speak privately with James. Evidently, he had heard the news on his way to church.

"Rest easy now," he encouraged her later later. "They caught the robbers and their leader, Sweet Berry's father. You're going to get asked lots of questions at school, though."

"I don't mind questions. Were my things recovered? Did the men confess to having threatened me? Were they linked to the theft of Fred and Martha's team of horses?" Hattie asked anxiously.

"Deke hasn't confessed to any of the charges," James replied. "All I know now is that he's in custody and very angry."

Thinking ahead already, Hattie wondered aloud. "Now that he's out of the way, I can visit the home and start helping his family!"

"Just wait a while, Hattie. Let's be certain he'll be held in jail through the trial. We don't want anything to jeopardize you," James warned.

But she heard something else. To Hattie, the arrest got Deke out of the home long enough for her to make a good start. She probably had a few days before the case got a judge's attention. That meant she could go to Sweet Berry's home immediately.

Hattie prepared for a barrage of questions at school and made plans for concealed projects with Levi and Ida. But sensitivity was called for, as Sweet Berry would be devastated by her father's incarceration. Hattie's gain was Sweet Berry's loss; the child's only parent had just gone to jail. She was sure to be crushed. So, despite her own relief, Hattie's first priority as a kind teacher was to support the children and help them understand.

※ ※ ※

The moment Sweet Berry started crying big tears, Hattie did her best to explain. An arrest was complicated, so she appealed to childlike reasoning. Sweet Berry had no clue whatsoever that her father was a thief. The loss of her mother was still quite fresh, as well. On top of that, Sweet Berry's history with her grandmother happened to be quite short. The little girl felt awfully alone.

At least Sweet Berry knew her father drank too much whiskey. That was only a first step in Hattie's logic, however. Getting across the rest of the bad news could be harder. Hattie knew it was appropriate to respect the family unit, now led by Grandmother Salali. But how much did Salali understand? This question raised the issue of providing for the three children. Salali probably felt overwhelmed.

In the midst of these complications, Hattie said as little as possible and kept Sweet Berry right by her side. The little girl watched her, turned to her for guidance and permission, and trusted Hattie with her loneliness. Little Sweet Berry just wanted to be close. And Hattie understood, for that's exactly what she wanted from James.

"I miss my Papa," Sweet Berry moaned. "I like the present he gave me, Miss Hattie."

"That was nice of him," Hattie replied, slightly distracted as she planned the home visit.

※ ※ ※

Hattie kept her ears open for news about Deke from Fort Smith, the site of the jail for the U.S. District Court for the Western District of Arkansas. Its jurisdiction included Indian Territory, much to the chagrin of Agent Butler. In a couple of days, word came that Deke and his gang would be held over for trial. This was confirmation that he would not be at Salali's home any time soon, if ever. Hattie was counting on a conviction. Giving thanks through a long, deep sigh, she concluded that God had cleared a big obstacle.

Now she would make her teacher's visit, although Sweet Berry would have to translate. Perhaps Salali needed empathy or even encouragement to read Rev. Foreman's translated Bible chapters. Abijah had continued to share helpful information which helped Hattie plan. Salali was a sixty-year old widow who had been born in Georgia. In 1825, when she was a young woman, the Cherokee Nation adopted Sequoyah's life-changing alphabet. Soon afterward, Salali learned to read and write.

On occasion, she had attended Rev. Worcester's church in Park Hill although she didn't speak English. Since the church drew mostly mixed-blood Cherokees, she kept her distance. Hattie wondered if this was more evidence of growing pressure not to socialize much with mixed-bloods. Salali's attitude about mixed-bloods had improved, however, since she started caring for Sweet Berry, Levi, and Ida, all of whom were mixed-bloods, just of different sorts.

Grace seemed unusually quiet, but attentive. "I can see the relief in your eyes, Hattie. Deke can't hurt you anymore."

"You have no idea," Hattie responded. "I'm already sleeping better."

"My husband said to tell you that Deke was undoubtedly behind the bad things happening to you," Grace added. "He emphasized that your worries are over and life can calm down now."

"Really? Tell him thank you. Am I ever going to meet your husband?" Hattie asked.

"Well, his life is complicated right now. I'm worried about his nervousness," Grace confided solemnly. "He says that old, unsolved murder of the mean woman is getting fresh attention. The sheriff is sniffing around."

As that first full month of school drew to a close, Hattie took Sweet Berry all the way home. The time was right. She could meet Salali and lay some groundwork for a teacher's visit later. Sweet Berry's family would still be reeling, no doubt, from the accusations against Deke. That presented an opening for Hattie to connect with them and establish herself as someone they could trust.

As Salali's house came into view, Sweet Berry jumped down from Comet and ran ahead, calling to her grandmother. By the time Hattie reached the door, Salali stood waiting to greet her. The woman looked older than her years, her tanned face weathered and care worn. Threads of silver streaked through her long, black hair.

"I can explain her words, Miss Hattie," said Sweet Berry, looking back and forth from her grandmother to her teacher.

"She say thank you for coming home with me," Sweet Berry translated.

"Tell her I am sad for your family," Hattie began slowly. She had to speak the right things. This was the first time she had been face-to-face with any woman facing such an uphill battle.

"Grandma say to come inside," Sweet Berry added.

The house, consisting of four rooms, was constructed of heavy, hewn logs. Hattie glanced from the lime mortar between them to the whittled chairs that anchored each side of the stone fireplace. Fascinated, she rubbed her hand across a brown and white spotted animal hide and then followed Sweet Berry past the spinning wheel. She was glad the house was solid and had a wood floor. As she entered the main room, Sweet Berry suddenly began to jump up and down.

"Look, Miss Hattie," she chimed excitedly.

When Hattie turned, she experienced one of the most dumbfounding, unforeseen jolts of her lifetime. There, sitting in the corner, was her treasured trunk! Somehow, she managed to keep her mouth from flying open and tears from pouring out of her eyes. A sudden, extra heartbeat thundered so heavily that she flushed. The gravity of what had happened started to sink in.

For a moment, Hattie was so stunned she couldn't even think. Deke was far more manipulative than she ever imagined. The situation had just grown terribly complicated.

"My son brought your gift here," Salali told Hattie through Sweet Berry. "Thank you."

Hattie blinked again. The robbery was characterized as a gift! It was no small consolation to know the whereabouts of her trunk. But what deception! Yet his family knew nothing of it! That was why they weren't ashamed or hiding the trunk.

"My father made it," she heard herself comment. "Isn't it handsome?"

Her first thought was how accurate Abijah's description of Deke had been. The words he used were *charming but angry*. Deke had a particularly chilling talent for telling captivating falsehoods.

"It's the best present anyone ever gave me," Sweet Berry sang. Then, leaning toward Hattie, she added, "and the biggest secret, too!"

So, little Sweet Berry believed Hattie's trunk was a gift brought here in secret. That was why she had not mentioned it before. What else could Deke have told this child to keep her quiet? Whatever it was, it allowed her to remain innocent, free, and happy. Criminals were always good liars.

Shortly, Hattie realized the depth of the swindle went even farther. Deke probably made up tall tales to embellish the surprise. How underhanded and mean of him. He must harbor contempt toward Hattie. But for what? Did he want to punish her for being a white teacher or for supporting temperance? Hattie needed to ponder the reasons much more carefully.

Why didn't he sell her trunk? Or maybe he got caught before he could. Perhaps he used the trunk theft as a warning, knowing Hattie would find out eventually. What if he was on a binge of drinking alcohol after the theft and couldn't make a trip across the Arkansas border to get rid of it? Perhaps he just meant to stash it temporarily, but then Sweet Berry recognized it. That could have led him to make up an elaborate story. And Sweet Berry, as well as her grandmother, believed it.

"What did you think when the trunk came to your house?" Hattie asked, unable to add much heart to her voice.

"When I saw it, I ran to Papa to wake him up," Sweet Berry explained. "He said he was sick, but had made a special trip to get it."

"What was wrong with him?" Hattie followed up, hoping for more clues.

"It was whiskey sick, Miss Hattie."

"My granddaughter knows too much for her years," Salali cut in through Sweet Berry's translation.

That was all Salali said. Clearly, she didn't want the child to know more. Placing a hand over her heart, she shook her head and then pointed at the trunk. After that, she walked away and might be grieving the turn of events, or Deke, or her responsibility for the children.

Hattie knew enough. It was what it was. This was not the purpose of her visit anyway. Instead, she had to regain her composure and focus on problems and needs more important than her trunk.

"Are Levi and Ida here?" Hattie inquired, not looking at Salali.

To Hattie's surprise, Sweet Berry ran from the room and returned with her two siblings. Ida, round-faced and bright-eyed, looked Hattie up and down for a long moment. Levi, tall and lean for his age, was older but more shy. They stayed close together and gazed at Hattie with neither shy nor frightened expressions. Hattie read their earnest innocence and felt great compassion. The only good thing she knew was that they spoke English.

"Hello, I'm Miss Hattie Sheldon, Sweet Berry's teacher," she introduced with a warm smile. "It's so nice to meet you. I hope we can become friends."

"I'm Ida, Miss Hattie," the girl replied openly. "Sweet Berry tells us everything she learns at school. I can read a little, but don't have no books. Levi knows some Cherokee words."

"I have many books and lessons in both English and Cherokee," Hattie replied, struggling to keep her sympathy in check. "I'd like to bring you some later if your grandmother approves. But we must keep it secret."

Ida smiled, but looked at Sweet Berry after a second and put her finger to her lips. This must be her way to let Sweet Berry know not to tell their grandmother in the other room.

"If someone finds out or Granny Salali can't keep us, will me and Levi … have to … leave?" Ida asked. "Deke was so mean to her, Miss Hattie. We didn't know what to do. Is he coming back?"

Hattie opened her mouth to reassure Ida but then watched Sweet Berry cloud up with tears. Before she could respond, Levi's quiet voice added to the emotional scene.

"We know we can't go to school, Miss Hattie," he whispered. "What's gonna happen to us?"

After she left, Hattie rode directly to James's cabin at Murrell's. He would calm her down. When he didn't answer, she redoubled her efforts and then marched to the front door of Hunter's Home. The burden in her heart had to be heard. There was no holding back after she had encountered the crying needs at Sweet Berry's house. She could barely accommodate all the levels of obstacles and emotions.

"Hello Miss Hattie," Susan chimed upon opening the door. "I ain't seen you in a month a Sundays."

Hattie was glad to see Susan. They made brief small talk before she explained that she needed to find James Latta. As Susan led her out back, she mentioned Louisiana. Susan had heard about Mr. Murrell's responsibility for his late brother's property there.

"I've heard Louisiana is about the hottest place on earth," Hattie commented.

"That's exactly what Mr. James said," Susan chuckled. "He told me he never forgets what his close friends say about it. It takes bad words to tell the truth about that sticky heat, them thick swamps, and, worst of all, them awful big mosquitos."

Hattie immediately linked the mention of James's friends in Louisiana to Erminia's comment about a sweetheart there. It must be true. The image of a beautiful girl with flowing blonde hair and endearing blue eyes filled her imagination. What should she do about it?

When they reached the barn, Susan told Hattie to wait. Several handsome hounds snooped around after eyeing her. Beautiful horses tied there seemed perfectly comfortable with the dogs. Because she had overheard James telling Fred about the particulars of fox hunting with Mr. Murrell, Hattie knew these horses and hounds were trained to work together.

Momentarily, James entered the barn striding at top speed from the grain mill. At his heel was a big, handsome hound dog. He looked none too relaxed, Hattie realized. Maybe this was a poor time for her to just show up.

"What brings you back here?" James called, the dog barking at his heels. "Be quiet, Joshua. Down! Stop barking."

"I made a discovery that John Stewart needs to know about."

"Oh, alright. But you'll have to wait," James apologized. "Mr. Murrell's got me occupied."

"Don't give it a thought," Hattie smiled, hiding her disappointment. "Can I go talk with Susan by the spring house?"

"Be my guest," James approved. "Shoo those dogs off if they bother you."

Susan smiled as Hattie approached and asked if she could wait out there. A couple of dogs had followed Hattie and were jumping up for attention.

"Them hounds keeps Mr. Latta busy," Susan giggled. "Master Murrell bless each dog with a prophet name. We all's got a favorite. Mine's that spotted one, Samuel. Mr. Latta likes old Joshua."

"They sure are friendly," Hattie laughed, patting a hound that had followed her. "What goes on at this spring house, Susan?"

"The water flows through night and day to keep food from spoilin'. My master's old spring serves folks along Park Hill Creek. Some folks just call it the branch," Susan explained. "My master got help from the slaves of Mr. Latta's father years back. They're skilled craftsmen known for buildin' on this place. They did this sandstone spring house, the house foundation, and the chimneys."

Hattie flushed at the surprise connection between the Latta and Murrell families. "Is this the only spring around here?" she managed to asked, looking up and down the creek in her amazement.

"No, ma'am. The chief's got one and Lewis Ross and Arch Campbell," Susan replied. "They's got one down in Cold Weather Hollow called Blue Spring. It's full of nice, fat perch!"

"Do you fish there?" Hattie inquired. She was glad to get off the subject of the family connections.

"Ever' chance I get," Susan whispered. "Mr. James let us take all we can eat."

"I bet they're good," Hattie returned. "Grace said there's nothing more delicious than perch from a sweet spring."

"Yep. And I've heard that Grace is an answer to prayer for you, Miss Hattie. Well, lemme say somethin' else, too. That Mr. James is an answer to prayer for me," Susan mouthed, suddenly serious. "I cried to heaven for an honest overseer and the Good Lord sent us a fair-minded, God-fearing man."

"You can always count on James," Hattie blushed with pride.

"My cousin—she was free—run off from her slave husband and his mean overseer," Susan whispered, shaking her head. "She went way up north but almost froze and starved to death. Folks up there talk big 'bout lettin' Negroes work, but mobs chased her off from workin' in the knittin' mill. They burnt the place where she slept. No white folk let her live nearby. She got stopped and questioned near ever' day. Lord, she give up and come back to Arkansas!"

Once again, here was a story about the flaws of the northern United States' stance on ex-slaves. Was it just coincidence or something more that led Hattie to hear such things? What did it all mean? The system she had been raised to believe was the best one, the only one that could endure with fairness, now seemed full of holes.

After Susan went back to the house, an hour passed. By dusk, James had not returned to talk with her and Hattie grew hungry. While she had the energy, she pretended to be nonchalant and took her leave. Only Comet would listen to her despair tonight. What had been so important that James couldn't even give her five minutes? It seemed only some people could always count on him.

Hattie still needed to get word to John Stewart. The telltale evidence she'd discovered at Sweet Berry's home would help convict Deke. But she must remain mindful of Agent Butler. There was no doubt but what, with Deke in jail, Levi and Ida were in jeopardy. How could anyone prove that the children were free Negroes? Even that wasn't enough, however. She had just learned by accident that if free Negroes in the Cherokee Nation had not been freed specifically by Cherokee slave owners, they would be expelled. What if Butler found out the true circumstances of Levi and Ida, not to mention discovering them in possession of books from Hattie? The children could be expelled and the mission itself could be charged with breaking the law. Hattie's project would be a tedious one and could only succeed with much prayer.

She realized she had complicated things for herself. Because of Sweet Berry's innocence—and the secrets about Levi and Ida—she must insist that her trunk not be returned. John Stewart must promise not to take it out of Salali's home. The reasons must remain private. Besides Deke and perhaps his gang, surely nobody else knew the trunk was stolen property.

Hattie felt sure she would discover more evidence eventually. She already suspected how wily Deke was. He had protected his daughter from the truth in a way that left Hattie with no recourse if she cared about the child's feelings.

From that day forward, Hattie vowed to do everything in her power to support temperance efforts. A clever drunk was no friend of hers. The devastation wrought upon Sweet Berry's family as a result of drunkenness rippled in every direction.

The only good news, she concluded, was learning a valuable lesson. She thought better of some of her big goals from before the attack and theft of her trunk. Given the dangerous complications, she decided her dreams were often just naive musings. Because she had investigated too little about Indian Territory, those dreams had brought trouble to her life.

In the future, people—not hopes or dream—must become the most important priority in her life. She had gained maturity and refined her sense of purpose. It was the care and teaching of people who had lost their liberty or homeland. People were all that truly mattered. When they hurt, she wanted to be available with compassion. And Sweet Berry, the epitome of goodness and purity, was hurting even as she treasured the lie that Hattie's trunk was a gift. That trunk served as a powerful reminder that things, objects, and possessions were all temporary and replaceable. People and relationships weren't.

Hattie realized her beliefs and her work could always be compromised if she grew too attached to material things or objects like the trunk. They could be stolen or lost or ruined. But humans were spiritual beings with eternal significance. She should free herself from attachments to anything but people. *I can more than endure the loss of my trunk*, she began to tell herself. *No trunk—or any other item—is important enough to destroy the love and trust of a child, especially one in a desperate situation.*

❖ ❖ ❖

John Stewart rode off after the serious, revealing conversation with Hattie. She said a prayer of thanks that he now knew about the trunk. The challenge didn't stop there, however; it contained many more elements that needed attention. But first, she had to finish the school day.

"It's too nice to stay indoors," she told the children as their reading session ended. "Let's go outside for some sunshine while the weather is decent."

But Percy lingered by the door.

"Miss Hattie," he shared quietly when the others were out of earshot, "Buck said Grace's husband has big, red sores on his face."

Hattie drew back, wondering what to think. "Is it true or is Buck just making trouble again?"

"Sweet Berry said he told her."

"Then it sounds to me like second-hand talk. He likes to scare people. I thought you were avoiding Buck and his pestering," she reminded.

But to herself, she wondered what would make Buck say such a thing?

"I kicked him real hard last week, so he doesn't bother me anymore," Percy shared proudly. "We're friends now."

"I'm glad you stood up for yourself," she congratulated, while wondering if Grace's husband was sick.

❖ ❖ ❖

Sunday dawned with brilliant sunlight shining like crystals off the otherwise scant dew. The drought had grown tiresome. Hattie was but a few steps toward church when a cloud of dust came rolling down the narrow lane ahead of someone's wagon. Overnight, fall's veil had changed the wind direction. She pulled a borrowed black wool shawl up around her neck with a shiver and stepped aside. Once the approaching wagon and its dust cloud had passed, she would continue.

But as it came into view, Hattie could hardly believe her eyes. Emerging from a grove of trees was a sumptuous carriage pulled by a magnificently matched and groomed team. Something about the horses looked familiar; they gleamed in the sunlight. One had an unusual marking just above his right hoof and the other a white streak in his mane. There was also no missing the majesty of the carriage's black elegance; it was varnished to a high shine and edged in gold. Stylish brass lanterns adorned either side of the box. The side doors featured actual glass windows.

The ownership of this expensive carriage could only be attributed to two candidates: Chief John Ross, leader of the Cherokee Nation, or Mr. George Murrell, James's well-heeled plantation boss. Her father would have oohed and aahed at the fine leather work on the substantial harnesses.

Then Hattie remembered. These were the horses that had carried the children and her to the temperance rally. They belonged to James's boss.

Thinking of him brought recollections of studying in his magnificent home after she first arrived in Park Hill. How kind that in his absence he allowed his home to be opened so charitably. Furthermore, Dwight had explained that Mr. Murrell continued to support the mission even after the American Board pressed Rev. Worcester to cut off ties with slaveholders. Was he in town long or on his way to Louisiana?

But something altogether unexpected riveted Hattie's attention the next second. She couldn't help but stare at Mr. Murrell's Negro footman attired in scarlet and white livery with gold buttons and trim. She had never seen a footman like that even in Utica. The spectacle in all its grandeur was a shock in a place like Park Hill.

As the carriage drew close, to her great surprise, it began to slow. She could scarcely believe it. Then she caught a glimpse of the gentleman inside. Hat in hand already, he nodded and smiled at her kindly. Mr. Murrell looked far more distinguished than she'd expected, with his cleft chin and heavy brow. A vision flashed across her mind. What must he and James look like racing across the meadow on one of their fox hunts?

"Good morning," he called in a deep, booming voice. "Are you Miss Sheldon, the new teacher? I saw you emerge from the teacher's quarters."

"Yes, sir," she returned, smiling widely. "You must be Mr. Murrell."

"How do you do," he practically bowed. "Your reputation precedes you. I heard good things in my correspondence with Rev. Worcester last summer. He sounded more than pleased that you accepted the teaching role for the mission school."

Such a nice comment lifted Hattie's spirits considerably. If only she could have met him at one of his elegant socials, instead of here on the dusty road. Compared to the quality of his surroundings, she felt colorless and drab. However, it was of little consequence and she must not apologize for her plain, ordinary dress. After all, he didn't seem to notice.

"Why, thank you. It's a pleasure to meet you, Mr. Murrell," she responded brightly. "I owe you many thanks for the chance to study in your library and for transporting my students to the temperance rally."

"Any time," he replied, the sweep of his southern accent filling her ear. "If you're on your way to church, I'm going right by there on my way home. It would make me feel better to deliver you there safely."

"Why, thank you," Hattie returned, almost awed. He wasn't just saying hello. To her disbelief, the footman took her hand and helped her into the opulent carriage! She appreciated Mr. Murrell's indirect way of referencing the murder that nobody had solved. Leaving that topic alone was best.

James had said the Cherokees revered Murrell, giving him the nickname "Skiosti," which meant Good Man. He was a successful planter and a man of means known for his loyal participation in the community. But since his young wife's untimely death, many things had changed and he traveled often. Hattie found herself updating him about Park Hill.

"Rev. Worcester should return in the near future," she wagered after they had chatted for a few minutes. "I hope you won't leave for Louisiana before then."

"As a matter of fact, my plans are still uncertain," Mr. Murrell replied thoughtfully. "A great deal of work and hard decisions await me at Tally Ho."

"I've been hearing about the bayou country. But Park Hill is as far south as I've ever been. You can guess my northern family's thoughts on the plantation system. I didn't even know that some Cherokees owned slaves," she shared hesitantly. *Where in the world had that comment come from?*

"I don't usually discuss such things, yet I respect the concern of missionaries," Mr. Murrell responded quite openly.

"Forgive me for my impertinence," Hattie begged. "I'm still getting used to being called a northern abolitionist missionary. Someday, I pray we will replace slavery with something more humane and equitable."

"Your point of view comes from a portion of the Christian perspective, like Worcester's," he allowed. "Mine is from another portion. Nevertheless, I make sure the slaves on my properties are treated better than any others I know of."

"Yes, I've met Susan, who speaks well of you. And I've read about labor challenges. If you freed your slaves, would white or Cherokee laborers be willing to do the work?" the bold voice inside Hattie asked.

"That would be difficult for many reasons," Mr. Murrell replied hesitantly. "But I share the sentiments of wise men and friends nearby, like Mr. John Latta in Arkansas. Someday, the slaves will be free. There may have to be a dispute of Biblical proportion to bring it about, though."

"As a teacher, I hope some of the Cherokee limitations on slavery loosen up. I am passionate to educate every child, even slaves."

"Cherokee law prohibits the formal education of Negroes, you know. I'm obligated to abide by that," Mr. Murrell responded soberly.

"I understand, but it grieves me. If only Agent Butler could be a little less rabid," she returned.

"He is aggressive, but not an enemy," Mr. Murrell advised. "Did you know he and some other lawmen are currently tracking a rumor to prevent crimes against Negroes? Some robber has threatened to steal and sell Negro children. You might think Agent Butler would turn a blind eye. But he's concerned."

Hattie's heart jumped as she pictured Levi and Ida. Meanwhile, Mr. Murrell turned to instruct his driver as the carriage slowed. They had arrived at the mission church already. He must be a good man indeed to entertain her unplanned questions, Hattie concluded. She didn't know where the time had gone as they talked.

Smoothing her hair, she realized she was seated behind a little curtained window that almost obscured her from a significant number of onlookers. *Oh my goodness*, she exclaimed to herself. *They're all staring*. How might they and the others interpret her unexpected arrival? Most had likely never ridden in such elegance.

Then, she had an unbelievable idea. If she had spent months arranging such a show of access-to-power as this, it could not have transpired any better. For, there stood James Latta and Erminia Worcester, waiting respectfully to greet Mr. Murrell. Pinching herself out of amusement, Hattie readied herself. In another few seconds when she stepped out of the carriage, a delicious, calamitous reaction was about to unfold.

From outside, the footman grasped the brass handle with his pristinely gloved hand and swung the shiny black door open. Mr. Murrell nodded politely and then flicked his coat tails back as he glided out the door. Both feet planted on the ground, he turned back and reached for Hattie's hand. Smiling innocently, she emerged from the carriage without a hint of haughtiness, her gaze focused squarely on James's face.

No one uttered a sound at first. James stopped short of dropping his teeth upon seeing Hattie in the company of his boss. Recovering, he nodded and greeted them both, his eyes darting uncertainly from Hattie to Mr. Murrell for clues.

Similarly, a sound of surprise came from off to the side. Erminia had taken an unrestrained, humiliated gulp of air and stood there agape. This sound was the most satisfying comeuppance Hattie had ever experienced. From the look on Grace's face nearby, quite a few other people also realized the truth: Erminia could not bear for someone lower in her artificial social standing to ride in Mr. Murrell's coach. So much for insisting she must act as intermediary to introduce Hattie to Park Hill's powerful and wealthy citizens.

While it lasted, the scene was rich beyond belief. Hattie acknowledged her shallowness in loving it so much, but there it was. She couldn't predict what the consequences would be, but for the moment, she didn't care. None the wiser, Mr. Murrell shook hands with James and Erminia, who dabbed at her face nervously with her lace handkerchief. She forced a smile in a failed effort to appear unfazed. Then, in the course of a few more seconds, Mr. Murrell returned to his carriage and was gone.

❖ ❖ ❖

Hattie committed to saying very little to James about her ride with Mr. Murrell. She had had her satisfaction, which almost made up for him leaving her waiting the other afternoon.

"I can't figure how you pulled it off," James laughed, a bit puzzled. "Are you awestruck? Is that why you're so quiet? Or has all this violence overwhelmed you?"

"No, I'm alright. He saw me come out of my quarters," Hattie explained. "I just went along with the invitation when he offered to keep me safe."

"I sorry I didn't think ahead and come after you myself. But let me share something you're gonna love," James retorted, a hint of glee in his eyes. "When the coach pulled up, I had just been talking with Mrs. Worcester. She commented that she knew we were keeping company."

"Oh, really?" Hattie exclaimed, her eyebrows raised. "Well, at least she's informed now."

"Where was Grace today?" he asked.

"I'm wondering that same thing," Hattie contemplated. "She's been quiet and not really herself. I don't know what she's thinking half the time."

"I bet things will improve when Rev. Worcester gets back," he estimated.

❖ ❖ ❖

Before anyone else arrived on Monday morning, Sweet Berry bounded into school full of stories. She was still overjoyed that Hattie had come to her home for a visit. It got her attention off her father's arrest, so she seemed much more herself than the previous week. Without Deke's drunken behavior and temper, the household could finally grow more quiet and orderly. And Sweet Berry seemed to gain comfort from the mood of her new environment.

"We had a visitor for supper on Saturday," Sweet Berry chirped. "And I helped cook."

"Good for you," Hattie replied, genuinely pleased for her. "How many people?"

"One nice man. He's a preacher from Bread Town," Sweet Berry replied.

Hattie knew immediately that something was amiss. Her pulse quickened, but she sought to maintain a calm exterior.

"What is his name?" she managed to croak.

"Rev. Evan Jones. He talks funny because he's from across the ocean. It's called Wales," Sweet Berry returned, obviously taken with Jones' brogue.

"What made him come to your house?" Hattie pressed, hoping to get the truth so she could figure out what to do next.

"Grandma said he likes full-bloods. Lots of full-bloods go to his church. He said maybe he can help get Papa out of jail," Sweet Berry added.

Hattie felt her stomach lurch. "Has he visited the jail?"

"He told Grandma that Papa has a rival on the outside. What does that mean, Miss Hattie?"

A rival? Someone competing with Deke? For what? Stolen goods? Whiskey sales? Perhaps it was just the chronic full-blood versus mixed-blood feud.

"Isn't Bread Town far away?" Hattie asked to distract her little student.

"Yes, but he wants to preach here, too," Sweet Berry explained. "He's coming back."

Hattie bit her tongue. Park Hill was far from the Baptist Mission at Bread Town. Rev. Jones's presence must be part of a strategy and certainly not just a coincidence. It didn't bode well. After all these years of Rev. Worcester's patient love toward Park Hill residents, was Rev. Jones taking advantage of his absence to compete with him?

Rev. Worcester's church was already small. Could this new development divide the loyalties of nearby full-bloods to make it even smaller? All the more, it might signal that Rev. Jones wanted to bring his brand of preaching to Park Hill, the heart of the American Board mission. So much for the historical adage that one's region signified one's religion. Rev. Jones was something of an invader to Hattie.

But that wasn't the worst of it. The more perilous side of his interest in full-bloods was his abolitionism. Hattie wondered if he had taken leave of his senses. Without doubt, his presence would taunt numerous mixed-blood slaveholders, the likes of which included Mr. Murrell and Chief Ross. No doubt, Agent Butler would keep an eye on Jones, as he did on all the missionaries.

Hattie wondered if she should inform the others connected to the Park Hill Mission. The news might set off a chain reaction, like with stacked dominoes falling down, one after another. In the absence of Rev. Worcester's leadership, someone should also write the American Board immediately. What if a confrontation occurred before the American Board could sort out the correct action?

Hattie paused for a moment, realizing she was getting ahead of herself. Henceforth, on behalf of the Park Hill Mission, she must simply remain watchful, lest Rev. Jones build more quiet inroads through the region or Rev. Worcester's congregation. How would Jones compare against Rev. Worcester's quiet, penitent, and law-abiding nature? She just hoped she could stay calm if Rev. Jones tried to free Deke from jail!

❖ ❖ ❖

After the children left that afternoon, Hattie decided to

accompany Grace to the tiny Nave General Store. On the way, she could try to catch up on her friend's life without asking prying questions. Grace always knew the latest stories.

Today, Grace seemed a bit tired. She perked up soon and told Hattie about the early years of the mission, when Rev. Worcester experienced difficulty getting supplies. After removal of the Cherokees to Indian Territory, few general stores had even existed. Many items had to be ordered all the way from New Orleans.

"The American Board sent some things. Others were procured from Ft. Gibson. But, still, the Worcesters barely had enough to get by in those early days," Grace explained. "River shipments met the bulk of all missionary needs before they, or even the Cherokees, built permanent homes. After removal, it took a while to bring this place to life."

The little wooden store looked much like a house, resting just north of Park Hill Creek in a rough clearing. Finding it primitive, Hattie had to completely release all her expectations built by Utica standards of commerce. Once inside, she grasped why she had been advised to shop in Tahlequah for most of her needs. This store's goods were in short supply. It did not carry clothing at all. Hattie wondered how stocking decisions were made, given that Ft. Gibson was the main supplier of food for the Cherokees. She reminded herself to be grateful for local availability of necessities like combs, soap, and sewing utensils.

Further perusing the food and household items, she also became aware that nobody was present to tend the store. Curious, she looked to Grace while pointing toward an open back door. They headed that direction only to hear two voices rise. But, just shy of the door, Grace grabbed her arm.

"Stop, Hattie. Stay inside," she warned, an unusual sense of alarm in her voice. "I think I know who's out there. You don't want to ... to interrupt."

"Is it someone dangerous?" Hattie queried as she drew back.

"Possibly," Grace whispered from a corner. "Come back over here. The horse out front has a federal stamp on the saddle. I think its Agent Butler's."

"But I'd like to talk to him," Hattie hesitated.

"Something tells me this isn't the right time," Grace replied.

Stealthily, Grace slid back along a wall toward the open door. Hattie was startled as the men's voices grew louder. Listening from behind a crate, she would pretend to shop if the men came inside. But they didn't and seemingly remained unaware of the women.

"I would swear Worcester's been up to no good back east," Butler was saying to the missing store clerk. "You've got to help me watch. I bet he's working every abolitionist channel. If he tries to preach against slavery like Jones, he's a fool. But we need evidence. Then, I won't hesitate to expel northern abolitionist missionaries, believe me."

At this, Hattie's pulse jumped. Grace had been right. It was no time to have a conversation with Butler. In fact, maybe there was no need for a conversation at all. His comment revealed his disdain for Rev. Jones. On that, he and Hattie agreed.

But, on second thought, that was the least of her worries now. More urgently, Butler was also hot on the trail of Rev. Worcester and other missionaries. That meant he was suspicious of her! Miraculously, fate had tipped her off. She felt fortunate to witness first-hand how Butler enlisted the clerk's help to watch and listen to missionaries.

Even though Butler couldn't possess new information about Rev. Worcester, he had a whole scenario outlined. His intention was to intimidate and expel missionaries, which might coincide with Rev. Worcester's hoped-for return. How unfair! What a twisted circumstance!

Hattie waved to get Grace's attention. To her horror, she knocked a box of cigars to the floor instead. Tipped off, the men stopped talking. Hattie cowered, uncertain what would happen. But just as footsteps reached the back door, Grace called out innocently.

"Hello? Is anybody here," she inquired and then released a convincing laugh.

Impressed by Grace's quick thinking, Hattie rose and replaced the box of cigars. The clerk was alone as he entered and looked around. Hattie nodded politely while stepping toward the front door. She caught sight of Butler when he mounted his horse and rode off.

"Hello Mrs. Barnes," the clerk greeted. "How may I help you?"

"We didn't see what we needed, so we'll stop back another day soon," Grace replied hollowly, nodding to the clerk as she took Hattie's arm.

❖ ❖ ❖

"How did you know to be wary?" Hattie questioned while regaining her composure. "You can't imagine how grateful I am."

"I listen a lot," Grace answered tentatively. "When my husband has visitors, there is much to learn. They disregard me, but talk openly. In many ways, I will always be an outsider because I am white. So I ... choose to ... keep still. It's better to be subservient and quiet around many Cherokee men."

"Oh. I never thought of that," Hattie responded quietly. "Every time I turn around, something in this place becomes the opposite of my expectation. But I know one thing for sure: Rev. Worcester is innocent. Rev. Jones is the one who needs to be expelled."

"That sums up my thoughts, too," Grace nodded, her gaze far away. "It's foolish to ever let our guard down."

·14·

Confusion, Confrontation and Catastrophe

"If the river's high enough, we're going over to Tullahassee for Thanksgiving," little Percy offered brightly. "Mama told Pa she misses her sister."

Hattie remained in awe of Ann Eliza Worcester Robertson, the oldest sister of Hannah and Sarah. Someday, she intended to meet Ann Eliza and her administrator husband. Rev. William S. Robertson had been born and raised on Long Island, right in her home state of New York. He sounded like a man of many interests and talents, like her father.

Hattie already revered them for another reason. The Robertsons loved and kept Miss Thompson like one of the family. Since she had learned the full story from Miss Thompson herself about why she went to live at Tullahassee instead of staying in Park Hill, Hattie saw the idea of family in a new light. She had saved Miss Thompson's dear letter and poem in her letter box.

Remembering that the Robertsons would welcome a new baby before Christmas, Hattie replied to Percy with enthusiasm.

"I'm anxious to visit Tullahassee and the Three Forks, as well. You must tell me all about it after you return, alright?"

Tullahassee, a region of beauty with rich, loamy soil, was not easy to reach. Some nine miles west of Ft. Gibson and two miles north of the Arkansas River, it was home to a place many referred to as "The Point." The large area encompassing The Point had long been known as the predominant crossroads for emigrants on the move to the expanding west.

Nearby, in the Three Forks region, a mass of interests entangled themselves one with another as military, exploratory, tribal, trade, and river travelers pursued their own agendas. The California Trail met the old Texas Road just east of the Three Forks. Product-laden wagons drawn by oxen had worn deep ruts in the ground, Martha had mentioned some time back.

Intrepid explorers met idealistic gold prospectors there. Trading posts outbid independent whiskey dealers. Meanwhile, the federal troops at Ft. Gibson tried to keep peace in the midst of this activity along the converging waterways of the Arkansas, Verdigris, and Grand Rivers. Hattie pictured the grizzled men, the soldiers, and the excitement. Truth be told, she would have liked to go along with the Hicks family to Tullahassee.

Sweet Berry informed Hattie that her grandmother wanted to discuss the Bible since she'd finished Rev. Worcester's translation of I Peter and II Peter. Evidently, she was confused. Then Sweet Berry showed Hattie an entirely unfamiliar publication of the same translation. It was also marked I Peter and II Peter. How curious that Salali was in possession of two separate versions!

On closer examination, Hattie discovered that the familiar one was Rev. Worcester's, while the other had been translated by Rev. Jones. He must have left this copy of his own translation when he paid Salali the unexpected visit.

"Grandma says one tells a story, but the other one tells it different," Sweet Berry related. "She thought there was just one Bible. Do all preachers make their own Bible?"

Abruptly, Salali's confused question brought to mind what Hattie had read weeks back. Although Jones and Worcester corroborated their translation work in the beginning, Jones had broken away and began to translate his own version with the help of his son. Salali had read widely differing versions of the truth! Of all the obstacles in Rev. Worcester's dogged pursuit of Christianization, this one could hurt him the deepest. His lifelong goal was to rebuild trust, not leave the Cherokees wondering which version of the Bible was best. Faith was primary with him.

Here was a woman in need, but Jones's independence ended up confusing her. How ironic that the Bible itself could fall into question. The Cherokees always seemed to end up in a situation where white men led them astray.

Hattie now questioned Jones's efforts closer. His interest in Deke's imprisonment worried her more every hour. If she didn't miss her guess, factionalism and the white man's influence were involved somehow. Interested parties were rallying to Deke's side just because he was a full-blood.

Then a thunderbolt of concern struck her. Jones might have discovered far more than he bargained for at Salali's house. He could have encountered Levi and Ida there in a full-blood Cherokee family! It was possible they were no longer anonymous or safe. Would he tell? Who? What would happen to them?

❖ ❖ ❖

"That preacher is coming back tonight," Sweet Berry happened to mention on her way out to play that afternoon.

Hattie nearly tripped in her eagerness to learn more. Indeed, Sweet Berry was certain that when Rev. Jones thanked her grandmother and left her house, he said he would return on Tuesday night to talk with more full-bloods there. Grace heard Sweet Berry, too, and looked worried.

"Last week, my husband ran into Jones near here," Grace revealed to an open-mouthed Hattie. "He's traveling far and wide to make nice with as many full-bloods as possible."

"Rev. Worcester would never ride all the way to recruit like that in Bread Town," Hattie raved.

"Jones is tricky," Grace frowned. "He made my husband mad enough to start talking against abolitionists again. He also underestimates mixed-blood resentment when he only reaches out to full-bloods."

"Oh, Grace. This is so complicated," Hattie declared. "Your own husband is now against your anti-slavery beliefs?"

"He talks about it a lot," Grace related, her voice losing strength. "So, I have less and less to say."

❖ ❖ ❖

Instantly, a plan formed in Hattie's mind. It was risky. But she had vowed to do the right thing for Sweet Berry's family. Fear must not hold her back.

After school was dismissed, she grabbed the black shawl and told Sweet Berry today was the day of the teacher's visit to her home. Sweet Berry seemed pleased. They climbed on old Comet and set out. Thankfully, she had not been specific with Salali about when she would return for this visit.

After seeing Sweet Berry inside, Hattie reassured Salali about the differences in the Bible translations. Then she stressed the importance of talking about Sweet Berry's school work. Even though they were communicating through the little girl, Sweet Berry patiently answered Hattie's questions about the school and her lessons. In a short time, Salali smiled at Sweet Berry's progress. When Salali also asked questions, Hattie considered the visit a success.

Then she took up the topic of Levi and Ida. Careful not to say anything that broke the law, Hattie showed sympathy for Salali's challenge and the pressure on Sweet Berry to translate between English and Cherokee. When she asked to talk with Levi and Ida, Sweet Berry brought them into the room.

Hattie took her time as she talked with them to ascertain their level of education, if any. She also listened to their stories attentively. All the while, she kept nodding to Salali to make the right impression. It appeared she could stretch this conversation until Rev. Jones showed up.

Before long, various full-blood friends and neighbors would arrive. Hattie said Sweet Berry told her about Rev. Jones's visit, but she wasn't finished talking with Levi and Ida. She inserted the idea that they might be compromised if Rev. Jones discovered them. So, Salali left Hattie with the three children and went to greet her guests. This was a more perfect scenario than Hattie could have hoped for.

She was present on a legitimate visit. There was no need, therefore, to explain the presence of Comet, if asked. He remained fastened to a branch behind the house. Once the other room was filled, Hattie repositioned herself by the door. She warned the children to listen carefully, as she would, and cracked the door for air.

The message Rev. Jones delivered was traditional in nature, a fairly standard Calvinist approach. His voice was low and serene. An interpreter shared the words in a calming tone. Hattie knew she must not fault Jones based on her emotions, for his history with the Cherokees was just as long as Rev. Worcester's. But she still didn't trust him.

After Rev. Jones developed his theme, he veered off using words like yoke and subjugation. Employing a few Biblical examples, he also began to raise his voice slightly.

"How many of you remember the loss of choice?" Jones accelerated. "The State of Georgia and others dealt harshly with you or your forefathers. Your land was taken. Some in the Cherokee Nation went along with that. And it was wrong. The old values were put aside and a heavy burden of loss came over this people. Soon, you had no property. You had no choice. You had no freedom to disagree."

"Tonight, I want you to think about others among you who also have no choice, no property, and no freedom," Rev. Jones continued. "Their enslavement is an abomination to God. The Cherokee Nation is shamed by mixed-bloods who yoke another race of people. That is not true to the Cherokee ways of your forefathers. Like whites in the South, the mixed-bloods gained wealth and enslaved Negroes. But the burden of it falls on the *whole* tribe. Too many slave owners are now the leaders of this nation. And the missionary among them in Park Hill refuses to confront that sin. How can you let that stand?"

At this obvious swipe at Rev. Worcester, Hattie gritted her teeth, but said nothing. This was no time or place to become a martyr who stood up for Rev. Worcester. She could barely contain the desire to jump out of her skin, though. Here was growing verification that Jones fed the factional divide. All the more, he used Rev. Worcester's law-abiding ways to stir up the full-bloods! The attendees responded with growing murmurs.

A white preacher was fomenting disharmony between members of the tribe, Negroes, slaveholders, and missionaries! Gauging from what she already knew, Rev. Jones had just crossed the line. Rev. Worcester would never, ever do that; he was all about peace and rebuilding trust with the Cherokees after removal. Rev. Jones, in her estimation, must want to lead an insurrection by one contingent of the Cherokee Nation against another.

Luckily, his message was not lengthy. When he concluded, there was singing and a benediction in Cherokee. In less than a quarter of an hour, the Cherokee attendees had departed. Hattie's disbelief and conviction buoyed, she still struggled to collect herself and interpret what had just transpired. But it was late and she must respect the risk she was taking. Growing more confident of her evidence, she encouraged the children and thanked Salali for trusting her. Instead of leaving a book or any other material linked to the Park Hill Mission or Rev. Worcester's press, she gave them a book from her childhood that she had brought all the way from Utica.

Climbing on Comet, she hurried him along to the main road and returned to her quarters without incident. Thankfully, no one stopped her. And there didn't seem to be anyone on guard at the mission when she put Comet away. It really wasn't necessary now that Deke was jailed. After she went inside, she got out her pen.

❖ ❖ ❖

October 28, 1856

Mr. George Butler, Esq.
Agent for the Cherokee Nation
U.S. Department of the Interior
Office of Indian Affairs
Tahlequah, Cherokee Nation
West of Arkansas

Dear Agent Butler,

This letter was prompted by comments made by Rev. Evan Jones at a clandestine gathering of full-blood Cherokees near Park Hill. I can attest to the fact that Rev. Jones's message had a motive of causing dissent between factions already struggling within the Cherokee Nation. Since I understand your position to be one of unifying the tribe and working toward its peaceful existence, I deemed this matter appropriate for your attention. Rev. Jones disparaged a fellow missionary, Rev. Samuel A. Worcester, who has consistently been proven to abide by the laws of the Cherokee Nation. Those laws currently make the practice of slavery legal. This criticism by Rev. Jones directly encouraged the full-blood Cherokees who were present to revolt against the law and against their fellow mixed-blood Cherokees because they are slaveholders. Finally, Rev. Jones, not a trained linguist like Rev. Worcester, has distributed translated chapters of the Bible which are causing confusion to the Cherokees. This effort is further proof of his fomenting. I implore you to take action.

Yours very sincerely,

Harriet A. Sheldon, Teacher
Park Hill Mission School
Cherokee Nation

❖ ❖ ❖

Hattie made an exciting announcement to her class on the last Wednesday in October.

"Just like teaching the girls how to knit, I have plans for the boys, as well."

The boys looked at each other in wonder and then practically jumped to the ceiling in anticipation. She had to quiet them before continuing.

"On Saturday—just three days from now—you boys are going to learn how to provide your family with meat. Mrs. Barnes and I will take you to learn about butchering at Percy's home. Mr. Abijah Hicks has invited us to help dress out the mission's meat for the first part of the winter. I will take you girls another time."

At Hattie's prompting, Grace rose and explained what would happen. She told the children that Mr. Hicks was readying the smokehouse to dry beef and had gathered salt from nearby deposits to preserve pork. The time was right for butchering both, since cooler weather had arrived and the flies of summer had died off. At a clean, prepared outdoor shelter, Mr. Hicks had constructed a pulley using a strong rope over a large tree branch. After he killed each animal by a sudden, merciful blow, he would give each student helper a knife to help cut the hide away from the strung-up carcass. Following that step, gutting and the removal of organs would happen swiftly.

"Then, I will help Miss Sheldon remove the suet found in a leaf mass around the kidneys. It's covered in a waxy coating," Grace described. "We must save it for other uses."

Once the butchering was complete and the clean-up over, this suet was to be trimmed of all gristle and flesh before being chopped into chunks. In the mission kitchen, Rhoda knew to ready large pots to cook the suet over low heat for five to six hours. During that time, impurities always rose to the top for removal through a straining process later. The resulting product was then called tallow. After it was poured into pans to cool and dry, Hattie, Grace, and Rhoda would put their knives to work again chopping it into bars. The final step was storing the tallow bars at room temperature. It was a necessary ingredient for making candles and soap in the near future.

No sooner had Grace and the children left school that day, than Hattie heard horses approaching outside. Going to the door, her heart leapt to see James leading a second, saddled horse. She waved, wondering what he had planned.

James didn't slow the horses down, however. He kept cantering until they skidded to a stop in front of her, kicking up dirt, gravel, and grass.

"Well, hello, what's......?" she began, but James cut her off.

"Shut the door and come with me," James ordered curtly, not even a hint of a smile on his face.

"Is something wrong?" she questioned, searching his stony face.

"You could say that. Hurry up," he ordered again.

Concerned, Hattie grabbed her shawl and pulled the school door closed behind her. Usually, James dismounted to help her onto her horse, but today he just looked sideways to avoid facing her.

"Where are we going?" she inquired once her feet were firmly in the stirrups and situated. Maybe he was up to some game. Did he think he could outride her? Did he want to intimidate her for some reason? But she didn't really think that was it.

Without answering, James tossed her horse's reins her direction, causing the horse to pull back skittishly. She caught one, but dropped the other. Luckily, the horse didn't buck. Retrieving the dropped rein, she looked up again. Something was terribly wrong. Her heart ached already, but she vowed not to cry. No matter what.

"Follow me north and don't lag behind," James demanded, turning and spurring his horse.

The wind was warmer that afternoon, for which Hattie was grateful. Yet it whipped the horse's coarse black mane and her shawl. What was wrong with James? She had never seen him like this. Where were they headed?

Cantering behind him, Hattie did her best to remain calm. *Take stock*, she demanded of herself, *don't let your emotions get the best of you.* This unexpected flight with James was mysterious. But no matter what problem hung in the balance, she knew in her heart of hearts that James was trustworthy, even when he was mad. She might not like what was going to happen, whatever it was, but she needed to remember that.

As they rode further north out of Park Hill, she calmed down a little, letting herself feel the wind, imagining it sweeping wisdom into her. Riding like this demanded attention; she couldn't ponder much of anything but the wind. It might actually help blow away the clouds of uncertainty.

Hattie's only option now was to pray. *What do you want from me, Lord,* she questioned? She hadn't even lived in Park Hill six months. So far, she had survived it. That wouldn't have been possible without tenacity and faith, which she knew were gifts. And James had helped her overcome many intimidating barriers.

Before long, they passed groves of trees she had seen on the day they went to Tahlequah. The trees were crowned in fall hues of gold and red. She found rugged beauty in the loamy mounds, windswept hills, and sharp rock outcroppings. They made her new home exciting and strangely beautiful, although her parents would probably think it was desolate and depleted. Hattie continued to look around as she followed James. Like the smoke curling from nearby chimneys, she wondered where they were going.

Within another quarter of an hour, Hattie felt windburn on her face. She prayed they weren't going all the way to Tahlequah. Through bloodshot eyes, she scanned the grey horizon. Her energy was flagging because she was hungry. The longer she rode, the less this journey made sense. All she could do was hang on.

Shortly, they approached a small building in the distance. What was it? Hattie's hips and legs ached, especially the leg she had broken. When first mounting this horse, she hadn't anticipated being saddle sore. Now, she knew that was a certainty tomorrow, if not tonight.

Arriving at the utilitarian structure, Hattie noticed that the saddle of the horse out front had a federal stamp on it. She had seen it before at the Nave General Store. James dismounted and reached for Hattie's reins. Helping her down, he still said nothing. But because of the gesture, maybe some of his frustration had lessened while riding. Hattie stood silently and waited for him. She felt it best to say nothing.

James led the way and opened the door, ushering Hattie in ahead of him. This did not look like any federal official's office should, Hattie thought. It must be temporary. Inside the makeshift place, Agent George Butler sat behind a decrepit desk. Standing, he offered a stiff greeting, but did not appear surprised to see them. Pointing to two chairs, he gestured for them to sit down.

"Thank you for coming," Butler opened.

Hattie blinked as she contemplated the setting. Did this relate to their meeting about the murder and the threat letter? Was Butler going to share something important, perhaps that a suspect was in custody for the crimes? If so, why was James upset?

"Miss Sheldon, you know that I met with Mr. George Murrell after leaving Dr. Hitchcock's home," Agent Butler began. "In the course of our conversation, the subject of Rev. Evan Jones came up. You seem to be aware of his actions."

Suddenly, Hattie's heart fell. A sensation of distress flooded her in an instant, pulsating into her head as he continued. This meeting was about the letter she had written accusing Rev. Jones of fueling abolitionism among full-blood Cherokees. Word certainly got around fast. She recalled her frustration when Jones spoke at Salali's house. His statements had brought a surge of protective and defensive sentiments for Rev. Worcester, whose reputation she could not let Jones damage.

But, how was Rev. Jones's name linked to Mr. Murrell? And why was James involved? Hattie breathed in shallow starts wondering what was coming next.

"I had already been investigating Rev. Jones before receiving your letter," Butler continued. "In the course of that inquiry, I traveled to Bread Town and a number of other locations trying to gather evidence. I wondered if anyone would confirm that Rev. Jones made blatant, abolitionist statements. That is the gist of your letter, is it not?"

"Yes," Hattie confirmed meekly, growing more apprehensive about the coming conclusion, whatever it was.

"Among the full-blood Cherokees I encountered, none would speak against Rev. Jones. Your letter changed things. Therefore, I proceeded as if evidence had been secured. Prosecution, however, involves the filing of formal charges and the determination of jurisdiction," Agent Butler explained.

Hattie felt like she was already in court. The language was so formal, the tone so serious.

"I was prepared to take your sworn statement and ask if anyone else could corroborate your charges," he added. "But then that plan changed, as well. Without going into detail, Miss Sheldon, you would be wise to remember that you're being watched."

Just as she was beginning to comprehend that she could help expose Jones's guilt, Hattie grew uncertain. What did Agent Butler mean exactly? Watched by whoever threatened her or watched by people who didn't want Rev. Jones's reputation in question? Her mind sped nervously. This was confusing and involved. Maybe she didn't have everything as straight as Agent Butler wanted.

"Mr. Murrell asked Agent Butler to postpone any further action against Rev. Jones. He also requested this meeting, considering that you were new and might not know as much as the rest of us. Mr. Murrell and others now ask that you withdraw and leave the matter to Agent Butler," James specified bluntly.

Hattie drew back in surprise and then stood, deep in thought. How had Mr. Murrell figured into this confusing maze, she wondered? Folding her arms as she moved behind her chair, she strove to clarify her thoughts before speaking. Did James mean that Butler would pursue the enforcement of the law, but no longer needed her evidence? Who were the "others" that didn't want her to speak out? These men—so official, so intimidating—had not told her the whole story. They were trying to pull the wool over her eyes. How was she going to deal with it?

"What is the missing information here?" she asked, turning back to face them. "All I've heard is a lot of rhetoric. The question of *WHY* is still unanswered."

"I don't have the necessary releases to explain that now," Agent Butler stammered rather formally.

"What have I done wrong that requires me to withdraw? Why are you being evasive?" she challenged. "I'm upset by this intimidation. I have a right to be upset. And you know that's what you're doing."

Neither man responded.

Hattie licked her lips nervously, hoping against hope that the scene before her would go up in smoke, that she would miraculously find herself back at her quarters in her own bed, warm and toasty. But that was a childlike wish. A grown woman would face the suspicious situation in her midst and deal with it directly. Hattie pulled herself together and spoke.

"You know that I am a missionary from the north," she reiterated, facing Agent Butler directly. "If you have concluded that that makes me an abolitionist, then that is your decision. Rev. Jones said intolerable things to breed animosity toward mixed-bloods by full-bloods over slavery. He came to Park Hill with questionable motives instead of keeping his attention on his own territory. Most disturbing to me, he confused the Cherokees by breaking off cooperative

relations with Rev. Worcester and by distributing a poorly translated portion of the Bible. I'm standing up for Rev. Worcester,
whom I revere, and whom you also know to never condone or preach
abolition publicly. He keeps the Cherokee Law."

Turning briefly as she spoke, she watched James stare out a
window. He looked so blank, but probably knew so much more than
he revealed. Was he in hot water, too?

"I hereby withdraw my complaint. May I go now," Hattie concluded boldly, holding her head up.

"Yes, thank you, Miss Sheldon," Agent Butler stuttered,
standing clumsily.

Hattie walked out without another word. Securing her shawl
over her head against the coming evening chill, she untied the horse,
mounted and rode south toward Park Hill. In order to fully digest
what had just happened, she needed plenty of time and air. Maybe
she could even beat the dark.

There was no denying they were concealing information. The
confusion felt painful like her first weeks in Park Hill. With regard
to Rev. Jones, however, she realized she had possessed too little
understanding when making her ideological complaint. That action
obviously carried much more weight than she ever grasped. Today's
confrontation and whatever would follow was far beyond a student
tattling to the teacher that a fellow student misbehaved.

Moreover, when it came to misconduct, Hattie stumbled
on another conclusion. Agent Butler had purposely revealed to
unknown others that she submitted a complaint letter. She had

told no one about it. This lone fact proved that he was loose-lipped, untrustworthy, and questionable. And he was against her because he was against all abolitionists, real or imagined, confirmed or not.

But what was James doing in the middle of this mess? And why had he taken such a stance against her? He hadn't looked so confident while staring out the window.

"Hattie, wait up," James called from just behind. "Why didn't you tell me you were going to accuse Rev. Jones?"

Slowing, Hattie hadn't realized a single, disobeying tear streamed down her face until she tasted its unwelcomed brine. She must look a fright. The lump in her throat maintained its control, though. Until he explained some things, she had little to say.

Why hadn't she told anyone about the letter, she chided herself? Because she had formed her opinion based on reading Rev. Worcester's *private* files! Rev. Jones was already guilty in her eyes before she ever heard him preach. That was why she decided to fight this battle against him on Rev. Worcester's behalf. Obviously, the impact of it—and other things still hidden—ran deeper than she grasped.

"I don't owe you an explanation for everything," Hattie snapped. "And I don't deserve your attempt to make me feel guilty either—or that unnecessary embarrassment in front of Butler."

"Look, Hattie," James complained. "That was a ridiculous decision. You don't even know what you don't know. I've tried pretty hard behind the scenes to keep you out of trouble. But I'm going to stop protecting you."

"Instead of protecting me, why don't you just tell me what's going on?"

"Figure out your own life. It's in your hands now," he retorted.

Flushed with too many emotions, Hattie held her words, nodded, and then turned her horse toward Park Hill. How annoying that he would still ride beside her all the way home.

That evening, Hattie's neck and shoulders ached with tension. Intent upon keeping her composure, she still felt wooden and cold, even though the fire in her stove blazed. She had arrived back at her quarters well after dark and left the horse outside, still saddled. James would have to care for the poor, tired creature. On the way home, a wolf's howl in the distance had accompanied the weather's wild turn from chilly to damp and raw. It also seemed to mimic her misery, loneliness, and confusion.

Gradually, relaxation slowed her down to the point of feeling her exhaustion. Dozing off, her head drooped forward, which led to the swelling of her sinuses and a throbbing headache that stirred her unintended nap. Fitful images seemed to mock her from beyond the curtain of deep sleep. She heard a sound. Wasn't it just the wind? But when the sound returned with more urgency, it roused her. She thought she heard a woman's soft voice. Opening the door was risky, but something encouraged her to check, just in case.

When Hattie peeked out, there stood Sarah, dripping wet, holding a lamp. Hattie gasped, and drew her inside. She couldn't stop her questions as she blotted Sarah dry and led her to the warmth of the stove. Sarah should not be out in this weather.

"Forget about me," Sarah cautioned. "I'm here because of you."

Unable to stop herself, Hattie blurted out, "This was a horrid day!"

"If ever a woman needed a loving reminder of her worth, it is you tonight, Hattie Sheldon," Sarah said devotedly. And then she took Hattie in her arms and held her tight.

Such empathy touched Hattie as deeply as if her own family had just arrived. She couldn't help but replace a portion of her sorrow and regret with appreciation. But she wasn't sure which emotions her tears represented. Sarah's understanding and comfort meant more than she could express.

"This latest development ... I can't even grasp it, Hattie. I just had to come to you. Both Dwight and I want to be supportive and sensitive in your dark hour. He's waiting impatiently, and insists that I can't stay. But, dear Hattie, you can count on our prayers. Many of us have been touched profoundly by your courage, perseverance, and loving heart," Sarah whispered, shedding a tear herself.

"But, how did you find out?" Hattie softly inquired.

"The most important detail to know tonight is that you are loved and respected. We will do anything to help make things better," Sarah concluded as she kissed Hattie's hand and took her leave.

Waving goodbye, Hattie marveled at the timing of Sarah's visit. Whatever led to her learning about the confrontation by James and Agent Butler was a blessing from God.

Unbelievably, Saturday was already the first of November. Hattie remained somewhat shaken after Wednesday's events but had put one foot in front of the other and moved forward. The day of the butchering, she was ready when Grace arrived, determined to project a strong façade at the Hicks place. She wouldn't have to talk about her complaint letter or meeting with Agent Butler because Grace didn't know about them.

She had had her good old cry, but wasn't sure how much it helped. Nothing much had changed, except that she felt more distant from James than ever before. The sensation of harboring fury against someone she loved so intensely posed an odd riddle. Confusion ruled as she entertained both emotions simultaneously.

Even more perplexing was the way the awful meeting with Agent Butler had transpired. James hadn't seemed himself. His actions, words, and emotions didn't coordinate with one another. In fact, he had surprisingly adverse opinions about her that he'd never mentioned before. How long had he held those back? What had changed his attitude toward her so thoroughly and quickly?

Without James's link to information, Hattie relied on Grace, who sounded anxious when she shared that lawmen had unearthed few facts about the murdered preacher found in the tree. What a troubling end for a faithful carrier of the gospel.

The authorities had no theories on a motive, either. Most murders usually satisfied some grudge involving factions. When the missionary's body was removed, he had but a few dollars in his pockets and a crumpled ticket of passage to the Three Forks region.

Meanwhile, Hattie just had to endure the uncertainty linking that murder with her attack, threat letter, and trunk theft. The more she reflected on Deke, the more she wanted to believe he was responsible for all of those crimes. But she wasn't going to succumb to her impulse to see James even though he could probably help untangle some complexities. James must figure out that secretiveness accomplished nothing. She would require an apology for subjecting her to Butler and things unexplained. Would she ever find out the whole story? There was plenty of time for that, but she was getting impatient for an apology.

On the way to the Hicks place, Hattie commented that she and Grace needed to make today an unforgettable experience for the boys. Grace looked at her with a subdued expression and nodded. Neither of them seemed inclined to share their woes, but there seemed to be plenty on both sides.

Hattie was suffering more than second thoughts about James, but couldn't explain without bringing up Agent Butler. Grace disliked Butler so thoroughly. There was nothing to gain in reconstructing the frustrating confrontation for her.

Even though it was hard, Hattie concluded they must try to overcome and be happy. The upcoming demonstration would be an eye opener. She pictured a great fattened hog and a muscled bovine. Her mother would never let her near anything like the spectacle she was about to encounter. It would add to her circle of understanding about Park Hill, however. Today would require maturity and she was becoming well-seasoned at viewing everything from that point of view.

"Look," Hattie cried suddenly, pointing toward Park Hill Mountain. "There's a great big panther up there!"

Instinctively, Grace pulled the reins back, handed them to Hattie, and reached for a loaded rifle at her feet.

"Are you really going to shoot it?" Hattie whispered in amazement, trying to follow Grace's line of sight.

"Good grief, Hattie, yes," Grace argued. "Panthers kill cattle, goats, sheep, and horses. They do tremendous damage that wipes out people's hard fought living."

Hattie slowed the horses further as Grace steadied herself again to take aim. Then they both lost sight of the panther. Momentarily, it emerged from behind some trees, climbing effortlessly from rock to ledge and on up.

Almost crouching in anticipation herself, Hattie cringed while waiting for Grace to fire. But, the next second, she gasped. Her knees suddenly turned liquid from disbelief. The panther wasn't the only living creature moving stealthily up there. A partially hidden man was looking straight at her. Something about him appeared vaguely familiar.

"What's wrong?" Grace asked, bringing the gun down and looking sideways at Hattie.

Hattie went cold as a clam. She had persevered silently for so long under the threat of being watched. Agent Butler had confirmed it, too. She hadn't just imagined the man on the mountain, but could no longer see him. On second thought, maybe he was up there hunting. Agitated, Hattie decided it was probably wise to keep quiet.

"Oh, nothing. I'm sorry for breaking your concentration," she apologized.

"Well, the panther's gone now," Grace sighed as they continued to the Hicks place.

Abijah and Percy waved as Hattie and Grace arrived. Across the meadow, several boys approached, as well. It wasn't exactly a beautiful day, but better than a dry dusty one. By the hour, clouds had rolled in. Occasional showers promised to moisten the parched landscape. Hattie prayed that Buck and Lucas would behave and participate. Abijah said Hannah and the little girls had joined some others going to Fort Gibson for supplies.

Shortly, Hattie called the children together so Abijah could explain more thoroughly the steps Grace had enumerated earlier in class. All his equipment looked carefully organized and ready for the undertaking. Hattie didn't find the idea of butchering repugnant, but felt a little flutter of uneasiness about encountering the unknown.

To her relief, Abijah knew exactly what he was doing. With swift strokes, his knife did its work and served as a marvelous example for the boys to follow. Hattie found herself fascinated by his skill and how it mesmerized them. There hadn't been one complaint or prank all day. In fact, plenty of cooperation and even some laughs made everyone's efforts lighter.

By early afternoon, the day's task was completed and the cleanup underway. Abijah showed Hattie the hog's bladder he would clean and dry for Hannah to cover food in crocks. She couldn't believe how efficiently he used every morsel from the animals. Very few scraps remained. Proudly surveying the buckets of suet ready for rendering into tallow, she and Grace loaded the wagon, said goodbye, and headed for Rhoda's kitchen.

Momentarily, steady rain began to fall accompanied by claps of thunder. They couldn't turn back despite the rather uncomfortable, wet conditions. But they were too energized to be bothered anyway. Hattie went back over the day's events, expressing excitement that she—and hopefully, the boys—had learned more than she predicted.

"Our spirits are a far cry higher than when we set out," she laughed.

"But you saw something this morning, didn't you?" Grace questioned a few seconds later.

"I thought I did because I keep anticipating trouble. That's faithless though," Hattie chided herself. "Things have quieted down, and I haven't heard another threatening word."

Grace looked serious. "Well, it's past time to tell you that I did."

"What? When?" Hattie returned, incredulous.

Grace shook her head. "Other bad things may happen, Hattie."

Hattie's old fear welled up. "Who told you?"

"That's the hardest part. I think I know who's doing it," Grace answered, her voice low and grave.

Hattie let out a long moan of dread as she searched for words.

Grace continued. "The clue was misunderstanding *why* you were being watched..."

Suddenly, a blinding flash ripped past them accompanied by a boom of deafening proportion. Hattie was thrown violently and, in the mayhem, couldn't follow what was happening. Likewise, the horses jumped crazily, fought the reins, and jerked the wagon sideways. Hattie heard herself scream. She smelled smoke and the wagon almost tipped. It must have been a lightning strike!

Within seconds, the horses' wild veering jolted the wagon upright again. They began to gallop at breakneck speed. Wet soil and stones flew up, striking Hattie and forcing her to cover her head and close her eyes. Eerie groans and frightening rasps from the wagon's strained wood and joints filled the air. Hattie struggled to feel for anything she might hold onto amid the swift, disorienting motion. Where was Grace? Had she fallen?

The horses had gone crazy in only seconds. Hattie hadn't

witnessed the terrifying spectacle of uncontrolled, furious horses for years, and then only at a distance. Her father had warned her and her siblings to stay clear of the immense strength of horses, especially when something startled them suddenly. When horses stampeded out of control, they could kill, he cautioned. A while back, his client's horses had stampeded, wrenching the reins away. One snapped back suddenly, blinding the poor man.

Hattie pictured this as she was thrown from side to side, a thousand other terrors racing through her mind. After one particularly violent bump, she came close to touching the horses' huge, muscular buttocks as their uncontrolled force tossed her with abandon. Gasping from fear, her mouth and throat went dry as she reached for anything to hold onto.

Even amid the rain storm, she couldn't hear anything but the deafening gallop of hooves, snapping of leather, clinking of bits, and heaving snorts of the horses. Her heart seized to think she could be maimed or trampled any second, but that possibility doubled as the horses barreled forward with devastating speed. They seemed to grow more frenzied each second and soon pulled violently in different directions. Seeing how they strained the harness to break point, she shuddered, but was still helpless and at their mercy. The thunderous pounding of their hooves warned that she had few choices and little time.

Staying alive became her sole focus, but how could she regain control of the situation? Widening fractures threatened to crack the hapless wagon open each time the horses changed direction or jerked it over old ruts. Grasping the buckboard with one hand, Hattie managed to push against the seat with the other hand and gain enough stability to pull her legs under her. But the minute she gained a footing, another bounce threw her down again.

Finally recovering enough balance to steady herself, she scrambled onto her knees and was able to grab the reins. Rising, she pulled hard, which afforded enough resistance to stand up. Yelling the horses' names after planting her feet solidly, she bent her knees and pulled with every fiber of her being. Her voice was loud and purposeful, but intended to calm the great animals.

Fulfilling her worst fear, the horses' flattened ears continued to signal acute distress. They did not respond to her voice. If she couldn't slow or calm them, their muscular dominance would pull her to her doom when the doubletree split.

Hattie knew the danger of looking away as she tried to survive, but she was filled with despair about what might have happened to Grace. So, she took a deadly chance and glanced around. Reckless in her worry, she stole a particularly dangerous look behind her, but Grace wasn't even in the back of the wagon. There was no sign of her whatsoever. Heartsick as the wind whipped her matted, muddy hair into her eyes, she cried, *Oh, no! Did she jump? Was she thrown?*

Her mouth now parched from terror, Hattie drew a ragged breath as the winded horses' intensity finally diminished somewhat. Hopefully, they were running themselves out. But the danger remained. Then, astonishingly, Abijah raced up on his lean, fast pony and flanked the team of horses bravely. With immense precision, he called the horses' names and repeatedly bellowed *whoa, whoa.* Neck and neck with the team, he leaned over expertly and managed to grab their harness. It was a terribly dangerous move Hattie had never heard of. But, wonder of wonders, the horses heard and responded to him. Slowing as he continued to speak, the horses' ears rose, which signaled the return of responsiveness. Surely, the nightmare was finally ending.

Hattie acknowledged her utter helplessness when she made

eye contact with Abijah. But instead of encouraging her, he seemed panic-stricken. Abijah looked like he had seen a ghost, or maybe the devil himself. The end of the frightening runaway did not comfort or calm him.

Bewildered, tears streaked across Hattie's pale expression. She grew more worried as he turned the team back in the direction from which it came. Endless moments of suspense passed while traversing the now soggy road. Miserable, cold rain continued to pelt them.

Soaked to the bone, Hattie decided the weather conspired against her. There in the drenched, fog-laced misery of disaster, she knew in her heart of hearts that something awful had happened to Grace. Still holding on nervously, her stomach gripped tighter and tighter in fear. Hopefully, Grace was back where this nightmare started and wasn't hurt badly.

A sudden attack of shivers racked Hattie's body. Yearning for cover, she reached down to peel the soggy fabric of her dress from her skin. To her amazement, it was soiled all across the front with forebodingly dark, irregular spots. How could the mud have stained it so quickly? Something about the look of it made Hattie's shivers reach all the way into her soul.

Then, to her disbelief, she caught a glimpse ahead of her friend's calico dress on the ground. *Please God, help Grace*, Hattie prayed. Grace lay there in a crumpled heap and did not move. Hattie was beside herself to reach Grace's side but had to wait until Abijah could finally halt the horses.

Jumping down, Hattie called out as she rushed to her friend, almost losing her balance in the slippery mud. Calling again, she jerked her dress out of the way so she could slide on her knees to get close as fast as possible. Still, Grace did not stir there with her head tucked down and her hands drawn to her chest. Clasping her shoulder, Hattie gently turned Grace face up. Expressionless and smeared with mud and muck, Grace fell limp in her arms, those caring blue eyes staring past her sightlessly. Grace was dead, a dark and jagged bullet hole burned through the blood spattered bodice of her dress.

15

Letting Go of the Past

From the moment Hattie laid eyes on Grace's dead body, she shrieked for what felt like a lifetime. She had only heard lightning, not a gunshot. Who had fired and from where?

How could such an unthinkable accident happen? What kind of fool was out hunting in the rain? The rush of emotion tore at her and almost stopped her heart. Grace had been her constant, guiding star. She had given of herself unselfishly as a true friend. Hattie almost felt like Grace was her protective, older sister. She didn't think she could bear losing another sister.

Clearing the mud from Grace's porcelain face with shaking hands, Hattie grew suspicious because the bullet wound was so well placed. Poor Grace was shot through the heart. If God had any mercy, she hoped he had taken Grace to heaven in less than a second, before she realized what had happened. Maybe the coincidence of the lightning strike was a sign.

But then, Hattie stopped cold. OH NO! Someone meant to do

this! Suddenly, rage welled up and overtook every part of Hattie. As she sobbed, the anguish threatened to burst her lungs. She hugged Grace's helpless corpse close to her heart with all her might. Since the cry of a panther was said to be like a woman's scream, Hattie heard herself as a hunted creature mourning the mortally wounded Grace. Even though Abijah came to help, she would not let him.

Then, in the blink of an eye, the most repugnant thought made itself known. Rising, she stepped back silently as it gathered and grew. Abijah reached toward Grace as she walked off with only this one, awful truth in mind.

The gunshot must have been meant for her! She was the one everyone was trying to protect. She was the one who had been threatened, attacked, and robbed. Grace was dead because of her! And the strange man lurking up on the Park Hill Mountain had been the shooter.

There was no other explanation. Unspeakable confusion and guilt began to boil up, blotting out the earlier terror of the runaway wagon. Death might be easier than living with the gruesome reality of seeing Grace like this.

When Hattie cried herself out, she was forced to stop for air. But then the unthinkable bubbled up again and blotted out everything else. *Oh, Grace. I'm so sorry,* she repeated until she felt she would go crazy.

The torment hollowed out a well of grief into which she felt herself sink, as if she were drowning. Every few moments, the nightmarish scene returned. Repeatedly, she wanted to duck while picturing the man on the mountain. He must have followed the wagon and skulked through the shadowy woods not far away, seeking the place where he would get the perfect shot. Then, when the earsplitting discharge occurred once again in Hattie's recollection, she began to shake all over again. Abijah, helpless and exhausted, patted Hattie's shoulder.

With each repetition, Hattie's unfathomable suffering mounted. The bullet meant for her had hit Grace instead. Sweet, helpful, honest, faithful Grace. Forgiving Grace. More than any other quality, it was Grace's forgiveness and ability to go on with life that made Hattie suffer paralyzing remorse. *I talked her into going to Abijah's,* she punished herself, full of condemnation.

Because of the lightning bolt, gunshot, loud voices, and commotion, Rev. Stephen Foreman and little Percy came running to the scene. Immediately, Percy began to howl in fear. Through her torrent of emotion, Hattie pleaded with Rev. Foreman to save Grace, to do something. The distress in his expression lowered her soul further into the oblivion that was now reality. Without so much as a word, he knelt beside Grace and felt for a pulse on her lifeless neck. Finding none, he said a prayer and then scooped up little Percy to remove the child from the ugliness. That's how Hattie learned that Rev. Foreman was Abijah's uncle. She regretted that innocent, little Percy had seen the dreadfulness of the tragedy. Hopefully, the other school boys were home by now.

Together, Hattie and Abijah rushed back to the wagon and dumped the soap-making fat out onto the muddy ground. The buckets were almost empty after the runaway. But something had to be done to soak up the fat in the wagon bed.

Turning in desperation, Hattie realized she could break off fistfuls of prairie grass and stalks of sagebrush to line the wagon for receiving Grace. When that was done, Abijah lifted her body from the crude spot of ground where she had fallen. Hattie helped him lay her in the wagon ever-so-gently for protection. Grace might as well have been asleep except for the appalling condition of her body from the gunshot and her fall.

Unable to bear such an indignity to her friend's earthly remains, Hattie had another idea that sent her behind the wagon for privacy. With angry force, she began to tear at her petticoats until the fabric gave way and allowed her to rip a swath of yardage loose. With Abijah's help, she wrapped Grace lovingly in the purity of that white cloth before anyone else could stare at her exposed wound. To Hattie, this was like a warm blanked hugging Grace tightly.

Before long, the roadside swarmed with neighbors, the Sheriff, and others she had never met. All the while, she kept watch for someone familiar, someone she could hold onto. But no one came. To make matters worse, nature's cold tears turned to a downpour blown by churlish winds.

When Dwight arrived, Hattie cast him a heart-breaking glimpse of utter helplessness. But he had to confer with the Sheriff and pronounce Grace dead before comforting Hattie. If only he or Sarah could help her stop shivering, which had nothing to do with the rain or cold wind. But Dwight was kept busy by the Sheriff, so Hattie remained there alone, minute after excruciating minute passing as her bereavement and revulsion continued. There was no sign of James.

Soon, theories sprang up about the shooter's identity. Hattie's misery mounted steadily. If only she had paid closer attention. Why had she let the lightning and the storm and the mad horses steal her away from tending to Grace? There was no doubt in her mind but what this excruciating tragedy came down to some failure on her part. If she had stopped the horses sooner, maybe she could have stemmed the bleeding, offered resuscitation, or prayed with Grace.

About mid-afternoon, Rev. Foreman broke away from the scene and offered her his coat after commenting that her lips had turned blue. His fatherly presence was her first sign of hope or rescue. By that time, she had prayed fervently to escape. At least she knew him and felt secure that Rev. Worcester trusted him. She had already done her best under the horrific circumstances to answer the Sheriff's questions through chattering teeth.

"Miss Sheldon, please accept my condolences," the Sheriff had concluded after learning what she knew. "I can't comprehend this violence or your sadness over the death of Mrs. Barnes. But I know you need to get somewhere warm and mustn't stay by yourself. Rev. Foreman worried that Mrs. Worcester will hear of this tragedy and suffer terribly without her husband. Since she's alone, please go to her home so you two can comfort each other. I will find you there for further questions."

Hattie only nodded, her emotions so frozen she couldn't argue. Her last face-to-face encounter with Erminia had been a surprisingly pleasant one. The Worcester household sounded warm and homey in comparison to this crude and ugly place. It also sounded better than the confines of her quarters.

On the way to the Worcester residence, against all likelihood, Rev. Foreman's children, Jennie and Taylor, waved him down while returning home from a friend's house. Unaware of the tragedy, they grew distressed just from Hattie's appearance. Their father could not stop them from peppering her with questions and worries about her destroyed dress, the mud, her hair, and her tears. It was all he could do to keep Grace's murder under wraps until they got home. Hattie was grateful he respected her exhaustion and profound shock enough to save her from having to explain. She struggled to be responsive to her little students, but was desperate to escape any further conversation.

As soon as the carriage drew up in front of the Worcester home, she thanked the Foremans and insisted they not be delayed any further. Bidding a hasty goodbye, she ran for cover. But she was also running from questions. And exhaustion. And misery. And guilt.

No one answered the front door, even after she knocked so loud it must sound like an intruder. Desperate to get out of the cold, Hattie raced to the back door. Finding it open and no longer able to accommodate the dripping cold, she burst inside and called to Erminia. There was no answer. She waited. But the house was silent. Erminia, as well as two women guests she recently agreed to keep, must be out.

Under the circumstances, Hattie dispensed with the confining rules of propriety. Trailing drips across the kitchen floor, she approached a stack of freshly laundered linens resting on the table. Not hesitating, she took the liberty of drying herself with one and wrapping another around her shoulders. She lit a lamp and the stove, longing for warmth and a soothing cup of tea. All the while, her heavy heart released its anguish.

While the stove heated, she let down her final guard. Grief possessed her frame with shudders, moans, and whimpering. Because she shook so badly and the day was waning, a frightening chill prompted her to do something about her wet dress. But she wasn't about to disrobe at the Worcester home. So she started a fire, wrapped herself in a bed sheet, and stood by the warm hearth.

In many ways, she saw herself as captured by what had happened.

No other thoughts could compete with the agony of dear Grace Barnes taking the bullet meant for her. All was lost. She would never see Grace again. If only James would hurry and find her. Never before had she needed his embrace so badly.

Exhausted from crying, it occurred to Hattie that a person could actually run dry. If such a thing happened, how would she release the awful hurt seizing her very spirit? That question hung in the air unanswered, however. She had fewer answers to more questions than ever before.

Truth be told, although she had been desperate for James's touch, she felt relieved now just to sit in the quiet. Pure silence ministered to her in her exhaustion. Her body felt better even though her mind was far from quiet. She was praying desperate prayers. But then she realized she was unconsciously bargaining with God to reverse Grace's death.

When the stove grew hot enough to boil water, Hattie made her way slowly to the kitchen again. Impatient, she discovered that the tea kettle was empty. Why would Erminia not have ample water? Where had she gone and when would she return? The last thing Hattie wanted to do was go back outside and up the hill for water.

Frustrated, she peered out the back window at the stone well. Curiously, a Negro man was there working in the rain. Perhaps it was the same man who had helped Hannah on the day of the social. Maybe he would draw some water for Hattie's tea.

Taking a cape from the wall hook by the door, she covered her head and shoulders and walked toward the well. Offering a polite wave to signify her intent, she greeted the man as politely as she could under the circumstances.

"Excuse me," she called, suddenly remembering how red her face was. "Can you help me with some water?"

"Evenin' ma'am," he said, lowering his eyes and tipping his decrepit, wet hat.

"I'm Hattie Sheldon, the new mission teacher," she explained. "I think I saw you the night of the social."

"Yes, ma'am. They call me Rufus," he returned courteously.

"Is something wrong with the well?" she inquired, wondering if he might be linked to the mission in some capacity or another.

"It's plum contrary," he explained, shaking his head. "I ain't never worked on it before. When a deep well's broke, it's big trouble."

"That sounds serious," Hattie returned. "Can it be fixed?"

"I'm hopin' for the best," Rufus chuckled good-naturedly. "But I'll say this. Working way down there is scary. Rev. Wooser said to fear God—and when I'm down there, I do."

"Oh, I'm sorry," Hattie replied. "Where do you live, Rufus?"

"Over yonder at my master's," Rufus returned. "Miz Wooser's all undone cuz she can't work nobody no time as a slave. She fears trouble, but needs water."

"I see," Hattie responded, recalling the American Board's specifications about hiring somebody else's slave. He must be hired on his off time for money he could keep.

"Miz Wooser begged for help since the Revrun's gone," he continued. "She made me swear to get a pass from my master, or Revrun'll lose his job. I pledge my free will and she pays me fair wages."

"I hope it goes fast," Hattie replied, concerned. "Can you get me some water? Do you work on wells often?"

"No, ma'am, I don't," he responded. "They just sent me cuz Mr. James can't. He fixed this old well before."

"I guess I don't know Mr. James," she responded.

"He's my overseer, but my master sent him off to another

plantation in Loozeyana," Rufus expounded. "Gonna be gone a long while to get that place in order. They got lots of slaves."

Hattie's knees almost buckled. Mr. James must be HER James! James Latta. He was gone to Louisiana? When had he left? Her face flushed blood red and her heart pounded so hard she saw stars.

In a weak voice, she excused herself and started to back away.

"You change your mind, ma'am?" Rufus questioned. "I'll put a bucket here when I leave directly."

Answering that she didn't really need the water, Hattie walked fast toward the house. Her legs grew almost too weak to carry her. How could this be true? Surely James would have stopped to tell her. Or something. Only he was probably still mad at her.

On top of losing Grace, how could she endure any more loss, any more heartache? Why was all this happening at once? She had assumed the last few days amounted to a cooling off period between them. When would James come back—or would he? What about that possible sweetheart?

Rushing back through the open door without closing it behind her, Hattie all but collapsed again. Her soul felt colder than her body as she rocked with abandon by the fire. An unrelenting emptiness joined the woe in the pit of her stomach. Almost sick, she dropped her head in her hands.

Something behind her made an odd sound like a boot bumping a chair leg. It was unnatural and out of place. Before she could turn to look, however, the particular odors of whiskey and sweat preceded a coarse man's voice that broke the silence. Hattie froze as he spoke.

"Stay right where you are, Miss Abolitionist," he ordered gruffly. "I've finally got you right where I want you: in front of my gun barrel."

Hattie began to shake as a whole, different level of fear overtook her. The man was walking slowly around the side of her chair. She dared not move.

"You messed up my plans over and over," he complained bitterly, brushing a greasy lock of hair from his eyebrow.

Finally in her line of sight, Hattie bristled because she recognized the disheveled criminal with the flinty stare. Unshaven, the skin on his upper cheeks was unnaturally marked with blemish-like lesions. He wore the same buckskin shirt as the man up on the mountain just this morning. But her heart skipped a beat when she noticed the notch missing from his ear. It seemed too unbelievable to be true, but he was the same man who had rudely approached her at the social. They had called him Smoky.

"You go around this place like you own it," he nearly spat. "Making friends with the likes of Negroes causes trouble for mixed-bloods. You thought you could sneak around slavery to get ideas from that Baptist abolitionist, too. The both of you make me sick."

Hattie's jaw was clenched so hard it threatened to crush her teeth. This despicable man had been following her, maybe all along! But he misunderstood. She was opposed to Rev. Jones, not getting abolition ideas from him. Yet, that didn't make sense to this man. The thought had never occurred to her before that she and Rev. Jones held the same anti-slavery beliefs. They just handled themselves in such opposite ways.

"I decided it was time to get things behind me. Smoky, I told myself, these women are ruining everything. So, this morning, I dealt with one part of the problem and tonight I'll take care of the other," he said slowly with dripping disdain.

Feeling her jaw clench, Hattie realized he had just confessed to Grace's murder! He had meant to kill Grace! What kind of impossibly twisted character was capable of such a thing? Even worse, he intended to kill her, too. But why? Who was he? Could she figure a way to stop him?

By now, Smoky stood between Hattie's rocking chair and the open door. His gun was still pointed directly at her as his evil gaze bore daggers of hate through her.

"You can't get away any more. If you had taken my warning seriously, I wouldn't have to kill you. But you kept right on," he carped, moving sideways to grab his bottle and take a swig.

He had written the threat letter! Surely he was also her attacker! This whole time she had assumed it was Deke and that she was safe with him locked away. What was this man's link, if any, to Deke? But then she recalled little Sweet Berry's words after Rev. Jones's visit. Jones said Deke had a rival. Smoky must be that rival!

"You northern abolitionists come here and ruin people's lives," Smoky continued between drinks. "Why don't you just leave us alone? I got so tired of hearing about your do-gooder intentions. And it got embarrassing for a mixed-blood like me loyally upholding the laws of slavery."

Hattie's chest tightened painfully. She felt like an animal killed instantly after stepping on the trigger of a steel trap. Yet, her ears heard every, tortured sound the man made. By talking in such a way, he was giving clues about who he really was. The thought of it, the coming together of the hints, and the realization brought the worst torture of her life. And if it ended here and now, her most painful regret was never again seeing Grace or feeling the precious embrace of James.

She was flooded with memories of statements that hadn't quite made sense and comments with double meanings, just like the one today. When alerting Hattie to who was after her, Grace had said "I think I know who's doing it." She had also commented about being foolish to have let her guard down. Mixed-bloods had ignored her, but talked openly. And finally, she had passed along the false tip that Deke instead of Smoky had targeted Hattie. He emphasized that your worries are over and life can calm down now."

"You were using Deke for cover, weren't you," Hattie heard herself ask in a voice that did not reveal any fear. "You wanted my trunk, but he beat you to it. That trunk could have raised plenty of money to buy your whiskey."

"With people like you around, I would end up in jail just like him," Smoky grumbled as he unconsciously lowered his gun while taking another drink from the whiskey bottle.

The moment that gun went down, everything changed in an instant. From the doorway behind Smoky came the unmistakable metallic click of a gun cocking. Jerking his head up, he went rigid. Hattie's mouth flew open, which confused him even more. Suddenly, she knew beyond the shadow of a doubt that her silent prayers had been answered.

"Drop it, Smith," Reverend Worcester demanded, looking more like a marshal than a preacher. "You have three seconds or I'll shoot to kill. And my aim is steady."

Smith Barnes's expression fell suddenly, as he turned slowly to face Hattie's boss. He dropped his own weapon, looking deflated in his cowardice. To Hattie's further relief, he lost his balance slightly, just as he lost his nerve.

By then, Rev. Worcester stood inside his own home telling Grace's husband it was all over. Hattie couldn't take her eyes off her long-awaited boss's face because he had now become her hero. Every

bit as tall, but barely half as vigorous and stately as she remembered, his reputation remained intact among the likes of one so fallen as

Smith "Smoky" Barnes. To Hattie's amazement, Smoky fell apart before her very eyes.

"Don't shoot me," he begged Rev. Worcester in his drunkenness.

❖ ❖ ❖

October 30, 1856

Dear Hattie,

Just like ships marooned on the dry bed of the Arkansas River, you and I have run aground, too. Somehow, we've come to cross purposes and we don't have a way to go forward. Maybe that's not by accident. At any rate, it's out of my hands.

I'm telling myself you are free of my opinions now. Maybe I've been trying to steer you like a new wagon. But we weren't following the same trail. With me out of your way, you can carry on as you see fit. One too many times, I reminded you that you're not the first young missionary to encounter tough times in Indian Territory. But, Hattie, without question, you are the one I'll never forget.

The controversy surrounding your letter to Agent Butler troubled Mr. Murrell greatly. He said the last thing the Cherokee Nation needed was a big, public ouster of a preacher with a long record of service. That's how he started when he sat me down for a serious talk and announced he was sending me to Louisiana. It was a move I didn't expect. He insists I can do lots of good there. Maybe he really meant I wasn't making enough of a difference here. Whatever the case, I know you will get along better, too, without me saying you don't know what you're talking about.

As for Agent Butler's investigation of Rev. Jones, you deserve to know what really happened. After receiving your letter accusing Jones, Butler put out a bad word on you. He thought he could get rid of both an abolitionist teacher and an abolitionist preacher. Instead, it backfired and saved the both of you. That's because my father heard of your letter and appealed to Butler privately. He urged Mr. Murrell to do the same. They are powerful men who help keep relations balanced. In this case, they agreed the timing was poor for bringing your proof forward to prosecute Jones. Many Cherokees revere Jones, after all.

There is a key piece of information I thought I told you, but evidently I didn't. You remember that my brother, Will, and I were wagon masters to Texas in 1850? After that, he married Rev. Jones's daughter, Anna. Tragically, she's sick and dying, so it's a very bad time to prosecute and kick Jones out of the Cherokee Nation even though he will continue to gin up the full-bloods and preach against slavery.

But, Hattie, you need to abandon that fight and stop acting like Rev. Worcester's avenger. Just focus on teaching. I know you'll have a truly good impact on the children. And, for your sake, I pray that Rev. Worcester returns soon. By the time you receive this, I will be long gone and you can get some peace and quiet.

—James

❖ ❖ ❖

Outside the close-knit Worcester family, few would grasp the devastating coincidence that Hattie's loss was compounded. At exactly the same unspeakable time Grace had been murdered, James had left. Without her faithful friend and the love of her life, Hattie felt alone in a way words could not describe. That was just as well, because none came. She moved through her hours in silence. More than any others, Grace and James had filled her days and become her closest companions. They had also satisfied her need for friendship … and love.

After she cried herself into exhaustion over one, the absence of the other punished her further. This back and forth torture finally led from confusion to a strange sense of mourning that Hattie couldn't sort out or prioritize. Death always demanded the utmost respect and consideration. But losing James felt exactly like a death. He was suddenly gone with no mention of returning.

Hattie had not realized before that so many of her hopes and dreams had shifted almost imperceptibly from her original goal of teaching to her new love for James. Did others grasp this? Were they just remaining silent due to the circumstances? Hattie kept quiet about him, even though his absence tore another gaping hole in her already broken heart.

Tending to duty only helped a little. She dismissed school until further notice and gave herself to the work of grief and the logistics of Grace's upcoming service. Even that disquieted her because she couldn't seem to hold onto her own thoughts very long. Her mind had gone far away and left nothing but raw emotion in its place.

❖ ❖ ❖

November 2, 1856
Dear Mother and Father,

The inexplicability of fate just visited us here in Park Hill.
Since my last letter to you of just a few weeks ago, weighty
events carried the mission and the whole community beyond
imagination. As you may have gleaned, I wanted to present
the happy and constructive side of Park Hill to you when
I first arrived. Because you had not held me back from
my dream, I felt it unfair to burden you with worries that
remained unsolved here. The truth is that dangers plague the
Cherokee Nation and its people. I don't mean that we live in
constant fear. But we do live mindfully as we watch out for
one another. I have learned to accept the bad, appreciate the
good, and keep moving forward. After all, this is my new
home.

These last months, I was blessed with the help and friendship
of a loving woman who had worked around the mission
for years. She left the south as a girl and later married a
Cherokee man. Rev. Worcester mentored her and she worked
closely with me at the school. But, tragically, she was killed
yesterday. I am saddened beyond description over the loss
because she was such a dear soul and a true friend.

Equally as heartbreaking, the man I described for you in such
glowing terms last month has been sent by his boss to work in
the state of Louisiana. I cannot hide my feelings for him, nor
do I even want to any longer. This man, James Latta, became
the light of my life and I am devastated that he is gone. All
attempts to be philosophical about the future without him have
failed me.

And yet, I knew you would never understand him or my
love for him. James, a southern man but a pragmatist, is a
slave overseer caught in a web of unjust laws and rationalized
practices. Were it not for all that, you might like him very
much and come to understand the tremendously good qualities
I found and appreciated in him. Not only was he kind,
respectful, and good to me, but he also was never mean, selfish,
or abusive to the slaves. Nor will he mistreat the ones he now
manages at his new job in Louisiana.

I envisioned spending the rest of my life with this man. But
that is now in the past. He is gone, so I am seeking to ground
myself once again with my work and redefine my purpose.
I hope you will find a place in your hearts to forgive me, no
matter how badly disappointed you may be. And I continued
to love you more than ever.

Your daughter,
Hattie

There were no children to mourn or survive dear, dear Grace.
Her murderous, criminal husband sat in prison, certain to be convicted
and hanged for his hideous act. Thank goodness Rev. Worcester
had returned. Although he was tired to the bone, grey in the face,
and lacking robustness, he led his family and his congregation in an
embrace of Grace's life. That sent a powerful message out into the
community—about the nature of love and its deep connections.

They dressed Grace for burial in one of Sarah's dresses the color
of a peaceful, blue haze. One by one, Hattie, Sarah, and Hannah sat

solemnly beside her lifeless body as families were supposed to do. Onlookers would have sworn that Grace was their blood relative. Finally, Rev. Worcester's touching eulogy memorialized her faith, loyalty, loving kindness, and exceedingly good humor.

No sooner was Grace laid to rest, than the investigation for a motive expanded. Soon, it resulted in revelations that left Hattie too stunned for words. When the awful truth came out, it also struck a low blow against other friends of Grace's. Over time, many in the community recalled Grace making light of her own clumsiness; she called herself accident prone. But that was her clever ruse to protect the secret she'd hidden so well. Oh, how the others wished they had paid closer attention. The telling discoveries reminded them of their positions of responsibility and then highlighted their lack of it. They despaired and entered another woeful chamber of grief.

That was because Smoky was revealed to be a violent, paranoid man who had always blamed Grace for his losses, frustrations, and failures. He had beaten her. A coward, he could not resist the whiskey that convinced him everything was her fault and that she had associated with people who could expose his flaws and bring him to shame. There was no question but what he abhorred Grace's association with Hattie.

As he slid deeper into the disappointing abyss of his own creation, he sought a reprieve by getting rid of both Grace and Hattie. Evidence confirming this was found at his hideaway. Grace hadn't taken the bullet meant for Hattie. Both had been marked for death that day. Hattie would feel the pain, the loss, and the confusion over that point for the rest of her life.

The most crucial source of convicting information against Smoky turned out to be an unlikely innocent. As Hattie turned this over and over in the weeks ahead, she stared for many hours at Park Hill Mountain or the cemetery. Henceforth, she swore to never again react harshly when a child's behavior seemed uncharacteristically bad—because children lacked the ability to reason circumstances through. When a situation went wrong, they could only respond emotionally.

That's exactly what Buck, the bad boy at school, had done. For reasons she couldn't explain, Hattie had mentioned casually to Abijah about Buck's strange reticence around Grace, as well as his boastful loyalty to Chief John Ross. That led to the Sheriff's interview with Buck, who obviously knew something, but was terrified after Grace's murder. If Buck told, he remained convinced he would meet his maker violently and soon, just as Smoky had threatened. The child had absolutely no voice of experience to inform him about the frightful things he heard and saw around Grace and Smoky's place.

Finally, Abijah and the Sheriff went to the chief, who agreed to personally comfort and assure the boy of his safety. Buck finally told how the cursing and crying had drawn him to sneak nearby to investigate. Perhaps blessedly, he still lacked adequate words and the maturity to make sense of why Smoky abused Grace so badly.

When everything was finally over, the only vestige of Grace that remained was a lasting memory that pulled at the hearts of all her friends. That dear woman's influence was like a long musical note that lifted one's heart even after it gave way to silence. As she healed, Hattie could call up the memory of her friend at any time. It came back to her like a favorite, familiar tune and her heart yearned for the former days of seeing Grace's kind eyes and hearing her helpful words.

❊ ❊ ❊

One day, as Hattie cried about James in private, Sarah arrived unexpectedly. Her empathy showed Hattie that she was the only available friend who really understood. When both were young, Hattie had lost two sisters, while Sarah had lost her mother. Sarah sympathized with Hattie in ways that didn't need an explanation. To Hattie's great relief, Sarah began to nurture her, feed her, and tend her wounds.

"No one should have to endure a broken heart alone," she soothed as Hattie wept.

It was as if Sarah gave her permission to experience the depth of her own grief. When she had mourned alone, she hated the sounds of her sobs for they represented a side of herself she never wanted to encounter again. Hattie decided that was due to old, painful memories of her entire family when they were overcome by loss. That was ten long years ago, but it had shaken her so badly she vowed unconsciously to never become that distraught again. Yet, this new mournfulness over losing Grace and James was just as awful.

"Hattie, come with me," Sarah instructed firmly, but kindly. "It is time to go out into the wilderness to lament."

The symbolism of such an act had Biblical connections, so Hattie agreed. It was a cloudless, temperate day marked by soft breezes. The golden, drying prairie grasses of late fall swished steadily and created a rhythm-like accompaniment to her feelings. She wished the wind would sweep her hurt away to a place far, far beyond her conception.

"You need to go into the darkest corner of your lost love," Sarah advised unexpectedly. "When we get to the place I've chosen, we will be miles from anyone or anything. I've encountered this before and you must trust me. It is time for you to scream and cry out loud. Give voice to the agony, Hattie."

Visions of wounded, wild animals struck Hattie, but she believed in Sarah. It felt true that grief had to be bested by physical power and hard fought prayers. Without God's help and the unrelenting force of will, such a powerful emotion could destroy a person. All the while, Hattie held the thought that God had created her bereavement and that it surely had a purpose. She might never know what it was, though.

Before they arrived, Sarah continued to narrate. This was the first time she had taken Hattie into her confidence with stories so personal or private.

"I fought paralyzing anguish when my mother died after Mary Eleanor's birth. In answer to my prayers, Miss Thompson's abundant love cultivated healing and brought meaning back into the void."

But just as her family appeared to make its way forward again, Sarah found herself saddled with a stranger for a step-mother. Erminia was the opposite of her mother and Miss Thompson. All gentleness, patience, and support disappeared; living with Erminia was like suffering the presence of an unseasoned imposter. Her annoying attempts at mothering smothered Sarah, crushed her spirit, and eventually forced her to beg God for the gift of forgiveness.

"It didn't come immediately," Sarah continued. "In fact, for a long while, I believed myself unable to endure or thrive. In that inconsolable state, I wrote a letter I regretted. It was a cry for help to Ann Eliza. She was soon to return to Park Hill from her schooling back east. I warned her of the grave relational challenges that awaited her. Balancing my regret, however, was the fact that that letter and its desperation marked a turning point after the lowest low."

So, at Sarah's urging out in the far fields of Indian Territory, Hattie released the torment from her wounded soul. Without regard for any other, she used her voice to force it out. In her mind's eye, it rose from the pyre of her hurt like smoke only to be purified by the winds and blown all the way to heaven. A certain helplessness accompanied it, which she likened to a prayer. She hadn't felt helpless since breaking her leg. But there was merit in giving one's weakest moment as a sacrifice, just as the Bible said.

Like with Sarah's letter, the releasing experience marked a turning point for Hattie, as well. Her emotional wounds began to feel the balm of relief. When her dark moods lifted, she realized the reprieve was not from freeing herself of the agony, but was a gift from God in reply. There was no artificial way to orchestrate peace in a person's heart. It had to come as a gift in order to be real or, all the more, to be appreciated.

Sometime afterwards, Hattie contemplated how she hadn't given much energy or emotion lately to her hurt. Looking over her calendar, she marveled at how time had given her the perspective to appreciate her blessings. The worst of her suffering had finally retreated.

Replacing it were new hopes and plans for the future. She had been embraced by her adopted family, the Worcesters, with open arms. The school children reminded her to remain tomorrow-oriented, as well. The past was where her grief belonged.

> *December 1, 1856*
> *I'm close enough to touch a whole new, expanded reverence for God's plan of life and death. Yet, I may never grasp its worth completely. His power has transformed my outlook and grown my vision of all creation, especially this mortal world. To have experienced such radically profound parts of life only points to mysteries I cannot conceive of, but which await me in whatever time I'm granted to achieve my purpose.*

Acknowledgements

To grasp the essence of Hattie Sheldon's long journey in 1856 from Utica, New York to Indian Territory in what is now eastern Oklahoma, I loaded my car in northern Virginia and hit the road.

Hattie made her way to the middle of early America by train and boat. The last part of her trek, which was by wagon, posed the greatest unknown, so I wanted to recreate that part of the trail and cover the distance she traveled. Only after I had driven small, side roads for five hours at a modern speed limit from Missouri into Oklahoma could I possibly imagine the grueling journey Hattie made in a wagon at less than four miles per hour.

What's more, the geographical differences between her old and new homes illuminated the cultural divide she must have experienced, as well. The more I learn and write about Hattie, the more I appreciate my modern, comfortable life. But the simplicity and quiet of her era draws me back constantly and makes me wish that time had not separated me from knowing her.

Many others I have known deserve attention and thanks for other parts of my journey, which have been literary. I offer my deep appreciation to Oklahoma anthropologist Shirley Pettengill for inspecting my manuscript's precision regarding the history of Oklahoma's only antebellum home, The George M. Murrell Home, because Hattie Sheldon taught there; for guiding me through 19th century life and customs, and for detailed tours of Park Hill, Oklahoma, that brought the old community alive, including The

Park Hill Mission where Hattie Sheldon lived and worked. I am indebted to Dr. Alan Snyder, Professor of History at Southeastern University in Lakeland, Florida for developing my love of American History, as well as for his expertise editing and reviewing my manuscript for historical accuracy. My book would not have been possible without the endless resources of Ancestry.com, FamilySearch.org, GenealogyBank.com, and Fold3. Thank you to The University of Tulsa's Alice M. Robertson Collection, part of the McFarlin Library's archives, for its inherent richness, as well as for the immense help its digitized holdings offer online researchers like me. The documentation in that collection of real people's written voices made it possible for me to breathe life back into their 19th century lives, for they were the dedicated missionaries and family members who associated with and revered Hattie Sheldon. I am grateful for the friendships of those who proofed my manuscript, offered suggestions, and kept me encouraged during the process of completing this second book in my series. Those include: Attorney Linda Ann Long, Dale and Jewell Duval, Regina and Dale Jahr, Barbara Nelson, Lea Helmerich, Rebecca Schenk, Mickey Miller, and Stephen C. Funk.

Thank you to award-winning artist Gary Bowers (visit www.garybowers.net) for the immense talent that led to the creation of his original painting, "Western Sky", which graces the cover of this book.

ABOUT THE AUTHOR

A descendant of Oklahoma homesteaders on both sides, Lane Calhoon Dolly grew up hearing stories of perseverance from her accomplished physician father and revered preacher grandmother. Dolly worked in the Reagan White House and then earned a Masters in Public Policy. A voracious researcher, she followed all-but-forgotten leads to fill a mysterious gap in her family tree. Hundreds of hours of research in the Library of Congress, Harvard's Houghton Library, and The University of Tulsa's McFarlin Library Archives rewarded her contention that Hattie Sheldon's life was traceable and inspiring. Other rich sources of information that helped Dolly strike the "mother lode" of historic connections were the Oklahoma Historical Society, Oneida County Historical Society in Utica, New York, and George M. Murrell Historic Home in Park Hill, Oklahoma. Her resulting first novel, *A Distant Call: The Fateful Choices of Hattie Sheldon*, has led her to speaking engagements before historical fiction fans in the states of Virginia, Delaware, New York, Oklahoma and South Dakota.